# RAINBOW IN THE MORNING

## Eileen Stafford

HEADLINE

First published in 1993
by HEADLINE BOOK PUBLISHING PLC

10 9 8 7 6 5 4 3 2 1

British Library Cataloguing in Publication Data

Stafford, Eileen
Rainbow in the Morning
I. Title
823.914 [F]

ISBN 0–7472–0762–3

Phototypeset by Intype, London

Printed and bound in Great Britain by
Clays Ltd, St Ives PLC

HEADLINE BOOK PUBLISHING PLC
Headline House
79 Great Titchfield Street
London W1P 7FN

For Ted
who was always there to encourage

In memory of the seven hundred American servicemen tragically killed in Operation Tiger, April 28th, 1944. Operation Tiger was a training exercise which took place off the south coast of England in preparation for the D-Day Normandy landings. This tragic mishap, although known to a number of local people, was a discreetly kept secret for several years.

# ONE

## 1943

'You needn't be so insolent, my girl. No other man is likely to take you!' Maud Lindhurst looked pointedly away from her niece towards the small child playing with her doll on the hearthrug.

Pamela heard the scorn in the words, and felt a searing anger. She knew that what her aunt said was true, and that it was no earthly use trying to refute the unpalatable facts. She was uncomfortably aware, too, of the hint of obsessive love as Maud glanced at the little girl. Pamela wanted to snatch up her daughter and run from the room, run anywhere away from this woman who controlled both their lives with such absolute power. Instead she clasped her hands together tightly beneath the table and forced herself to reply quietly.

'But you know that I don't love Alan. He's good and dependable, but that isn't enough, Aunt. I need to be really in love before I commit myself for the rest of my life.'

The older woman rose from the breakfast table and snorted irritably as she folded her napkin with elaborate care. 'Love only brings trouble – as Olivia, your dear foolish mother, found out. Dependability and kindness are the things that matter. You'll do well to settle for those.' She walked to the door and opened it. Then she turned and fixed her niece with a penetrating stare. 'And don't forget the advantages of having a man who hasn't to go and fight. As a farmer he has an honourable reason to stay at home.'

1

Privately Pamela thought that if she was to be forced into a loveless marriage then an absentee husband might be a very good thing. She watched her aunt leave the room and tried to summon up every vestige of resolve and courage that she could muster. It was 1943 after all, she thought, not the last century.

Her dog moved from his place beside the fire and came to her, sensing her distress. She reached down and stroked him. Binks was one of her greatest comforts. They had been almost inseparable ever since Uncle Richard had given her the shaggy little puppy three years ago at the time of her deepest need.

Now Richard Lindhurst seemed to be totally engrossed in his *Daily Telegraph*, the only newspaper his wife allowed in the house, but eventually he lowered it and looked at her, brows creased in solicitude. 'You wouldn't have anything to worry about,' he said, repeating his wife's comments. 'Alan won't have to join up, I mean.' He glanced back at the newspaper. 'Lots of our boys being killed in Sicily now. There seems to be no end to it.' He put the paper down and poured himself another cup of tea from the big earthenware pot that was always used at breakfast. 'He's educated too,' he went on. 'There aren't many round here like him, with the brains to win a scholarship to a good school.'

'Meaning that I wasn't quite clever enough and you had to pay for me?' Pamela said, but she smiled a little as she spoke. She didn't want to upset Uncle Richard.

'That was your aunt's wish,' he replied. 'I missed you when you went away, just as I shall miss you when you go and get yourself wed.'

'But, Uncle, I don't want to marry Alan Saunders, or anyone else for that matter.' Pamela too poured herself another cup of tea and added some of the rich jersey milk from their own cows. It was fresh and creamy, brought in straight from the early milking. 'Why should I marry just because Aunt wishes it?'

Richard Lindhurst held the cup between his big farmer's hands, warming them in a manner that Aunt Maud would have frowned upon. He looked into the cup and appeared to be studying the tea-leaves with the greatest concentration.

'Because she usually seems to know what's best for everyone,' he said at last, with no hint of sarcasm in his voice. His words were tinged with a sense of inevitability.

It had always been like this, Pamela reflected. It was as though her aunt determined the inescapable and pre-ordained paths for all who came under her control. There had been Belmonts at Burlcombe House for generations, and she considered herself the family's undisputed head. She often used her maiden name, and Pamela always had the feeling that she bitterly resented having had to change it. She obviously considered that marriage to a Lindhurst was of far less importance than being born a Belmont.

Much of the estate land had been sold off but there was still enough left to make a viable farm and Pamela guessed that her aunt had married Uncle Richard merely so that he could work the remaining acres more efficiently. It was an unofficial family secret that he had been a farm labourer on the estate long ago. He had always been, to his niece, a friend, a kind of equal, with Aunt Maud dominating the two of them. It was she who gave the orders and her will was never disputed. For Richard the situation appeared to be satisfactory. He had a kind of happiness.

'But she can't know what's best for me!' Pamela's voice was full of rebellion, yet in her heart she knew that she would probably agree in the end to whatever plans were made for her. Like her uncle she would submit, for the time being anyway. And why? She sat at the table, hands gripped fiercely together, tea growing cold in the delicate china cup.

The nightmare returned as it constantly did, even now, more than three years later. A country lane, a terrifying figure in the darkness pulling her down into the mud. He had approached her from behind and she had had no chance to see his face. Her torch had been knocked from her hand and had smashed on the stones at the side of the track leaving only total blackness, for the Devon lane cut deeply into the land just here and the trees met overhead cutting out even the faintest glimmer of light from the night sky. She had fought desperately for a few moments, striking out blindly against his superior strength. She would

3

always remember her own screams, sounds that seemed to come from some other source, from some terrified animal. Then there was the humiliation and the pain. She had not understood what was happening to her, what he was doing. Surely she was being killed in some horrifying way. But he had left her at last, bleeding and almost insensible. She had no idea how she got home. Perhaps it was some blind instinct that led her stumbling back to Burlcombe, but she knew that she would never forget her aunt's hard face and the scathing comment that greeted her, 'Only to be expected, just like your mother.' Pamela had needed love and comfort just then but it had not been forthcoming, except a little from Uncle Richard whose rage at her attacker had, in the end, overridden everything else.

'Like your mother, like your mother.' Maud's words went round and round in her head even now. They haunted her dreams and sometimes her waking hours too, their power to hurt often seeming as great as the thing that had happened to her. It wasn't that she was ashamed of her mother, or indeed didn't want to be like her, but it was important to try to understand, even to defend this incomprehensible thing that Olivia had done. Pamela had never known her mother, the beautiful Olivia, the younger sister whom her aunt had apparently adored.

'She died when you were born. You were her punishment for what she did!' Her aunt never ceased telling Pamela about the dear sweet girl her mother had been until she went off one day and sinned. Pamela hadn't discovered what the sin was until she herself was raped. But the fact that her mother could have enjoyed something like that and had gone willingly with a man, was completely unthinkable to her.

Pamela had dared to ask her aunt about it one day, but Maud had flown into such a rage that the mystery still remained unsolved. Olivia had definitely had a lover. That much was clear – she herself was the result. Pamela always felt uncomfortable when she thought about it. Even the word, lover, was strange, almost unpleasant, yet oddly disturbing too. And this unknown young man was her father. Did he know about her? Who was he anyway? Pamela often felt that only when she had answers

4

to all her questions would she be able to find any real peace.

Suddenly the child on the rug got to her feet. Sturdy baby legs carried her unsteadily across the room. She ran past Pamela, not looking at her, and pushed open the unfastened door. 'Want Aunty,' she said. 'Jane wants Aunty.'

Pamela watched her go and experienced a surge of impotent rage. She longed to put her arms around her little daughter and hug her, but such demonstrations of affection had always been frowned upon by Maud. Brooding upon her own proposed marriage to Alan Saunders made Pamela remember with greater clarity the events of the past few years and her aunt's rigid sway over every aspect of her life.

'You will have the baby,' Maud had told her when the disastrous fact of her pregnancy had been confirmed. 'And if it is a girl we shall keep her. I shall bring her up myself and try to eradicate the bad blood she will obviously possess. You will not interfere, ever. On those conditions we will help you.'

Pamela, then a helpless and terrified fifteen year old, had agreed. There was no other choice. She had secretly hoped for a male child. Her aunt had no time for boys, he would be adopted, and it might have been possible for Pamela herself to begin a new life with no constant reminder of the horror and the shame.

But Jane was born fair and beautiful, a contented happy baby, and Pamela had loved her ill-begotten child from the first moment of her birth. But it was a love that must never be openly shown. For reasons of her own Aunt Maud had insisted on that, and had decreed too that, as she grew, Jane must not know her true parentage. Pamela must always be merely a sort of older cousin to her own child. That way, argued Maud, the story of the rape need never be told. The baby would be passed off easily as an orphaned young relative.

Apart from holidays, Pamela had been away at boarding school since she was eleven so no one in the village knew of the two terms spent at a different establishment. Those months, when she had been banished to a home for fallen girls run by a religious order, had been the most miserable of her young life. She had watched her figure grow bulky and repugnant; the studies that she loved had been replaced largely by domestic work. She remembered the total helplessness of that time and how she had resolved that one day she would be independent and strong, free for ever of Aunt Maud and of men. Never again would she allow herself to be in this degrading and impossible situation.

There was an uncomfortable barrier between herself and most of the other girls in the home, too. She had been unable to make friends for none of them had been raped by a stranger. Their liaisons were even giggled about sometimes in the dormitory. She felt hardened and isolated, determined that she would never again be hurt by anyone.

The whole experience had ended with horrendous hours of pain and terror. She had witnessed the birth of calves and sheep on the farm but nothing had prepared her for this!

But then they had put Jane in her arms, for she was one of the lucky ones, the nuns told her. Her baby was going home with her, was not going to be adopted. For a few golden days she had been happy, cradling her child, feeding her, loving her, trying to believe that life could be good again. Her bitter resolutions were forgotten. Until Aunt Maud arrived! Pamela remembered the strange look on her aunt's face when she first held the baby in her arms, and since then, in spite of the strictness, a bond had grown between the grim older woman and Pamela's child.

Watching it, knowing that she was excluded, was the most difficult burden Pamela had ever had to bear and she was well aware that there was nothing at all that she could do about it. Yet she was determined that one day she would put everything right. Sometimes when her rage at Aunt Maud was greatest she wanted revenge, yet she knew that, of itself this seldom brought happiness. First and foremost it was her child's love that she craved.

Uncle Richard frequently tried to comfort her, to explain something that was almost inexplicable. 'The baby looks just like your mother,' he often remarked. 'Just like Olivia.' And then Pamela would sigh and feel more left out than ever, totally alone, for Olivia had been very beautiful, and was kept permanently so

6

by her romantically early death, and by the exquisite painting that hung at the bottom of the large staircase.

Richard Lindhurst got to his feet, disturbing Pamela's painful memories. He looked at her with compassion. He knew that ever since she could toddle Maud had conditioned her, implying by words and actions that she was to blame for her mother's death, and latterly not totally innocent either of the horrific rape three years ago by an unknown man.

It was Maud who had decided that they would not tell the police, would make no effort to find the culprit. Richard had argued with his wife but had finally given way to her as he usually did. He couldn't understand her reasoning and still felt angry sometimes that the fellow had not been brought to justice.

Of course he had always blamed the tinkers. He had foolishly allowed them to camp on a bit of his land, the field farthest from the house, of course. Maud had not been pleased, but he'd stood up for them, said they needed somewhere for a few days. Sometimes he clenched his fists in anger at his own misplaced goodwill. If he'd seen them off as soon as they arrived it might never have happened. There'd been a fellow there that he'd not liked, a big man always wearing an old trilby, and Pamela had said something about a hat when he'd questioned her. That was the only thing she could remember, a hat of all things. The tinkers had gone early the next morning, before dawn in fact, and although he'd made enquiries he'd never been able to trace them. Not that it would have done any good anyway. In fact, when he thought about it, he knew that vengeance would solve nothing, might do a lot of harm in fact. He told Pamela of his suspicions and she'd seemed inclined to believe him, reassured at least that the tinkers had moved on and her attacker was unlikely to return. After Jane was born the subject hadn't been mentioned between them. He hated to think of Jane with a tinker for a father!

His glance strayed to the door through which the child had disappeared. Perhaps after all Maud had been right. To know who the rapist was would probably be a bad thing. Jane was a precious treasure to all of them, a gift, proof that good might

7

occasionally result from something evil.

He loved Pamela too, though, and often felt that she was the one who had lost in all of this. She had lost her child for sure. She was not allowed, on Maud's orders, to think of her baby as a daughter, and this was another thing that made him angry. Yet he was on the whole a mild man, usually willing to exchange compromise for peace.

And Pamela was tough, a survivor. He had watched her grow up sturdy and strong and with a fierce independence that she might not have possessed if she had been more molly-coddled. It comforted him to believe so anyway, though over the years he had tried to give her some security and affection. Showing his feelings didn't come easy to him, but he hoped she knew that he loved her like a father. He and Maud had never had children. Pamela was the daughter he would have liked.

He couldn't help thinking that this proposed marriage might solve her problems even though she didn't appear to be too keen at the moment, and if Maud could be persuaded to let her take Jane it would be better for all of them. He and Maud were getting old. The child needed proper young parents and now that she was past the baby-stage she was more difficult. There were toddler tantrums now and then that wearied both of them. Maud had told him that Alan Saunders knew and accepted the fact of the rape even though it was still a secret carefully kept from everyone else in the neighbourhood.

He looked affectionately at Pamela, guessing her thoughts. 'I know you're not sure about Alan,' he said. 'But he'm a good lad on the whole. Think very hard about it, maid, and I'll do what I can to make sure your aunt keeps her promise over Jane.' He went to the door and then turned and grinned at her. 'Stop looking so wisht,' he added, lapsing deliberately into the speech of his youth which Maud hated and which he knew amused Pamela. 'I could do with some help with they calves today. You'm good with 'em.'

She smiled back at him. 'I'll not be long, Uncle Richard.'

As the door closed behind him she stared out of the window at the soft Devon rain. A blackbird was singing cheerfully in the rowan tree outside and Pamela's spirits began to lift. She was filled with the conviction that somehow she would succeed; one day she would have the right to determine the course of her own life. She would get herself and Jane out of Aunt Maud's clutches.

She left the table and picked up the doll that her child had left on the hearth rug. She held it close to her breast and smelt the baby-smell that lingered on it. The quickest way of escape open to her for the moment was marriage to Alan Saunders. She stood holding the doll and thought about it. He was acceptable, she supposed, reasonably handsome, keen on the idea of marrying her apparently although she would have liked to hear that he loved her. But perhaps that was asking too much! And he had said, albeit a trifle unwillingly, that he would take Jane too. There were plenty of other girls who would jump at the chance of marrying a man like Alan Saunders. Was she being too choosy? Was Aunt Maud right after all?

There was a large nub of disquiet in Pamela's heart however over her aunt's true motive in promoting this marriage. There was a sort of inconsistency to it. Surely she would never let Jane go? Was it a way of getting the little girl completely to herself, completely in her power? When the bait had been accepted, the marriage made absolute, would Aunt Maud bring all her formidable resources into play to keep Jane here? Pamela knew that if this happened there would be an even greater barrier between herself and her child. The marriage would have been partly in vain.

Would she ever be able to teach herself to love and trust again? she wondered. Since the rape she had erected a barrier between herself and others, not wanting any close relationship that might bring hurt. Perhaps a husband whom she didn't madly love might be the best thing after all? Love only brought unhappiness, Aunt Maud had declared. It wasn't a very pleasant philosophy, but maybe there was a grain of truth in it. But then Pamela shuddered. How would she manage the side of marriage that she dreaded, the nights that would certainly bring back those terrifying memories with greater clarity?

Still unresolved, she went out to the back porch, followed

closely by the comforting presence of her dog. She put on wellingtons and macintosh. She must go and help Uncle Richard. With
most of the men away in the forces there was a lot of work to
do on the farm and she seldom had any free time to herself.
Perhaps that was a good thing, she reflected. Hard work in the
fresh air helped allay everyone's anxieties, even hers.

A week later Pamela went out walking with Alan Saunders.
'So, have you made up your mind?' he asked. He was a big
purposeful man and strode along beside her looking neither to
right nor left. There was only the slightest trace of a Devon
accent in his voice. His years away at school had erased most of
it and he made great efforts to be considered one of the gentry.
'I'm still thinking, Alan,' she said firmly, and wondered if he
saw how beautiful the foxgloves were that lined the lane or was
aware of the scent of the honeysuckle that twined itself in and
out of the blackberry blossoms in the hedge. The rain earlier in
the day had given the air a freshness that was quite intoxicating.
There had been a rainbow shimmering in the sky when she first
looked out of her window that morning. The delicate magical
colours always gave her a sense of optimism for the day ahead.
As long as she was not alone, dusk was her favourite time, a
precious hour just between full light and darkness. She liked to
call it 'the dimpsey' as the village people did. It had a fairy-like
quality that affected her in a similar way to the early morning
rainbow. In the hard light of day there was no magic, no time
for dreaming.
Bats were swooping and darting around their heads but Pamela
had no fear of them. She loved their quick erratic flight and was
constantly surprised by their ability to avoid imminent collision
by swooping away suddenly just as a crash seemed inevitable.
The call of an owl affected her differently. There was a fearsome
quality about it. The eerie haunting cry was usually answered by
another in some secret place across the fields or woods, and she
shivered when she heard it. There had been an owl that other
time, that fearful time she wanted so desperately to forget. She
was too scared to walk alone here in the woods any more. Uncle

Richard had said many times that the tinkers wouldn't dare show their faces in the area again. The man who had raped her would see to that. It was quite safe he assured her. Now the war was on, there were hardly any visitors about, only locals whom they all knew. But although Pamela believed him in her head, the irrational fear would not go away. The lanes she loved had become quite out of bounds to her after dark. It was one of her greatest regrets. But she reminded herself that Alan was here now. She was quite safe. That was one good thing about him: he gave her a sense of security. She suddenly wanted to take his hand and share both her fear and her enchantment but sensed that he would understand neither.

She walked along quietly beside him, wondering what he was thinking. She was not to be kept in doubt for long.

'Your aunt is getting impatient for a decision,' he said. 'She wants the wedding straight after harvest.'

'And what do you want?' Desperately she hoped for a little tenderness, some small indication of warmth.

'After harvest would suit me fine,' he said. 'There's always a bit of a gap in the work then. You'd be able to get used to things at Morelake before the winter sets in.'

Alan had walked a few steps further before he obviously realized she was not going to rush to keep up with him. 'What's the matter?' he enquired, looking back a trifle impatiently.

'Nothing's the matter,' she said. 'I used to make up stories about this bridge. It's one of my favourite places. The old name for it is Fairy Bridge.'

The lane was an old packhorse route along the coast and an ancient stone bridge spanned the narrow stream that ran down from the hill behind Burlcombe House.

He came back and traced the stone with his finger. 'Needs some work doing on it,' he remarked. 'All this wants repointing or the whole thing will collapse in a few years' time. It's on your uncle's land, isn't it? I'll mention it to him.'

Pamela wanted to scream and laugh, both at the same time. Suddenly she saw the funny side. Alan was a good man, she decided, a very practical good man who would always see that

11

things didn't fall down, that his house was cared for, walls frequently painted, hinges oiled, and all the bothersome paraphernalia of life efficiently dealt with. What was wrong with that? If he left her to her dreams it might not be so bad after all. And she would have Jane. She was determined that she would have Jane at last. She looked up at him and only the laughter bubbled from her.

'What's funny?' He looked hurt.

She wanted to tell him that he was funny, suddenly hilariously funny, but she knew that he would never recover from the insult.

'Just life,' she said. Then she quickly kissed him on the cheek and turned and walked away towards her home, towards Burlcombe.

Surprised by the kiss, the first that she had given him, he stood still for a moment on the bridge and put his hand tentatively to the place where the brush of her lips felt like fire on his face. He had not kissed her yet, had deliberately not behaved in any way that might remind her of the rape. He fervently hoped anyway that she had forgotten the horror and that all the details had faded from her mind. He didn't want her to think about that on their wedding night.

He quickly caught up with her and took her hand. 'You kissed me,' he said, feeling rather stupid.

'Well, you have asked me to marry you!' She stressed the word 'have' as though slightly indignant at his surprise.

'Then you will?'

'If I can have Jane, I will.'

He hesitated and when he replied his voice was flat, unsure, but his answer was in the affirmative. 'Yes, you can have Jane if you're set on it.' It wasn't a deliberate lie, he told himself firmly. One day they would have Jane, if not immediately, but he needn't tell her that. One day a long time off, he hoped. Time was a healer. He'd get used to the idea of having Jane around eventually, and there would be other children by then anyway.

'Then I suppose I'll marry you,' she said.

He looked at her and felt that something was expected of him. He put his arms awkwardly round her, and her body against his seemed exquisitely soft and delicate. He was unexpectedly overcome with a desire to protect this woman who intended to give herself to him. He bent his head and kissed her, first on the cheek and then, with some hesitation, on the lips. Perhaps marriage might not be such a bad idea, after all.

The touch of his lips on hers was slight but she suppressed a shudder. No one had kissed her like that since that other time . . . Unbidden, the memory surfaced again. There were similarities, but she had never seen her attacker. He had been completely silent, never uttering a word, and the night was dark with no moon or stars.

She tried to calm herself. She opened her eyes and saw Alan's clean handsome face, with the fair hair brushed back and the blue eyes looking searchingly into hers. So far he had seemed to be rather lacking in the male passion she had read about and dreaded. Perhaps she could learn to put up with it when the time came, and if it led to babies – well, that was what she wanted, a baby or two of her very own that she could have and hold from the beginning, children whom she would be free to cuddle. And Jane would learn to love her too.

Pamela returned the embrace, her arms tightening around Alan suddenly. Somehow she felt a little sorry for him but had no idea why.

He moved away from her and she crossed her arms over her breast, hugging herself. This wasn't love but she was sure it would come some day, though how and when she couldn't tell. Would this marriage bring it? In spite of her doubts she knew that she would do her best, would try to make it successful, for had not Uncle Richard told her that you had to work at it, that marrying a man didn't automatically bring about the realization of all your dreams? Well, she had plenty of dreams, and a vast amount of determination too!

She looked away from Alan and saw Binks busily trying to remove part of a dead tree from the river. She was overcome with affection for the shaggy little creature. Apart from her dog, she felt that no one had ever really loved her. Only to him could she give complete love and trust. She called his name and he came out of the water, shook himself all over both of them, and ran to find a stick that was easier to carry.

'I'm not taking him as well!' There was contempt in Alan's voice as he nodded towards the excited animal.

Pamela looked at him in utter horror and for a moment was speechless. 'But we've never been separated,' she said at last. 'I love him, Alan. He's been my only friend. You can't mean you won't have him, surely? I . . . . I don't think I can marry you after all if you're going to lay down conditions like that. Binks is nearly as important to me as Jane.' She scooped the wet dog up in her arms. 'Where I go, Binks goes. So now it's you who'll have to make up your mind!'

He was completely nonplussed. Could he give in so early in their relationship? He shrugged his shoulders, unwilling to capitulate immediately. 'I've never liked dogs,' he said. 'Dirty things.'

Pamela wanted to run away. For a moment she wished never to see him again if he felt like that. But she suppressed her feelings. Perhaps she was being childish? She wouldn't give in though, on that she was determined. She kissed the dog on his wet face and was licked profusely in return before she put him down.

'They're not dirty if they're looked after properly,' she said firmly. 'Perhaps I'll manage to persuade you how nice they are?' She smiled at him, suddenly realizing that this was their first disagreement, and for her an important one. She would try to win him over with charm at first.

'You'll never make me believe that,' he said. 'We'll talk about it another day.'

'No, it's important. It can't wait. Please, Alan.'

He looked at her. She was definitely pretty. He had always thought so, always desired her. Surely a dog was not going to wreck his plans? It was a small dog. 'If it stays outside, I might agree to have it,' he compromised.

'Outside?' Pamela was shocked. Binks had always been one of the family, had shared her bedroom.

'Yes. Outside. In the barn.'

14

She frowned. 'Well,' she said, 'I'll think it over.' Privately she was sure that she would be able to change his mind. Binks was good and charming, a dog to wheedle himself into anyone's heart. Alan wouldn't be able to resist him. After all, he had never known a dog, never owned one.

'Good,' he said. 'That's settled then.'

'Settled?'

'You'll marry me!'

'If you don't always lay down the law, I probably will.'

'A man should be master in his own home.'

Pamela thought of Uncle Richard. He had never been master, never would be. And was it necessary anyway? He and Aunt Maud seemed happy enough. 'There's got to be sharing,' she said.

'Some, yes.' He said no more and they walked in silence the rest of the short way home. But it was not an unpleasant silence. Pamela felt that a kind of compromise had been reached. She was determined not to be a door mat to Alan Saunders and felt a little more confident now. Confident that, over some things at least, she would be able to manage him. At the gate of Burlcombe he kissed her briefly again before she rushed away from him up the path to the front door, closely followed by Binks. Once there she turned and watched him kick his motor-cycle into life and drive carefully down the rutted track. Then she went to the rowan tree, touched it for comfort and went inside.

# TWO

*Olivia's Journal – 14th February 1921*
*My fourteenth birthday! Maud and Richard have given me this beautiful book. I love the soft leather cover with my initials embossed in gold. It has empty pages of creamy paper and it will be my Journal. My writing is small and I think that it will be many years before I come to the end. Perhaps it will last until I am nineteen or twenty. How old that seems! I shall write all my dreams and secrets in it and no one will ever read them until I am dead, or perhaps until I am an old, old woman. Then I might give it to my great grandchildren. I cannot imagine what it must be like to be really old. My sister Maud is thirty-six and Richard a few years older.*
*I am so glad that this book has a lock and a key so that Maud will not be able to pry!*
*Olivia Belmont*

The first page of her mother's journal always made Pamela feel sad. Poor Olivia! Dead so young, never an old woman. Had she lived she would still be quite young, in her thirties. Pamela sometimes wondered what kind of mother she would have been. She pictured her full of fun and always loving, a friend as well as a mother. And now all that remained of her was a beautiful marble angel on her grave in the churchyard, her dog Mallory's small tombstone in the garden and this little leather book. Olivia Belmont had recorded her innermost thoughts in a journal and this book had been secretly given to Pamela by her uncle one day just recently. 'I found it when I was doing some repairs,' he had told her. 'T'was under a loose floor-board in her old room, all wrapped up in lace and put into a little tin box. Your Aunt Maud don't know that it have come to light. Best keep quiet about it or her'll want it, and I reckon 'tis yours by rights, especially now you'm getting wed. 'Tis just as I found it. I couldn't bring myself to read a word of it.'

It was now one of Pamela's most treasured possessions and she kept it hidden, its lock securely fastened, the key usually on a ribbon round her neck. Prying eyes would never find its secrets. They were for her alone. In the words the young Olivia had written Pamela had discovered that her mother had truly loved her father. That love between her parents was a talisman she held to herself, giving her a sense of self-worth when everything else in her life had worked in the opposite direction.

Aunt Maud and Uncle Richard seldom talked about Olivia. Pamela wanted to know more about Daniel, the man her mother had loved, but she dared not mention even the name to her aunt. Even Uncle Richard's face became solemn whenever Pamela tried to question him on the subject. 'Your aunt doesn't want him mentioned,' he always said, and that was an end to it. It seemed from the journal that Olivia hadn't wanted his identity known either. Yet Pamela was constantly curious about the man who was her father. One day, she promised herself. One day I shall find him. But that was for the future. Now she was obliged to turn her thoughts to her marriage to Alan.

Pamela knew that her aunt was feeling triumphant. Maud Lindhurst had schemed and planned for this wedding and everything was going just as she wished, as it always did. All the people around her were pawns whom she arranged at will. Even Alan Saunders fell in with her careful arrangements.

'You must go and look at your future home,' she said one evening. 'You're lucky to have a house waiting for you. Morelake is sound and sturdy.'

She could have been talking about a bull or a ram, Pamela

thought. 'It's a bit gloomy, don't you think, Aunt?' she replied. 'Not so beautiful as Burlcombe.'

Maud sniffed. 'Maybe not. But beggars can't be choosers.'

Pamela was caught off guard. Was she such a bad bargain then for Alan? 'What do you mean?' she said, aggrieved.

'You know perfectly well what I mean.'

Pamela turned away and went outside, suddenly needing to be alone. There it was again, the inescapable shadow of the rape! It had followed her throughout the years. She clenched her fists in anger, determined that she would not allow the cruel words to hurt. She had already decided that she would be no abject and submissive little wife to Alan. She was as good as he was and was not guilty, definitely not to blame in any way for what had happened to her.

Alan took her to see his house a few days later.

'What do you think of it then?' There was a trace of pride in his voice as he led her from room to room, but she looked around in despair and struggled not to let the dismay she felt show in her face.

Morelake Farm was situated in a valley with no view of the sea and little sun in the winter. In an area of great beauty Pamela often felt that it was unique in having none of its own. The house was covered with a kind of rough grey pebble-dash outside and its shape was uncompromising. It was the kind of house that children draw when they are first given pencils and crayons. There was a door in the middle, four square windows, two up and two down and no shrubs or trees to soften its lines.

'Mother didn't like plants near the house,' Alan explained impatiently when she mentioned the barren state of the garden. You could hardly call it a garden at all, Pamela thought. It was just an area of grass.

'Too many insects come in the windows,' Alan added, perhaps feeling her criticism.

Inside, the house was just as bleak, and although Pamela had visited once with her aunt she had not realized quite how bleak

19

it was. It had not mattered then, but now it did. It mattered a lot, for this was to be her home. The entire house had the feeling of a hollow shell to her. In spite of the heavy Victorian furniture and drapes there was an emptiness, an echo of the blank personality of Alan's mother. She remembered the old woman who had died a year or so before. Nothing had existed for her but her son. She'd had no interests other than those which concerned him and the farm. There were no books in the house, no paintings, but on every wall hung photographs of Alan, in his christening robe, at school, in his first long trousers, with his prize bull.

'If I'm to live here I shall have to make some changes,' Pamela said adamantly. 'At first, of course, it will only be those that I can manage without buying anything. I should like to feel that . . .'

'Nothing drastic and none in the parlour,' he interrupted. 'That was mother's room and I've always liked it. It's special. I don't want it altered at all.' His words were abrupt and firm and Pamela looked at him in disbelief. The parlour, as he called it, was the most important room of the house.

'But, Alan, your mother's been dead over a year now. I'm sure she wouldn't want . . .'

Again he interrupted her swiftly. 'Do what you like with the kitchen, the scullery, the dining room, the rest of the house,' he conceded, 'but the parlour stays as it is.'

Angrily Pamela turned from him and at that moment a dog barked outside, somewhere on the hill in the distance, and she thought swiftly of Binks. Binks and then Jane. Alan had made concessions for her. He had compromised eventually, agreeing to have Binks on condition that he was put out at night. Yes, he had said, she could have the animal in the house during the day, but he must sleep in the barn. So, Pamela thought, perhaps she must make allowances too. She would leave the parlour to his memories, but she would never sit in that room if she could help it. Never!

In spite of her fear she walked alone that evening. Although she was frightened to be on her own in woods and lanes where there were concealed private places, the road that ran along beside the beach seemed to hold no menace. She had always felt safe there. The beach was mined for fear of invasion now so she kept to the road.

As she walked she glanced now and then at the great rolls of barbed wire that made an almost impenetrable barrier between herself and the sea. Binks was not too pleased when she came this way for he had to be on a long rope. A small dog might get through and step on a mine. In fact one had done just that. The depressing remains of the once rather splendid hotel on the shore stood witness to the tragedy. Pincher, a dog she knew, a small black and white sheep dog not unlike Binks, had crawled beneath the barrier and had blown himself up as well as part of the now abandoned building. Everyone had been sad when it happened, and the ominous event had made the war suddenly more real on this hitherto peaceful stretch of beautiful Devon coastline.

She looked at the ruined building and at the long curving forbidden beach and remembered playing there as a little girl years before the wire went up. Her childhood had been harsh, but there had been moments of fun – never with Aunt Maud, but Uncle Richard had brought her here now and then, and they had played with an old football, had thrown pebbles into the sea, and on days when the waves were small competed with each other to see whose stone could spin the farthest across the water. There had been another dog then, a collie much loved by both of them, and she remembered how he repeatedly dashed into the waves, enjoying the fun.

And there was Mallory, too, the great Irish wolf-hound who had belonged to her mother. His grave was in a corner of the orchard. He had been accorded the honour of a small headstone by Aunt Maud, for this dog had been special. To Pamela, as a small child, he was enormous and his dark eyes had often regarded her solemnly as though he too was blaming her for the death of his mistress. Yet she had loved him, and could just remember putting her small arms around his shaggy neck and longing for the parents she had never known.

She looked through the wire at the sea. It was calm today and a light mist dampened her hair and made the tweed of her old coat wet to the touch. She wondered if she would ever be able to take Jane down on to the beach, if it would ever be safe again, if they too would throw pebbles and paddle without fear, perhaps even swim. She remembered making sandcastles sometimes too, not here at Slapton but on the sandy cove just below Stoke Fleming. Uncle Richard had taken her there in the pony-trap occasionally as a very special treat.

Building castles . . . That house . . . Her thoughts turned to the home she would try to make for Jane and herself – and for Alan. Would love ever come, and were security and kindness enough as Aunt Maud told her? She strode out swiftly, trying to keep up with the excited Binks who was impatiently running as far as his rope would allow.

The wedding was arranged for the beginning of October. There were just a few weeks of freedom left. Or at least a kind of freedom. Perhaps she had never known freedom? Perhaps she was just exchanging bondage to Aunt Maud for another sort of captivity?

Abruptly the words of the Bing Crosby song flashed in to her mind and she laughed a little and began to hum the tune. It was something about not being fenced in. She had heard him last night on the wireless set but Aunt Maud had turned it off before he got further than the line about being turned loose. Pamela wished she could recall the exact words and wondered how the rest of it went. But the tune was catchy and it cheered her. She walked home with a lighter step.

A few days later Alan came over to Burlcombe to make some more arrangements for the wedding. He sat with Pamela on the settee and discussed various matters with Aunt Maud, for all the world as if the girl beside him was just some unconcerned bystander.

Pamela seethed with anger and resentment but said nothing until her aunt went out to fetch more hot water for the teapot.

When they were alone at last she turned to him. 'What about

Jane?' she asked. 'Nothing has been said about her and when she's coming to live with us.'

There was a look on his face that she couldn't fathom and she felt a shaft of fear. Surely she was not to be disappointed after all? She had entered into this marriage mainly in order to have her daughter to herself at last. There had been no promise, but it had been implied that this would be possible.

'Jane will stay here for a time,' Alan said firmly. 'It won't do to uproot her too suddenly. It must be gradual.'

Pamela looked at him. She acknowledged grudgingly to herself that what he said might make sense, but wondered if he was being sincere and thinking of the child. Or was he just putting her off? She couldn't tell.

'Not for long,' she said. 'A few days at the most. I don't want her staying here for long, Alan, not after we are married. She'll soon get used to the idea of living at Morelake.'

He was looking down at the plate in his hands and refused to meet the anxious plea in her eyes. The suspicions that she had tried to set aside became stronger and fear and anger rose in her again. Suddenly she was confirmed in what she had already suspected and tried to deny – that she couldn't wholly trust either of them, her husband-to-be or her aunt. Both were concerned only with their own schemes. Her happiness came nowhere in the considerations of either. There was something she didn't understand . . .

'And Binks,' she continued forcefully. 'Binks will come with us straight away, of course.'

'Certainly not.' His voice was full of distaste. 'We need time to get used to each other. I don't want to see you pouring out all your affection on a dog. We must have our honeymoon first.'

'Honeymoon?' Pamela couldn't believe that he had said the word. Coming from Alan it made no sense!

'We'll not go away, of course. I couldn't leave the farm. But I could manage a bit of time off. Go to Exeter perhaps.'

'Then there's no reason why Binks shouldn't come with us after the reception.' Pamela was quite determined not to give way on this one small thing. 'I'm not leaving him with Aunt Maud, not even for a day. I told you before, Alan, and I thought we'd agreed.'

'All right, if you feel so strongly about it, but he goes in the barn. Don't try to change that.'

'Very well.' Compromise was still not submission, Pamela told herself firmly. Her life so far had been one long submission to Aunt Maud, and she guessed that if she was to win any independence now she would still have to struggle for it.

'But I'm not giving in over Jane,' Alan went on resolutely, confirming her fears. 'If she comes, it'll be much later on. I'll decide when and how.'

Pamela's disappointment almost erupted into fury at these words but her aunt came back at that moment and it was important not to show her distress which would be seen as weakness.

Maud was carrying a jug of hot water with which she carefully refilled the teapot. She poured second cups and the watery liquid was weak and insipid. 'Can't spare any more tea,' she said. 'We've used too much this week already.' She looked at Pamela critically. 'You'll have to learn to manage your rations, my girl. It's not easy even on a farm. You've had me to do it for you until now.'

'I know, Aunt. Thank you, Aunt.' Pamela resisted a desire to scream, and gulped her tea quickly. She had to get away from these two. One of them at a time she could cope with, but both together was too much.

Before she could get to her feet, her aunt finished her own drink and stood up dismissively. 'I think everything is arranged then,' she said. 'See Alan to the gate, Pamela, and then come back and clear this away. Don't dilly-dally out there, please.' She brushed a few biscuit crumbs from her dress and walked to the door. 'And wash up, too, when you come in. There are saucepans soaking in the scullery.'

Pamela gritted her teeth but watched Maud go without comment and then turned to Alan. 'Come on then,' she said. 'I'll see you out as instructed.'

Unexpectedly he at last took her hand and gave it a small

squeeze before dropping it as if he had been stung. She was surprised and immensely touched by the gesture. It comforted her, dissipated her anger a little. Perhaps this marriage might not be so bad after all? At least she would be getting away from Aunt Maud. And he had talked of a honeymoon! Even if it was to be in his gloomy farmhouse, his very use of the word gave a little lift to her heart.

She suddenly smiled at him and was glad that she hadn't allowed her anger to get out of control. She led the way out of the room, into the hall with its staring stag heads proudly fixed there by some long-dead ancestor. In contrast there was the portrait of her beautiful young mother, Olivia, painted before her disgrace, her sin. Pamela stopped in front of it. 'She was my mother,' she told Alan unnecessarily for he was well aware of the Belmont family history. 'I never knew her. She died when I was born. She was Aunt Maud's sister, much younger of course. There was more than twenty years between them and they were very fond of each other, apparently.'

He too stopped and stared at the girl in the straight twenties-style dress, the long pearls hanging almost to her waist, and her eyes looking back at them, bright and sparkling, challenging them perhaps to be happy.

'She wasn't . . .' He paused, sounding embarrassed. 'Wasn't married, I believe?'

'No. She was in love, very much so, but they weren't allowed to marry. I don't know why. There's some mystery about it. I've always longed to find out more about my father. He might be alive still, probably is. I've no idea whether he knows about me.' She shrugged her shoulders, trying to sound as though it didn't matter too much. 'I don't suppose he does know. I'm illegitimate, of course.'

She said the word 'illegitimate' with relish. It was something her aunt had told her since she was little and she took delight in almost hurling the well-known fact at him. They had never talked about it before. It was part of the bargain, one of the reasons that she was not a good catch and must therefore be grateful for his generosity. With that in her background and Jane too, another illegitimate child, she was highly undesirable, as Aunt Maud kept reminding her.

They stood together and continued to look at the girl who smiled out from the elaborate gold-painted picture frame.

'She's very beautiful,' Pamela said. 'I wish I was like her.'

Alan turned his eyes away from the long-dead woman to the living one at his side. 'You're not so bad,' he said, and then laughed and went to the front door, opening it so that the dank and misty night air wafted into the hall. 'Pretty enough for me,' he added. 'Beautiful women are all right in pictures. Not so good in galoshes in a muddy farmyard.'

'Thanks a lot,' Pamela said. She followed him outside, almost closing the door behind her, but not quite. She was not allowed a key. 'Goodnight then.' She stood waiting for his kiss and he bent, finding her lips with his. But it was a kiss totally without passion, almost without feeling, merely an acknowledgement of their status. She watched him go down the path to the gate where he had left his old motor-cycle.

Binks had followed them out, and as the noise of the engine died away he bounded joyfully up to Pamela and then ran across the grass and fetched an old rubber ring which he laid expectantly at her feet. She bent and picked it up and threw it for him, wanting to laugh and cry all at once. Laugh at her dog's delight in the simple pleasure of his game, laugh at Alan's chaste kiss for it augured well for the future. She certainly didn't want a passionate and lustful husband. And his remark about her looks merely amused her. At least he had said that she was pretty enough. But she wanted to cry with the sudden knowledge that Binks didn't like his new master at all, kept out of his way as much as possible. Dogs were supposed to be good judges of character.

The harvest came and was over, and then the wedding too in the same manner, in the same church. Pamela endured both with a feeling that she was somewhere else, as if all this was happening to another person.

It was only in Alan's home later that day when everyone had

gone, and later still in Alan's mother's vast feather bed, that she faced the reality of the decision she had made, the gamble she had taken. She had done all that was required of her during the day: made the correct responses, eaten the sandwiches and meagre fare provided for the reception, smiled at her guests and received their presents. She had looked nice too in a pretty tight-waisted dress, not long, not white, but smart. Her wavy blonde hair had been forced into a neat roll twisted round a ribbon at the nape of her neck and another one on her forehead, and Aunt Maud had produced a little hat that fitted between, added some netting to cover her face, and had stared at her with something like pleasure for once. 'A proper bride,' she had commented. 'A proper bride. And just be grateful, my girl. It was something your poor mother wanted and never got. Be grateful.'

Pamela could hear the words 'Be grateful' as she felt the feather bed engulf her. It was slightly damp and she shivered, though whether from cold or from the sight of Alan taking off his clothes she couldn't be sure. Nervousness and fear almost suffocated her but she hoped desperately that his previous lack of amorousness was going to set the pattern for their marriage. The fact that he had never shown any passion towards her had been something of a comfort.

He was removing every garment with elaborate care, placing each one on large wooden hangers and pushing aside his mother's dresses to find a place for his own clothes in the old musty wardrobe.

As she watched him, memories that she thought had faded a little returned in all their horror . . . memories of the rape that had blighted her life. She clutched her arms across her body and tried to think instead of the romantic novels she had read. She had saved all her meagre pocket money for years in order to spend it on these books, and on batteries too for her precious little torch. Her reading had been done secretly under the bed-clothes, all in an effort to erase the bad things, to replace them with the so-called magic that the paper heroines achieved. But it was a kind of love, a magic, that she doubted she herself would ever discover; certainly it was pretty unlikely with Alan.

27

At last he was naked and she looked with awe and fear at his powerful back muscles and slim buttocks, but he didn't turn to her. He pulled on an absurdly funny nightshirt and she thought he looked just like . . . she searched her mind for a likeness and the only ones she could recall were characters from her old nursery rhyme book. Didn't 'my son John with one shoe off and one shoe on' wear a similar garment? Then there was Rip Van Winkle and various others. Fear and nerves together made her want to laugh aloud at the picture she was creating in her mind, and she stuffed the sheet into her mouth so that she should make no sound. She was completely terrified in spite of all her efforts to remain calm.

He climbed into bed beside her, and the nightshirt seemed to be somewhere up around his middle. His long legs were powerful and hairy and she could feel them against her. And then all the remembered terror of the past took over. Pamela was lost in a sea of terror. She tried desperately to distance herself from what was happening to her. She knew that she must try to let her body lie there and accept the horror while her spirit flew free. It was a way she had evolved of managing other unpleasant situations in her life and it rarely failed. And if her mind could dwell on something funny, then she was saved. Madly she searched her memories and suddenly the outrageous activities of the man on top of her reminded her idiotically of the fierce Jersey bull of whom everyone was scared – everyone except Uncle Richard who could manage him. Uncle Richard . . .

Her thoughts flitted mercifully away from the bed, from Alan's tremendous weight and triumphant power, away to Uncle Richard. Did he really do unimaginable things like this to Aunt Maud? She lay there beneath her husband, crushed and humiliated, and thought not of England but of her aunt and uncle, and suddenly everything was almost all right, lost in the hilarious concept of those two in a situation like this.

At last, drained of energy, Alan rolled from her and within seconds was asleep, his ridiculous garment still around his middle, legs bare and slightly revolting sprawled across the bed. Carefully Pamela slid from her side of it and in the darkness went to the bowl of water that, remembering, she had prepared on the marble-topped table in the bay window. She took a flannel, wiped it over the soap – a special scented block that she had saved for this purpose – and cleansed herself as best she could, wiped as much of him as possible from her skin. The water was cold but she rejoiced in its freshness. Then she crept back unwillingly into the bed and eventually slept.

When she awoke he was gone. He had told her that she would usually have to get up to prepare breakfast for him after the early milking, but for this one morning he would allow her to sleep on. They would breakfast later, together. She stretched luxuriously and thought of the night. And she knew suddenly that if she could always laugh silently to herself during his love-making, she would survive. Her sense of humour would save her. Then she heard Binks barking from the shippon and she leapt from the bed.

At least she still had Binks, and if only Alan would grow to like the dog, and allow Jane to come to live with them soon too, then she was sure that she would be able to manage everything else in her life.

She washed again, all over but as quickly as she could. She pulled on some old twill trousers and a blouse and ran down the stairs. Binks would be lonely.

# THREE

*Olivia's Journal – 18th May 1921*

*My little book is filling up with all my thoughts and dreams. I love writing in it. I suppose if I had a friend to talk to I should not need to write so much.*

*Richard has been cutting the clover field today as the weather has been good lately. I love this month. The hedges and lanes are full of flowers, and everything looks so beautiful.*

*Maud and I are going into Kingsbridge tomorrow to buy some material for new dresses. I wonder if she will dare have any of hers made up in the new short length? I don't suppose so. I must admit that my sister is very old fashioned. Richard doesn't seem to mind though. He is the perfect husband for her.*

*Will I find someone who is just right for me one day? He must be handsome of course, tall and dark and romantic. There is no one like that around here!*

Richard Lindhurst was allowed an hour to himself each evening. He usually went to the Red Swallow for a beer and also to forget the veneer of gentility that he had been forced to wear ever since he had married Maud. He had fulfilled all that she required of him and in return had a comfortable home, good food, or as good as wartime rations and their own farm produce allowed, and Maud was a satisfactory bed-mate into the bargain! He had been surprised at her ready compliance with his needs in that

31

direction when he first married her. In fact she had been eager, and he obliged happily twice a week!

The most difficult part of their marriage had been his agreement to try to change his comfortable Devon voice for the tones and accents of his betters, as she called herself and her family. It had been a hard struggle but he had almost conquered his tongue, and it was only in times of stress and also for this one hour each evening that he reverted to the speech of his childhood. He could switch at will now and sometimes used his broader vowels to amuse Pamela.

He thought of his niece as he trudged along the coast road. She'd been wed for a couple of weeks or more and he hadn't heard a word from her. Alan Saunders was a decent enough chap but always kept himself to himself. What he'd be like with a woman Richard had no way of knowing, and Pamela needed a bit of loving after the cold way she'd been reared. Sometimes he blamed himself a little, felt that he should have stood up to Maud more.

He could hear the sea rolling gently over the shingle of the beach as he walked and an owl called from the wood on the landward side of the road. He quickened his pace, longing for the company of his mates. Already the November nights were dark and cold. Winter seemed to have settled in earlier this year and he would be glad to get out of the drizzle into the warmth of his favourite pub.

At last he turned away from the sea and up the road to the village. He knew every step of the way, and that was a good thing for every cottage window was covered with the obligatory thick black curtains. There had never been any street lamps for gas was unknown in this remote bit of Devon. He had a large torch but its beam was covered with a piece of brown paper fastened over the glass with an elastic band. Only a small circle the size of a farthing was allowed to shine and this must always be directed towards the ground, never up into the threatening skies.

At last he reached the pub and pushed open the door, shutting it quickly behind him so that no light should escape. He settled himself at the bar with a brimming tankard at his elbow. He lit his pipe and felt a glow of contentment. All things considered, he was happy. Apart from the lack of children, his marriage with Maud was quite pleasurable for he was a man of no ambitions and simple requirements, and there had been Pamela to bring up and now Jane. He sighed a little at the thought of baby Jane, wondering for the hundredth time if Maud would really let her go with Pamela now that she was wed. She was her rightful mother after all even if the poor child wasn't allowed to know. He had never held with all the secrecy about that regrettable affair, and the thought of the wretch who had done it going free was one of the few things calculated to make him furious. But Maud had insisted at the time and when Jane was born he had to admit grudgingly that perhaps she was right. No child wanted to grow up knowing that she was the result of a rape!

None of his cronies was in the bar yet and he moved closer to the fire, savouring its warmth. It was funny, he mused, how both Pamela and her child had unknown fathers; or at least unknown to them. He knew very well who Olivia's lover had been but this too must not be talked of. Olivia had been beautiful and wild, the complete opposite of her elder sister, his Maud. He shook his head and wondered if his wife could possibly be right in her stern opinions about her young sister's fate. Was Olivia's death in childbirth, Pamela's birth, a punishment for her sin? He very much doubted it. If the Almighty was up there with a big stick ready to punish like that, then Richard wanted nothing to do with Him. Although in most things Maud was undoubtedly correct, he was convinced that in this she was definitely wrong.

The flames of the big log fire leapt up in glorious abandon and he chided himself for his blasphemous thoughts and turned thankfully as the door was pushed open, letting in a gust of cold air and the welcome sight of Ben Yates. Now he would be able to have some men's talk. Those other things were women's affairs, and he frequently told himself that he was better keeping his nose out of what he knew little about!

Ben hung his coat on a hook behind the door and came over to share the warmth. ''Tis a nasty old night,' he said. 'A couple of them Jeeps full of Yanks just passed me. Nearly knocked me into the Ley. Them'll be wishing they was home in that old Californy, I'm thinking, what with all this weather.'

Richard nodded his head in agreement. 'There be a lot around the place,' he said. 'Something be going on, I reckon. Us better not talk 'bout it too much. "Careless Talk Costs Lives,'' and all that,' he quoted.

'Can't help noticing though. There be a lot of them around. Giving an eye to our women too,' Ben said dubiously. 'Taking the place of all our lads overseas, if you ask me.'

Richard found himself feeling a momentary thankfulness that Pamela was safely wed. No fear of Yanks giving her more than a wink while that great Alan Saunders was around.

The bar was filling up, the dart board in use now, and cigarette smoke was wafting over him with a warm enveloping sense of security. He puffed appreciatively at his pipe. It was another thing forbidden at home.

'I see Parson 'ave called a meeting at church tomorrow,' Ben said. 'Missis be going. They say 'tis important and someone from each family got to attend. It bain't church business.'

'What be it about then?' Richard had heard some mention of this event but Maud had said very little. He imagined that, like most things, it didn't concern him.

'Don't know. Something about the Yanks, I reckon. Missis hopes that none of they are going to be billeted hereabouts, not in the houses anyway. Us 'ave had enough with all they kids.'

There were murmurs of agreement. The evacuees had filled every available spare room in the area at the beginning of the war and although some of them had drifted home, fetched by anxious mothers unable to come to terms with the separation, a considerable number remained. Maud had thankfully waved goodbye to the four that had been billeted at Burlcombe long ago and was frequently consumed with anxiety in case more should arrive.

Richard could never refer to Maud as 'the Missis', the term always used by his friends for their wives. 'My wife wouldn't like Yanks in the house!' he said. He was filled with dread at the possibility. He could just imagine the ructions if she was faced with a load of GIs.

'I be a bit bothered about my Moll.' Ben Yates looked worried. 'Any chance of another pint, Ted?' he asked the landlord hopefully. 'I needs it for comfort.'

Ted Colwill grinned at him. 'I reckon I might just squeeze another for you, Ben.' Beer was in short supply. It was one of the worst aspects of the war according to some regular patrons of the Red Swallow.

Ben Yates remained lost in gloomy thoughts until the beer arrived and then he gulped anxiously. 'Us got a spare bedroom,' he explained. 'I don't want they Yanks at close quarters with my lil maid.'

Molly Yates was sixteen and very pretty. Richard sympathized fully. Thoughts of Pamela's experience still haunted him. 'The meeting might not be about the Yanks,' he said hopefully. 'I reckon 'tis likely to be just the bosses telling us to get more food out of the land. Us got good soil hereabouts and every bit be precious now.'

The landlord interrupted their speculations. 'I heard that there be eight or more meetings planned,' he said. 'Parson went to a special one for clergy a week ago, so he knows what it's about, don't he? They must have been told to keep their mouths shut. I reckon 'tis something big. Parson wouldn't be involved if 'twas just about growing more potatoes!'

On the following afternoon Maud set out for the church. She arrived early to procure a seat in the front pew. Pamela was beside her, for she had been instructed by her husband and her aunt to be sure to attend and not to be late. Maud was bristling with importance for the Vicar had called on her personally and asked for her co-operation in seeing that each household in the parish was represented. She had done her rounds efficiently and was confident that the church would be packed. But she had not thought it necessary for Richard to leave his work on the farm. She had declared that she was quite capable of seeing what it was all about and would inform him when she got home.

35

Alan was not present either. 'It can't be anything important,' he had said. 'I don't want to spare a whole afternoon away. There's too much to do. You must go, Pamela. I want to plough the stubble field before the weekend, as well as look to some of the hedges.'

Of course she had obeyed as she always did. It was a congenial order anyway. Like everyone else she was curious about the strange command to go to the church but she was not unduly worried. And she would be able to go back to Burlcombe afterwards for an hour and see Jane. So she sat happily beside her aunt, her mind filled with thoughts of her daughter rather than with any pronouncement that the Vicar might be about to make. Her plans to take Jane to Morelake to live soon after the wedding had been frustrated when the little girl had caught measles. When she was better they would talk about it again Aunt Maud had said ominously, but she shouldn't be out in the cold November air just now.

Maud swivelled round in her pew, watching each person who shuffled into the church. There were quite a lot of men probably using this meeting as an excuse for taking the afternoon off, she thought with disapproval. Many of the women had small children in tow and that didn't please her either. Children made a noise, were a disturbance. She should have stipulated that there be no children! Jane had been left firmly behind in the care of Mrs Baines, the housekeeper.

For a moment her thoughts turned to the child. She was still poorly and Pamela had been forced to agree that she should remain at Burlcombe for a little longer. Maud had been triumphant. The measles was bad, of course, but it had played right into her scheme of things. Now that Pamela was safely married and out of the way, Maud was more determined than ever to be the greatest influence in Jane's life. She was a tiny image of her grandmother, dear dead Olivia, the precious sister who had gone astray, and Maud fervently wished to bring her up strictly so that there was no chance that she too would err and bring disgrace on herself and her family. Somehow she felt that she had failed both with her sister and with her niece. Now perhaps the Good

Lord had given her another chance. Baby Jane would grow up pure and good. Maud was determined to see to it!

Her thoughts didn't remain with Jane for long. She was consumed with curiosity about the purpose of the meeting but she tried not to show it. Although the Vicar had asked her to stress the importance of the gathering to all and sundry, he had not thought fit to confide in her and that fact caused her great annoyance. It impinged considerably on her feelings of superiority. It was a definite embarrassment to be just as ignorant of the gathering's purpose as the most insignificant of the common villagers behind her. She hoped that none of them knew of her lack of enlightenment.

She sat on the edge of the hard wooden seat and glared at those who had come dressed in their working clothes or smiled condescendingly at others who had struggled into their one and only Sunday suit or dress. She herself had put on a severe navy blue coat, added hat and gloves, and had fastened her best cameo brooch to the white brocade collar of the blouse which was visible at her neck.

She had just turned towards the altar when a startled gasp was clearly audible from all those sitting nearer the back. The woman behind her whispered loudly in amazement, 'Yer, look who's with Parson. 'Tis some big-wig for sure.'

The remark brought an angry frown from Maud, and then she too saw the man who was accompanying the Vicar up the aisle and her heart beat a small tattoo of surprise for it was none other than Lord Fortescue, the Lord Lieutenant of Devon. She fluttered a smile at him hopefully as he passed for had they not met at a reception a few years ago? She hoped that he remembered her. But if he thought it necessary to be present today it must surely be something very important. For the first time that afternoon she felt a tremor of apprehension.

The Vicar introduced his guest and the general buzz of interest and shuffling of feet on the stone floor ceased and was quickly replaced by almost total silence, only broken by the odd sniffle from a child here and there and the deep and surprisingly apologetic voice of the speaker.

He was hesitant at first, as if his usual air of authority had deserted him. In spite of all her efforts to concentrate, what he was saying didn't make sense immediately to Maud. Then he paused and repeated his words all over again as if he suddenly realized that the import of his message was so staggering that most of his hearers were still in almost complete ignorance.

Gradually, as some of his audience began to understand what was being asked of them, looks of disbelief and outrage appeared on their faces. Maud sat rooted to her chair, hands clasped together so tightly that her fingers ached and her head began to throb. Her mind wanted to reject utterly everything that he had said.

There was a stunned silence in the ancient church followed by a gradual outburst of protests which became louder and louder until some of the men were shouting angrily.

'Do ee really mean us 'ave got to leave, clear out like, and all for they Yanks? Why can't us stay alongside of they?' Bill Bayley had a small mixed farm that had been his father's, and his grandfather's before that. 'Makes no sense,' he stormed. 'This be the best land in Devon. Country needs the food.'

There was agreement from everyone. 'Us won't budge,' said another militant voice. 'You'll 'ave to drag us out, or get they Yanks to shoot us first!'

Maud tried to pull herself together. If anyone was going to make any sense of the ludicrous situation that had just been outlined, it was herself. She rose majestically to her feet and turned to the rabble behind her, quelling them into silence. Then she looked at Lord Fortescue and smiled glacially.

'Do you really mean, sir,' she said with acid sweetness, 'that this whole region is to be completely evacuated? I just cannot believe that you are proposing anything so monstrous! And what is the total area you propose to take, may I ask?'

She saw the Vicar bend towards his illustrious companion and just caught the whisper of her name.

'I am afraid that is the import of my sad news, Mrs Lindhurst,' Lord Fortescue said, and Maud noted that he looked pale and strained. 'It will be about thirty thousand acres altogether. But please understand that it is not I who made this decision. It has come from the highest sources.'

'Churchill he means,' a voice called from the back. ''Tis Winston Churchill, I suppose. 'Ee be the one who told us to get every bit of food from the land. Ave 'ee taken leave of his senses then?'

Once more there was near pandemonium in the church and the Vicar clapped his hands ineffectually, trying to command some attention. Then the cultured authoritative voice of their visitor cut across the din once more and gradually the noise gave way to grudging quietness.

'I assure you that Mr Churchill is far from having taken leave of his senses. This action has been considered and planned carefully and there is no other piece of land so suitable for our purposes. We need your co-operation, ladies and gentlemen, in order to further the progress of the war. Your help will see that fewer of our lads are killed when it comes to the real action, and that we have peace more quickly.'

Maud, watching him carefully, saw him close his eyes momentarily almost as if beseeching help from the deity whose building he had commandeered. Suddenly she thought of the church, of the treasures, the font, the screen and much more.

'What of this building?' she asked. 'Are the churches included in your plans?

The Vicar answered her. 'I'm afraid so,' he said sadly. 'We intend to move all that can be taken out, and will try to protect the rest as best we can. With sandbags probably.'

His words more than those that had gone before brought home to Maud, and probably to the other lesser mortals ranged behind her, the inevitability of what was about to happen to their beloved villages and fields. There was something infinitely sinister in the idea of sandbags in or even around a church.

One of the men, forgetting totally the sanctity of the surroundings, leapt to his feet. 'They must be expecting the bloody Jerries,' he shouted. 'Else why do us need sandbags?'

Unease, fright even, rippled through the ancient building. It was an almost tangible thing.

'Us been close to they Jerries for long enough,' he went on. 'They be only just across the water after all.' He sat down, white-faced, and another man jumped up.

'Us always said that ol' barbed wire and they mines that be under the sand wouldn't be enough to keep the Jerries out. Be going to mine whole area then, Lord Fortescue?'

There was much angry noise and whispering while the two men at the front conferred together. It was the Vicar who faced them at last.

'If we are to expect such sacrifices from you we must obviously tell you a little of the reasons that lie behind the government's actions,' he said. 'But "Careless Talk Costs Lives" as the posters everywhere say. I would urge you all to keep silent about what has taken place here today, and certainly do not talk about these events in the public house, or to any strangers.'

He took a deep breath. 'You must have noticed that there are a vast number of American troops in the area – all over Devon, in fact. They need to practise various manoeuvres, and to make this practice really effective live ammunition will be used. That is why you will have to leave. This whole area is to be a mock battle field!' He paused and then continued, trying to make his voice sound more hopeful, trying to minimize the fear and resentment that he knew every one of his hearers must be feeling: 'It will only be for a few months, and all your expenses will be paid. Your houses and farms will be put back into perfect condition by the authorities before you return. Meanwhile billets will be found for you and all your livestock. Farmers fortunate enough to be living outside the designated area will be able to offer pasture and barns. There is nothing for you to worry about. Everything will be taken care of.'

'They be going to blow us all bloody up!' It was the first objector again and Maud turned to glare at him. She got to her feet again.

'And we shall be blown up for sure, Jeremiah Perritt, if we refuse. I for one would vastly prefer Americans behind the guns than Germans!'

The speech was conclusive and the two men in front looked at her thankfully.

She inclined her head to them, acknowledging their gratitude. 'I presume there will be somewhere we can go for advice?'

'Of course. The Women's Voluntary Service, the WVS, will be contacting you. Farmers may stay behind now if they wish to find out more.'

For a second Maud regretted that she had not asked Richard to accompany her. She was certainly not going to wait with the rabble.

'We can get additional information later, privately,' she said to Pamela. 'I shall make a point of calling on the Vicar in a day or two when the panic has subsided. Meanwhile we must go home and present the facts to the men. They won't be pleased.'

It was the biggest understatement of her life, and she turned and swept out of the church, nodding to one or two and hoping that the trembling that she was beginning to feel in her legs wouldn't make her completely incapable of getting to the safety of the pony and trap before she collapsed completely. The strain of appearing calm and in command of the situation had taken its toll, and she was surprised at the weakness that threatened to overtake her.

Jim Baines was sitting in the trap holding the reins lightly. He was seventeen and anxious to join the navy. Meanwhile he worked for the Lindhursts, as did his mother. He jumped down when he saw Maud.

'What be it all about then?' he asked as he helped her into her seat.

For a moment she felt quite faint. 'You'll hear soon enough,' she said curtly. She mopped her brow and beckoned to Pamela who was standing uncertainly beside the path.

'Will you come back to Burlcombe?' she asked.

For once there was a slight tremor in her voice and Pamela thought she looked suddenly very old. All the assurance Maud had shown in the church had gone.

'I have my bike here,' said Pamela. 'I'll cycle along beside you, but I mustn't stop long. Alan will be wanting to know what it was all about. It'll be a terrible shock.'

She pedalled slowly, not quite keeping pace with the clip-clopping of the pony. She couldn't find anything to say to her aunt just now. The news was the most terrible, the most unbelievable, that she had ever had to give. She wondered how it would affect all their lives. She felt numb, unable to fathom the full implications yet, and had no idea how she would tell Alan. What words could she use that would soften the terrible blow he was about to suffer? How could he ever leave Morelake; leave the newly growing wheat just showing in lines of green on the brown earth; leave his precious herd of pure-bred South Devon cattle – a herd that he had carefully bred over the past years and of which he was so proud? And then there were the sheep, most of them in lamb now, and the sow with her young litter of squealing piglets. Where could he take them? Where would they go?

The total impossibility of what was being asked of them all stupefied her and she cycled along almost blindly on the familiar road that ran between the sea and the Ley. Usually she loved this place, the sound of the waves on the shingle to one side of her competing with the eerie whispering of the wind in the rushes on the other, but today she could think of nothing but the coming trauma. It had the substance of a dream . . . no, more a horrifying nightmare from which she would awake thankfully, the call of the owl in the dark fastness of the wood changing to the dawn chorus of the blackbird and thrush, and the winter darkness giving way to spring.

But she knew in her heart that it was no dream, that something was about to happen which would change all of their lives for ever. And as she considered it, gradually a strange excitement began to replace the horror. Wasn't it what she craved? Excitement! Change!

By the time she reached Burlcombe she was beginning to feel decidedly disloyal. In an atmosphere of total dismay she must surely be quite alone in experiencing this curious elation. Trying to dispel it, she leaned her bicycle against the rowan tree, helped her aunt down from the trap and followed her into the house.

# FOUR

*Olivia's Journal – 20th November 1921*

*What a gloomy month November is. Most of the trees are quite bare now, yet some of the oaks still have beautiful golden leaves to cheer us all. Richard has been hedging most of the day. The long hedge at the end of the garden must be just so. He is always very proud of it when he has finished.*

*I often wonder why Richard and my sister married. I love them both very much but they are so different. I frequently laugh secretly at Richard's efforts to speak properly. Maud gets so upset if he lapses! This morning I heard him tell one of the horses that it was 'mazed as a brush', and sometimes he winks at me and calls me 'lil maid'. My sister would be so cross if she heard.*

'I'm going to have a brandy,' Maud said to a surprised Pamela as soon as they were through the front door of Burlcombe. 'I only keep it for emergencies as you know, and I judge this to be one.'

She took off her coat and hat, threw them down in the hall without her usual care and walked slowly into the sitting room. Then she took two glasses from the cabinet and opened the cupboard in the vast sideboard. She pushed aside a great quantity of home-made wine and triumphantly brought out the carefully hidden bottle. She poured herself a very large measure and a very small one for her niece. Then she sank on to the sofa which

43

had been pulled up beside the fire and placed the bottle on a table close to hand. 'Now go and fetch your uncle,' she said. 'Drink your brandy first, mind.'

Pamela flinched as she felt the burning golden liquid on her tongue. She had never been allowed it before. Its smooth fire flowed through her and she closed her eyes momentarily with surprised pleasure. Then she watched, fascinated, as her normally very abstemious aunt drank three times as much.

Maud flushed and looked up at her. 'Well, go on then, girl,' she ordered as she crashed the glass on to the table. 'I told you to go and fetch Richard, didn't I?'

Pamela turned and rushed out of the room, the drink giving wings to her feet but making her stretch out her hands to the doorpost for support when she reached the cold clammy dusk outside. It was not the magical 'dimpsey' tonight but a threatening chill that enveloped her.

Although it was nearly dark she knew that she would find her uncle in the long field. Aunt Maud had told her earlier that he was working on the hedge that bordered the garden. It was important to make this especially secure or the sheep would be through and trampling the precious vegetables.

Richard Lindhurst took great care with all his hedges, pruning carefully, cutting some branches a little way through, then gently bending them so that they lay horizontally, twined into the upright stems. He had been working most of the day on this hedge and now it was almost dark he had finished at last. He was pleased with his day's labour as he stretched upright, placing his hands against his aching back. He was just thinking that it would be good to get inside for a wash and a meal when he heard Pamela's agitated shouts. He looked in the direction of the sound, wondering at first why she was here and what the trouble could be for he could hear the distress in her voice. Then he remembered that she and Maud had been to a meeting at the church.

'I'm coming,' he called. 'Whatever's the matter? Not more evacuees, is it?'

44

'No, Uncle. Nothing like that. Much worse. Much, much worse.'

Richard was quite sure that there could be few more disastrous prospects as far as his wife was concerned than a houseful of noisy children. He hadn't minded the previous lot but Maud had been so strict, so neurotic about their behaviour, that life had been completely miserable for everyone. He often wondered why she wanted so passionately to keep little Jane, but supposed that was a different matter. He sighed at the premonition of trouble.

'What's wrong then?' he said.

'I'll let Aunt tell you.'

There was a strange note in his niece's voice and she didn't wait for him as he had expected. He followed as quickly as he could. From long habit he pulled off his boots, but Pamela's disturbing words didn't allow him to find his slippers or wash his hands. He felt the cold of the slate floor through his socks as he rushed along the passageway towards the sitting room where he could hear voices, anger and distress clearly discernible.

The unusual sight of his wife in a state of near collapse on the sofa with a brandy glass beside her caused his heart to pound in his body like a piston. Forgetting his dirty hands, he went over to Maud and knelt on the floor at her side.

'What's the matter then, love?' he said gently. 'Tell me what's the matter.'

Maud stared for a moment at her husband, but seemed to be looking through him rather than seeing him. Then she pushed him away.

'We have to go, to leave, leave everything, for the Americans,' she proclaimed dramatically. They're coming to practise here, right here on our land, in our house, everywhere!' Maud was silent for a moment as her glance swept the room. She poured another measure of brandy unsteadily from the bottle and gulped it down, holding the glass so tightly in her hand that he feared it would break. She glared at Richard as if he were personally responsible. 'And I acquiesced, heaven help me! I agreed to it,

45

to their diabolical plans. Without any protest to speak of, I meekly acquiesced!'

Richard looked at his wife and then at Pamela with total incomprehension.

'Since I came home,' Maud continued, 'I have changed my mind about what I shall do. I let them think I would co-operate, but I will not. They shall not have my house,' she thundered. 'I'm not leaving, ever. They can shoot me. I shall not leave!'

She emptied the glass and placed it once more on the table beside the bottle. Then her eyes closed and her head sank back on to the cushions.

Pamela looked at her aunt and found it difficult to believe that she could behave so stupidly. It was quite out of character. Her face was red and ugly and her skirt had slipped up over her knees revealing dark green bloomers, the elastic cutting into her ample thighs. For a moment Pamela felt a tremor of disgust, but this was quickly followed by pity. She bent and pulled Maud's skirt down and tried to arrange her lolling body more comfortably on the sofa.

Richard stood up painfully. There was an unreality about everything and he felt more perplexed than worried. 'I've never seen her like this before,' he said. 'Not in all the years we've been married. What's up, Pamela? You'd better tell me all about it. I can't believe what she said. It can't be true surely, not here, not on our land? 'Tis the best in Devon. Where could we go anyway?'

'It's true, Uncle Richard,' she declared. 'All this area is to be used as a battle training ground for the Americans. They're going to use real guns, live ammunition, so everyone has to leave. All the farms will be evacuated.'

She paused for breath feeling for a moment the full horror of the monstrous things she was saying. 'They'll pay all expenses,' she continued lamely. She tried to make her voice sound a little more confident. 'They assured us that we wouldn't lose anything – money, I mean. They'll pay for everything, and the government will provide cars and lorries to take us and all our possessions and animals away. They couldn't say for how long, but some months, I believe. Lord Fortescue said that if we co-operate the war will end all the sooner and many of our soldiers' lives will be saved, so we have no choice, have we?'

She looked at her uncle and remembered that she must say this all over again soon to Alan. The words had tumbled from her almost non-stop but now the room was quiet.

Richard remained quite still as she spoke, his eyes fixed on her lips and not a muscle moving in his face to show how he felt. The things Pamela was saying were so awful that he was completely unable to make any response at first. Then he glanced at his wife again. No wonder she had reacted so strangely!

'She'll sleep for a bit. She's not used to the drink,' he said unnecessarily. 'A good thing too if you ask me.'

He got up and with clumsy hands refilled her glass and drank its contents slowly himself, savouring the unaccustomed liquor and hoping that it would calm his pounding heart. Then he sat down again, lowering himself slowly into the most comfortable chair, not caring that his clothes as well as his hands were stained with the precious red-brown earth. He turned to look at Pamela and repeated what he had already said.

'This be the best land in all Devon.' He slowly emphasized each of the words that were to be repeated by other voices round and round the villages and farmhouses of the area for days, in amazed incredulous tones. The shock made him forget his carefully achieved grammar. ''Tis needed to feed all they folks up country.' He shook his head in total disbelief. 'They up in London must be mazed as a brush to choose round here for their practices or whatever 'tis.'

There was a long silence for there seemed nothing sensible to add. Richard pulled a large handkerchief from his pocket and mopped his face and ineffectually rubbed some of the mud from his hands. Eventually he spoke again, staring at the fire as he did so, taking comfort from the glowing coals. 'If 'tis really true, then surely 'tis the most terrible thing I've ever rightly heard in my life.'

Pamela suddenly realized that she must now be the strong comforting one. She guessed that both her aunt and uncle would find it very difficult to cope, and even Alan might need her too when he heard about the impending tragedy.

'It'll be all right,' she said, trying to sound cheerful again. 'The houses are going to be sealed up. No harm will come to them, and we shall be able to come back next year.'

'I've seen something of bombs and shells in t'other old war,' Richard Lindhurst said. 'Remember that, Pamela.' His voice was full of misery. 'Us'll never come back, believe me!'

Her uncle's doom-laden words shocked her more than anything else that day. She looked around the lovely room and decided that what he predicted must not be allowed to come true. Burlcombe was her inheritance. She would definitely come back. It might not be for a long time, but no stranger should ever own Burlcombe. Of that she was quite determined.

'I've to go and tell Alan,' she said. 'I must go, Uncle Richard. Will you be all right?'

'Yes. You go. I'll look after your aunt. And there's Mrs Baines in the kitchen with something nice in the oven for our supper, I've no doubt. You go home to that husband of yours and be a bit of comfort to him.'

Pamela kissed him on top of his bald head and pressed his hand in a gesture of sympathy before going to the kitchen where she guessed she would find Jane. There was just time to give her daughter a quick forbidden kiss while Aunt Maud was fast asleep!

It had been some time since she'd had any close contact with Jane. Whenever she thought of the way Maud had cleverly had her own way in spite of the promises she'd made, Pamela became very angry. She thought now of the treasured memories, the few times that she'd been able to snatch alone with Jane when Maud was out. There was a picture book Jane had particularly loved and they had looked at it together now and then in the days before she left to marry Alan. The book was about a little fat elephant who wanted to fly, and Pamela would read the words to her and they would laugh together, Jane cuddling up in her arms. Pamela wondered where the book was now and if anyone else read it to her. She almost hoped, selfishly, that no one had. It was a precious memory, too good to share.

The child was sitting at the table mixing something in a bowl, and as Pamela looked at her shining curls and the baby hands tightly holding a wooden spoon, she was consumed with love. She wanted to gather Jane up in her arms and crush the little body to her own. Instead she said calmly, 'Hello, darling. Are you making some cakes for . . .' She almost said 'Mummy' but changed the word quickly. 'For Pammy,' she finished.

Jane looked up at her for the first time and there was a hardness in the blue eyes. 'For Aunty Maud,' the little girl said. 'They aren't for you. They're for Aunty Maud. You don't want me any more. Naughty Pammy has gone away to live, gone away and left me.'

Mrs Baines turned from the sink where she was peeling potatoes. 'Don't take no notice of her, deary,' she said. 'She don't mean it. She've just been listening to your aunt. She'll get over it.'

But suddenly Pamela's forbearance changed to fury with the woman who had taken everything from her and given nothing, denied her knowledge of her parentage, starved her of love all her life, and was now taking her child away from her in this unforgiveable way.

Only one thing made any sense to her now, only one line of action appeared to remain. She must have Jane, have her straight away regardless of any other consideration.

Quickly, and without thinking of the difficulties, she took a coat from the hook beside the back door and threw it round the child. 'You're coming home with me,' she said. 'Now, before she fills you with any more poison!'

Jane began to scream, but before Mrs Baines could dry her hands and intervene Pamela picked up her daughter and rushed to the door. Thankfully it was not locked and she was able to push up the metal latch with one hand. Then she was through and out into the orchard, running and stumbling beneath the darkening November sky. She took the path that led through the wood and had no time to feel afraid. In spite of the weight of the struggling, screaming child she was exultant. She had her baby in her arms and she was not going to give her up!

49

But the child went stiff with rage and her tantrum was so fierce that Pamela was almost unable to hold her. Brambles clutched at her legs and damp branches slapped into her face yet she stumbled on relentlessly until at last the small powerful feet thrashed out, kicking her fiercely on the shins. Then she tripped and fell to the ground, and the child with her. For a terrible moment there was a silence so frightening that Pamela wondered if Jane was dead, if she had killed her. The whole wood seemed to be silent too as though sharing her agony.

Then Jane's shrieks started again. She lay on the wet grass, filling the night with her terror, thumping the ground with her arms, pounding viciously with her legs. And Pamela sank down beside her and knew that she was beaten. Maud had won again as surely as she had done all down the years. The afternoon's news was as nothing to Pamela in that moment compared to the sudden realization that it was too late now to earn her child's love. Jane had been wickedly stolen from her by her aunt. Perhaps she and Alan had planned it together from the beginning?

'Want Aunty Maud, want Aunty Maud!' Jane screamed, confirming her fears. 'I hate you! I hate you!'

Pamela heard the terrible words and reacted automatically. She knew that she must get back quickly to the warmth of the kitchen. She staggered to her feet, pulling at the bare and dripping branches of a tree to steady herself. At least Jane appeared to be unhurt and there was infinite cause for relief in that. 'I'll take you to Aunty Maud,' she said grimly. 'Just stop crying and I'll take you back.' She could hardly bring herself to utter the words, but before she could consider how she was to put them into practice, how to quieten Jane and accomplish one of the hardest tasks of her life, she heard an anxious voice calling her name.

'Pamela, where are you?'

'Here, Uncle Richard,' she shouted. 'We're here!' And when he strode through the bushes towards her, she threw herself into his arms and wept for her lost child and her lost hopes. 'Take her home. She hates me.'

He kissed her gently and then stooped to pick up the still-rigid, screaming child while Pamela stood and watched him. There was love and care in every line of him, and she was comforted.

To her relief, Jane stopped the terrible screaming and allowed herself to be held close by Richard who wiped the tears from her face and warmed her little shivering body with his own.

'She'll be all right with me,' he said. 'Don't worry about her, love. I'll see she's all right. You go home to that husband of yours and he'll be none the wiser. I'll not say a word to a soul.'

'And what about Aunt Maud? Whatever is she going to say?'

He laughed grimly. 'No need to fear that her'll know anything about it. That brandy! It's got her good and proper. She's not used to it. She hasn't wakened yet. I'll carry her up to bed later and that's the last we'll see of her till morning probably! And I'll make sure that Mrs Baines don't say a word neither.'

'But Jane will tell her, won't she?'

'Stop worrying yourself, girl. I said I'll see it's all right, and I will. You've just got to trust me, haven't you?'

Pamela nodded, knowing that for the moment there was nothing else she could do. She walked silently behind the two of them, back the way she had come, full of gratitude to this kind, good man. She realized that she had been wrong about not being loved. All those years of her growing up, Uncle Richard had loved her. He was not very good at showing it, that was all. The thought gave her a glow of warmth and she was comforted. He had been a sort of bulwark between herself and her aunt, a quiet presence in the background, and he would be the same for Jane.

As if in confirmation of her thoughts, the little girl was quiet now, tucked warmly into Richard's coat. When they reached the back door of Burlcombe, Pamela kissed her child gently on her soft baby cheek, holding her face close until the chubby dimpled hand came up automatically and brushed the feel of her away.

'Reckon you'll be all right now, deary?' Her uncle's voice was concerned, breaking into Pamela's thoughts.

'Yes, I'll be fine,' she assured him, hoping he believed her. 'My bike's here.' She kissed him too and then marched round to the front of the house where she had left her bicycle propped

51

against the rowan tree. That tree featured in her mother's journal, she remembered. It was supposed to bring security and to ward off evil. She touched it superstitiously as she often did before pulling on her gloves, but it was the old black bicycle that gave her most comfort. She felt safe on it, as though the sturdiness of its uncompromising frame imparted strength and security. The road back along the shore to Morelake was flat and open. She could cycle the few miles quickly, and there was just a glimmer of light still in the western sky. She pushed the gate open and pedalled away in the direction of Stokenham.

She was halfway home when she saw the dimmed headlights of a vehicle coming in the opposite direction. It stopped beside her and she saw that it was a Jeep, one of a number that had been causing some consternation in the area lately. Reluctantly she stopped and gripped the handlebars tightly as an unfamiliar male voice addressed her.

'Excuse me, lady, I guess I'm lost. Can you direct me to some place called the Red Swallow?'

The request was reasonable, nothing out of the ordinary. With all the signposts removed for fear of a German invasion, the Americans who had already arrived, the advance party, were constantly getting lost, constantly asking for directions. Yet she felt the old familiar terror rise in her and was furious with herself. She had thought that marriage would erase the fear, the nightmare memories of the rape of all those years ago, but the panic began to rise again.

She couldn't see what the man looked like. The light on the front of her bicycle was dim and went out anyway when she stopped pedalling. She forced herself to answer sensibly. 'Keep along by the sea and take the first turning inland,' she told him.

'Gee, thanks,' he said. 'You sure have some funny names around here. I've never seen a red swallow!' He leaned out of the cab and she could feel his sudden interest. 'You all right, lady?'

'Yes, I'm quite all right, thank you.' It could only have been some tell-tale note in her voice which told of her alarm.

'OK then,' he said uncertainly. 'If you're sure. Thanks for the directions.'

Then with a roar of the engine he was gone, leaving her to the near darkness and the blessed silence, broken only by the familiar rustle of the wind in the reeds on one side of her and the lapping of the waves on the other.

She wrapped her scarf more closely around her neck against the cold and chided herself for her reaction to the American. He had sounded pleasant, and she was dismayed that even after more than three years she still felt a shiver of fear whenever she was alone with any unknown man.

She started out along the road again, pedalling more slowly and trying to sort out in her mind all the events of the quite momentous afternoon. The last hour was uppermost and she realized that her relationship with her little daughter was in jeopardy now as never before. Yet she determined that she wouldn't blame herself too much. Yes, it had perhaps been foolish to snatch the child in that impulsive way, but surely she had been goaded into it? She gritted her teeth in anger again as she remembered Jane's words. Aunt Maud was trying in the most subtle and despicable way to drive a permanent wedge between them. Yet strangely she felt less hopeless now as she began to wonder what her next plan of action should be.

But there was this other thing too, this monstrous order that the whole area was to be evacuated. Her thoughts returned to the meeting and the news that she would have to give to Alan. Her mind still refused to grasp it fully and she wondered if she would wake up soon and realize that it was just a horrific nightmare. Yet she knew of course that it was no dream but a frightening, unimaginable reality.

It wasn't just the direction of her own life and Jane's that would be altered, perhaps irrevocably. The evacuation would change the lives of everyone in the area. She knew that although she had heard and taken in all the facts and plans that had been outlined this afternoon in the church, she still hadn't truly grasped the full impact that the evacuation was going to have.

She would have no home! Uncle Richard and Aunt Maud would have no home! After December nothing would ever be quite the same again.

But she was young and unencumbered. Perhaps it could be the start of a new life? Could she see it as a challenge? Suddenly excited in a strange and tremulous way, she didn't stop to put her bicycle in the shed but just propped it carelessly against the wall. She remembered that her coat must be muddy and quickly brushed it as clean as she could with her glove and then ran up the path and pushed open the unlocked front door.

The early darkness had brought Alan inside. He came from the kitchen and looked at her. 'Well?' he asked. 'What was it all about then?'

'I think I need a brandy,' she replied, thinking of her aunt, and suddenly she swayed on her feet and closed her eyes against the sudden light and warmth. And then, to her own amazement, she heard herself saying a trifle hysterically, 'Alan, have you ever actually seen a red swallow?'

# FIVE

*Olivia's Journal – 30th November 1921*
*Burlcombe is lovely even at this time of year. I wonder if it will ever be mine? Maud says that I shall inherit because she and Richard have no children, and of course dear brother Philip was killed in the trenches.*
*Today Richard planted a new tree at the front of the house. He says it is a rowan and that in Scotland they plant them to ward off evil spirits. Maud scoffed at the idea of course, but I rather like it. I shall touch the tree every time I go out and in!*

'Have I ever seen what?' Alan looked at his wife in alarm. She was not usually given to making stupid remarks. She looked decidedly strange, though. There was something about her that he couldn't place and it seemed that she had retreated further from him than ever. Filled with unusual concern, he helped her take off her coat and scarf. He draped them carelessly on the hallstand and when he looked at her again he saw that she was watching him yet appeared to be looking right through him.

'A red swallow. You know, the name of the pub. Have you ever seen one?'

'Why are you asking me such a silly question?'

'Someone just asked me how to get to there, to the pub. He was surprised at the name.'

'No, I've never seen a red swallow and I have no idea why the

55

pub was called that. What has it to do with the meeting? You were going to tell me about it, remember?'

She walked through into the kitchen and sat down on the settle beside the stove. He followed her, wondering what had caused this strangeness and what he should do next.

She solved the immediate problem for him. 'I should like a cup of tea,' she murmured. 'Not brandy after all.'

He stood for a moment, unsure of himself. During his mother's last illness he had done almost everything in the house as well as on the farm and had mentally decided never to do so again, but Pamela's present state demanded concessions. He took the teapot from its place on the mantelpiece. It had always been kept there so that it would be warm and ready. A nice cup of tea had been his mother's constant comfort and was frequently his too, a remedy for most ills. He measured tea leaves carefully into it and lifted the heavy iron kettle, already steaming on the hob, on to the glowing coals so that it should come fully to the boil.

Eventually he handed Pamela a brimming cup of strong tea, first stirring into it a heaped spoonful of sugar.

'Now drink that, and then calm yourself and tell me what's the matter,' he commanded. 'You look . . . odd.' He examined her face anxiously and hoped that she wasn't going to be ill. An ailing wife was certainly not in his scheme of things!

Pamela didn't enlighten him at first. She sat there enjoying her husband's unusual solicitude. It had been a traumatic day. She silently reviewed its various events and decided that for a start she must banish from her mind, for the moment at least, her aunt's betrayal over Jane. She knew that later on she would have to sort out her thoughts about it and determine what was to be done, but now there was this other unbelievable thing that was about to happen to them all.

She finished the tea, drinking right down until some of the leaves were in her mouth. Then she took a deep breath and looked at Alan. 'All this area is to be requisitioned,' she said. 'We have to be out by December the twentieth. Everything, everybody, animals, all we possess, has to be moved out!'

Alan sank on to the chair opposite her. He was staring at her as if she was possessed. 'You must have dreamed it,' he stated. 'You're out of your mind. Go up to bed and have a sleep, Pamela. Maybe you should have some brandy after all. I'll bring you some in a glass of hot milk. We'll talk about whatever it is in the morning.'

Gradually she perceived that he thought she was truly ill, had taken leave of her senses. Her stupid remarks about the Red Swallow had made him think she was beside herself! She stared at him and spoke quietly, rationally, willing him to believe her.

'It's true, Alan,' she said. 'Lord Fortescue was there with the Vicar and he explained it all to us, or as much as he could. We have to keep it secret, of course. The American forces need this whole area to practise for some big military purpose. They're going to use live ammunition, so we all have to go.'

It took some moments for him to comprehend that there might be some truth in what she was saying, and during that time she sat there, the large saucer balanced on her knees and the cup with the dregs of tea in it clenched in her hands.

She saw him struggling to understand, trying to imagine the vastness of it. She could even hear the ticking of the large grandfather clock that stood in the hall as they sat either side of the fire in the threatening silence. That and the crackle of the coals were the only sounds. Both usually comforted her, but just now they brought no solace, more a sense of irony, This spurious security was about to be taken away, forcibly removed like . . . She put the cup and saucer down at her feet, refusing to think about Jane.

Why was he silent? Why was he looking at her like that? His blue eyes were staring into hers and she couldn't comprehend his thoughts at all. She wanted to break through the blankness that was all about him and stifled a strong desire to scream out to him to say something, to react somehow. Instead she said quietly, 'I can hardly believe it. Nor can anyone, I expect. It hasn't sunk in yet really.'

At last he spoke and his voice was measured and cold, all feeling obviously hidden. 'You must have got part of the story wrong somehow,' he said. 'This is some of the best agricultural land in the country. The wheat's showing through already. We need it. There are the potatoes too, fields of potatoes, and most of the cows in calf, the sheep in lamb.' He got up, took the cup and saucer from her, and put them with his own on the table. 'I shall go and see Ben Yates. He went to the meeting. Wish I'd gone myself now, not left it to a woman.'

Pamela tried to ignore the last sentence. She hoped that the distress and anger he was surely feeling beneath that calm exterior was the cause. 'It's true, Alan,' she whispered. 'I know I might appear rather distraught, but I assure you it's true. There's to be an information centre set up right in Stokenham. The Women's Voluntary Service will be manning it. The government are to pay all our expenses.'

Alan snorted in disgust. 'I'll believe that when I see it!' he commented angrily, showing a little emotion at last. 'Go and have a lie down. You look washed out. I'll put your bike away.'

She smiled at him, glad of a further unexpected kindness. He was like that, she thought. Just when you imagined he had no thought for your welfare at all, he would suddenly come out with a sentence that lifted your spirits. She jumped up quickly. 'I'm not ill and I'm not going to bed,' she said firmly. 'I left a casserole in the oven. We'll sit and have our meal as though nothing's happened. Then we can talk about it.'

He looked at her doubtfully, yet she could see the relief in his face.

'If you're sure you're all right?'

'I'm all right.'

He went out to put her bicycle in the shed and she stood for a moment and looked around the kitchen, *her* kitchen, for she had tried to make this room her own. There were jars of herbs on an open shelf that she had picked and prepared earlier in the year from the garden at Burlcombe. She had dried them in big fragrant bunches tied to the old beams in the kitchen. And here in the cool and spacious larder which she had scrubbed and re-organised were her first jars of home-made jams, and four Christmas puddings made only last week. These were the small things that gave a permanence to life, she thought a little sadly. Yet as she turned towards the big oven that dominated the room she was cheered. At least she wouldn't have to blacklead that awful monstrosity each week! She opened its heavy door and lifted out the big earthenware pot. She placed it on the draining board and lifted the lid a little. A comforting smell of meat and herbs and onion filled the kitchen, and she was proud of the fact that she had taken time over the preparation of this meal earlier in the day.

She laid the table with care, selecting one of their best table cloths and the silver cutlery, wanting somehow to make everything special. The day had been so momentous that she just wanted to sit for a while with the luxury of the clean embroidered cloth in front of her, the sparkling cutlery and best china. Those things gave a sense of permanence and peace, and it didn't matter that this was quite an illusion now.

When Alan returned he washed his hands at the sink then looked at the table but said nothing. He lifted the lid of the casserole, sniffed appreciatively and sat down. Pamela could feel him watching her as she ladled out the stew. She carried the plates to the table and prepared herself for the detailed questions that she guessed would come.

But it seemed that he still doubted her account of the afternoon and she was grateful for the unexpected silence. She realized that he would have to hear her story all over again, preferably from another farmer, before he would believe her. She tried to be generous, tried to understand how he must feel.

'You still think I'm talking rubbish,' she said as he cleared away the dishes.

'Sorry,' he muttered. 'But it can't be true.'

That was all he would say about the matter and later she heard him going out. He banged the door as he left, and as she lay alone in the large bed and listened to the wind whistling round the house and the owls calling from the trees in the wood on the hillside, she shivered and wondered what the future held for all of them.

Alan apologized in the morning, telling her that everything

she had said had been confirmed at the Red Swallow. But he refused to comment further and it was a full week before he would talk about any of his plans. He went about the necessary work on the farm quietly and efficiently, but frequently disappeared for long hours and wouldn't mention where he had been or what he intended to do. He was kind to her in a remote sort of way but refused to answer any of her questions or treat her as a partner in any decision-making.

Eventually, at the end of a week of worry and uncertainty for both of them, he put his newspaper aside one evening after they had eaten and looked at her. His face was white. 'I've made up my mind,' he said.

'But we haven't talked about it,' she complained. Yet she knew as she looked at the set lines of his face that whatever she said would have no bearing on anything he had decided to do. She remained outwardly composed yet inwardly felt both hurt and defiant.

Alan was completely unaware of her feelings. 'There's no need to discuss anything. I've made my decision,' he said again. 'First I shall sell all the sheep and cattle at the next market in Kingsbridge. There's going to be a special one set up for farmers who are being turned off their land. If I wait any longer the prices will drop. Now is the right time. We've only the one pig and piglets after that. I can soon find a home for them. The poultry . . .' He shrugged his shoulders. 'They aren't any problem.'

'But what will you do?' She couldn't imagine Alan without the background of the farm, this gloomy house, the animals.

'I shall join up. I shall have to anyway. With no land, I shall have no reason to stay.'

She stared at him in disbelief. 'But there's no need for that,' she exclaimed. 'It won't be for long. When the Americans have left, we can come back and . . .' She paused. There was a look on his face that she had not seen before and it slowly dawned on her that he might be glad to go. Men liked to fight, didn't they? Perhaps he thought it was a great adventure, better than staying here in this ordinary hum-drum place? Perhaps he felt just as hemmed in as she did? The thought amazed her. 'You want to go, don't you?' she said. 'And I never realized!'

He didn't comment but continued, 'I've given some thought to what you should do too, of course. I believe that you would be happiest in the Land Army. It's the kind of work you're used to, and you'll have a roof over your head, a wage and some security. I shall send you money as well. When we get the house back you can come home and get it put to rights. The land and most of the farm can wait until after the war when I return. You can rent out the fields that you can't manage, to a neighbour probably.'

Pamela gasped. 'You've got it all worked out, haven't you!' She was filled with rebellion, suddenly anxious to do anything as long as it was not what Alan had decreed for her. 'What if I have other plans?' She had always fancied herself in the Wrens. The uniform was smart and the life seemed to be decidedly glamorous.

Alan raised his eyebrows. 'You're my wife, or had you forgotten? It's my job to decide what's best for you. The Land Army is obviously the most satisfactory solution.'

She didn't argue any more at the moment, knowing that there were other ways of getting what she wanted and that if he was away she would be free to do as she pleased. She was determined that she would be mistress of her own life, but there was no point in declaring this aloud. 'You may be right,' she said, not believing a word of it, and her voice held a trace of carefully hidden excitement as she rose from the table and started to clear the dishes away into the scullery. She tried to think about Alan instead of herself.

'Which service do you want to join?' she asked him when she returned to the fireside.

'RAF, I suppose,' he remarked without looking up. 'I've always been interested in aeroplanes. I shall see about it when all the stock is sold and everything settled here. We shall probably have to help your aunt and uncle with their move too.'

Pamela was pleasantly surprised by his concern for her family. She had put the dishes to soak in the large stone sink and now sat down opposite her husband, her thoughts roving over all the events of the past few days. In spite of her anger with her aunt and her grief at Jane's rejection, she had forced herself to cycle over to Burlcombe more than once. She had struggled not to show any resentment, and to face Maud with a measure of poise that she was far from feeling. She had tried to keep her sense of injustice under firm control, for she realized that her future access to Jane depended on that. She knew that careful diplomacy would probably achieve far more than angry scenes.

Now she held her hands to the blaze and thought with gratitude of Uncle Richard. He had been as good as his word and no mention of her bid to remove Jane from Burlcombe had been made. The child seemed to have forgotten it, and Mrs Baines, whose sympathies were definitely not always with her autocratic employer, had been compliant too.

For a peace offering on her first visit, Pamela had made a batch of home-made sweets with a precious tin of condensed milk and had offered them to Jane in an effort to restore their relationship. The little girl had smiled at her, showing none of the fear that Pamela had expected.

'Nice,' she had said after she had crammed her mouth full of the round sticky toffees. 'Nice sweets for Jane.' Then she had run over to Mrs Baines with one in her hand and reached up to put it in her mouth. 'Pammy made sweets for Jane,' she said. 'One for Aunty Baines.' Then she had delved into the bag again, retrieved another with grubby little fingers and had given it to Pamela, pushed it into her mouth in fact, and the tears had come quickly to Pamela's eyes. She had tentatively put her arms round her child and kissed her on her clean shining head, but then Jane had pulled away and run back to the safety of Aunty Baines, holding her skirt, regarding Pamela with sudden apprehension.

Many thoughts surged through her mind as she looked at Alan sitting there reading his paper as though nothing of any great note was happening to them all. She had come to the awful conclusion lately that he *had* been in a conspiracy with her aunt over Jane. She was sure that they had arranged everything to their mutual satisfaction long before the wedding. She should have known, of course, that he had never wanted or even intended to have Jane. The knowledge made her colder than ever towards him and her aunt. Yet she was determined to wait and see what happened. The evacuation and his proposed departure into the forces might change everything. There was no point in having any kind of show-down now.

She stared into the embers and then added more coal, covering the glowing red and gold with the black. She picked up the long cast-iron poker and attacked the fire viciously, willing the flames to leap up again in glorious abandon as they had done earlier.

'Should we be using all that coal?' Alan said accusingly.

'Why not? We'll only have to leave it to the Yanks, won't we? Might as well enjoy it.'

She looked at him as she spoke and tried to bring some order to her feelings. So he was going to join the RAF and she had hardly commented on his momentous decision. She attempted to visualize him in uniform. 'Are you sure you want to go into the Air Force?'

'Yes, I'm sure.' On this subject as on all others he brooked no dissent. He obviously didn't want her intruding on his plans and dreams.

But he put down his paper and at last seemed prepared to talk a little. 'Do you know what your aunt and uncle are going to do about the move?' he asked, changing the course of her thoughts. 'Have they said where they want to go?'

'When I went over two days ago they were still dithering. But I do think they'll need our help eventually.'

'What do you mean, dithering? They'll have to make up their minds soon.'

Pamela recalled her aunt's strange behaviour after the meeting in the church. She had always been a strong woman, fully capable of managing her own life as well as the destinies of all around her. This crisis seemed to have strangely unhinged her. 'Aunt Maud was in a state of near hysteria for a couple of days. I told you about it.'

He nodded. 'Not like her at all.'

'It was really strange. She was splendid at the meeting, and I thought she'd start bossing everybody around, arranging things for the whole area.'

'There's time yet! I've never yet known your aunt to be involved in any situation she couldn't handle!'

His words were prophetic. Maud took a few days to come to herself and decide on her course of action and that of her husband, then she whirled into action. When she thought back to the episode of the brandy and the way she had let herself go after the meeting she was secretly a little ashamed, but resolutely made excuses for herself and eventually came to believe that there had been nothing untoward after all in her behaviour. She had not seriously meant that she would defy the authorities. It was merely an instantaneous reaction with no substance.

Now, however, she knew that she must put things right and set a good example to the lower orders. And so, in a very short space of time, she saw that everything was arranged to her satisfaction. The small herd of cattle was sold privately to some-one in Cornwall. There were not too many Jerseys in that part of Devon so the deal was made with relative ease. The few sheep were entrusted to a neighbour who lived outside the evacuation area and the poultry either similarly disposed of or destined for the pot.

Slowly a new idea had taken root in Maud's mind. In spite of her outward assurance a niggle of doubt over the way she had treated Pamela sometimes disturbed her peace.

Since Pamela's marriage, the tiny worm of doubt had grown and now she saw a way of escape. If she could, for the first time in her life, go somewhere far away, even if only for a few months, away from Pamela, away from Alan Saunders, then perhaps she could forget the guilt which was beginning to bear so uncomfort-ably upon her? And there was somewhere she had always wanted to see. Now was her chance. She went about the work of disman-tling her home and farm with a sense of urgency and enthusiasm that totally mystified her husband until she informed him of her plans a few days later.

# SIX

## Olivia's Journal – 5th December 1921
*It will soon be Christmas. I shall go with Richard to choose a tree from the wood and then we shall decorate the house with holly, but Maud will not allow any of those pretty paper chains that I see in the village shops. She says they are common!*

*I have asked for a puppy for Christmas. I want something, someone, of my very own. I am often so lonely here. I wonder if I shall get one. Maud isn't too keen. She doesn't approve of dogs in the house.*

Pamela looked with consternation at the empty fields and farm buildings when she next visited Burlcombe.

'You got rid of everything a bit quickly, didn't you?' she commented to her uncle as she looked round the quiet yard.

'Yes, we did. Your aunt did,' he corrected himself. 'I was pretty sad to see the cows go. I was fond of them. Gentle creatures. Even that gert bull I could manage.'

Pamela was sorry for him. He seemed lost, like a little boy deprived of everything he valued. 'Where have they gone?' she asked.

'To a good home apparently. Someone who knows about Jerseys and has some of his own.'

'What are you going to do now then?' For the first time she noticed that her uncle looked old. He had always been such a source of strength and energy. She had never considered his age. He was always there to give reassurance and stability. But there was a sadness about him now, a vulnerability that tore at her heart.

'Have the authorities found you anywhere to live?' she asked anxiously. 'What about all the farm equipment and the furniture and things? And will you be able to have Sheppey?' The sheep dog was his constant companion.

Richard took a long time lighting his pipe and then leaned on the lower stable door and didn't look at her. 'No, not Sheppey,' he said. 'Your aunt has taken it into her head to go to Scotland. She wants to visit her cousin in some place called Craemore, I believe. This woman is married to a Scotsman. He's in the navy, she says, and stationed there on the Firth of something or other. Moray Firth, I believe it was. I don't rightly know what a Firth is – a sort of inlet of the sea, I think. 'Tis like a foreign country!'

He took a long comforting draw on the pipe. 'Well, this cousin has always wanted us to visit. Perhaps you remember your aunt talking about it now and then? It couldn't be done, of course, much too far away and the train fare so expensive. Now it seems the government are so anxious to get us out of the way that they'll pay for us to go anywhere if we can arrange it ourselves. We can even get them to pay the rent of a cottage up there too.'

Pamela was horrified. 'But it's so far away! I remember Aunt Maud mentioning the cousin but I haven't any idea where Craemore is. I don't think I've ever heard of it!'

'A long long way, and cold.' Her uncle shivered. 'But your aunt thinks that it's too good an opportunity to miss. She's got a sudden wish to travel. With the house and everything taken over and nothing to worry about, she says she's got something called wanderlust. Jolly funny at her age, if you ask me.'

Pamela found this latest news almost as hard to believe as the original bombshell. 'Are you going too, Uncle Richard?' she gasped.

He looked at her at last, and smiled a long slow smile before he replied. 'Now I couldn't leave your Aunt Maud to face a journey like that on her own, could I? Always wanted to see a mountain for that matter,' he said quietly. 'No mountains around here, and Ben Yates will take Sheppey for me. He's got his brother's cottage out Shercombe way, and a few fields as well. 'Tis outside of the area so he's lucky. He'll be kind to the old dog.' He bent to pat the little bitch who was standing as close to him as she could get, perhaps sensing his unease.

Then his glance strayed to the wooded hillside behind the house. 'Yes,' he said, 'I'd like to see a mountain before I die.'

For once the rain had ceased and the sun was shining through the clouds. There were glimpses of blue sky and Pamela knew that the sea would be beautiful today. Behind the barbed wire coils there would be little waves lapping on the shingle. Tears glimmered in her eyes for this man whom she had lately come to realize she loved very much. Then her grief for him was replaced by sudden hope. 'What about Jane?' she demanded. 'You can't take her right up there, surely?'

It was her uncle's turn to show compassion.

'It might be for the best,' he said slowly. 'She's happy with your aunt. Mrs Baines is coming too. Her son's old enough to join up, it seems, and so she'd be alone. She's glad to come. It'd be cruel to separate little Janey from them two, I'm thinking.'

Pamela was taken aback. She had always thought he was on her side. 'It's not for the best!' she stated desperately. She was amazed that he could say such things. 'It can't possibly be for the best, Uncle Richard. She's *my* child. I love her and you're taking her away from me!'

She was about to push past him through the back door of the house, anxious to confront her aunt and to have the great show-down that had been boiling up inside her for days, weeks and months perhaps, but surprisingly he put a restraining hand on her arm and barred her way.

'Just a minute, my dear,' he said. 'Just listen to me before you go charging in there. Maud has a visitor too – one of they Yanks.'

Pamela paused in surprise. He was so seldom assertive.

'We have to do what's best for Jane just now,' he said. 'Nothing else matters at this moment.'

'I know that, but I'm her—'

He interrupted her swiftly. 'Not like she understands it,' he said. 'Your aunt and Mrs Baines are the two who've brought her up. She thinks of them as mothers. You were just a little thing yourself when she was born, only fifteen, more a sister.'

'Mrs Baines could stay with me. I'd find somewhere.' Pamela was desperate, seeing the whole world against her.

Richard sighed. 'Be practical, maid. We shall have plenty of room up there in that cold old Scotland. There's houses to rent. Round here's crowded out already, and when all us refugees have been shifted it'll be worse. On your own you'd be free to do anything, go anywhere.'

For one wild moment Pamela thought of suggesting that she too should go to Scotland, and then as quickly as it had come the idea subsided. To be at such close quarters with her aunt when at last there was hope of freedom from her was not to be contemplated.

'Jane's difficult now, a real little tyke with a will of her own,' Richard continued. 'She's not the sweet babe she was. She gets them tantrums now and then, and if she can't have her own way the whole house be filled with her screams. You go and feel free for a bit, Pammy. It won't be for ever, only six months or so, and what's that in a lifetime?'

She sat down wearily on the old wooden bench beside the door. There seemed to be a glimmer of sense in her uncle's quiet wisdom and it influenced her as her aunt's autocratic commands never could. Perhaps six months was not worth making a great fuss about? After that, life might return to normal. She would have Morelake back and she'd probably be alone there if Alan was still away. Perhaps then Jane might come to her more easily, more happily? Slowly hope began to rise in her heart. If she could forge a new relationship with Jane it would be worth waiting for, and much better than forcing something quickly now.

Binks pushed his wet nose between her hands. She looked at him and then up at her uncle, and managed a smile. 'Thanks, Uncle Richard,' she whispered. 'You're very wise.'

He was obviously embarrassed by the praise. 'I just love the lot of you,' he said, turning his head away. He had never mentioned the word 'love' to her in all of her eighteen years.

'I hear Alan is going to join up,' he said, anxious to cover his self-consciousness.

'Yes, and he thinks I should go into the Land Army.'

'Good idea, if that's what you want. But make up your own mind for once.' He turned back to her and smiled. 'Be free like I said, free for the first time in your life, Pammy. I'll look after your little maid, never fear about that. And when she's a bit more grown, I'll see that she knows the truth. Your aunt's getting old. You'll have your babe one day for sure.'

Pamela felt a further lifting of her spirits. Nothing was permanent. She must come to terms with the temporary separation from Jane, let her go without too many regrets. Uncle Richard loved both herself and her child and would be a sort of anchor, a link between them. She knew now that in his quiet way he would see that she was not too strictly dealt with and would keep an unobtrusive rein on Aunt Maud's over-possessive love and desire to dominate and rule. And nice sensible Mrs Baines was going to be there too. She would give Jane the kisses and the cuddles that had been so disastrously missing from Pamela's own childhood. She thought of Jane's tantrum in the wood and experienced doubts about her own ability to manage a child alone and without her own home, perhaps in cramped and difficult lodgings. The idea seemed less and less desirable. In contrast there was the bait of this wonderful freedom that her uncle held out to her. For the very first time in her life, and for just a few short months, she would be free!

'Thank you again, Uncle,' she murmured. She smiled at him, and then kissed him shyly on his bristly cheek. 'I'd better go and see Aunt and offer to help. I think I can just about face her now. There must be a lot of packing up to do.' She glanced round at the pile of wooden tea-chests stacked in the yard.

Richard put his hand on the place where she had kissed him. 'You're going to be all right, maid,' he said. 'Enjoy yourself for a bit.'

Then, obviously still embarrassed, he followed her glance as she looked at the chaos of the once tidy yard. He shook his head doubtfully. ''Tis all going to be stored by the authorities somewhere or other,' he said. 'Everything has to go – all the furniture, the farm things, everything. It fair turns my brain to think of it.'

'Never mind,' she said. 'We're all in the same boat. It turns my brain too!'

'By the way,' her uncle said as she was about to go inside, 'I told you we got a visitor, didn't I? An officer no less. Don't know what he wants. Your aunt's offering him tea. I'm told they don't like tea. I hope he knows how honoured he is! Jane's out,' he added. 'Mrs Baines have taken her to a party in the church hall, arranged by the Sunday School. The last before 'tis all closed down.'

'I met one of the Yanks the other night,' Pamela said. 'He asked where the Red Swallow was. The name seemed to amuse him.'

'Shouldn't wonder,' Richard commented. 'Decent chaps they be, though. Go on in and see what this one's come for.'

Pamela smiled and pushed the back door open, followed by Binks who had run beside her bicycle all the way from Morelake.

She flung open the sitting-room door and then stopped, arrested suddenly by the sight of the young American sprawled in the large armchair beside the fire. She put her hand to her hair, wishing she had combed it, wishing she was wearing something more flattering than the shabby old tweed coat and heavy black stockings, wishing she was beautiful like Olivia.

The man stood up immediately and Maud looked from one to the other crossly. 'My niece, Mrs Saunders,' she said to her guest. She stressed the 'Mrs'. 'Pamela, this is Lieutenant Lawson.'

He took a few steps across the room to her, held out his hand to her, looked into her eyes. And the room, the furniture, the heavy brocade curtains, all became insubstantial, ethereal, having no meaning or substance. Only the old lamp seemed to remain, shining more brightly behind him, making a halo around his head. His hand was firm as he grasped hers.

70

'It's sure nice to meet you, Ma'am.'

She could say nothing at first. She just stood there as if hypnotized, her hand in his and the whole world encompassed in his smile and intent brown eyes.

As soon as the American released her hand, Pamela came to her senses. She chided herself for her reaction and stood looking at him a trifle more critically. He was definitely out of place here at Burlcombe, his youth and colourful personality at odds somehow with the quietness and unchanging serenity of the place. He wore his uniform with a careless elegance, and towered over Aunt Maud, making her appear insignificant for once. This fact pleased Pamela.

Then she realized that his voice was vaguely familiar and wondered if he could be the driver of the Jeep she had encountered on her way home a few days before. She hadn't been able to see his face then because of the darkness, and guessed that there were many other GIs who sounded similar, but surely this was the same man? There was a special quality in the way he spoke that she couldn't quite define.

'Was it you who asked me directions to the Red Swallow the other evening?' she enquired. 'Someone did. I'm afraid I might have sounded rather abrupt.'

His eyes searched hers. 'My fault, Ma'am,' he said. 'Sorry if I frightened you. I guess I shouldn't have stopped like that.'

Pamela smiled. 'You didn't frighten me,' she said untruthfully. 'I was a bit upset. We'd all had quite a shock that afternoon.'

She was aware of his sympathy and quick understanding.

'I guess all you folks must be pretty sore about things just now,' he said. 'Gee, I'm sorry about having to move you all out of your homes.' He turned to include Maud in the conversation and his glance swept the room with its lovely furniture, the window with its brocade curtains hanging to the floor, and the fireplace that dominated everything. 'We don't have many old places like this in the States,' he said. 'Nor real fires too often.'

'The evacuation isn't your fault,' Pamela remarked flatly. She couldn't think seriously about the house or anything else while

71

he was looking at her. All she could see was his smile, his eyes, his hands with the long artistic fingers. Hardly the hands of a soldier.

Almost as if he read her thoughts, his glance strayed to the grand piano that filled a corner of the room. 'Do you play that?' he asked.

Maud answered his question and her voice was almost defensive. 'Pamela isn't gifted in that direction,' she stated firmly. 'It was my sister Olivia who played, Pamela's mother. She was very talented.' There was a finality about her statement and the American turned from her to look at Pamela.

'You seem the artistic sort to me,' he said. 'You should try again some time.'

'As my aunt says,' Pamela replied, 'I have no gift. My mother failed to pass on her talents.' Her voice held a trace of bitterness. For as long as she could remember she had yearned to play but the piano was always kept locked when she was a child. The top was covered with old silver-framed photographs which were only removed for dusting. There had been a piano at school but extra money was needed for lessons and had not been forthcoming.

'That's a pity,' the American drawled. 'But you really should try again. It's often different when you're grown.' He moved over to the piano and stroked the wood lovingly. 'I'd sure like to play this instrument. It's a beaut. I guess you'll have to be careful where you store it?'

'It'll go with all the other stuff,' Maud replied dismissively. 'It hasn't been used for years, needs tuning. I'll have it done when we return.' She was perched rigidly upright on the edge of her chair before the fire, but had not invited Pamela to sit down. Now she stood up, indicating that the conversation was at an end. 'Thank you for coming, Lieutenant,' she said, holding out her hand to him. 'It was good of you – of your unit, to send you. We appreciate it. This evacuation is going to be a great burden to all of us, but if it helps to win the war, then we must put up with it.'

She turned to Pamela. 'Will you see Lieutenant Lawson out?' she said. 'I have a lot to do. Don't be long. You can help pack some of the most delicate china for me while you're here. I can't trust that to Mrs Baines or your uncle.' She swept from the room, leaving the two of them staring at each other.

Now that they were alone, the war, the imminent threat from bombs and guns, had no meaning. Or perhaps they added to Pamela's sense of excitement? For this precious moment she was aware only of the man looking at her as if she held his whole life in her hands.

They stood quietly, neither speaking. She was the first to come to her senses. 'Come on then,' she said quietly. 'I must show you out as my aunt said.' She walked deliberately away from him, leading the way through the hall and out of the front door. Without stopping, she allowed her hand to brush the trunk of the rowan tree and did not turn round until they reached the end of the garden path. Then she stood back and allowed him to pass in front of her. With the sturdy wooden gate between them, she looked steadily at him. But she was silent, having no words to define how she felt, and nothing to say which would make any sense of what had happened to her.

'Shall I see you again?' he asked gently. She was gripping the top bar of the gate and he put his hand over hers.

Yes, oh yes! she wanted to shout. Instead she forced herself to smile sedately. 'I live with my husband at Morelake Farm. Maybe you'll be visiting us too? We're in the evacuation area as well. Alan has a big herd of prize South Devons. He's spent years building it up. He's very upset about having to part with them of course.' The words tumbled out and weren't what she wanted to say at all. In fact, they were the opposite of all the things she felt. She couldn't understand herself. She was feeling just like one of the heroines in the little novelettes she used to read when she was younger and wanted to know about love. The thought jolted her out of her reverie. Love! Well, if this was love then she must resolutely turn her back on it. It was threatening to her whole way of life, to common sense, to Alan, to everything.

Her reply obviously brought the American to his senses too. He stepped back, taking his hand from hers, and all the magic receded. 'This war's for real over here,' he said thoughtfully.

'The folks back home have no idea what you Brits are putting up with.' He shook his head and then smiled at her. 'Well, so long then. I might be visiting your place. Morelake, did you say? Depends what my instructions are.'

For a scarcely perceptible moment his eyes belied the casual words. 'I'm only going to selected farms,' he explained. 'If Morelake is on my official list, then I'll be there. If not, perhaps we shall meet some time in your . . . Red Swallow?' He laughed. 'What a name! I've never seen a red swallow.'

'So you said before. Goodbye then, Lieutenant Lawson,' she said. 'We shall probably bump into one another somewhere.'

'I sure hope so, Ma'am.'

His Jeep looked slightly incongruous in the muddy lane, and before jumping into it he addressed her once more. 'Would your husband allow me to give you some nylon stockings? I'm told they're much prized by the ladies around here. We have a stock of them at camp for little presents. It might compensate for the South Devons!' He laughed ruefully. 'That's just a joke, honey, and in bad taste too. I apologise. I've been wondering what to do with my share. I don't think your aunt would appreciate them, would she?'

Pamela grinned at him, the moment of heightened emotion completely gone now. As always she was able to see the funny side, both of her inexplicable fascination with this man and of the impossible vision of her aunt's face should she be confronted by the gossamer-thin nylons that most girls had only read about and desperately coveted. 'No, she certainly wouldn't,' she agreed. 'But, yes please, I'd love some.' She glanced down at her legs, encased today in thick black lisle stockings and heavy lace-up shoes. 'I don't quite know when I'd wear such frivolous things, but the right moment might come.'

'It sure will, honey,' he said as he jumped into the vehicle. 'It sure will. I'll see to it.'

With a roar the jeep was away and she stepped back from the splashing puddle. She couldn't help wondering whether he meant that he would see that she received the much prized stockings or that he would see that she had an occasion to wear them. She hoped fearfully that it was the latter. And he had called her honey! She went slowly indoors, the charming unusual term running round and round in her mind like a refrain. It sounded slightly out of place. Perhaps his earlier 'Ma'am' was more suitable, but 'honey' was wonderful, just wonderful. With a lift to her spirits she skipped a few steps and then composed herself and went to help Aunt Maud with the china.

# SEVEN

*Olivia's Journal – 20th December 1921*
*I shall not be allowed to have a dog. Maud told me that*
*Richard's sheep dog is enough. I cried myself to sleep last*
*night. There is a new litter of puppies at the cottage and they*
*are so sweet.*

Alan was in the house when Pamela cycled back to Morelake
later that afternoon. She could hear him banging about upstairs
when she went inside and wondered what he could be doing. She
put the kettle to boil and took potatoes from the shed to peel
for their supper. Then suddenly she stopped, knife in hand, and
frowned. There had been a strangely empty look to the fields now
she came to think of it, just like Burlcombe, but in the early
dusk and with her mind filled with thoughts of the American,
the unusual quietness hadn't immediately registered.

She finished the potatoes and put them to boil, then she made
a pot of tea and carried it and two cups to the scrubbed kitchen
table before going to the foot of the stairs and calling to her
husband. 'Are you coming down, Alan? There's a pot of fresh
tea ready and some scones that I baked this morning.'

It was a few minutes before he appeared and when he did so
there was a ravaged look to his face like someone suddenly
bereaved. He went to the settle beside the fire and flopped
heavily upon it.

'They're gone,' he said. 'Years of work, all gone. I got a good

77

price though, and the chap who bought them looked a decent sort. He'll look after them well. I was lucky. Got in early. If I'd waited no one would have wanted them, no room in the fields. I couldn't see them go for slaughter, not a good herd like that.'

He almost seemed to be talking to himself. She knew how much the beautiful South Devons meant to him and tried to share his sorrow. 'Perhaps you'll be able to buy them back after the war?' she said. 'Or stock bred from them.' She handed him a cup of tea, spread home-made butter on a scone and gave him that too.

'Maybe,' he grunted. Then, unexpectedly, 'These are good. I shall miss your cooking.'

'I'm glad you'll miss me,' she said. 'Even if it's only for my scones.' Then at last, plucking up courage, she kissed him gingerly, not on his face but on the top of his head. She wanted to say, 'The cows are gone but you still have me. We still have each other.' But the words refused to come, and even if she could say them, she guessed they wouldn't comfort him very much.

Yet he looked up at her and smiled. 'I went to the recruiting office,' he said. 'I've asked to go into Bomber Command. The future of the war will be determined by the mess we can make of the Jerries now. They said that my school record will stand me in good stead. I should be able to get into the mechanical side. I was always good with engines.'

So everything was changing all around her! Pamela stood and looked at him, and perversely felt that she was sorry he was going. In the few weeks of their marriage she had become used to him, used to his company even if he didn't talk much, used to the security he gave her, and yes, even used to his big overwhelming presence in the double bed. Without him she would be lonely, anchorless. Uncle Richard and Jane were leaving too, going somewhere miles away to a place with an outlandish name and almost impossible to visit. Craemore! It sounded remote and cold and strange. It had nothing at all to do with anything she had known or would ever know.

For the first time in her life she would be alone. Then she thought of the American and felt colour rising to her face. Guiltily she put her hands to her cheeks and hoped that Alan wouldn't notice. 'How long will you have to wait?' she asked.

He shrugged his shoulders. 'I'm not sure. There'll be call-up papers shortly, I suppose. I've started packing. That's what I was doing upstairs. Mother lived here all her life and there are her things to see to as well as my own. I want to get that all done before I have to go.'

'We still have about four weeks before we have to be out,' Pamela said. The shortness of the time suddenly horrified her. Four weeks from now she would have no home. Both Burlcombe and this gloomy farmhouse would be empty and cold. As well as no people, there would be no place of her own to go for warmth and refuge. And it would be almost Christmas. There would be no paper chains, no tree brought in from the little wood on the hill to be decorated with the baubles that were stored away in the roof at Burlcombe. And her plum puddings? What would happen to them now? she wondered. Where would she be on Christmas Day, and with whom would she share her first married Christmas dinner?

'I don't suppose I'll have four weeks,' Alan said, and then went back upstairs. While she prepared their meal she could hear him bumping around again and was grateful that he had not asked her to do those things, turn out her dead mother-in-law's clothes. He clattered down many times and she could see a great heap growing bigger and bigger just outside the back door. Resolutely she went on cutting up vegetables for the stew, trying not to think about what he was doing. It was his own affair, yet she was very curious. Some of the clothes were good. There were furs and long floor-length gowns obviously kept from the days of his mother's youth. Pamela had resented the presence of his mother's shadow here in the house ever since she first came into it.

Later that night she could smell the smoke as it billowed up into the dank November sky, and knew that all those treasures were burning to ashes.

Pamela met the smiling young lieutenant again, not at the Red

Swallow but at the information centre which had been quickly set up in the village hall. A vast number of helpers were needed and in spite of Alan's initial reluctance she had volunteered.

'Where am I going to find a few hundred tea-chests?' she said wearily to her supervisor at the end of the first hectic morning. 'We shall need masses of the things for everyone to pack their belongings in.'

The woman laughed and Pamela saw the bizarre side of the situation.

'At this moment I have absolutely no idea, but we shall get them from somewhere, I'm quite sure,' Mary Turner replied.

The work went on during the afternoon too and there was the occasional angry scene to deal with. Some folk found their outrage difficult to contain for there seemed to be no enemy at whom it could immediately be directed.

'I'm having no truck wi' it,' one old man told Pamela adamantly. 'I've lived here all my life. I was born in my cottage and I'm not moving now. They Yankees and Jerries can do all their fighting right round me!'

She spent a long time with him, persuading, trying to explain that there was no choice and eventually making the arrangements whether he liked it or not. She noted that someone very forceful must be there with him on the removal day. At last he hobbled towards the door and then turned back. 'I'll take a shot gun to anyone who comes near my cottage,' he shouted angrily when he realized at last that no one was taking any more notice of his refusal to budge.

At that opportune moment Pamela heard a vehicle screech to a halt outside and Lieutenant Lawson arrived at the hall entrance just in time to hear the threat and to have the stick brandished in his face. She wanted to laugh but restrained herself with difficulty.

The American appeared not at all nonplussed. 'Gee, Grandad,' he said with a smile, 'I thought for sure I'd come here to learn to fight Jerries, not you Brits. Are you certain you'd take a pot shot at me?'

The old man glanced at him, and then surprisingly turned and winked at Pamela. 'You first, and then the Boche,' he said. 'I fought the Hun in the first go, and I'm ready for them in the second.'

With that he tottered out of the doorway and away down the road.

The lieutenant laughed and then came straight over to Pamela's desk, obviously pleased to see a familiar face. 'Well, hi there,' he said. 'You got yourself a job then, Ma'am, and you seem to be having a heap of trouble too.' There was still a trace of amusement in his voice.

Pamela made an effort to appear calm and efficient. 'A little, now and then,' she replied. 'But most people are resigned. It's just a case of getting all the organizing done.'

'You've got a mighty big job ahead of you,' the lieutenant said. 'Don't forget that they've made me the liaison officer. I'm the guy to sort out any problems, and the US army is here to help.' He gave a mock salute. 'Just tell me what to do and we'll do it, Ma'am.'

She wished that he would revert to the 'honey' of the first time they met. The formal 'Ma'am' made her feel ancient, and well and truly married.

'It's not up to me,' she said. 'But I know we'll need transport, of course, lots of transport to get people and furniture away. Farm machinery too.' She thought of the new tractor of which Alan was so proud, and some of the cumbersome bits of apparatus that went with it. 'The big stuff is going to be difficult,' she added unnecessarily.

'Sure thing. Your tiny lanes and those great hedges, they just frighten the life out of me when I'm driving round them. Why can't they be nice and straight so's you can see the other fellow coming in the opposite direction?'

She laughed at him. 'We're used to them, I suppose, and not many of us drive around here. The lanes are very old. They were all right for horses and carts. In fact, some of us still use horses, especially now that we can't get petrol.' She suddenly felt protective of her way of life. 'It's the war,' she said. 'We've been fighting the war a long time.' There was a trace of rebuke in her voice, but as she looked at him her own personal defences rapidly diminished and she wanted to ignore the queue of people waiting in the hall for her attention, wanted to see only him.

Without taking his eyes from her face, he put his hand into his pocket and brought out a small packet. They were both oblivious of the impatient and yet interested stares from people around them as she took it, as their hands touched for a brief second.

'The things I promised you,' he whispered. 'And I hope I'll see you wearing them some time!'

Alan stood looking at his empty fields so recently stocked with his precious herd of beautiful red-brown South Devon cattle. He thought of the silent milking shed and the yard, clean now in a strange and sterile way. He had never known any of it like that before.

A few hens still scratched around the back of the house and he regarded their carefree pleasure with surprising sadness. Their days were numbered. The poultry that had always been around so long as he could remember had meant little to him except as a ready source of eggs and the occasional roast, but now, in their cheerful and unsuspecting clucking, they seemed to symbolize all the familiar things that were vanishing, perhaps for ever. The pig had gone, along with her squealing babies, and the ewes were far away in someone else's fields. He was glad that he had sold the great shire horse two years ago to a good home well away from this benighted area. There had been a sadness in that but the fact that he was progressing from horse to tractor had comforted him. There was no room for emotion on a working farm he had told himself then, and tried to think that way once again.

Suddenly he heard a yapping from the shippon. That blasted dog! He had never liked dogs, had always refused to have even a sheep dog and was glad about that now. It was another burden that he hadn't had to think about. But what was to happen to Binks? Stupid name for a dog too, he thought. Well, that was Pamela's problem. He was surprised that she hadn't taken him along with her to the hall in the village where she was helping out at this new-fangled information centre. Information! What did Pamela know about how it felt to have your life pulled right away from beneath you? How could she deal with all the angry farmers he had talked to in the Red Swallow and at market? She'd been determined to do it, though, so good luck to her!

He ignored the dog, and went inside. He tried also to ignore the half-empty rooms, bare now of ornaments, pictures, all the things that made a house into a home. Only Pamela's belongings and a few necessary items of his own remained. He had spent every spare minute packing all the trappings of his past life into old tea-chests and cardboard boxes and they were stacked sadly in the dank, cold parlour.

He went up the stairs two at a time and into the almost empty bedroom. There was no bathroom and he washed in the cold water that Pamela had left in an old jug. The marble-topped wash stand with its china bowl and jug were packed away. He stripped off his shirt and shivered with the shock of the water on his skin. Then he went down into the kitchen to shave. It was a habit he refused to change in spite of Pamela's disapproval. It saved having to carry hot water upstairs, and his razor and soap had always been kept on the mantelpiece above the fire. Then he returned to the bedroom, finished his ablutions and finally dressed again in fresh clothes, and with more care than usual. He put on a clean white shirt, his one suit, selected a tie, and added an overcoat for it was cold on the motorcycle.

The papers had arrived that morning. He was to report at the recruiting office for a medical. If it was satisfactory he would be sent to a training centre, and his days of working the land would be over for a time at least. He felt a shiver of excitement at the prospect. Perhaps he might even learn to fly? Maybe at last he would get a chance to have a go at the Jerries. Ever since the Battle of Britain he had longed for that. But there had always been the farm, the need to produce food, the need to look after his mother. His success as a farmer had assuaged his ambitions a little, but now he was no longer needed here, his fields would be mock battle grounds, his house empty.

His earlier sorrow over the cattle gradually slipped from him and was replaced by a new sense of freedom. To be in the forces would be liberty of a sort. True, almost every hour of his day would be ordered and his path decreed by others, but he would be unencumbered, have no worries, and that would be a new and releasing experience.

He looked at himself in the long mirror behind the old wardrobe door and grinned at his reflection. He was only twenty-four. Sometimes during the past years he had felt so much older than that, but now that the burdens had been forcibly removed the years seemed to vanish too. He felt carefree and buoyant, young for the first time in his life. He had a wife, of course, but judging by her behaviour in bed she wouldn't be too sorry to see him go. He had wanted the marriage to work, wanted to make up to her for what she'd suffered, and although he'd made that despicable bargain with Maud about Jane, he had felt sure that one day he'd be able to take the child to live with them if Pamela still wanted to have her.

But everything was changing. The evacuation was standing his world on its head. There was nothing he could do about the past now. The war would probably sort it all out, and he had other things to think of anyway. Praise God he had other things to think of at last! The RAF was bombing Berlin and he wanted to do something to contribute. He hoped it wouldn't be all over before he had finished training. He ran down the stairs, didn't bother to lock the house, and was soon out on the winding lane that led to the town, the wind blowing coldly around him, the grey sky suddenly flaming to red as the contrary sun deigned to appear just before its demise behind the hill. He was going to his medical, to a new life.

At Burlcombe Maud was supervising the packing. There were three large trunks to go to Scotland and everything else was to be moved to safe storage arranged by the authorities.

Richard had just come in, had removed his boots, washed his hands and was sitting beside the stove in one of the few chairs that was not already stacked ready for the pantechnicon that was due the following morning. He had retired behind his *Daily*

*Telegraph* and from time to time lowered it to survey the chaos around him.

Eventually Maud came into the room. She was carrying a tray set with a cracked teapot, old cups and home-made scones. She carefully placed it on an upturned box that had replaced the small shining table that usually stood beside his chair.

'I've got our travel warrants for Scotland,' she said. 'We leave in five days' time, and our trunks go before us, by freight.'

She handed him the precious pieces of paper and he looked at them dubiously. He read the words aloud. 'Craemore via Edinburgh and Inverness. Outlandish-sounding places,' he commented.

Maud ignored his obvious disapproval. She was beginning to feel excited. This house had been her home for as long as she could remember and she had hardly ever been away. Perhaps an adventure was called for at last!

'I'm sorry we can't go sooner,' she said. 'Never mind. For the last few days we'll just have to camp out here with the bits and pieces that we can either leave behind or carry. We'll manage.'

'And have you heard from that cousin of yours yet?' Richard enquired. 'Are you quite sure about this place in . . . in this Craemore?'

'Yes, I've news about that too,' Maud said in triumph. She pulled a letter out of the pocket of her apron and opened it. 'This came in the morning's post. Cousin Ivy has arranged for us to have the little house I told you about. Of course it won't be like Burlcombe, but we must be thankful for small mercies. We're very lucky.'

'Wish I could take Sheppey with me,' Richard said. 'Can't bear to think about parting with her.'

'Don't be daft,' Maud said acidly. 'She's a stupid dog, not even house trained. What would we do with a creature like that on a train journey that seems set to take near two days, and no shippon to put her in, only a small house? She'll be fine where you've arranged for her to go and you can get her back first thing when we return.'

Richard sighed. He knew that his wife was right in this as in almost everything else. 'She'll miss me,' he said sadly. 'And I'll miss her. But she'll be taken care of, and like you said, 'tis only for six months or so and then we'll be back.'

Maud sniffed. 'That's what they say. I wonder, though.' She returned to the labels she was writing in large black letters on pieces of card which were to be fixed to the trunks. 'Number four Lighthouse Lane,' she said aloud. 'It sounds as though you'll be near that precious sea of yours, anyway. But it'll be a cold sea, I reckon.'

'The Firth, the Moray Firth,' Richard commented. 'I looked it up on a map. It's a long way.' Privately he couldn't imagine why Maud had told the authorities that she wanted to go so far. They could have found somewhere down Dartmouth way if they'd tried. He knew that she wanted to see this Cousin Ivy of hers, but the woman was not a close relative really. He sighed again. There was no knowing what his Maud would take into her head to do. Perhaps it was one of the things that made life with her interesting! If you went along with her plans and had few of your own, well then, everything was all right. And that was what he had resolutely decided to do long ago when she asked him to marry her.

'Can you drive, Mrs Saunders?'

Pamela, tired now and wondering when her long day would be over and she could cycle back to Morelake, was slightly taken aback by the question. There had been no car at Burlcombe although her aunt had occasionally suggested that they get one as soon as the war was over and petrol available again. However, since her marriage Alan had rather surprisingly taught her to drive the tractor.

'I can drive a tractor,' she replied, and couldn't help noticing the supervisor's raised eyebrows.

'That's splendid then. We urgently need more drivers. You'll have to get a bit more practice first, though. Our nice young GI-liaison-what's-it has asked how he can help. He can take you out for a couple of hours tomorrow, I should think. That all right with you?'

Pamela gulped. 'Yes. Yes, of course that's all right,' she said quickly, hardly believing it.

'Not in the Jeep, of course,' the supervisor explained. 'You won't have to drive one of those. You can have your lesson in one of the Ford Ten Vans that have been loaned to us. We're having a couple here and we need another driver.' She smiled encouragingly at Pamela. 'I think you'd do the job very well. You've proved yourself to be sympathetic and responsible.'

She was filled with a glow of pleasure at the unexpected praise. 'What exactly would I have to do, Mrs Turner?' she asked.

'Various things. You'll have to go all over the place when you're proficient: take people to see accommodation that's been offered to them, see old people into nursing homes, transport boxes and crates. You'll need a lot of tact and understanding! Does the idea appeal?'

Did it appeal! Pamela was filled with enthusiasm. At last she was to do something worthwhile, something where she could use her brains and her initiative, something other than working the land, working in the kitchen, washing, ironing, baking! Oh, yes, it suited her all right!

'I'd love it,' she said.

Alan viewed the proposal with misgivings. His wife was to learn to drive a car, something that he himself had never done. She was to be taught by a Yank, and an officer at that, and then she would be employed as a driver!

'I don't want you to do it,' he announced. 'It's not right. You're my wife. Giving a few hours to help out is one thing. Being employed full-time and gallivanting all over the place in a motor car is another.'

Pamela looked at him in disbelief and dismay. He was sitting in the kitchen with a large cup of tea on the table and a hunk of bread and cheese half eaten. 'But you can't stop me now, Alan,' she stated firmly. 'You can't possibly. It's all arranged. And I'll

87

be able to see to our things too, and help Aunt Maud and Uncle Richard. I shall have the van most of the time, I think. I might even be able to bring it home here at night, and I shall have a special allowance of petrol. I shan't have to cycle home in the dark and the rain. I'll have a motor car, Alan, a motor of my own. Of *our* own. You can drive it too. I'll ask especially if you can drive it. You're quite capable. You know all about engines and driving and all that. Oh, Alan!' She stopped her long tirade and glared at him, daring him to disagree again.

He saw her determined face and felt suddenly unable to cope with her outrage if he refused. In fact, how could he? The medical had been satisfactory and he was to report for initial training soon. He wouldn't be here. He would have no idea what she was up to. The thought took him by surprise. But then, he might be flying, he reminded himself. That was better than driving a Ford van! He looked at her and did not see her. He saw a Lancaster instead, saw himself at the controls, saw the starlit sky and the lights of a German city below, saw the flashes and the fires.

'Very well then,' he said at last. 'I shall be away. I'm going in a few days' time.' He tried to bring his mind literally down to earth, to concentrate on her life instead of his own. 'You'll have a lot to do here. A van will be a help, I suppose.'

'Thank you, Alan.' She went to him, surprised by his sudden turn-about, not quite understanding his reasons, and kissed him putting her arms around him and holding him for a moment. Then his words suddenly had meaning for her and she stood back and stared at him. 'You're going?' In her excitement she had forgotten his medical. She had been so taken up with her own news that she had not thought about him and was ashamed.

'Was it all right then? They're taking you? The Air Force?' The questions tumbled out one after the other. She didn't quite know how she felt. She knew that happiness was something you had to work for and she had been trying to do that, trying to make a kind of happiness for both of them, hoping that their mild affection for each other would grow into love eventually. Now it seemed that it would have to wait.

There was no sign of a baby yet either in spite of all the tossing and thrusting in bed almost every night. She had been sorry about that for she felt that it might create a bond between them, and she needed to have a baby of her own to cherish and to love, to replace her lost Jane. All these thoughts chased themselves through her mind as she stood back and looked at him.

'Yes, the Air Force,' Alan said, jolting her back to the eager questions she had asked him. 'I hope to get on a pilot's course eventually but I may not be good enough for that.'

'Of course you will.' Her tone was confident now. 'You've had the right sort of education and you've quite an impressive array of exam results.' She had helped him fasten down a large box of papers only the previous day and the certificate with its list of distinctions had been on the top. He had removed it and put in in his old leather suitcase, ready she guessed for some selection board or something similar. 'You were best in scientific subjects,' she reminded him. 'That'll impress them. And you're a good mechanic.'

'That's what I'll probably be,' he said. 'I have to be realistic. There'll be a lot to learn. Aeroplanes aren't like tractors you know.' He laughed, a little grimly. 'I expect I'm too late to fly, but I can always hope. If I'd been able to go right at the beginning, things might have been different.'

Pamela looked at him with compassion for she knew a little of all the dreams and ambitions that he had buried here in the productive Devon earth. 'Never mind,' she said. 'You'll get something good, just mark my words. And you'll look very handsome in uniform. I shall be proud of you.'

He smiled at her and then, unexpectedly reached for her hand and squeezed it in his big farmer's one. 'How about something to eat?' he asked. 'I'm not used to a working wife, and this bread and cheese isn't exactly exciting!'

Smitten with sudden guilt she quickly laid the table and brought out some cold chicken, home-made pickle and fresh bread. She glanced at the meat with a pang of sorrow. One thing that could be found in abundance at the moment, she thought ruefully, was roast chicken! Which of her engaging clucking hens had most recently met a sad end? she wondered. She tried not to think of them as she carved.

She and Alan sat at the table and ate and Pamela felt that at last there was the beginning of a bond between them. How incongruous that it should happen now! Yet perhaps not so strange after all. Maybe because of their enforced separation there might come a strengthening of their marriage, even the blossoming of love one day in the future. Could it be? she wondered as she looked at her husband. Could they ever be soulmates, ever understand each other? Was enduring happiness possible between them? She finished her meal, cleared away the dishes, washed them quickly and went to bed still wondering.

Alan followed her shortly afterwards and they lay side by side in the large feather bed, not speaking.

'There haven't been any babies,' Pamela said at last. 'There can't be, now you're going away.'

He moved closer towards her. 'Are you sorry about that?' he whispered.

'I should have liked a baby right away. To have conceived one I mean. Jane will soon be miles away in Scotland with Aunt Maud.'

There was a long silence and then he spoke softly, comfortingly. 'Perhaps it's for the best that you aren't expecting. We don't want our child born with no home, do we? Wait until we've got Morelake back.' Then, surprisingly, he turned from her and was soon asleep.

It was a sensible, practical statement, completely typical of Alan, and she smiled in the darkness and agreed with him. Now was no time to be making babies. She ran her hands over her flat stomach and was glad. She was really free for the first time in all of her eighteen years, or would be soon. In a few days she would be totally unfettered. No baby, no husband, no Aunt Maud, no Morelake to be slaved over, no Burlcombe even. And tomorrow Lieutenant Lawson was to give her driving lessons!

# EIGHT

*Olivia's Journal – 28th December 1921*
*I wonder if Maud and Richard will ever leave Burlcombe?*
*I cannot imagine it, and yet I should love to travel. They*
*have never been for a holiday. Maud talks about Scotland*
*sometimes. We have a cousin there, and Richard says he*
*would like to climb a mountain. I think it would be wonderful*
*to see Venice and Rome and Florence! My brother Philip was*
*killed in France, so perhaps I should be content just to be*
*alive. I hope there will never be another war. There cannot*
*be. Men could not be so stupid again.*

'I need to figure out this automobile myself before I can teach
you anything about it,' he said. 'D'you mind if we go for a bit
of a drive first, Ma'am? Will you go in the passenger seat for a
while?'

'Of course.' Pamela was apprehensive but excited too, though
whether because of the lesson or the teacher she couldn't tell!

'It's all the wrong way round for me,' he said. 'We drive on
the other side of the highway back home.'

He held the door for her and she climbed in, arranged her gas
mask and handbag behind the seat and tried to appear composed.
When he was settled beside her she looked at the controls and
decided that it didn't seem too complicated. She was grateful to
Alan for teaching her to use the tractor. The big lumbering thing
had been difficult at first, but she had won eventually and this

smaller vehicle seemed much more manageable. Obviously Lieutenant Lawson thought so too for they were soon away, along the curving road at the sea's edge and then inland through the quiet stricken villages.

Pamela had not had time to cycle far lately but now she could see more fully the results of the coming evacuation. Small cottages stood with staring curtainless windows, and most of the fields were empty and cheerless. Beside many open front doors there were boxes stacked waiting for transport, some with inadequate tarpaulins covering them against the steadily falling rain. Some of the little shops were closed already and in one village, helpers with an emergency kitchen were ladling out soup to families who had packed all their food and pots and pans.

They drove slowly past, looking at the cold strained faces of the people holding their bowls like victims from some faraway famine.

'We're sure causing some trouble round here,' her companion said quietly. 'Makes me feel kinda guilty.'

'No need,' Pamela replied. 'Just think of what's happening in France and Holland and all the other occupied countries. It must be terrible to have Germans soldiers everywhere, and that awful Gestapo.'

'Too right,' he said. 'I guess we Yanks are a better bet.'

She smiled at him and then they drove for a little while in silence until eventually he pulled the van into a field gateway and turned off the engine. 'How about we start the lesson?' he said. 'You ready?'

'Yes, I'm ready,' said Pamela, trying to calm her nerves.

'Suppose we change places right here then, and you drive now?' He grinned at her encouragingly.

'Good idea,' she replied. 'I'm a bit scared, but I can't wait to be a fully fledged driver. It sounds important!'

They both laughed and Pamela opened the door and jumped down on to the rain-soaked earth so quickly that she slipped and only just managed to prevent herself from falling into the mud.

'Steady there, honey,' he said, and was round to her side and holding her before she could stand fully upright. 'We don't want any casualties before we've fired a shot!'

She saw his brown eyes close to her face, felt his arms tighten round her as she struggled to regain her balance. She knew that she should push him away yet she wanted him to go on holding her.

The first move came from him. He released her, steadied her, held her away from him and looked into her eyes. 'Well now,' he said. Then, 'Are you hurt?'

'No. No, not at all,' she said. 'It's just that I . . .' The golden moment had passed, leaving her both shocked and delighted and quite unable to put any of her feelings into words. She shook herself free of him, for his hands were still loosely on her shoulders, and walked round the back of the van, carefully this time, anxious not to lose her footing again on the treacherous mud. 'I'll take over then,' she declared, dismissing any further embarrassment, and climbed decisively into the driving seat.

She hoped she hadn't shown any glimmer of how she felt during that fleeting second or two in his arms. She had been brought up to believe that any display of affection to a comparative stranger would immediately label her cheap, a little tart. The harsh words were used by her aunt to describe local girls who had 'gone wrong' and she felt that they were often secretly applied to herself as well. The words went round and round in her head as she listened to his instructions, but she gritted her teeth and banished them, and then concentrated her mind on the driving lesson. By the end of an hour she was driving competently. She had regained her composure too and he was obviously pleased with her success.

They were passing the old lych gate of a church when he asked her to stop. 'Will you just look at that?' he said. 'I'd sure like to take a closer view of it.'

Reluctantly she pulled into the side of the road and waited as he climbed out. She intended to stay firmly where she was while he did his tour of inspection. But he came to her side of the vehicle and opened the door.

'Aren't you coming too?' he asked. 'I'd like you to tell me

93

about it. You know something, I've always wanted to see inside one of your old churches but I'm kinda scared.'

She sat back and looked at his tall lanky body in the casually smart uniform, his intelligent face with the startling brown eyes. She was used to blue eyes. Alan's were blue like her own.

How could he possibly be scared of something so ordinary as an old church? she wondered as she considered him. This man who was here to storm enemy beaches, fight his way into France? It was incongruous. He must be saying it just to get her out of the van. 'I don't know your name,' she said, wondering at the fact. 'I don't like calling you Lieutenant all the time!'

'I was going to get round to that,' he said. 'You forestalled me. I'm Lawrence. Can't think why my mom put those two names together, Lawrence Lawson, and with Lieutenant tacked on to it the result is quite ludicrous! My friends call me Larry, of course. So I'm Larry, Ma'am.' He gave a mock bow.

'I like them,' she said. 'Your names. They sound very English and they're . . . sort of distinguished.'

She was beginning to feel a little easier with him. While she had been coming to grips with learning to drive the van, her mind had been busy with the problem of her relationship with her instructor. There must be no more romantic feelings, she decided, for that sort of thing only led to the unpleasantness she experienced night after night with Alan, and if some fictional heroines achieved a great state of something called passion, she certainly had not managed to do so. And after all, she was a married woman, she reminded herself, and he was in all probability married too. But as a friend he would do very well, and she needed a friend. So with this resolution firmly made she felt more confident, more able to deal with him.

'You think my names are distinguished?' he said. He sounded amused. 'I've never heard them called that before. English, yes.'

'Did your parents come from England?'

'My father did, a long time ago. I guess I've no claim to fame though, no reason to have distinguished names.' He took out a packet of cigarettes and offered it to her 'Smoke?'

94

'No. No thanks. I've tried but they make me cough.'

'Mind if I do?'

'Of course not. Uncle Richard smokes a pipe. He says it makes him feel happy.'

'You know something? Right now I don't need a cigarette to make me feel happy.' He put the packet back into the pocket of his coat. 'I'll wait until I need cheering up! Are you coming to show me your church then?'

She decided that she needed to stretch her legs anyway so she would oblige him. She stepped out of the van, carefully this time, and stood beside him wondering if she too felt happy. What was happiness after all?

They stood for a moment looking at the ancient building.

'Thanks a million for stopping here,' he said. He opened the old wooden gate, holding it for her. Then as it clicked shut behind them he turned and looked at her, and she blushed.

'Before we go any further,' he said, 'I'd like you to tell me about yourself, Ma'am. I told you my name but you didn't tell me what I may call you. I can't go on saying "Ma'am," can I?'

She wanted to say, 'No, but "honey" is lovely. You could call me that for ever.' But she replied sedately, 'My name is Pamela, and you may call me that. Please don't call me Ma'am. It makes me feel about a hundred. I'm eighteen actually, married to Alan Saunders as you know. We have, or rather had, a farm which my husband is in the process of dismantling, and he's about to join the RAF. I was brought up by my aunt and uncle and sent to boarding school. Is that enough?'

He smiled. 'I guess it'll do for now, Pamela honey. But what happened to your mom?'

'Died when I was born,' she replied simply. 'She was called Olivia. She was very beautiful and talented as my aunt told you, and not at all like me!' As soon as she had said the words she regretted them. They sounded cheap, as though she wanted a compliment, wanted his denial.

He didn't laugh at the remark or respond as she expected. 'Well, I guess that's real sad,' he said. 'Not having a mom.'

He took her hand for a moment and squeezed it in his, and

together they walked along the path between the old grey tomb-stones. Pamela wondered if the long dead occupants of the graves were aware of their presence, knew of their thoughts and emotions on this cold winter day. Everything was quiet, even the birds seeming to join in the eerie silence as though in expectation of some great trauma to come. She wondered if the ghosts of those lying for so long in peace here would be disturbed by the guns that were soon to be shattering the stillness of their quiet resting place.

She paused and looked at one of the graves. It was more splendid than many of the others, marked by a beautifully carved angel in fine marble. She read aloud the words at its base. 'Olivia Belmont, Died May 1st 1925 aged eighteen. Very much loved sister of Maud. Loved and ever missed.' She touched the angel, tracing her finger round the upturned face. 'My mother,' she said.

As she spoke she could feel Lawrence's immediate sympathy. It caused her to feel her loss more keenly, and yet there was within her too this sense of guilt and inferiority, two emotions that were always strongest here in this ancient churchyard. 'She died the day I was born,' she whispered. 'I don't know who my father was. My aunt blames me for her death.'

She was still touching the cold marble as though her hand had a will of its own. Gently, Lawrence put his own hand over it. 'That's an awful thing to grow up with, honey,' he said, and the warmth in his voice and in the touch of his hand brought her back to life.

Together, without more words, and hand in hand, they turned and walked on up the gravel path to the church door. There was a paper pinned to it and they stopped to see what it was. Lawrence read a few lines and then broke the silence.

'Gee,' he said, 'will you look at this? It's for me. It's written here just for me.' And he quietly read aloud the whole message, not stopping until he reached the end.

Hearing the measured English sentences spoken in his lovely mellow voice, Pamela felt that this was a special moment, something she would remember and treasure.

## TO OUR ALLIES OF THE USA

This church has stood here for several hundred years. Around it has grown a community which has lived in these houses and tilled these fields ever since there was a church. This church, this churchyard in which their loved ones lie at rest, these homes, these fields, are as dear to those who have left them as are the homes and graves and fields which you, our Allies, have left behind you. They hope to return one day, as you hope to return to yours, to find them waiting to welcome them home. They entrust them to your care meanwhile, and pray that God's blessing may rest upon us all.

Charles,
Bishop of Exeter

There were tears in his eyes when he finished and he was not ashamed, making no effort to brush them away.

Pamela, looking at him, was filled with something quite different from her feelings for anyone else. She guessed with a sense of foreboding and shock that this man was destined to mean something to her and it was not in her power to deny it.

But as they entered the empty church she was immediately distracted from her own problems. She gasped as she saw the desolation inside. She had known that all this was happening, but actually seeing it made the facts more immediate, more terrible.

Everything that could be taken out had been removed or packed. Huge wooden boxes with straw showing beneath their lids were stacked just inside the door ready for removal. The ancient building was now almost a shell and Pamela gazed around in sorrow. The cold cheerlessness of it seemed to engulf them both.

'Gee, I don't know what to say.' Lawrence stood beside her and she could feel his sadness matching her own. 'I'm just sorry I didn't make it in time to see the place like it was. We've been briefed about all this and it meant little until now. One of my jobs is to head up a team to see to the sand-bagging.'

He released her hand and went to the bare altar window. He ran his fingers along the wall and then traced the form of the recumbent stone knight who lay beside the effigy of his wife, their eyes closed and hands clasped together in prayer.

'I guess they've been lying here a very long time.' His words were full of amazement, and reverence too.

'The church is about seven hundred years old, I think,' Pamela told him. 'Perhaps more.' She stared at the space where the beautiful wood screen should be. 'I can't believe it. They've even dismantled the screen. You'll have to come back and see it after the war.'

He laughed at her gently. 'I hope I'll be able to do just that, honey.'

She heard the seriousness in his voice and her heart gave a jolt of fear. It seemed an almost impossible dream. Would he survive the fearsome thing he was here to practise and ultimately do? She turned her thoughts resolutely to the present. 'I suppose the screen is packed in those boxes by the door,' she said. 'I wonder where they'll store it?'

'Some place a long way from here, I hope,' he replied. 'I'll see our guys make a good job of the sandbags.' He looked again at the recumbent knight and his lady. 'We sure don't want to do any damage to these old folks, do we?'

'They've survived a long time,' Pamela said. 'Cromwell and the Civil War and all that, so I expect they'll manage a bit more strife!' She began to shiver. 'Can we go?' she whispered. 'I can't bear it any longer.'

It was only a little warmer outside and the rain was still falling gently. They walked the long way round to the van, going through the older part of the graveyard, making their way slowly so that they became gradually wetter and wetter with the softly falling drizzle. Lawrence kept stopping, trying to read some of the older and almost indecipherable tombstones. At last, just before they turned the corner towards the road, he pulled Pamela into his arms and kissed her. His lips were firm but gentle and his body tense. At first she was apprehensive, then as his mouth closed over hers she knew complete accord with this man, complete happiness for just those few golden moments beneath the darkening Devonshire sky. He seemed to be the missing portion of herself. She had never felt whole before, always incomplete, always searching.

But very gently he put her from him. 'I'm sorry, honey,' he murmured, and she wondered with a stab of pain how he could possibly be sorry.

He still held her hand and led her to the van, opened the door of the passenger seat for her, tucked a blanket comfortably round her knees and smiled at her as he closed the door. Then he walked around to the other side and folded himself into the driving seat.

'Thanks, Pamela honey,' he said. 'Thanks for showing me that lovely old place. I'll do my job better now that I've seen it with you.'

There was nothing that she wanted to say in reply. She sat beside him clutching to herself the memory of those brief moments of enchantment in the cold churchyard, and he was silent too, holding the magic. They drove through the narrow twisting lanes, the steep hedgebanks either side mostly bare now of leaves, back to the sea, back to the busy troubled world, back to reality. There were a few glimpses of reflected sunlight in the western sky where the winter sun had departed, giving up the struggle with rain-clouds and night.

It was almost dark when Lawrence switched on the dimmed headlights. Eventually they reached the village and the door of the information centre. He pulled the van into the space outside, next to his Jeep, turned off the engine and gripped the steering wheel tightly.

Without looking at her, he said, 'I shouldn't have kissed you like that. I'm sorry.'

She stared at him. He was gazing straight ahead through the rain-spotted windscreen.

'Don't say you're sorry,' she pleaded. 'Please don't say it.' The distress in her voice was clear. 'I wanted you to kiss me, Lawrence. It was the most . . .' She tailed off, not knowing how to finish, how to convey to him that she was not some common little . . . she flinched as her aunt's constantly remembered words flashed into her mind. She wanted him to know that he was special, that her newfound feelings for him were precious, the most wonderful thing she had known in her life, and not to be held cheaply.

Lawrence turned then and looked at her. He saw the tears in her blue eyes, and wanted to hold her in his arms again, to feel the softness of her.

'For me too,' he said at last. 'For me it was very special, Pamela honey. I'll carry the memory with me always.'

There was a finality about his words that made her want to reach out to him and hold him for ever. Instead she pressed his hand lightly and opened the van door, letting in a gust of damp November air. Then she climbed out of the vehicle, holding her head high, and walked into the warmth and bustle of the information centre.

Mrs Turner looked up enquiringly as she entered. 'Everything satisfactory?' she asked.

'Yes,' Pamela replied. 'Quite satisfactory. I can drive now. Lieutenant Lawson has been a very good teacher.'

'Excellent. You'll be one of our volunteer drivers then. There's loads of work waiting for you.' The woman turned to Lawrence who had followed Pamela inside and was standing at the door. 'And you, Lieutenant. I've had orders that certain churches are ready for sandbagging.' She rummaged amongst some papers on her desk and retrieved a sheet. 'Here's the list,' she said briskly. 'Can you get your men on to it soon?'

'Sure thing, Ma'am,' he replied, but his eyes were searching Pamela's as he spoke, and as she smiled her farewell to him she knew that those moments in the sad abandoned church would remain in her memory for ever too. The remembered emptiness of the ancient building echoed the cold emptiness of her heart.

'Take care, won't you?' Mrs Turner said. 'Don't let your men damage anything if you can help it. You'll be working under the direction of the Ecclesiastical Sculptor and his team, of course, but our churches are precious. We hope to get them back when all this is over!'

'You'll have them back, Ma'am, and I hope that I'll visit some day to see them in all their glory.'

Lawrence's words were filled with an optimism that Pamela longed to share. She wondered if he could have any thought of the double meaning that she was reading into them. She gave a little wave as he turned and then was gone. There was still a queue of anxious people waiting for her advice and her comfort. She took off her coat and headscarf and smiled at the weary woman who was next in line. 'How can I help you?'

'My little Tommy has just gone down with measles,' the woman said, 'and my old father, well, he's a bit funny in the head now and don't rightly know what 'tis all about. How can I get somewhere that'll take them both, as well as me and the hubby and our other three and our dog and ten hens?'

Pamela quickly hid her amusement. It was the hens, the ten hens! But it was easy to see that the woman was quite over-whelmed with the monstrous problems confronting her. Pamela resolutely put her own concerns to the back of her mind. Settling herself behind the trestle table that was her desk, she reached for a pen and notepad, unscrewed a pot of ink, dipped the pen into it and then carefully wrote down the family's name, number of people, and the complications. She could feel the woman's worried eyes watching her, trying to read the upside-down hand-writing from the other side of the table. When she had finished, she looked up and tried to make both her smile and her voice reassuring.

'I'll see to everything, Mrs Tremayne,' she said. 'Come back tomorrow and I'll have found an answer for you. Don't worry. No one will be left with nowhere to go.'

Dear God, she prayed as the next anxious enquirer shuffled into the seat before her, please make it all come right and make this awful war end soon!

She was not yet allowed to take the van home, so an hour later she mounted her sturdy old bicycle and pedalled wearily back to Morelake and Alan. The rain was heavier now, the darkness total and the dim lights of her bike hardly adequate. Alan had fixed a dynamo for her and the harder she pedalled the brighter the lights shone so she tried to go faster, willing her legs to work like pistons. The exercise was good, she decided, and in spite of her tiredness she was able to think more clearly out there in the cold with the familiar calming sound of the sea beside her.

By the time she reached home she had made up her mind. She was quite determined about what she must do. Alan was her husband and she would be faithful to him. Lawrence must remain a dream.

Binks ran out from the shippon and greeted her exuberantly as she pushed her bicycle through the gate, and then Alan came to the back door.

'I've put the pie you made last night in the oven,' he said. 'Hurry up, woman. I'm hungry!'

# NINE

*Olivia's Journal – 1st January 1922*
   *The first day of a new year! I have made a lot of resolutions*
*and I could not possibly put them all down in this book for*
*some are very secret. One is rather selfish I suppose, but I*
*have made it nevertheless. I am going to pray every night for*
*two things, a friend and a puppy. I am so lonely.*

The winter chill seemed to strike right through to Pamela's bones
on the morning she was to drive her family to catch the train for
Scotland. So at last it was here, she thought, the day when she
would wave goodbye to them, the first real separation. It was
the thought of not seeing Jane that upset her most although she
knew that she would miss Uncle Richard's comforting presence
too.

   She had been allowed to take the van home the night before
and drove the short distance from Morelake to Burlcombe
through the eerie early morning dark. She wound down her
window in spite of the cold wind that blew straight in from the
sea and could hear the waves worrying at the shingle beyond the
barbed wire. The cry of a night bird and the smell of sea-weed
that had been washed up on to the beach during a recent storm
added to her feeling of desolation.

   She turned eventually into the familiar drive of Burlcombe and
the van bounced and rattled along the uneven surface to the
house. As she pulled up at the front door she could see that a

number of candles were flickering unsteadily here and there. The electricity had been disconnected of course. It all added to the feeling of unreality.

The door was open and she could hear voices inside. 'Hello,' she called. 'Are you ready? I'll carry some bags for you.'

Aunt Maud came to meet her. She was holding Jane firmly by the hand and both she and the child were shrouded in thick coats, scarves and knitted pixie-hoods. She peered out of the door and looked at the vehicle in some disdain. 'Is there going to be enough room in that?' she enquired. 'Looks pretty small to me. They might have managed something larger.'

Uncle Richard followed them and in the dim glow of the stable lantern which he was holding Pamela saw him wink at her. She was immediately comforted.

'Sorry, Aunt,' she said. 'I know it's going to be a bit of a squash but I think we'll manage. There are two seats behind me. Who's going to sit in front?' She held her breath, hoping that it would be her uncle or even Mrs Baines.

'I will, of course,' Maud said. 'The other three will go behind. I hope Jane will sleep.'

The child was excited. She broke loose from Maud's restraining hand and started hopping about the yard. 'I'm going on a puffer,' she said. 'Ch ch ch ch ch ch ch. A puff puff.'

Pamela smiled at her and for a moment took her hand. 'That'll be fun,' she said. 'And if you're good in the van, I've got some more sweets for you.'

Jane stood still and looked up at her. 'Nice Pammy,' she said. 'Pammy's nice now she makes nice sweets.' Then she pulled her hand free.

Pamela laughed. 'Cupboard love,' she said in an aside to Mrs Baines.

Eventually the luggage was packed in the back of the vehicle and all the candles blown out. Mrs Baines and Jane were happily ensconced in the rear seat when Maud, just about to usher Richard beside them, changed her mind. 'No,' she said, 'I shall go in the back after all. Richard, you go in front.'

Pamela wondered with a tiny flash of amusement whether her

aunt was unwilling to allow Mrs Baines and her husband to be in such close contact for the journey. 'Right then,' she said. 'You'll have to help me find the way, Uncle Richard.' She handed him a map and torch. 'With no sign-posts and in the dark it isn't going to be easy.' Then she turned to look nostalgically at Burlcombe, the Belmont family home, empty now for the first time in years. How many? Two hundred perhaps. Maybe more. She could just make out the curtainless windows looking stark and austere.

'I wonder if the rowan tree will survive,' she murmured to no one in particular. Then, before climbing into the van, went over to it and put both her hands on its trunk. 'It brings good fortune,' she said.

She drove steadily, hardly talking. The first few miles were dark and difficult but gradually the eastern sky was filled with glowing colour, the sun rapidly banishing the darkness and the remnants of mist. It was a dawn such as Pamela had not seen for weeks. 'I do believe we're going to have some sunshine today,' she said. 'Look, the sky's all red.'

Newton Abbot station was busy, full of men and girls in uniform, and Pamela was relieved when she managed to pack her family on the train at last. It was only as she walked along the platform waving goodbye to them, finally running to keep up with the train, that the reality struck home. For the first time in her life she was alone. Not lonely exactly, for throughout her growing up she had been lonely. This was different. All those who cared, even a little bit about her, would be far away. From now on she was responsible for her life. There was no one to make decisions for her. It was an odd feeling, but the more she thought about it, the more she considered that it probably had its compensations.

She walked slowly back to her vehicle and manoeuvred it out of the station forecourt, thinking about Jane whom she wouldn't see for months. Jane of the fair curling hair and blue eyes whom she loved to distraction. She put her hand up to touch the slight stickiness she could feel from the quick kiss the child had imprinted on her cheek just minutes ago. She didn't want to wipe it away. Jane had been bidden by Mrs Baines to kiss her goodbye, and, perhaps persuaded by the gift of sweets, had obeyed happily.

Pamela allowed a few tears to run down her cheeks as she drove through the busy streets of Newton Abbot and then out into the countryside. Only Binks was with her now. He had jumped on to the passenger seat as he always did when the van was empty and she was comforted by his presence. She patted his head for a second and felt his answering lick.

The only vehicles on the roads were military ones and she drove carefully, expecting to encounter a Jeep or lorry around each corner. The Americans were not used to Devon lanes and high hedges and frequently took the bends far too fast, or conversely their vast convoys could be encountered crawling along and causing almost as much of a hazard. In spite of this she gradually began to enjoy the journey. The early promise of sunshine had been fulfilled and the sky was blue, the clouds white and fluffy replacing the heavy grey blanket that had covered everything of late. During the past gloomy days all colour seemed to have been obliterated from the hills and fields, but today was different – a golden winter day, sent it seemed especially to cheer her.

She didn't hurry, and after a while pulled into a field gate and took out a bag of sandwiches. Binks ran round and round joyfully, barking his pleasure at being free, and then he sat beside her, hopefully waiting for his share. A robin watched them from the safety of a bush nearby and Pamela looked at his cheerful plumage and saw the bright holly berries behind him in the hedge. It was like a Christmas card and she remembered that there were not many more days before the holiday. Holiday? She almost laughed at the word. The entire evacuation area had to be cleared and handed over to the authorities by December 20th so it wouldn't be a very happy season this year for the families she was helping to move. There were only five more days left in which to finish the gigantic operation.

She closed her eyes and held her face to the sun, feeling its gentle winter warmth and enjoying this small respite. Then a feeling of guilty pleasure swept over her. Morelake was to be closed tomorrow and she was glad. When she was able to claim it back she would be able to put her own stamp upon it. As each piece of furniture had been carried out into store she had felt that a bit of her dead mother-in-law had gone too, her ghost purged from its gloomy rooms.

And what about Alan? He had been happy to join up, eager in fact. Yet during those last days together she had to admit that there had been an improvement in their relationship, something on which a successful marriage might be built in the future if both worked hard at it and cared enough.

When she opened her eyes she saw that the robin had flown away, but the other birds, thrown into confusion by the spring-like quality of the day, were singing, and suddenly she felt like singing too, her earlier sadness receding rapidly. Bing's new song about a white Christmas didn't seem like coming true at the moment, but she whistled the tune to herself and jumped up, anxious now to complete the final closing up of Morelake. While the desolation of Burlcombe had been a terrible grief, the emptying of Morelake was a secret triumph, a miracle that had sprung from the tragedy of everything else.

Another small miracle had occurred in her life too. Lieutenant Lawrence Lawson! She thought of him with a flutter of guilty pleasure as she drove the remaining miles back to Morelake, and knew that even if their destinies lay in quite different directions, as they probably did, she would never forget him.

The blue skies and gentle warmth of that one day was just a tantalizing glimpse of summer. Early the following morning everything was back to normal with thick clouds and a penetrating raw coldness that made Pamela shiver as she opened the door to let Binks outside. Today Morelake was to be closed. She was glad that it had come at last. She had been uneasy during the last few days since Alan left. It had been hard to stay in the almost empty house at night. The cold barren rooms seemed to hold a menace that she couldn't explain, but she had been determined that she would remain until everything was completed, all the formalities seen to and the keys handed over. Alan had moved an old bed into one of the empty rooms for her. 'It doesn't matter about this,' he had said. 'We don't want it any more. We don't need to pack it away.'

She made a cup of tea on the primus stove and cut herself a thick slice of bread. She sat on one of the boxes and ate and drank, wondering how Alan would feel if he were here, and glad that he was not. He had given her strict instructions about how everything was to be done and she had secretly laughed, for she had helped so many other families with these final soul-destroying rites that she was well aware of all the formalities.

He had seen to the placing and storage of everything that mattered to him. Only Pamela's few personal possessions had been left to her care.

'Lock everything up securely and then report to the centre,' he had instructed. 'And don't hand over all the keys. Keep a set with you, and make sure you don't lose them.'

She had been impatient with him, yet desperately tried to hide her irritation. She had endeavoured to reassure him that she was perfectly capable, and had kissed him as lovingly as she could manage. He had roared away on his motor-cycle, and as she watched him go she had felt a mixture of emotions. She hoped that he would be happy and fulfilled, and safe too. But mostly she was thrilled because she was to be free at last of his stuffy gloomy house.

And now the day had really arrived! She finished her meagre breakfast and went outside to call Binks. He had a worried look about him when he came which made her laugh. She gave him some milk and the remains of the loaf of bread. 'Never fear, Binksy,' she said affectionately. 'You'll not be vanishing like all the other animals. Come on, let's go and make sure once again that every window is latched and everything in order, and then we'll lock it all up.' She stressed the last words with a sense of triumph.

The dog caught her mood. The worried droop of his body changed and he wagged his tail and jumped up at her, his muddy paws making marks on her navy skirt. She picked him up and hugged him and then skipped her way along the desolate passageway, ran up the bare staircase two steps at a time, glanced into each bedroom, then danced her way down again and into every room there. In the parlour she paused and was still and silent for a moment. This was the sacred room, the place that Alan had refused to alter, the sanctuary to his mother's memory. She wanted to shout and sing and cheer to the barren walls. She took up her dog's two front paws, bringing him to an uncomfortable position on his back legs, and pirouetted round the room with him. He manfully stepped out with her, enjoying her happiness, and then when she released him, ran round and round on the bare boards and barked so that the whole house was filled with the joyful echoing sound.

An hour later, with the house finally locked, she was businesslike and efficient again. She drove to the information centre and dutifully handed in the two large bunches of keys, keeping one set, along with those belonging to Burlcombe, safely stowed away in her suitcase. She reported officially that the move was complete and then gave answers to the usual list of questions which were noted down carefully. She was familiar with the routine, for frequently she herself was the one sitting behind the desk. Finally she signed the paper stating that she and her family were now officially 'out'.

'How does it feel when it's your own home?' The girl who was taking her place looked at her curiously.

Pamela considered the question. 'It depends,' she said. 'I've never liked Morelake so it wasn't too painful.'

'Where'll you live then?'

'Mrs Turner has offered me a room,' Pamela replied. 'We get on well.'

She had been very grateful for this offer. She liked the older woman with whom she had been working, and would have a room to herself overlooking the Bay. Binks was welcome too.

'You're lucky,' the girl said, then looked at the sheaf of papers

on the desk. 'That reminds me, Mrs Turner gave me details of
the next job for you. Some family to move.' She handed over an
address. 'Can you go now?'

'Straight away.' Pamela was suddenly full of energy.

Outside Binks was waiting for her. He was sitting up proudly
in the driving seat and wagged his tail when he saw her.

'Shove over,' she said, pushing him across. 'Let's get going.
We're footloose and fancy-free at last.'

'Hi there!'

She was just about to start the engine when she heard the
familiar voice and her heart flipped annoyingly.

The lieutenant was at the wheel of a US military lorry this
time and she could see that there were several GIs in the back.

'It's some days since I saw you,' he said. 'I was getting kinda
anxious.'

'I've been busy,' she replied, and hoped that the blush she
could feel rising steadily was not visible to the interested spec-
tators behind him.

He grinned at her. 'We'll have another talk some time,' he
said. 'With all these guys in the back I guess now isn't quite
right!'

'I've to drive a family over Kingsbridge way,' she said
unnecessarily and not quite knowing how to end the conversation.

'And we've got to fill bags with sand to protect one of those
churches of yours,' he told her. 'See you then, honey.'

She watched the lorry pull away along the narrow road towards
the sea. The men in the back whistled and waved and she waved
jauntily back at them. Then she drove carefully in the opposite
direction and tried to banish all thoughts of him. But she could
not. 'Lawrence,' she whispered to no one but the dog. But as
soon as she had spoken was furious with herself. 'Stupid creature!' she said angrily, and Binks cowered in the seat beside her.
She laughed and put a hand briefly on his head. 'Not you, lovey.
It's me who's being stupid. Totally and completely stupid.'

The grey blanket of cloud was thicker than ever. The memory
of that one lovely day seemed completely unreal now. The drizzle

and sea mist that had enveloped the beach and hills had returned, and were perhaps more fitting than sunshine to the mood of most of those who had to leave everything behind and move from homes and land. There had been no glimmer of a rainbow either. It seemed that all colour had departed.

Yet Pamela was filled with optimism as she helped the family to whom she been directed. Her cheerfulness was infectious, passing quickly to the burdened woman and her worried husband as well as to their two small children.

'It'll not be so bad,' the man said at last when all was done and they were on their way to their temporary home. 'In fact, us'll look on it like a holiday.'

The woman smiled at Pamela. 'Well,' she said, 'if you can be so cheerful with your man gone off to join the forces and your farm all emptied, then I reckon us can keep happy too.'

Pamela wanted to shout at them that it was just because he had gone off to join the forces and his house was all emptied that she felt liberated. But she forbore, said all the right things, deposited them at the door of the small barren cottage that was to be their new home, helped them unload their packages and left them sharing her optimism.

She found herself happily humming a tune she knew as she drove home. The words eluded her, something about praising the Lord and passing the ammunition she thought. She made a mental note that she must ask someone to teach her the rest of it. Lawrence would probably know. She blushed guiltily and changed to the one about a white Christmas. It was a dream that she hoped wouldn't come true this year!

# TEN

*Olivia's Journal – 14th February 1922*
*I am fifteen today, Saint Valentine's Day. I should love to*
*receive one of those beautiful embroidered cards that I see*
*sometimes in the shops when we go to Totnes or Dartmouth.*
*I have never talked to a boy.*

Pamela wondered how she would get on with Mrs Turner when
she went to live with her. They would be together so much,
evenings and weekends as well as every day. But on that first
evening when she carried her bulging suitcase into the house it
was very quickly obvious that she need not have worried at all.
She was soon at ease and grateful for such a comfortable billet.
She was greeted boisterously by the two dogs, and the sniffings
that went on between them and the apprehensive Binks turned
embarrassment into laughter.

After a simple meal in the kitchen Pamela looked round for a
tea-towel. 'Over there in the bottom drawer,' Mary Turner said,
indicating a chest in the corner of the room. She had her hands
in a bowl full of suds. 'I'm glad you've come. This is a big house.
It needs someone, just as I do. By the way, I think you should
call me by my Christian name,' she added. ' "Mrs Turner" makes
me feel old.'

Pamela felt awkward about giving her hostess anything other
than her full title. Aunt Maud had always been very formal about
such things. 'Thank you,' she said a little uncertainly.

113

Mary Turner smiled at her. 'There aren't many people who call me Mary now.'

Pamela detected a slight sadness in her voice and remembered that Captain Turner had been killed in the earlier days of the war. She felt awkward, wondering what to say, but her hostess gave her no time to reply.

'I put a match to the fire when we first came in,' she said. 'There'll be a nice blaze in the living room now. I intend to curl up in my favourite chair with a book. There's plenty to read if you've nothing else to do, shelves and shelves of all sorts of things.'

'I've letters to write,' Pamela said. 'I have to write to my uncle in Scotland as well as to Alan. And to Jane,' she added. 'I promised her that I'd do little drawings. She can't read yet.'

Pamela was not sure how much her hostess knew of the family history. Mary Turner had only lived here in Stoke Fleming since the beginning of the war so she was probably quite unaware of the problems and odd relationships of the Belmont family. And she wouldn't be inquisitive, Pamela thought with relief. She was no gossip, always taking people at their face value and believing only the good. She had discovered that much about Mary during the time they had worked together.

Pamela had brought her leather writing case down from the bedroom earlier and also the new fountain-pen that had been Alan's leaving present to her. 'I shall want some letters,' he had directed anxiously, a request that had surprised her. She ran her hands over the soft leather. She had always loved the feel of it. This too had been a present. Uncle Richard had bought it for her sixteenth birthday and she remembered looking at the blue deckle-edged paper with its matching envelopes and wondering to whom she could write.

They went into the comfortable living room at the front of the house and Pamela settled herself on the settee in front of the now cheerfully blazing fire. She unzipped the writing-case. Most of the paper was still there, only three or four sheets used. She took the top from her pen and carefully wrote her new address on the first sheet of paper.

They sat in companionable silence during the next hour until the letters were written, sealed, and stamped ready for the post. Then there was the wireless to listen to, the news to comment upon, and later a drink of Ovaltine. Eventually Pamela lay snugly between flannelette sheets in the comfortable double bed provided for her. Binks was contentedly in his basket in the corner of the room. She listened to his even breathing and the occasional snuffle of contentment, and thought about her life. The letter to Alan had been difficult, but she considered that she had accomplished it satisfactorily. Yet as she had folded the two pages and placed them in the envelope, she had been aware that if she had been writing to Lawrence it would have been a very different letter. She would have written of her feelings instead of only the practical day-to-day things. She might even have told him of the pleasure she found in the sound the sea made on the beach and the wind in the rushes of the Ley. Its pages would have been straight from her heart. She knew so little of him, yet she felt she knew instinctively how it would be between them.

After a while, with sleep refusing to come, she resolutely tried to banish the disturbing thoughts which shattered her peace. She recalled instead the things she had written to Alan. The letter was full of the details of her day, mainly about the closing up of Morelake for she knew that this would be his prime consideration. She'd been careful not to allow one glimpse of her joy to escape on to the page. She had not wanted to lie to him, but she couldn't express any sorrow. She hoped she had achieved the right note. She had finished with polite enquiries about his welfare and three prim little kisses following her very formal declaration of love.

Then her thoughts turned to Scotland. The letter to her aunt and uncle had been just as difficult to compose. There was much she could have said to Uncle Richard, but it had to be addressed to both of them and this made her words stilted and slightly solemn. But she had drawn a little picture for Jane, an amusing caricature of herself and Binks with Burlcombe in the background. She wanted to make her little daughter laugh, and remember. It was important that she remembered.

115

When she slept at last there were two people who filled her dreams. Lawrence and Jane seemed to be the ones she cared about most in all the world, but Uncle Richard was there as well, a comfortable presence, one who made no demands, a sort of browny-grey background figure causing her no problems and always bringing a sense of security and peace. Binks too barked and yapped happily in and out of her sleep.

In reality the little dog slept all night just as soundly as his mistress eventually did, and it was his cold nose that awoke her the following morning. He pushed as close to her as he was able and she draped her arm over the side of the bed. He licked her hand exuberantly with his harsh tongue. She laughed at him and pushed the bedclothes aside. Then she jumped out of bed and ran to the window where she could see the great sweep of the bay and the faint beginnings of a rainbow where the rising sun was shining on the gentle early morning drizzle.

'Oh, Binksy,' she whispered. 'I'm eighteen and free and I think I'm in love, whatever that means!' She lifted him up and buried her face in his rough coat. But there were sudden tears in her eyes that belied the joy. Just like the sun and the rain she thought, together making a rainbow that was full of colour and promise.

That final hectic week before the doom-laden date, Monday December 20th, was busier than ever before. The last few homes and farms still occupied must be emptied and sealed and the two or three remaining shops closed. The whole area must be handed over uninhabited and desolate. Pamela had very little time to think of herself. Everyone available was pressed into service. She worked with naval reservists, servicemen home on leave, even 'safe' prisoners from Exeter jail. It was important to salvage as much food as possible from the abandoned fields. When the last families had been moved out every vehicle was called upon to carry loads of kale, mangolds and turnips, sacks of corn and crates of hens.

Ben Yates and his wife Wendy, along with sixteen-year-old Molly, were almost the last to leave. 'Us be staying here to see that there's milk for all you folks,' he told Pamela when she arrived on the last Saturday morning to take the load of goods that stood by the farmhouse gate.

Uncle Richard's old sheep dog was there too, ready with a boisterous welcome. She hugged and petted the animal.

'Sheppey looks well,' she remarked. 'Is she missing my uncle much?'

Ben laughed. 'Cupboard love, that's all that matters to a dog,' he said. 'The Missis gives her lots of tit-bits as well as her meals and she'm doing fine. You write and tell your uncle that she'm as happy as Larry with us. Have you heard from them by the way?'

Pamela swallowed hard as she heard the word 'Larry', but it was just a saying, nothing more. She laughed at herself. 'Not yet,' she said. 'It's a long way.'

Ben Yates turned his attention to the disorganised piles of belongings that were stacked ready to go.

'Molly'll go with you in the van to show you just where our little old cottage be,' he said. ''Tis down by Shercombe.' He started to lift the sacks and boxes into the van. ''Twas my brother's, and 'tis mine now since he got isself killed in the desert. At El Alamein 'twas.'

There was pride in his voice and Pamela knew that this brother who had joined the army long ago rather than work the land had achieved hero status in the area ever since his death fighting with the Eighth Army in Africa.

'I suppose us be lucky to have somewhere of our own outside the evacuation area. 'Tis only just outside, mind, less than a mile. I'll be able to keep an eye on what be going on. Funny how things work out. 'Tis a bit damp and tumble-down but us'll soon have it put to rights.'

'When are you finally leaving then, Mr Yates?' Pamela asked, suddenly business-like. 'You must hand in your keys this afternoon at the latest.'

'I shall milk the cows and leave the churns full with a big notice that 'tis free for they Yanks and any others as come this way. Then us'll walk over, dogs and cows too. 'Tisn't far. Do 'em good! There are more churns over there, so us shan't need these.'

Pamela laughed as she imagined the little family with their last-minute packages as well as the animals travelling the short distance between the farm and the cottage, walking across the border for all the world like some refugee band that you saw in the newspapers. But that was in fact what they were, she reflected, and her laughter died. They might not be fleeing for their lives, but the war had put them out of their homes just like thousands of others all over Europe.

She knew however that the chief concern of Ben Yates and his wife was the welfare of their wayward and pretty daughter, Molly. Now that the Americans were arriving in ever-increasing numbers they had even more cause to worry. She had heard Uncle Richard talking about it before he left. He and Ben Yates had always been good pals, much to the disgust of Aunt Maud. Pamela wondered fleetingly if there was anything she could do to help. Perhaps she could try to make friends with Molly, but it wouldn't be easy. They would be living at opposite ends of the evacuation area too, and when the whole of it was sealed off it would be a long way around. Pamela tried to shrug off the problem. It had nothing to do with her.

Molly came out of the farmhouse door at that moment and her fair curly hair and pleasant round face looked all health and brightness. There was a childlike innocence about her that somehow annoyed Pamela, perhaps because she guessed that it was totally misleading. She felt a surprising and unpleasant surge of jealousy too, for the girl's freedom and conversely for her doting parents!

'Ready, maid?' Ben called to his daughter. 'Mrs Saunders be nearly set to take the stuff over to Shercombe. You'm going to show her the way and help unload it. Leave the heavy things at the gate, mind, and come straight back.'

'All right, Dad.' Molly tied a headscarf over her hair and buttoned up the old unbecoming tweed coat, pulling the belt tightly round her small waist. 'I'll be home by dinnertime.'

''Tis only sandwiches. That's all we got left. You like to come as well, Mrs Saunders?' Ben invited.

'I've got to be back at the centre as soon as possible. Thanks, though,' Pamela said. She turned to the girl. 'Right then, Molly. Let's go.' She climbed into the vehicle and opened the door for her passenger. Molly looked excited and Pamela guessed that she had never been inside a motor car before.

She drove carefully out of the lane and on to the road that led westwards along the coast. Then they turned inland past empty fields with no movement to be seen anywhere apart from the sea-gulls that rode the wind and called eerily overhead. The abandoned houses and cottages had a forlorn and desolate look and the occasional cat that had probably returned to its home or had been left to fend for itself ran from the sound of the engine.

''Tis all a bit dreary-looking,' Molly remarked. 'Good thing there's a dance tonight.'

Pamela glanced at her. 'Your father's letting you go then?'

The girl laughed. 'They'm going too. Mum's got to play the piano. 'Tis for everybody, so I shan't have much chance to do anything I oughtn't, shall I?'

'I suppose not,' Pamela replied, grinning at her. 'I hope everyone has a good time. It's in our hall. We've got to clear up a bit after we finish work tonight, try and make it look a bit less like a dreary old information centre.' She laughed. 'It's the last dance before it's officially closed. We've had special permission.'

'You going, Pamela?' Molly asked.

'I don't know. It depends.'

'Well, with your hubby away, I should think you needs a bit of cheering up. Why not come? It'll be fun, and some Yanks have been invited – the ones who've been helping out with the moving and things.'

Pamela knew about the invitations, and while she longed to be there tonight, she also felt a strange reluctance. 'I'll see,' she said.

They had turned off the main road and away from the empty villages. Here in these more favoured fields cows and sheep grazed and farmers still worked their land. The tiny cottage lay down a narrow side lane and the van bumped and clattered its way along and lurched to a stop outside the broken wooden gate. Pamela looked at the building in dismay.

'Is this it?' she asked unnecessarily.

'Yes, this is it!'

They both climbed out of the vehicle and stood for a moment, staring at the uncurtained windows and general air of desolation.

'Well, 'tis better than nothing,' Molly said with resignation. 'Dad couldn't bring hisself to come over here after Uncle Jim was killed. Silly really. Anyway, now us'll have to put it right.'

They worked together until everything was unloaded and stacked in the front room of the house or in the small shippon that was built onto the side. Then Pamela straightened up and rubbed her back.

'That was quite an effort,' she said. 'I'll give you a ride home, Molly. I'm going in your direction.'

'No, thanks,' the girl said. 'I'm walking.' She looked straight at Pamela with an unblinking stare. 'I'm meeting someone down by Southpool Wood. Mind not to tell Dad.'

Pamela wondered what to do. 'Do you think you should?' she said weakly.

'Course I should. He's a Yank. Nice too. How do you think I'm getting a pair of nylons to wear tonight?'

'Well, be careful.' Pamela felt a hundred years old as she gave the advice.

'You're a fine one to talk,' Molly said, and winked. 'That lieutenant be pretty handsome if you ask me.' With that she locked the door of the cottage, put the key in her shoulder bag and swung off down the lane. 'I'll be back home by dinnertime,' she called over her shoulder. 'Just tell Dad I'm doing a bit of cleaning up here if you see him. He won't know no different.'

Pamela stared after her feeling considerably shaken. So her friendship with Lawrence Lawson had been noticed. But how? Apart from the driving lesson they hadn't spent much time together, surely not enough to be remarked upon? She felt a little knot of fear in her stomach as she climbed back into the van and reversed it carefully. Then she drove back along the lane. There was no sign of Molly.

Halfway back to the centre, on a sudden impulse, she pulled

over to the side of the road and stopped. Here it was wide enough to park two or three vehicles without getting in the way of the many army convoys that frequently disturbed the quietness. She suddenly realized that from tomorrow all this would be closed to her. The beach had long been out of bounds but she had still been able to walk or cycle beside it. It held so many memories of her childhood. This little bit of coast was the place she loved more than any other. She stared out across the bay and wondered how long it would be before everything was back to normal, back to how it had been in 1939. And what would her life hold in that unknown future? A future with Alan? Mary Turner had said that he was welcome in her house whenever he had any leave. That was why she had given her the big room, the double bed. Pamela shivered.

She stood for a long time staring out at the grey-blue water, glad of an opportunity to be quiet, to stretch her still-aching back and breathe the fresh cold air that was blowing straight in from the sea. Then, just as she was thinking she should get back and do something useful, she saw the Jeep – first an insignificant thing in the distance. She watched its progress along the road and felt a quickening of her pulse.

The driver pulled the vehicle over and stopped beside her. 'Well, hi there. I've been hoping I'd see you. How are things, honey? You look kinda lonesome standing like that.' He was soon out and looking at her with that concerned expression in his brown eyes that made her feel that she was the only person in the whole world. But she was immediately conscious of her dishevelled appearance. She wished she was small and pretty like Molly Yates instead of tall and healthy-looking. 'Robust' Aunt Maud called her and she hated the word. She had always longed for tiny feet and small dainty hands, attributes that Alan would despise, but Lawrence Lawson would certainly find appealing. She pushed anxiously at her wind-blown hair. It had escaped from its restraining band and was blowing across her face. She tried not to think about how she looked.

'I was just thinking that I won't be able to come here after Monday,' she said.

'It's a real swell place. I can understand why you feel bad about leaving it. But it's not for ever. You'll have it back.'

They stood together and looked across the bay. The sun was shining now. It was another of those bright winter days that occasionally come to delight and surprise. The early morning brightness had not departed as it sometimes did and the air was cold and refreshingly clear.

'I've been invited to one of your dances tonight,' he told her, suddenly changing both mood and subject. 'Will you be there?'

Pamela made a swift decision. 'If I can arrange it,' she told him. 'But I can't be sure. It depends on a lot of things.'

'What things?'

She hesitated. 'Well, transport for one, and my landlady, for another.'

'Try to make it,' he said. Then he took her hand in both of his and lifted it to his lips. They were standing on the seaward side of the vehicles, protected from the road, and she looked up at him with startled eyes.

'Gee,' he whispered, 'you sure are beautiful. I guess plenty of guys have told you that before me!'

She turned away, embarrassed. No one else had ever said such things to her, and she had never thought of herself as beautiful, rather the reverse. In these ugly clothes, surely she could be nothing but drab? He must be teasing her. Even worse, laughing at her!

'You're making it up,' she replied. 'My mother was beautiful, not me.'

'The girl in the painting at your aunt's house? And in the graveyard,' he added more quietly. 'Yes, the picture was beautiful. And you're her daughter, Pamela honey, and just as lovely.'

He put his hand under her chin, forcing her to look up at him. Then he stopped and kissed her gently on the lips. 'Doesn't that husband of yours tell you?' he said. 'He should. He's a lucky guy.'

She shook her head. 'No.' The word was almost inaudible and was carried away on the wind and lost in the screaming of the gulls overhead.

Then suddenly she was in his arms, but he was gentle with her. There was none of the brute force that she was accustomed to suffer from Alan. And she responded. She wanted his arms to remain tightly around her for ever, but as swiftly as he had first held her, he put her away from him.

'I'm sorry, honey,' he said. 'I reckon apologizing to you is becoming something of a habit. I shouldn't have done that. Not again, and not to a respectable married lady. I guess I'm just a homesick guy wanting a little comfort.'

She looked at him incredulously. She stood and stared at him as she heard the careless words. So that was all it meant to him? A little bit of comfort! She hid her disappointment, the shattering of her dreams. She had obviously been naive and foolish, weaving schoolgirl fantasies about him that had no substance. He was just a GI out for a good time like all the rest. 'I'll have to go,' she said, and her flippant tone totally belied the misery she felt. She climbed back into the van, ''Bye then.'

'The dance?' He sounded anxious now.

She shrugged her shoulders. 'Perhaps,' she said. Then she started the engine and drove steadily along the road, soon turning inland back to the village and the information centre.

The doors were closed for the short lunch break when she arrived and she let herself in round the back. Mary Turner was on duty for the afternoon. She looked up as Pamela entered.

'Everything all right, dear?' she asked. 'Come and have something to eat. I've made us some sandwiches. Old Jeremiah Perritt brought a couple of eggs as a goodwill offering. Said he was sorry for being difficult when we moved him out.' She had the kettle boiling and the food ready on the trestle table.

Pamela sat down gratefully. She was suddenly depressed. Were all men the same really? She would have liked to talk about it to Mary, but couldn't bring herself to explain. It would mean telling her too much about her life, her marriage, her feelings for the American.

She experienced one of her occasional pangs of longing for her mother. Lawrence had reminded her of the painting of Olivia that had been carefully packed and stored away. Not to be able to see it whenever she felt the need was almost like an additional bereavement. Yet she had the diary. She was comforted a little by the thought of the precious little leather-covered volume that was now safely locked away in a drawer in her new bedroom. But Olivia was, to Pamela, still only eighteen, permanently eighteen, her own age. She felt the need for an older woman in whom to confide, someone of her very own who would understand and care.

'You look really weary,' Mary Turner said suddenly and there was concern in her voice.

Pamela looked at her in surprise. Could Mary possibly have read her thoughts?

'Come on, eat up,' Mary continued cheerfully. 'By the way, I thought that we might come over here tonight, to the dance. Do us both good. How about it? We can use one of the vans, I should think. It's a sort of farewell to the area as you know, and it's sure to be fun.'

Pamela smiled and began to feel better. Perhaps life could hold hope and fun and brightness again? She wasn't completely alone after all! And just as quickly she made up her mind about the dance. If Mary was coming, then so would she. 'All right,' she said. 'I'll come with you, and I'll wear my best dress and my nylons.'

Her moods seemed to go in great swings lately, she thought. One moment everything looked bleak, and the next – well, who knew what might happen? When you were young anything might come to pass. She put a hand to her hair, thinking that she must somehow get it washed before tonight, and then she laughed at herself and ate the last of the sandwiches with enjoyment.

There was a letter waiting for Pamela when she arrived home later that day.

'One for you,' Mary said, indicating the slim envelope on the hall table. 'From that nice husband of yours, I think.'

Pamela took it and looked at the writing. 'Yes, it's from Alan.' She recognised his large upright script, totally clear and firm. Like his physical presence, she thought as she put it down again.

She took off her coat and hung it on one of the pegs of the wooden hallstand. The letter, lying where she had placed it, seemed to have a life of its own. It was almost an intrusion into her newly achieved freedom, a threat to her efforts at self-determination, and a reproach that she was going to a dance tonight. She laughed at her fanciful thoughts, making an effort to banish them, and then she glanced at herself in the mirror before picking the envelope up again. She tidied her hair, tucking some straying wisps into the band that she had taken to wearing most of the time now.

She carried the letter through to the kitchen and found a fruit knife and then slit the top carefully, taking time, strangely reluctant to hear his voice again through the written word.

Dear Pamela,

I've been billeted in a block of flats here in St John's Wood. This is the training centre. It's strange being so close to a lot of other people after living on the farm. I shall be here for about another five weeks, I think, and then home for a short leave.

We have our food in a great disused garage and it's very dark and unpleasant, underground actually. But everything else is good and the important thing is that when I've finished all my training I shall be able to have a go at the Jerries. I don't know yet what section I shall be in. Of course I want to fly, but I could be ground staff.

Thank you for telling me about the closing up of Morelake.

Love from Alan

She sat down heavily on one of the kitchen chairs and held the page in her hand for a long time. It was a pathetic little letter she thought, not threatening, not bossy, not full of instructions. She tried to think of him surrounded by a lot of men. He had told her once, in a rare moment of intimacy, that he had never found it easy to make friends at school. She could understand this for there was something about him that forbade any kind of closeness. He appeared to be forever on the defensive, always imagining an insult where none was meant. He was more at home with his animals than with people, although even with them there was no friendship.

She read the letter through again and realized that, apart from the brief reference to Morelake, he had not acknowledged the two pages that she had sent to him, and there was not one word about her own welfare either. It was merely a statement, something that could have been written by anyone, a stranger.

'How's he getting on then?' Mary asked as she put the kettle to boil. 'Must be a bit of a shock for him after his life on the land.'

'Yes, I think it is. He doesn't say much. He'll manage, though. He always wanted to join up. It was only the farm that stopped him really.' Pamela put the letter back in its envelope. 'Anything I can do?' she asked.

'No. You go and have your bath,' Mary directed. 'I'll get something to eat and then you can wash up while I have mine. Only five inches of hot water, mind, like the powers-that-be tell us!'

Pamela laughed. 'I'll remember,' she said. 'And I'll be quick. It's too cold to stay long in the bathroom. It'll be a bit warmer when you have your turn.'

'It's a good thing that Alan wrote to you,' Mary called after her as she left the room. 'He must have known that you were going to meet some handsome GIs tonight!'

Mary intended the remark to be casual, a joke, but as soon as she had spoken she regretted her words. She had come to like Pamela very much. But the girl was vulnerable and lonely, and in spite of her sense of humour there was a sadness about her that no eighteen year old should possess. Yet she had a trace of toughness too, a certain strength of character that wasn't immediately visible but that Mary had come to admire. She wondered about her upbringing. Pamela often talked about the child, Jane, and seemed fond of her uncle, but Mary had grave doubts about the aunt. Mrs Lindhurst had a bit of a name in the area for being a stickler for having her own way. Certainly she

126

didn't sound very motherly, and after all, a girl needed a mother.

Meanwhile, in the cold bathroom upstairs, Pamela stepped gingerly into her allotted five inches of hot water and wondered if her hostess had any idea at all of her feelings for Lawrence Lawson. Then she reminded herself that there was nothing to know after all. To the American she was just a bit of comfort. Well, if that was how he wanted it, she would be casual too. She'd been stupid. She took the loofah, soaped it and rubbed herself fiercely all over. Grow up, Pamela Saunders, she said. Just try to grow up, will you?

# ELEVEN

*Olivia's Journal – 1st March 1922*
*Today Maud gave me a beautiful gold cross on a chain. It has my name engraved on it and the year when I was born, 1907. Maud said that my father gave it to my mother at my Christening. I wish I had known my parents. How sad that they were both drowned, yet they never grew old or lonely! This cross will be very precious. I shall wear it always.*

When Mary and Pamela arrived for the dance later that evening most of the local people who had not moved too far away were already there. Mrs Yates was sitting at the ancient piano vamping out some lively music that sounded vaguely like a quickstep, and a few couples were enjoying themselves trying to keep in step with her. Her daughter Molly, decked out in a tight-waisted dress and with a smear of bright lipstick on her mouth, had a discontented air about her. The GIs had obviously not yet arrived!

Pamela, in her gossamer-thin nylons, felt only half dressed. Used to thick lisle, her legs were cold, and the summer frock which was the only one she felt was colourful enough to wear for such an occasion had to be half covered with a heavy and unbecoming cardigan.

A gramophone and a hefty pile of dance records had been scrounged from somewhere for the evening in case Wendy Yates should tire, and later, as it scratchily ground out the Lambeth

Walk, almost everyone in the room began to join in. Into the midst of this noisy gyrating throng the Americans arrived. Just a few had been invited, the men who had been helping with the carrying and moving, those who had become known and trusted by the families they were displacing. They stood at the door, uncertain at first, and then they were gathered into the mass of laughing bodies, arms and hands stretching out to welcome them.

Pamela had no thoughts now for Molly Yates. Her whole concern was for herself. She knew that she must struggle to hide her feelings. She tried to tell herself that she was not important to Lawrence, nor he to her.

But here he was now, right beside her, laughing with everyone else – yet with eyes, it seemed, only for her!

The gramophone slowed to a gruesome wail as it came gradually to the end of its powers, and Mrs Yates was persuaded to the piano again while someone wound it up, changed the needle and put a new record on the turntable. Pamela found herself next to Molly. The girl grinned at her, happy now.

'She can only play them three or four tunes,' she whispered, nodding in her mother's direction. 'A quickstep and waltz. Them's all she knows!'

A quickstep seemed to suit Lawrence very well. He took Pamela's hand and whirled her into the dance, taking her breath away. He was a competent dancer, leading her into steps that made her eyes sparkle. She felt his arm tight around her and the memory of his remarks of the morning quickly faded from her mind. She wished that the dance would go on for ever. When the music changed to a waltz she was sure everyone else in the room would notice the way he was looking at her, but her face flushed with pleasure.

At last Wendy Yates exhausted her four tunes, and with an exuberant flourish, ceased playing. Then Lawrence led Pamela back to her place, bowed slightly, and left her for a time. She looked around at the assembled company, suddenly embarrassed, but saw to her great relief that no one was looking at her. They were all concerned more with their own enjoyment. Mary was deep in conversation with the Vicar, probably discussing some last-minute arrangements which must be completed by Sunday night. The landlord of the now closed Red Swallow was presiding at a table laden with home-made blackberry wine and lemonade given by an anonymous well-wisher, and the Vicar's wife was busy at the refreshment table handing out various goodies that had also been donated. Everyone who had the use of a kitchen had been asked to give a little out of their precious store of rations for this last get-together.

Lawrence was standing looking at the array of food, then Pamela saw him pushing through the throng towards her. 'Can I get you something to eat, honey?' he asked. He was holding a plate on which reposed a sad-looking sandwich. 'I see you've got our spam over here now,' he added, looking at it dubiously. 'There are some other things on the table, though. Anything you fancy?'

Pamela laughed to cover her embarrassment, and stood up. 'We ate before we came,' she said. 'But perhaps I could manage a little. I'll go over and have a look.'

He led the way back to the refreshment table and as Pamela stared at the abundance of little cakes, the jellies, and the sandwiches, her appetite disappeared. But it was not the food which caused her reluctance to eat. It was more the presence of the man at her side. 'I'll just have some wine,' she said. 'It's home-made and very good.'

She took a glass and sipped it gingerly, feeling herself relax a little. The room which had been chilly was now warm and filled with smoke from numerous cigarettes as well as from the ancient stove in the corner. She felt hot and stifled. 'I need some fresh air,' she said innocently, and then immediately regretted the words.

Lawrence rapidly finished his sandwich. There was much coming and going and Pamela hoped that their exit would go unnoticed. They walked to the front gate and stood together in the sharp, still coldness of the night. The sky was filled with a million stars and there was no wind. Only the sounds of dance music from the hall, another waltz, disturbed the velvet quietness all about them.

' "How wonderful this night is, a night to share with a girl you love!" ' quoted Lawrence softly. 'Do you know the song? It's from some crackpot musical back home, but those words sure do get to me just now!' He ran his fingers over her face and felt tears wet on her cheeks. 'What's this then?' he said, concerned. 'Life's too short for tears.'

The words gave her no comfort. 'That's just it,' she said. 'Life's too short for a lot of things.' She wanted to add, 'Like being in love with someone totally forbidden to you. Like being married to the wrong person.' But then she found that his arms were around her, his lips pressed to hers, and she gave herself up to him, to the love that she had tried to deny, to her feelings for this comparative stranger that she felt were quickly overwhelming all her common sense, all her loyalty to Alan, everything. It was the strongest emotion she had ever felt. Nothing else mattered.

Then, from the hedgebank that bordered the neighbouring field, she suddenly heard a childish giggle and the sound jolted her out of her euphoria as nothing else could. It was certainly Molly Yates over there on the grass. Pamela couldn't make out any distinct words but there was a male voice and more laughter, more sounds that caused her to think of Alan, of those unpleasant episodes in their marriage bed most nights. She pulled rapidly away from Lawrence and shivered. Then she turned and rushed back to the smoky warmth and security of the hall. She had been saved from foolishness just in the nick of time, saved by that silly little Molly Yates!

Lawrence did not follow her at once. He too had heard the sounds, realized what was happening there over the hedge and felt diminished in some way. He stood in the quietness and lit a cigarette. He had not been deeply affected by any woman in his life before, and knew that he must not allow Pamela to be cheapened by anything he might do. She was so young – eighteen, she said – and married. Perhaps he should abandon all thought of her, or maybe she should just remain a dream, an insubstantial fantasy that he could never possess for real. The thought suited the poet in him. Yet his feelings were not casual, he was sure of that, and the thought of giving her up was terrible. He was disturbed by the noises he could hear in the field, envious almost, but a brief careless liaison was not for him and he felt sure that Pamela wouldn't want that either. She was worthy of better things, yet what could he offer her? Nothing but his body and his love, fleetingly, before the war carried them apart for ever.

Inside the hall Pamela looked anxiously for his return, wishing she had not been so hasty and wondering what he must think of her. She longed to see him push through the door, longed to see the light in his eyes as he looked at her, longed to be dancing with him, feeling his arms about her. But her thoughts were interrupted by the sight of Molly Yates, face flushed, eyes bright and lipstick smudged, sliding surreptitiously into the hall, obviously hoping that her mother would think she had merely gone outside to the privy for a few moments. Mrs Yates was at the piano again and Ben was arguing about something with a few of his mates. It seemed that Molly was lucky. At least Pamela hoped that she was lucky. She coloured violently at her thoughts and looked with some compassion at the girl who was anxiously trying to brush mud from her dress.

Lawrence came back into the hall at last, but there was a difference in him and when they danced together again he said little. He was quiet, reflective, and she wondered if it was her precipitate flight that was causing his silence.

'I'm sorry,' she whispered, 'for dashing off like that, but . . .'

He put a finger over her lips. 'You don't need to be sorry, honey,' he said. 'Forget it. I felt like running too, but I guess they were just enjoying themselves!'

Pamela looked up at him, saw the brown eyes staring down into hers, and knew that if this friendship continued then she would want just what Molly Yates had wanted. She wanted it now, longed to have Lawrence hold her in his arms on the cold grass outside, and yet she knew with numbing fear that she must not allow it to happen. Whether it was a fear of Alan or a fear of God and fate she couldn't determine. But the blush that stained her cheeks rapidly ebbed as she thought of her husband, of his anger if he could see her now, if he could see into her heart!

'Could we sit this one out, please?' she asked as Wendy Yates thumped out an old-fashioned waltz.

Lawrence was immediately full of concern. 'Sure thing,' he said, leading her through the throng of sweating bodies to two empty chairs at the side of the hall. 'You OK? Anything wrong?'

'We shouldn't see each other any more, Lawrence,' she murmured. 'Please don't say anything or ask any questions.'

'That's about the hardest thing I've ever heard,' he said quietly. 'But I guess I must try to understand.'

'We must part now.' Her voice was low. 'People are looking at us.'

'Not like this, honey. Not right here with all these folks around.' His voice held absolute desolation. 'And I've something to give you. I'd like a remembrance of you too. Will you find me a small thing to keep, a talisman to take into battle?'

Pamela looked up at him. He sounded so old-fashioned, not at all what you expected from a GI. More like someone out of a history book. 'I haven't anything here,' she breathed.

'And I don't have my present with me. Can I come and see you on Sunday?'

Pamela thought swiftly. As he said, this was no place or time to make a final farewell to someone who held all of your heart. Sunday was another day. Perhaps hope might be rekindled on Sunday! Who knew what another twenty-four hours might bring? Yet she must not be alone with him. 'Come to the house during the evening,' she whispered. 'I'll find something for you. Mary will be in.' She added the last four words hastily, clinging to them, hoping he might guess at her meaning.

It had been a long and busy day, December 19th, the day before the final dreaded date when the whole area must be handed over to the authorities. Mary and Pamela had been driving to and fro from first light until darkness fell over the now silent and totally abandoned fields and villages. 'Thirty thousand acres, more or less,' Mary said. They were relaxing at last over an easily prepared meal of toast and sardines, a precious last tin from Mary's store. Neither had the energy to prepare anything more elaborate.

'That's the extent of the land we've helped to clear during the last six weeks. Think of it, Pamela. Six parishes, over three thousand people, nearly two hundred farms! All successfully evacuated. We've done a good job.'

Pamela, with her thoughts turning constantly to Lawrence during the day, had not concentrated too much on the enormity of the task that she and all the other volunteers had completed. Now that Mary put it in a nutshell like this it did seem an amazing achievement. She thought of the villages, most of which she knew well: tiny bustling places like Slapton, Blackawton, Chillington, or lovely Torcross sprawling along the sea-front, all now totally abandoned, their churches bare and empty, the houses sealed up, and the shops cold and desolate. And what fate was really going to befall the thatched cottages, the ancient stones and quiet meadows? What did Lawrence know, and how responsible was he for the desolation?

'By the way,' Mary continued, 'you'll be all right here on your own for a bit, won't you, dear? I have to go out for a couple of hours.'

The words cut across Pamela's thoughts like a knife. She wanted to shout out that no, she certainly wouldn't be all right, and yet at the same time she was filled with delight. Lawrence was coming tonight, and in spite of all her careful planning, Mary was telling her that she was going out! Was it God tempting her? 'Lead us not into temptation . . . oh, please God, lead me not into temptation!'

But there was no answer, no sudden surge of strength, and when the bell rang just after Mary had left – when the house was empty except for herself and the dogs – she opened the front door and hoped that Lawrence couldn't hear the thudding of her heart.

She made him coffee, and then held out the gift that she had decided to give him. It was one of the most precious things she possessed. He turned it over in his hands, the long artistic fingers holding it delicately and with reverence.

'Olivia,' he read aloud. '1907.' The name and the year were engraved on the back of the small gold cross, and as their meaning dawned on Lawrence, as he looked up at her in amazement, Pamela knew that in choosing this one special gift for him she had achieved her aim. She was letting him know, without words, that she loved him, that he was precious to her beyond telling, and that because he had this one cherished possession, she would remember him for as long as she lived. And she believed in its power. It would surely keep him from dying in this terrible war.

'But this was your mother's,' he said. 'The girl in the grave-yard. You can't give me something so special.'

'Take it,' she whispered. 'It was to mark her christening. Please, Lawrence, take it. It will be a sort of pledge between us. I want you to keep it always, and remember me.'

'Then I will,' he said quietly. 'And I'll always remember you.' He fastened the chain around his neck and tucked it down beneath his collar against his skin. 'My gift for you isn't so splendid,' he said. It was wrapped in tissue paper and he handed it to her with some diffidence. 'There's no value in it, but I guess it means a bit to me. Keep it safe for me.'

She took it from him, untied the string and then gasped with pleasure. The book was small, bound in soft brown leather embossed with gold leaf. She opened it carefully. 'Poetry!' she said in surprise. She read some of the lines over to herself. 'It's beautiful.'

'I bet you didn't think any GI was capable of writing poetry?'

'Do you mean that it's yours – that you wrote it?'

'All mine, honey.'

She looked at him incredulously. 'I thought that there was something special about you,' she said. 'So you're a poet?' Her mind had to make a big jump to take this in. She looked from him back to the book, and then up at him again. 'Do you really mean that this book is for me?'

'Sure. I'd like you to have it.'

'Oh, Lawrence,' she whispered. 'You couldn't have given me

anything more wonderful. It's like having a bit of you here with me for ever.'

He laughed. 'Wait until you read it before making any judgements.'

'I shall hear your voice in every word,' she murmured. Then she looked up at him and her heart melted for love of this man who had come here to say goodbye to her for ever. She held the book close to her with one hand and stretched out her arm to him.

They were sitting in Mary's front room on the settee and yet with a chasm between them, the chasm of the separation they had yesterday decreed. But yesterday was gone, today was today, they were alone and fate seemed to have decided otherwise.

He took her hand in his and together, as one, they moved to the stairs. Without words they went to the room that Mary had chosen for Pamela, the large room with the double bed 'for when your husband comes home on leave'.

It was intense joy that Pamela felt as she lay with Lawrence between the crisp white sheets. There was no fear, no withdrawing of herself, only happiness in giving pleasure, ecstasy and a wonderful fulfilment that she had never known before. She closed her eyes with the glory of it for he wooed her with love and with passion but with gentleness too. And when it was over she lay in his arms and felt no tremor of remorse. Instead satisfaction surged through her. She had not planned it, and had prayed that she should not be led into temptation. Those facts seemed to make it right. In her mind it was not an act of betrayal, just something wonderful that had happened without any premeditation. Perhaps the fierce God whom Aunt Maud believed in was being kind, allowing her to know for just this one precious time what the love between man and woman that He had ordained should really be like. Wasn't He supposed to be a God of love anyway? 'Thank you,' she whispered though whether it was to the Deity or to Lawrence she was not quite sure.

Slowly she sat up and stared down at the man beside her. She saw the cross, her mother's little golden cross, lying among the dark hairs on his chest and touched it gently. He put his hand over hers so that the cross was warm beneath both of their hands.

'This will be a symbol, a talisman, between us,' he said.

'A remembrance,' she whispered.

Half an hour later, when Lawrence had fallen into a gentle doze, Pamela bent down to pick up Lawrence's little book which she had laid by the side of the bed and began leafing through it. She saw that there was a photograph between the pages towards the end. She hadn't noticed it before. She took it out and held it in her hand for a long time. His face looked up at her smiling slightly. Then, to her dismay tears rolled down her cheeks, one of them falling onto the print. She quickly wiped it away, and her heart thudded with a superstitious fear. Was the smudging circle it made on his jacket some kind of omen? 'Please God no,' she whispered aloud. Then she brushed his face gently with her lips and tucked the precious photograph back into the book.

Alan spent most of his free time sitting alone in the pub. In the noise and the smoke and the bustle around him he could withdraw into his own private world. He found this crowded little place comforting. He was used to his own company, and here no one took much notice of him which was how he wanted it.

But there was the girl. She often glanced in his direction, and tonight, for the first time, she spoke to him. 'I live near here,' she said. 'I work in the factory making bits of aeroplanes that you chaps are going to fly.'

Alan looked at her with a mixture of curiosity and misgiving. She was small, much smaller than Pamela, older too he judged, and he noticed that she wore a wedding ring. He'd seen her before in the pub, usually with a man. Tonight she was alone and that surprised him. She looked a bit common but decent enough, he thought. Yet he had always supposed that it was only a certain doubtful type of female who would come into a pub on her own.

They were sitting next to each other at the bar and she was looking at him, her eyes searching his enquiringly. 'How long you been in?' she said.

Alan took another drink from the glass in front of him before he replied. He presumed that she meant in the RAF. 'Just a few weeks. I was a farmer, reserved occupation.' He always felt the need of an excuse for his late entrance into the war.

'Well, we need all the food we can get. Who's looking after your farm then?'

'A friend.' He had become used to the necessary small lies and deceptions. Anything more revealing led to difficult explanations.

'My hubby was killed in France.' Her voice was flat and devoid of all emotion. 'In May 1940, before Dunkirk. Seems a lifetime ago.'

Alan suddenly wanted to know if she had loved him, if she had been happy, how it was for her when they were together. He wasn't sure why she evoked all these questions in his mind. Suddenly his self-imposed isolation seemed less desirable. He thought of Pamela and his lips set in a determined line. The woman must have noticed the tension in him for when she next spoke she seemed to have softened a fraction. There was kindness and concern in her eyes and in her voice.

'Like to buy me a drink?' she suggested. 'I could do with another. Then we could go to the pictures if you've nothing else to do. There might be something decent on, and it'll be warm. The old flea-pit, I call it!' She laughed, a high brittle sound, and Alan felt himself colouring with embarrassment.

'OK,' he replied quickly. 'What'll you have?'

'Just a beer, please.'

The request surprised him. His mother would only allow herself home-made wine or the very occasional sherry. He didn't realize that women drank beer. He ordered half a pint for her and a pint for himself.

She drank it quickly and he looked at the froth around her mouth with distaste before she wiped it away. He knew that she was staring at him, trying to penetrate the hard shell of his reserve, perhaps understanding his nervousness. He wanted to bolt out of the pub, back to the doubtful safety of his billet. Yet the other men would be there, some of them anyway. He couldn't understand this fearful thing in him, this barrier coming between himself and everyone else, whether male or female.

'Coming then?' She slid off the bar stool and belted her coat tightly around her waist. 'It's not far. Just down the road.'

They sat together in the hot stuffy darkness and he closed his eyes now and then against the trashy American musical that was filling the screen. It reminded him of the Yanks at home, the GIs back in Devon who had turned him out. Because of them he was here in this alien place with this unknown woman beside him. He could smell her cheap perfume and he was very much aware of the warmth of her, of the feel of her thighs against his, pressing towards him, inviting him. Suddenly all caution, all the constraints of his upbringing, vanished in the dark intimacy of the place and he put his arm around her, pulled her close. She snuggled into his side and he was conscious of the smallness of her. She seemed to have a vulnerability that called out for his strength. He felt that she needed him. It was a new sensation. Pamela was never like that. He wished to be dominant, masterful and the boss, and yet at the same time he craved to be wanted and appreciated by a woman, by his wife. But if not her, then perhaps he might find these things elsewhere. He took hold of those words in his mind. Wanted, appreciated, needed! They were important, necessary to a man. If only Pamela felt some need of him, made some demands of him other than that he should provide a home for herself and the child.

At the end of the film they watched the newsreel. There were pictures of allied aircraft setting out to bomb Berlin. And then came President Roosevelt making a speech, and later Monty taking the salute somewhere. This was followed by detachments of cheerful singing GIs and the information of which he was already so painfully aware, that there were a lot of them in England! Nothing was said about the evacuation of his precious bit of countryside. That was not to be talked about. Alan thought of Morelake as he had last seen it, barren and empty, and he was filled with a sense of loss, a sudden lowering of his spirits.

'OK,' she said. 'Let's go. The main picture'll start all over again in a minute.'

Abruptly he was brought back to the present. They shuffled

along the row of seats and she took his hand, propelling him up the gang-way to the illuminated EXIT sign. Outside it was cold and dark and they stopped to button up their coats against the chill wind. Then she took his arm and they walked along the dismal blacked-out road. She suddenly turned up a side-street and he supposed that he would see her to her door wherever that was.

'Name's Brenda Barker, by the way.' She laughed suddenly. 'We've been together all evening and we don't even know each other's names!'

'Alan Saunders,' he said, astonished and slightly ashamed. He hadn't thought of her until this minute as a person with a name!

'Coming in? I've got a bit of coffee left and some biscuits, home-made ones.'

He laughed. Home-made biscuits! They didn't fit the picture somehow. 'Yes, I'll come in,' he said.

It was a small terraced house, the door right on the pavement. She groped for her key and pushed it into the lock. He could see nothing but the blackness beyond as she pulled him gently inside.

'Wait a bit,' she directed. 'I'll just put the blackout curtains over and then we can see what we're doing.'

He stood where he was in the darkness as she pushed past him and the pungent smell of her perfume was all around him again. He could hear the swish of curtains.

'Right,' she called eventually. 'I don't think there are any gaps.' She switched on the lights and he blinked in the sudden brightness. She showed him into the front room and he marvelled at the minute size of it. Then she struck a match and lit the gas fire, something he had never seen before. There was no gas at Morelake.

'Get yourself warm,' she said. 'I'll put the kettle on.'

He stood before the rapidly increasing heat and felt a mixture of excitement and apprehension, wondering what on earth he was doing here in this ugly little room with its strange cheerless fire. On the brown-tiled mantelpiece there were two garish blue vases set carefully on either side of a large photograph of a soldier. Alan studied the man. He was young, handsome, and was staring back, accusingly almost, with no laughter in the grey eyes.

Brenda felt small and warm and infinitely desirable when she lay beside him later in the double bed upstairs. Yet there was still that vulnerability about her that caused him to be gentle when he made love to her, more gentle than he had ever been with Pamela. She led him into joys and experiences he hardly knew and he was overwhelmed with gratitude to this stranger for the love and comfort she so freely gave. He'd had no idea it could be like this.

'Will you tell your wife about tonight?'

The question, whispered into the darkness, bewildered him. He pulled a little away from her, pulled himself up in the bed and leaned on his arm, looking down at her tousled head on the pillow. 'How did you . . . ?'

'I always know. It's a kind of instinct.'

'You mean that you . . . ?' Again he couldn't finish the sentence. 'Always know,' she had said. So there were many times like this! He got out of the bed, groped for the light switch and then started to pull on his clothes. Of course, he should have guessed. He had seen her with others. It would account for her skill! She had so easily picked him up and he had been completely taken in, deceived by the innocent look of her. He felt naive, a complete country bumpkin, yet at the same time he wasn't sorry it had happened. He had no regrets. Perhaps she would want to be paid?

Quickly she was out of bed too, pulling a wrap around her body, holding her arms out to him again. 'Don't be hard on me, Alan,' she whispered. 'I'm lonely and I miss my man, and I know I can comfort other lonely folks. I'm no hustler. I don't want money or anything. I told you, I got a respectable job. Don't judge me harshly, Alan.'

He was immediately ashamed of his thoughts. Her use of his name, not once but twice, her pleading, reached his heart in a strange way, as if their shared unhappiness gave them a special awareness of each other. But it didn't decrease his revulsion.

This kind of thing was her way of life! He felt sorry for her, wanted to leave her without any trace of accusation. He took her into his arms once more and kissed her. 'I don't judge you harshly,' he said. 'I have to thank you . . . I'm grateful. You've taught me things, helped me come to terms with myself.'

'Then I'm happy,' she said simply. 'That's all I want. Just to enjoy myself a little, to take a bit of pleasure from this rotten war, and to give some too.' She pulled away from him. 'Now you'll have to get back. Won't do to be late.'

He had almost forgotten the time. It was odd to have to be in by set hours, like school all over again. Quickly he finished dressing and ran down the narrow stairs.

She stood at the top, watching him in the dim light.

Just before he let himself out of the front door she called to him. 'Will I see you again?'

'Perhaps. Perhaps not.' It sounded abrupt and he turned and looked up at her lonely figure leaning over the banister. 'I think not,' he said. 'But thank you again, Brenda. Be happy.'

He reached his billet just in time, and as he lay in his narrow bed later that night he thought about the evening. No hustler, she had said. Yet perhaps he should have given her something, or would she have been hurt? She had inadvertently taught him much in that little time they had spent together. He had learnt that women could be tough and brave as well as vulnerable and lonely, that a hard shell like Pamela's didn't always mean a hardness of heart, that behind a self-sufficient exterior there might exist a longing and a need. He resolved to try to do better when he next saw his wife.

# TWELVE

*Olivia's Journal – 4th May 1922*

*We are to have new neighbours. A family has taken Ash Manor for the whole of the summer. There seems to be some mystery about them, for Maud will not speak of them. There are two children though. If they are my age I hope I shall be allowed to meet them.*

*There has been a burglary in the village and my sister is now saying that perhaps we should have a dog as a guard. Perhaps my prayers are about to be answered, but God has a very strange way of managing things!*

'Well,' Mary said on Tuesday morning, 'that's it. They told us that we must have the whole area evacuated by December the twentieth and we've done it.' She breathed a sigh both of relief and resignation. 'It's all theirs now and I hope they'll look after it!'

There was no need to rush breakfast today. They could spend as long as they liked over their porridge and tiny fresh eggs laid by the bantam hens that Mary kept in the garden.

Pamela, still in a daze, still thinking of Lawrence, looked at her and smiled. The previous day, the dreaded Monday, the final date of the evacuation, had been so busy with all the last-minute checking that she had found little time either to be sorry for herself or to feel any guilt over what she had done. Today was different. Tuesday morning, and no information centre to man, no heart-rending situations to sort out, no driving along muddy lanes ferrying miserable people to and fro, no pets to be taken to the RSPCA to be disposed of! She shuddered as she thought of some of the things she and Mary had accomplished during the past hectic weeks.

'I think we can all be proud of what we've done,' Mary said. 'The WVS isn't to be laughed at any more. We've proved our worth, the hundred or so of us!'

Pamela was silent, thinking about the words 'proud of what we have done'. Was she proud of the few precious hours spent with Lawrence? She knew that they had left her filled with sadness. Having vowed not to see him again, she doubted her ability to keep such an impossible pledge. She felt quite desolate. This loss, this grief, was different to the one she constantly experienced over Jane.

She wondered if her agonizing decision not to see Lawrence any more had been the right one. Should everything that her mind and body yearned for be denied? But what would happen if she gave in, capitulated? An affair? The word offended her, cheapened her dreams. A divorce then? That was much worse. A broken heart? She had that already. And her marriage? She had just begun to experience a deepening of her feelings for Alan before he went away, before Lawrence.

And what did it all mean to him? Did he have the will-power to keep to the resolutions they had made? She wasn't sure. GIs weren't particularly noted for their high ideals or strict morals! Yet he was different from most of the others she had met. He stood apart. He filled her heart with delight and her eyes with tears.

She became aware of Mary staring at her.

'My dear child, have I said anything? What's the matter?'

Pamela struggled for composure. She wanted to keep her thoughts to herself. 'No,' she replied. 'It's the anti-climax, I suppose. Nothing to do. I don't think I like the feeling.'

Mary smiled at her. 'They'll find plenty of jobs for us,' she said. 'You mark my words. There won't be so many of course,

146

no more rushing about, I hope, but we'll have to keep an eye on some of the families who've been moved. There'll still be problems, believe me!'

Pamela tried to picture some of the people she had helped, tried to divert her mind from her own grief to that of others. And then she gave a grim little laugh. 'I wonder what happened to the ten hens?' she said. 'Mrs Tremayne was so worried about them.'

'Eaten already, probably,' Mary replied. 'Or destined for Christmas dinner.' She started to clear the table. The breakfast things were still there, the toast limp and unappetizing and the tea cold in the pot. 'That reminds me of another job,' she continued. 'Did I tell you that we've to supply a mobile canteen for the Home Guard? They're to do night patrols around the outside of the whole area. It has to be guarded all the time to see that no one trespasses.'

Trespass? It meant going on to land that didn't belong to you, but this was their own land, their own fertile acres! Pamela thought of all the lanes and fields she had known since childhood which were now closed to her, a vast area now totally out of bounds. She felt a further sense of deprivation.

'How long do you think it'll be?' she asked. 'How long before we can all go home again? Have you any idea?'

'None at all. It's all top secret as you know. No point in speculating.' Mary broke the stale toast into equal portions and gave it to the three dogs who were sitting in a line, staring at her, mouths watering. 'If it was the Germans who were here instead of the Yanks we'd have something to moan about, though!'

Ashamed of herself, Pamela jumped to her feet and took the kettle from the stove to pour water into the washing up bowl. She would keep busy, keep doing as much work as she could find. There was a war on, she reminded herself. People were being killed and made homeless every day. What did her own little concerns matter? She put a handful of soda and a few precious soap flakes into the water and swirled it about, but all she could see in the froth and bubbles was Lawrence's face.

Later that week 'Out of Bounds' notices were in position all around the perimeter of the Area of Occupation. Pamela, looking at them, found each one threatening and intimidating. They loomed up at her in all the places that were most precious. She cycled to various parts of the boundary, stared over into the forbidden fields and felt overcome by a great sense of apathy, as though nothing mattered any more. For weeks she had driven herself to the ends of her endurance and now she had little energy, no more fight left. And there were so many American soldiers everywhere that forgetting Lawrence was a fruitless and impossible exercise. In every Yankee voice she heard his, in every uniform she seemed to see his tall handsome frame.

Then on Christmas Eve Alan came home. Only forty-eight hours leave he told her, and it had been suddenly granted. He had not been able to let her know in advance. He stood on the doorstep, for once unsure of himself, and Mary, coming along the passage behind Pamela to see who had been knocking at such an hour, beamed at him.

'Well, how nice to see you at last, Mr Saunder's, she said. 'And for Christmas too. Come along in and I'll get you something to eat. You'll be able to taste your wife's Christmas pudding tomorrow after all!'

She bustled about, leaving them alone in the front room, the room that Pamela felt she would always associate with Lawrence. She sat on the settee with her husband and wondered what to say. They were both awkward in this suddenly embarrassing situation.

They were no more at ease with one another when they lay side by side in Mary's bed, and when eventually Alan pulled Pamela into his arms and made love to her she could think of nothing but Lawrence's arms and Lawrence's body. Yet thinking of him she was able to respond as she never had before, and afterwards Alan looked at her in surprise. 'You've changed,' was all he said before he fell asleep.

For Pamela, sleep was a long time coming. She felt a sense of guilt, as though in responding to the man in her arms as if he had been someone else she had been unfaithful to him for a second time. She tried to tell herself that this was foolish. Her husband had made love to her and she had obviously satisfied and pleased him as she had never been able to do before. And there was a difference in him too. He had not been so urgent or so clumsy. She had to admit, when she stopped thinking of Lawrence, that there had indeed been a great difference in Alan's lovemaking. Had she in fact enjoyed it? The thought amazed her and she fell asleep, eventually to awaken on Christmas morning with some of her depression gone.

Alan was up when she opened her eyes. He was standing at the window looking out at the grey expanse of sea.

'Alan,' she whispered, and he turned and handed her a small parcel beautifully wrapped.

'Happy Christmas,' he said. 'It's scent. The chemist did it up for me. I hope you like it.'

She laughed affectionately at him. Although the gift was surprising, how typical the remark was, as though he wanted to make excuses for the extravagance. She untied the ribbon and lifted a little bottle from the box inside. 'It's lovely,' she said. 'Expensive. Chanel No. 5. You shouldn't have!' She could hardly believe it. The extravagance overwhelmed her. 'Thank you, Alan,' she said breathlessly. 'I bought you a diary, but it's in the post. I sent it. What made you buy me a present like this? How did you choose such a lovely perfume?'

As she spoke she realized that the amazement in her voice was not exactly flattering so bounced out of bed and threw her arms around him. Perhaps their marriage held some promise after all.

By the middle of January she suspected that she might be pregnant and at the end of the month she was sure. When it was officially confirmed she wrote to Alan. She hoped that the news would cheer him as it now cheered her. At first she had wondered about it. Her reactions were mixed, her dreams of independence and freedom thwarted. Yet as she became used to the idea she was glad. At last she would have someone of her very own, a baby over whom Aunt Maud could have no jurisdiction at all.

But in her heart was a gnawing fear. More than anything in the world she wanted Lawrence's child, a permanent memory of the man to whom she had given her heart, and just that once her body. Yet the guilt sometimes appeared monstrous. To have Lawrence's baby and to say that he was Alan's! Surely she would not be allowed to get away with such a terrible deception? Every time she thought about it she felt quick panic rising inside her so that her heart pounded and she shivered in anticipation of the day when she would have to tell her husband of her betrayal! She imagined the scene. They would be back at Morelake, the child would be in her arms, a dark-haired little boy with Lawrence's eyes. 'I committed adultery,' she would say. 'I committed adultery with an American. I've borne his child, his child, his child!' The words went round and round in her head when she was alone, when she was trying to go to sleep, when she wanted to feel young and carefree. She tried to replace them with the thought that the baby would have fair hair and blue eyes, Alan's son. A child with Alan's determined face and stocky build. But in spite of her guilt, in spite of the constant fear, it was a slim, dark-haired boy with poetry in his soul for whom she yearned. Sometimes, when everything was still and quiet, and especially when the moon wove patterns on her bedroom wall, then she would allow herself to think of Lawrence again. She would put her hands across her stomach and speak his name silently to herself over and over until the tears came and sleep eventually replaced her guilt with comforting dreams.

There had been no word from him. She wanted to tell him of the coming child and yet dared not. And how could he have any interest in it when he could never claim it as his? She thought about the coming baby almost constantly and wondered if there would ever be a way of knowing whether it was Alan's legitimate son or the love-child that in her heart she really wanted. Happiness and guilt strove together within her. Sometimes she thought that perhaps Aunt Maud was right after all in that judgement of her character. She tried to make excuses for herself, tried to preserve her ideas of her own self-worth, but it was difficult. To have a child and not to know who the father was seemed to Pamela a most depraved and immoral thing to do. And if you were married, then surely it was truly unforgiveable!

By not getting in touch Lawrence was obviously keeping to his side of their bargain yet his silence was a further source of unrest. In her heart from time to time she felt a little worm of fear that perhaps their relationship had not meant so much to him after all. When she read his poems she could feel his presence with her, closer than Alan could ever be, but during the humdrum routine of her days she wondered if she was merely giving way to fanciful dreams.

Now that Lawrence's part in the evacuation was over they would probably never meet accidentally again, and she frequently struggled with herself against the desire to write, to find out somehow if he still cared. But January passed and still she resisted. The news bulletins constantly told of the exploits and sufferings of the American troops in various parts of the world, and each time that she listened it was only of him she thought. Great waves of fury swept over her when she heard of the torture and deaths of thousands of American prisoners in the Philippines. Seeing Lawrence in her mind made each horror-story more real, gave each nameless soldier a face, and every time the GIs were successful, as they had been at Anzio, she shared the general pleasure. But her feelings were tinged with apprehension. She searched for an atlas, discovered that this faraway place was in Italy, and thought with a shiver of fear of the preparations going on right here in Devon for some similar battle.

A letter from Scotland arrived in the middle of February. There were congratulations about the coming baby, news of Craemore, remarks from Aunt Maud about men wearing kilts, a crayoned picture from Jane and a plea from Uncle Richard that Pamela should go once more to see how Sheppey was getting on with Ben Yates. He was anxious about his little sheep-dog, worried lest she should be missing him, and longing to have some further news. Pamela laughed affectionately when she read it.

'I shall have to cycle right round to get to the Yates' cottage,' she said to Mary. 'Uncle Richard doesn't realize that. I'll go on Sunday, shall I?'

'It's a long way,' Mary replied. 'All of twenty-five miles or more. Have you looked at the map?'

'Twenty-five miles?' Pamela was incredulous. 'As far as that just to get across to Shercombe? It's only six or seven along past Slapton. I know the road is closed, but surely it's not as much as twenty to go round?'

'Probably nearer thirty, my dear girl.' Mary rummaged in her desk and found the local map and spread it out on the table. 'There you are,' she said. 'And it's complicated too. Blackawton is closed as you know, and East Allington, so you have to go almost up to Halwell. If you take the wrong turning you'll end up at a barbed wire barrier or be blown up by a stray shell!'

'But I must go, Mary. I can't disappoint Uncle Richard. He adores that dog. I'd like to see how Molly Yates is getting on too.'

'Well, I'm not having you cycling all that way on your own and in your condition, and you'd have to stay the night. You couldn't do the two journeys in one day. How about us taking the van and doing some essential calls?'

'Could we?'

'I think so. I ought to make an official visit to some rather doubtful families that we evacuated over there. I could drop you off at the Yates' for an hour or two. It would be an interesting day out!' She grinned at Pamela. 'Our allowance of petrol will run to it next week, I think.'

The sun was shining on the day that they chose for the visit. Pamela felt a lifting of her spirits as they set out. Since Christmas the activities of the allied forces in the area had increased and the frequent shelling and gunfire was frightening. From her bedroom window she could often see a vast number of ships in Start Bay and it was with great trepidation that she watched some of the exercises going on there. Her thoughts at those times were always with Lawrence. But there was still no word and she didn't really expect any now. The only thing she had of him was the book of poems and his photograph. She had carefully fixed the print in the fly-leaf of the book and kept it with her mother's diary in the cupboard beside the bed. She read a little from each before going to sleep every night.

The journey round to Shercombe was not without incident. There was the constant sound of battle. They drove northwards, eventually reaching the steep wooded hillsides beyond Blackawton. A particularly loud explosion made Pamela shudder.

'It sounds like the real thing, doesn't it?' she said.

'Well, it almost is,' Mary replied. 'They're using live ammunition most of the time.'

'Why do they need to do that, for goodness sake? Isn't it bad enough to be killed by German shells?'

'They're preparing for the invasion of Europe, aren't they? And that's pretty important! I suppose it's vital that they get to know what they're doing.'

'Well, I hope they really do know!'

Mary smiled. 'It's that baby making you jittery,' she said. 'Don't worry. They won't kill any civilians. As long as we obey orders and don't sneak into the area, as I've heard one or two have done, we'll be all right.'

Pamela wanted to shout out that it was not of herself she was thinking, nor even of her baby. Lawrence was over there taking part in all those terrifying exercises. She closed her mind to the numbing fact that some time soon he would be in the midst of battle for real. The practice sounded fearsome enough!

When they turned seawards again Pamela felt that she could almost smell the heady scent of the sea. She hated driving inland. She had been born to the sound of waves crashing on to a shingle beach, and the calling of gulls was almost essential to her well-being and happiness.

The Yates' little cottage was much as she had seen it last time except that the front gate was repaired and bright curtains hung at the tiny windows. Molly came to the door at the unusual sound of the van, and as soon as Pamela saw her she noticed the pale drooping look, the hopelessness in the usually perky face.

'I'll pick you up in a couple of hours' time then,' Mary said. 'Sure you'll be all right?'

'Yes. Thank you for bringing me. I shouldn't have liked cycling all that way. It's so hilly as well as a long way.' She climbed down from the vehicle, called a greeting to the girl who was now coming down the path to meet her, and then watched as Mary reversed and then drove away down the rutted lane.

For a second Pamela felt vulnerable and alone and she realized how much she had come to rely on this woman who had so rapidly become a very good friend.

Then she was aware of Molly looking her up and down and eventually grinning at her.

'Well, hello then,' she said. 'What brings you over to see the likes of us?'

'I've come to see Sheppey actually,' Pamela said quickly, and immediately laughed at the unfortunate remark. Why did she always speak without thinking? It was one of her major faults!

But Molly was laughing too. 'Well, I might have knowed. Dogs be more important than folks to some! Come on in. Mum and Dad are out, and that dog as well for that matter, so you'll have to wait if you want to see en. Us can have a cup of tea and a comfy chat by the fire. I was wanting to see you.'

The room was tiny but clean now, and there was a cheerful blaze in the grate. 'Your mum has got it nice,' Pamela remarked while Molly brought out some of the best china from a box that was stowed away in a corner.

'I helped. Us had to scrub and wash for hours to get it like this, and it be small. Nowhere to put things, but 'tis better than living with other folks like some have to.'

When the tea was made and poured and they were sitting either side of the fire, Pamela wondered how she was going to

154

spend two hours in conversation with Molly Yates. They had
nothing in common at all.

Then suddenly Molly drained her cup and put it down before
looking at Pamela with large frightened eyes. 'I'm that glad
you've come,' she said. 'You got to help me. You'm the best
one to help.'

Pamela guessed at once what the matter was. Molly's pale
face and her own memories of the night of the dance told her
everything.

'I'm in the family way and frightened to death of me dad,' the
girl went on. 'He'll skin me alive when I tells en.'

Pamela gulped her tea and wondered what on earth she could
possibly say or do. 'Oh gosh, Molly, I'm sorry,' she managed.

'It's me that's sorry! I didn't know much about life and things,
did I? Me mam never told me all about what happens. I just let
Delmer do what he wanted and now I'm in this pickle. I ought
to have knowed, what with growing up with animals and all. But,
well, I just didn't think it could happen to me.'

'How do you know . . . I mean . . .'

Molly gave her a withering look. 'Well, I'm not completely
stupid. Pretty stupid I'll agree, but I knowed about how you
don't get your monthlies if there's going to be a kid. I knowed
that much. Since then I been to see my cousin Peg what lives
over Duncombe and she put me in the picture about everything.'

'Have you thought about . . . ?'

'Getting rid of it, you mean? Yes, of course, but when Peg
told me what they does to you, it put me off proper. No, I shall
have en. I thinks Mam'll take to the idea. It's just me dad that
I got to win over. Like I said, he'll flay me alive! That's where
you comes in . . .'

'Mightn't this Delmer of yours marry you, then?'

'Marry me? You'm joking for sure. Them Yanks is all the
same. Gets you in the family way, gives you a few pairs of fancy
nylons what's no use on a farm, and then off they goes home to
their wives – or more likely to get theirselves killed in all them
crazy games they be playing down there on the beach! Family

way, there's a laugh! 'Tis the wrong word to be sure for the state they leaves you in!' Molly grabbed the poker and viciously attacked the fire, adding a few more logs from the pile drying in the grate.

Pamela finished her now cold tea and put the cup down on the floor beside her chair. She looked at the girl with pity. 'What can I do then?'

'Well, seeing you got a Yankee fancy man, too, I reckoned that you might be in the same state. Only 'tis easy for you, having a husband. You can palm your kid off on him. I just thought that you might tell my dad that I was set upon one night and that I couldn't help it! I knows it sounds daft but 'tis my only hope. Unless you can come up with something what's better?'

Pamela was horrified, Molly's plight temporarily forgotten. So her friendship with Lawrence had been noted and commented on. If that was so then Alan was bound to find out.

'How dare you say things like that?' she said, stung into fury. She felt the palms of her hands moist with sweat and her heart was beating in furious agitated thuds. 'Don't you ever mention those lies again, Molly Yates, or I'll not lift a finger to help you. Do you hear me?'

'Yes, I hears you. Keep yer hair on. I knows what I knows, but I 'spect we best stick together, you and me.'

The last thing Pamela wanted to do was to stick to Molly Yates, but she realized that what the girl had said was not a lie but the horrible unvarnished truth. Whether she liked it or not they were in the same boat, or almost anyway, and she had to decide what was best, and quickly too. Their babies would be born about the same time, Molly's conceived on the night of the dance, and her own . . . On the night after that? Or safely and respectably within marriage a week later on Christmas Eve? Would she ever be sure? Anyway, it was obviously important to keep on the right side of Molly, to ensure her silence and her friendship.

Pamela tried to keep her head and to think about Molly's plight first of all. Suddenly cold, she held out her hands to the fire. 'You'll have to tell your mum and dad. That's the first thing,' she said. 'Then see what they say, and after that decide if you can persuade them that it wasn't your fault.' She continued to look thoughtfully into the glowing, spitting logs. 'I don't think it was all your fault, Molly.'

The excited yapping of a dog announced that they were no longer alone. The door opened and Sheppey bounced inside, saw Pamela and bounded joyfully up to her, licking her hands and putting muddy paws on her skirt. Glad of the sudden diversion, she made a fuss of the dog in return, burying her face in the animal's soft coat. Then she looked up to see Ben Yates regarding her with some curiosity.

'Long way for you to come,' he remarked. 'What brings you over to Shercombe then?'

'Uncle Richard asked me to find out how Sheppey was,' she said, glad to have something truthful to say. 'He's pining for the dog more than the other way round, I think.'

Ben laughed and sat on a stool to untie his boot laces. 'He always was a fool with dogs,' he said. 'But I says that you can tell character by the way a man treats a dog. Richard's all right. Where's that little mongrel of yours, by the way?'

'We thought we'd leave the dogs at home today,' Pamela said. 'There are too many to bring and they get jealous if we take one! There's a neighbour seeing to them.'

Ben grinned at her. 'Treating them like folks, that's what I call it. Anyway, you can write and tell that uncle of yours that Sheppey and me are good friends now. She comes wherever I goes and I'm thinking I'll not want to part with her.'

Pamela stared at him and couldn't believe in some of the dramatic things that Molly had said. There was kindness written in every line of him. 'He'll flay me alive' she'd said. It sounded extremely unlikely that he'd raise more than his voice when told of his daughter's condition.

When he went out to the back kitchen to wash and shave, Pamela turned to Molly. 'If you want my help,' she whispered, 'then tell him now while I'm here. Let's get it over with. Where's your mum?'

'Over to The Grange. She does a bit of work there to make

us a bit more money. She'll be back directly. All right, I'm thinking you've a point. With you here he won't be violent, and by the time you'm gone he'll have got used to the idea. And I can tell him you're like it too. Then he won't be able to say nothing, will he?'

'But how did you . . . ?'

'Oh, I knows. Never mind how. And 'tis that lieutenant's, I'll bet.'

Pamela felt the colour draining from her face again. 'Alan was home for Christmas,' she said as firmly as she could. 'It's his baby.'

'Us'll know that when 'tis born,' Molly said. 'I seen you together lots of times. He was dark-haired and handsome, like my Delmer. Mr Saunders be fair and blue-eyed.'

'You seem to know a lot about my affairs.' Pamela's voice was icy.

Molly laughed. 'Affairs be the right word,' she said. 'Affairs! That's rich that is . . . my affairs! How many more you had then?'

Pamela was furious. 'I'll not stay to help you if you're going to be so rude.' She got up and took a step towards the door but Molly forestalled her.

'Where you think you'm going then? 'Tis cold outside.' She paused and seemed to backtrack a little. 'Look, Pamela,' she said, 'we got to stick together, you and me. Don't go. I won't say nothing about the lieutenant if you help me out.'

'If you dare say another poisonous word about me to anybody, Molly Yates, it'll be the worse for you. Just you shut up with your wicked suspicions! I could accuse you of blackmail even. Just shut up, do you hear!'

'Oh, yes, I hears all right. Well, I suppose I'll keep me mouth shut. You going to help me, though? You'm OK. It's me what needs help.'

There was such a pathetic droop to Molly's whole body that Pamela felt her anger dissipating. She sat down again in the armchair, but on the edge this time. She felt more in command of the situation with a straight back. Her face was severe and determined. 'All right. You say something to your dad now and I'll try to help you. But I'm not telling lies, mind.'

'What's all them angry words about then?' Ben Yates wanted to know. He came back into the room, rubbing his face with a towel. He had removed his jacket and his braces were taut over his ample stomach.

Molly launched straight in. 'Well, Dad, 'tis like this, see. Pamela and me, well . . .' She paused, quite unable to go on.

Pamela came to her rescue although her courage almost failed her. 'Molly wants to tell you that she's going to have a baby,' she said bravely. 'Next summer.'

Ben let the towel fall to the floor and stared from one girl to the other. Pamela thought that she had never seen such a change in a man in so short a time. He stood as if transfixed and when he spoke his voice came out in a loud bellow.

'Them Yanks! Is that what you'm telling me? You been with them Yanks? And you only sixteen! Dirty little slut,' he stormed. 'Get out of my sight 'til I thinks what to do. Get out! Get out, d'you hear me?' Both girls had sprung to their feet yet he seemed to tower over them although in fact he was no taller than Pamela.

Molly fled the room. Pamela heard her pull open the front door and bang it behind her again as she ran outside. There was the sound of footsteps on gravel and then silence.

Ben looked at the door without moving a muscle and then sat down wearily.

'I might have knowed,' he said. 'I should 'ave knowed.'

Left alone with a distraught Ben Yates, Pamela felt ill at ease and completely at a loss for anything to say. She wished that Mary would return but there was still at least an hour to go before she could expect her, an hour to be passed here in this most difficult of situations.

'Sit down,' Ben commanded her. 'I'll not go after our Molly. She'll come back in her own good time. Her mother be due home any minute now. She'll know what to do.'

Pamela sat as she was told and held her hands stiffly clasped on her lap. She searched for something to say in Molly's defence.

'It was the night of the dance,' she mumbled. 'I think it might have been too much of that home-made wine. She's very young. She probably didn't know what was happening to her.'

Ben snorted. His belligerence hadn't entirely disappeared. 'Home-made wine! Didn't know what was happening to 'er!' he repeated. 'That's a laugh. 'Er *should've* known, any road. 'Er've grown up with animals all round the place. No need for not knowing.'

'It's different.' Pamela could feel her colour rising, flooding her neck now as well as her cheeks.

Then she was aware of Ben looking at her as though he saw her for the first time that afternoon. 'You'm in this, bain't you?' he questioned. 'You been seen around with that lieutenant fellow a bit.' He took a pipe from a rack beside the fireplace, opened his tobacco tin and pushed some of its contents into the bowl. Every movement was slow and mechanical as though his thoughts were far away. Then he got up and went to the window and stood there for a long time, staring out at the late afternoon sky. 'So you'm no better than she is for all your posh schooling. Worse, in fact, for you'm married!'

'How dare you?' Pamela said for the second time. 'How dare you say such wicked things? Yes, I'm going to have a baby too, but my husband came home on Christmas Eve.' Her protest was swift. For her baby's sake, for Alan's sake as well as for her own, it was important to keep a pretence of innocence.

Ben Yates looked stricken. 'Sorry,' he muttered. 'I shouldn't 'ave said that. Forget I ever said it, won't you, Pamela? I'm that mazed.'

For a time there was an uncomfortable silence in the room, broken only by the regular ticking of the clock on the mantelpiece. Then they both heard footsteps in the lane outside and Wenty Yates let herself in the front door.

She stopped to take off her wellingtons in the passage and then came into the room. She looked from one to the other. 'Nice to see you Pamela,' she said. 'How did you get all this way? 'Tis a fair old distance from Stoke now you got to go all round.'

'Mrs Turner had some calls over here. She's picking me up.'

There was another tense silence. Wendy Yates put her bag down on a chair and took off her coat. She placed it carefully on a hanger and put it on a hook on the back of the door. Then she stood and looked from one to the other. 'Molly have told you then,' she said calmly.

'Told us? Told us what, woman?' Ben stood up and pulled himself to his full height and glared at his wife.

'About the baby, of course. 'Tis obvious that you know.' She took the kettle from the fire and spooned some tea into a brown teapot. Then she gathered up the best china cups that were still on the floor where Molly and Pamela had left them.

'So she told you and you said nothing to me?' Ben was almost exploding with indignation.

'No, she never said a word. A mother knows these things. I was just waiting for her to say, then I thought we'd talk about it.'

'Well, she've said all right! Told me calm as a cucumber just now. Wanted to do it while Pamela was here.'

'What's Pamela got to do with it?' Wendy Yates looked at her with curiosity and then suddenly she laughed.

'You'm in the same pickle then?' she said. 'That nice lieutenant, I suppose? Well, there's a turn up for the books!'

Pamela felt cold all over, numb with anger and fear and a terrible impotent rage.

'My husband came home,' she shouted. 'Alan came home. Forty-eight hours' leave. It's his baby I'm having.'

Wendy Yates calmly poured herself a cup of tea. 'Of course, dear,' she said. 'You'm lucky then with a proper husband to give 'im a name. Our poor little Moll'll 'ave to make do with ours. Where is she by the way?'

'She'll be back,' Ben said. 'Her ran off in a huff.'

'Trust you, Ben Yates,' Wendy said. 'Trust you to frighten the poor maid out of her wits with your great bad temper.'

161

Ben looked suitably ashamed. 'I'll go and find 'er.'

He shuffled to the door and was about to put on his boots when Molly pushed through it.

Pamela felt that she was an intruder now, that she had no business to be here at this rather intimate family time, but Wendy included her in the little circle.

'Well then, miss,' she said to her daughter, 'us knows all about your trouble, and I been telling Mrs Saunders here that us'll give the babe our name so you need not be feared. I always wanted another kid, come to that.'

A look of relief crossed Molly's face and she threw her arms round her mother. The two of them hugged each other enthusiastically. Pamela felt more an outsider than ever, and experienced a trace of the old sadness as she saw the affection between mother and daughter. Then Molly released herself from her mother's arms and flashed a triumphant grin at Pamela. 'Thanks for everything,' she said to her. 'I hope your "trouble" works out just as well!'

# THIRTEEN

*Olivia's Journal – 3rd July 1922*

*God has answered my prayers. Because of the burglary in the village we have a dog, and what a wonderful dog – an Irish wolf-hound! Maud says that she wants nothing to do with him and so he is to be my dog, my very own. At last I have a friend! Already he follows me everywhere. He's beautiful, and not too big yet. He has the most enormous paws and lovely eyes. I have decided to call him Mallory after the explorer who climbed a long way up Mount Everest last month. I'm sure Mallory will be a compensation for not being allowed to talk to the Ash Manor children.*

Pamela held the telegram in her hand. She had dreaded this moment, and at first couldn't bring herself to open it. She knew that if Alan had been killed she would never be able to forgive herself for her disloyalty. His death would make it seem so much worse.

The boy who had delivered it was watching her impatiently. 'Shall I wait for a reply?' he demanded.

She hardly heard him at first, then glanced up at him and came to her senses. 'I don't know. I'll see.' She turned away and tore open the orange envelope, and read the words inside with relief and then shock. It was not about Alan. She read it again, and then a third time.

*Maud ill stop Stroke stop Could you come? Richard stop*

163

The boy was still standing on the path waiting for her answer, but for Pamela everything seemed to become one monstrous blank in which her mind refused to function. She had expected one thing and now here was quite another. She continued to stare down at the piece of paper and gradually the blur receded and she forced herself to think, to make decisions.

'Yes,' she said slowly. 'There is a reply.' Then, carefully, she dictated the few words that were going to take her hundreds of miles away from Lawrence for ever. In spite of the decision they had both made not to see each other again or to communicate, she had to acknowledge that secretly she had hoped it would not be so. Her pulse had quickened with every American Jeep that she saw, and when the postman stopped outside Mary's house, propped his bicycle against the wall and pushed an envelope through the letter-box, she always felt a slight excitement. Perhaps today or tomorrow there would be the forbidden but longed for letter?

She watched the boy until his motor-cycle disappeared round the bend in the road and then she closed the front door and walked as if in a dream into the kitchen, made herself a cup of tea and sank on to the nearest chair. A stroke, the telegram said. What did that mean? She had never known anyone who had suffered a stroke. Yet it must be serious or Uncle Richard would not have asked her to go so far. Craemore sounded like the very end of the world, especially now, especially in wartime – a wartime that had suddenly become more real with the constant sound of explosions and gunfire from the beach and the sea.

Then suddenly she thought of Jane. She could almost hear her voice. 'Nice Pammy. Jane likes Pammy's sweeties.' They needed her. To be needed was one of the most wonderful things in life, she thought, whatever it meant you had to do. She would go as soon as she could.

Two days later, with her suitcase packed and timetables worked out for the long journey, Pamela felt her initial panic subsiding. It was an adventure, the first of her life really, something that she was to do entirely alone. Yet in the midst of all the flurry of activity her thoughts returned time after time to Lawrence. She had packed his little volume of poems. It lay carefully wrapped in a silk scarf amongst her clothes. There was another book of poems beside her bed, for since reading Lawrence's work she had discovered that she enjoyed poetry, and there was plenty of it on Mary's well-stocked bookshelves.

On this last night she took this book and opened it at her favourite place. Then she whispered the special lines aloud, words that had seemed to jump from the page when she first read them.

> Nothing less than nothing
> Could each to the other be;
> Yet gossamer threads were woven,
> Too fine for eyes to see;
> Such threads as stretch through darkness,
> Through time and far-off space,
> And keep two lives still touching,
> When face is lost to face.

She had copied them out a few days before thinking that she would send them to Lawrence but had hesitated, resisting the temptation. She looked at the sheet of thick blue writing paper now for it was still where she had left it, just inside the front cover of the book. Should I send it after all? she wondered. Then, answering her own question, No! No, definitely not. I have to forget about him now. We shall never see each other again. This journey to Scotland is a good thing.

She was about to screw up the paper and throw it away, but re-read it and the poet's name: Auberon Herbert, 1894. I wonder if he had a love that he had to deny? she found herself thinking. Then suddenly it occurred to her that the verses could equally well apply to Olivia and to the unknown man she had loved . . . the man who was her own father. Pamela's heart gave a little thud. Who was he? she wondered as she had done so many times before. Where is he? Does Aunt Maud know? And if she does, perhaps now that she's ill she might tell me.

She refolded the paper and put it back in the book, placed it on the table beside her bed and fell asleep.

'I'll drive you to Newton Abbot,' Mary had promised. 'This is an emergency. We'll manage the petrol, and I suggest that you wear your WVS uniform. It'll give you some protection and a bit of status.'

'Do I need protection?'

'Well, probably not, but status, yes. And in that hat you're not likely to suffer any amorous advances!'

They had both laughed and Pamela had decided to follow the good advice. Now the morning of her departure had arrived and she settled herself in the passenger seat of the van and leaned over to glance at her reflection in the driving mirror. 'Well, I think you were right about the hat,' she remarked. 'It's about the most unbecoming thing I've ever worn.'

They said little for the first few miles. Pamela was grateful for Mary's quiet company. She had never been intrusive, never meddlesome. Pamela often wondered if she suspected that there had been more to her relationship with Lawrence than had been talked about between them. She hadn't been able to bring herself to confess what had happened on that wonderful forbidden night, and if Mary guessed she had said nothing.

There was no light yet in the eastern sky for they were making an early start. The dark dismal morning matched Pamela's mood and Mary seemed to read her thoughts as she so often did. 'In some ways,' she said, 'it'll be good for you to get away. There's nothing like a change of scene for coming to terms with . . .' She paused, obviously groping for the right word.

So she does know, Pamela thought. Aloud she finished the sentence for her. 'With falling in love with someone you can't have? Yes, you're right. I must forget him.' She looked at Mary's hands steady on the steering wheel and marvelled that at last she had a friend to whom she could say such things.

'Not forget,' Mary said. 'It will be a long, long time before you truly forget. In fact you probably never will, but the hurt

166

will lessen, and you'll find fulfilment in other directions. Believe me, I know.'

She was staring straight ahead at the weak glimmer of light on the road in front of the vehicle and Pamela was glad that they couldn't look at each other. With everything blacked out, no signposts and only dimmed headlights, she knew that Mary had to give every bit of her concentration to keeping the van on the road. She remembered doing the same journey herself with the van crammed with her family, her aunt and uncle, Mrs Baines, and Jane. It seemed so long ago. She counted up the weeks in her head and made it about twelve – nearly three months since she had seen her daughter. 'I'm longing to see Jane again,' she said. 'That will be one of the compensations.'

Newton Abbot was just waking up when they reached its cold wet streets but the station was busy: soldiers everywhere, a sprinkling of RAF uniforms, and a contingent of noisy laughing sailors on their way to Plymouth. Pamela pulled the uncompromising felt hat well down on to her forehead and none of the men gave her more than a passing glance as she and Mary pushed their way through to the platform.

'Now you've got your identification and all that you'll need for the permit when you get to Inverness, haven't you?' Mary fussed. 'And your sandwiches and flask? Don't lose anything!'

Pamela looked at her affectionately. 'Yes. And thank you a thousand times for everything.' It was like saying goodbye to a mother, she thought. Mary had almost assumed that role lately. 'I'll post a card from Inverness if I can, and then again when I get there. Stop worrying.'

Mary kissed her warmly. 'You've been a wonderful friend, more like a daughter,' she said, echoing Pamela's own feelings. 'I shall miss you, and I'll take good care of Binks.'

'I know you will. Kiss him for me when you get home, won't you.'

They both laughed, the tension broken, and then the train

snorted and puffed its way into the station, making further conversation almost impossible.

It was a long and difficult journey, but the accommodation Mary had managed to book for her in Edinburgh was clean and comfortable and Pamela got up early the following day refreshed and ready for the next stage. The morning sun was just rising behind the hills when the train carried her towards Inverness and she gasped in surprise at the unfolding vista of lochs and mountains. They made Devon's soft rolling hills look tiny and unimportant.

A pass was necessary for this part of northern Scotland and she was glad that Mary had organised everything for her in her usual businesslike way. The whole area of coastline around Craemore was an important naval base. It made Pamela feel strangely at home and she wanted to tell her fellow passengers on the little chugging train of her own bit of country, of the evacuation and all it had meant to everyone. But she said nothing. 'CARELESS TALK COSTS LIVES'. The notices stared at her from each little station and if there was any conversation it was carefully geared to simple, ordinary things as though everyone suspected that a Nazi spy might be sitting there disguised in uniform or anonymous country clothes.

The journey ended with a bus ride and then a ferry crossing from Invergarth to Craemore. Pamela sat in the little boat clutching her suitcase, her hat jammed tightly on her head against the wind. The sea was rough, but after all those miles crammed in railway carriages she was glad to be out in the cold fresh air again. She breathed in deeply and the sea-smell reminded her poignantly of home.

'You a stranger in these parts?' The woman sitting next to her peered as best she could in the near-dark.

'Yes. I've come to help look after my aunt.'

'Craemore is a bonny wee place,' she said. 'You'll like it, and we're a friendly lot. Your aunt is poor Mrs Lindhurst, then?'

'That's right. How bad is she?' Pamela immediately felt more apprehensive.

'They'll all be glad to see you. A fine lassie like you is just what they need.'

Those words made Pamela's heart sink still further. How would Aunt Maud really be? she wondered yet again. And how would she herself manage if she had to look after her aunt's most intimate physical needs? She shivered, both with the cold and the thought of the possible horrors that might be confronting her.

Until these last few hours of her journey she had kept her fears at bay, filling her mind with memories of Jane, and of Uncle Richard and his need of her. Alan too flitted in and out of her thoughts. He had been different during that short leave over Christmas, more tender and considerate in his love-making, more willing to talk to her, more interested in her life. It had been strange, giving a new and encouraging slant to their relationship, and she had asked herself frequently what had contributed to this pleasant change in him.

As she thought about her life and about Mary's comments made to her just before they parted, she decided that following a dream might be all right in a world of fantasy or fiction, but perhaps the solid reality of what you had, what you possessed, was a better foundation on which to build your life. She tried to force herself to think so. Alan was a real flesh-and-blood man who belonged to her and to whom she belonged. When he came home after the war maybe they could start again, and if this baby was his . . .

Then, suddenly, there was no more time for speculation. The shore was close and they were preparing to dock. She looked towards the unknown little town that was going to be her home for the next weeks, but could see very little. From the photograph that Uncle Richard had sent her some time ago she knew that the houses clustered round the small harbour. They were stone-built and sturdy, facing the sea. It was not unlike Torcross, she had thought when she first saw the postcard. But now everything seemed strange and foreign, and the voice of the ferryman was completely unintelligible.

Eventually she stumbled ashore in a daze, feeling totally alone

in this strange cold place, but then she saw Uncle Richard standing on the quayside in a circle of light from a dimmed street-lamp,
and suddenly everything changed. It was like coming home. She
realized in a flash that wherever he was, there home was. He
had brought her up, been as a father to her, and she felt secure,
knowing, in a way that had come late to her, that she was loved.
He strode towards her and kissed her on the cheek. He held out
his hand for her suitcase and she could see tears in his eyes.

'Thank the good Lord you've come,' he said, and in spite of
the words his thick Devonshire voice was the ultimate comfort
as it boomed out into the cold Scottish night. 'Mrs Baines have
got a meal all ready for you, maid. 'Tisn't far to walk to the
cottage, just a few steps.' He took her arm and together they
walked away from the sea, up the cobbled street towards the
little house.

'It's so good to see you, Uncle Richard,' she said. 'I've missed
you so much.'

'And we've missed you.' He paused in front of a terraced
house. 'This is it,' he said. 'Number four, Lighthouse Lane.' He
pushed open the door, which was not locked, and stood back to
let her pass. 'Jane's so excited about Pammy coming,' he said
quietly. 'She've been talking about it all day long.'

Pamela felt a lifting of her spirits at his words, but now that
the moment of confrontation with her aunt had come she was
scared too, wondering what she was about to find. She took off
her hat and glanced at herself in the mirror above the hallstand,
and then had no time for further qualms. An inner door burst
open and Jane rushed through it. Then she stopped and stared,
looked back to the comforting presence of Mrs Baines immediately behind her, and finally came forward again hesitantly until
she was within touching distance.

Pamela knelt on one knee and held out her arms to her daughter. 'Hello, darling,' she whispered. 'You've grown.'

The child was still standing there immobile, her big blue eyes
full of uncertainty.

'Give your sister a big kiss then,' Mrs Baines directed. She
came towards the two of them and pushed Jane forwards, and

slowly the little girl allowed herself to be wrapped in Pamela's arms, holding herself rigid still. The kiss was given and then she pulled away and continued to stare.

'I've brought you some sweeties,' Pamela said, smiling through her distress. 'They're in my case. I'll find them for you soon.'

'Not till you'm warm and cosy and have had something to eat,' Mrs Baines said. 'Take that damp coat off, lovey, and come on through. There's a nice cup of tea almost ready, and I've got a good warming stew for all of us later on.' She turned to Richard. 'Will you carry her things up? I've had hot water bottles in the bed for the last two days, so even if the room's cold, the sheets'll be nice and warm.'

'Aunt Maud?' Pamela murmured as her uncle went up the creaking twisting stairs. 'How bad is she? Is she in bed?'

'No. We get her up and sit her by the fire every day. Come on through and you'll see for yourself.'

Mrs Baines, with Jane close behind her, pushed open the inner door, and Pamela prepared to face the woman who had dominated her life for so many long years, the woman towards whom she would always feel a sense of resentment, and yet obligation too.

Maud sat in a chair by the fire, one hand supported on a cushion. She stared fiercely with those penetrating eyes that always made Pamela flinch. Her mouth opened but no words came, only a few grunts and a dribble of saliva which trickled down on to the hairs that grew now in profusion on her chin. She waved her left hand up and down and Mrs Baines went to her and wiped her face.

'Here's Pamela come all the way up from Devon to see you,' she said. She tucked the shawl more tightly round the older woman's shoulders and Pamela noticed the gentleness in the action.

'She can't talk no more,' Mrs Baines whispered. 'We got to try and make out what she wants. Go and kiss her. I think that might be what she be meaning.'

Pamela approached her aunt's chair reluctantly, forcing a smile. Then she bent and kissed the withered cheek and her

171

heart was suddenly filled with compassion, almost a kind of love, a strange emotion that she couldn't understand and which she had never been able to feel before. She was grateful for these new feelings for without them she knew that she could never face all the ordeals that she guessed lay ahead.

Yet the dreaded trials didn't materialize. In fact, her uncle's words the next morning at breakfast cheered her considerably.

'Mrs Baines and me does most of the work with your aunt,' he told her. 'It's Jane what's been the problem. We haven't got time for her now that there's so much to do. If you could look after her and do a bit of cooking and keep the place clean, then we shan't need much help from you with Maud.'

Consequently the following weeks were happier than Pamela had ever thought possible. She went for long walks with the little girl. They watched the coming and going of all the ships, and they went on to the beach. It became a favourite place, for Pamela discovered to her delight that the sands were not out of bounds here. There was no barbed wire, no hidden threatening mines beneath their feet. They made sand-castles too just like the ones she used to make at Goldpool beach when she was a child long before the war. And on a few rare occasions when Uncle Richard could spare an odd half an hour he would join them, and it would seem that she was back in the past enjoying once again those few precious hours when they had escaped from Aunt Maud's strict and unsmiling regime.

Craemore was cold, much colder than South Devon, but even this in some ways added to Pamela's pleasure, for the little kitchen was a warm cosy place. Aunt Maud slept in the front room now and was put to bed early. She slept soundly during those first evening hours and Pamela would find herself relaxed and at ease as she washed the dishes from their evening meal. Then she and Jane would sometimes bake little tarts or make the sticky sweets that they both loved.

Aunt Maud's condition didn't change. She got no better nor any worse. She just sat immobile, Mrs Baines and Richard waiting on her every need. A nurse came in each day to get her up, wash her and do other intimate necessities that the others felt unable to perform. Pamela was asked to do very little.

''Tis wonderful to have you here to look after the bairn,' Richard often said to her, and sometimes he would laugh at himself for his strange mixture of Devon and Scots.

Pamela often looked at her aunt and tried to achieve a measure of understanding. The old antagonism seemed to have gone from her face, and there was an unmistakable look of affection whenever she listened to her husband's words or submitted to his gentle though clumsy ministrations. How much she understood of what went on around her it was difficult to tell. Perhaps she had achieved a kind of peace at last beneath that silent exterior? Pamela also saw the devotion with which Richard performed all his duties to his wife, and was frequently moved almost to tears as she watched. They truly loved each other. She had never really noticed it before. At Burlcombe she had been too taken up with her own affairs, too anxious about her relationship with Jane, to realize that her aunt had another side to her strict unbending character. Pamela realized now that she should have been more aware, more discerning perhaps. Maybe it had always been there, this gentler side.

But one thing was quite disappointingly clear. If Aunt Maud did know the full name of Olivia's lover, the knowledge was locked away for ever. And now there was another enigma – one of her own making. Alan or Lawrence, which one was the father of her coming child? Whenever she felt the stirrings of self-reproach she vigorously fended off the feeling. She wanted a peaceful pregnancy. Her baby mustn't suffer.

During the day, when Pamela was cooking for the five of them, Jane would sit on a tall stool at the table and help. Gradually the relationship between them eased, became close, and Pamela realized that her aunt's awful misfortune had given to her the gift she had wanted for so long: her daughter's love and confidence.

With the passing days and the peaceful life she was leading there came a new contentment. It was a pleasant feeling, strange to her, and she realized that she had seldom been so happy. Sometimes she compared this pregnancy with that other one when she was so young, so frightened and vulnerable, and at those times would give Jane a quick hug, remembering what a precious treasure had come from that awful misfortune. This new baby too, whatever it looked like, whoever it resembled, would be loved and accepted by Alan. She clung to those positive thoughts and disregarded any others.

Jane's bedtimes were especially cherished, an hour of closeness that Pamela had never thought to possess.

'I love you, Pammy,' Jane said one dark February night. Her little arms were tight round Pamela's neck and her breath sweet and wholesome on her face. 'Don't go away again, will you?' she whispered fearfully. 'I want you to stay with me for ever and ever.'

'I promise I won't ever leave you, darling,' Pamela said, and breathed a prayer that she would be able to keep this promise, that nothing and no one would ever again snatch her from her child. Her own arms tightened around the little girl, and then Jane laughed and pulled away from her.

'You're squashing me, Pammy,' she said. 'And you're squashing Teddy too.'

The hugs ended in laughter, and then a story and more kisses, and when Pamela left her and went downstairs to the kitchen she was truly happy. Even her relationship with Lawrence, she thought, had not brought her anything quite like this, for in that friendship there was the underlying sense of guilt as well as the sorrow of inevitable parting, both emotions to be set against the joy and the ecstasy.

Alan wondered what to do with his forty-eight-hour leave. Morelake was closed to him, Pamela was miles away in Scotland, and he had no friends. Yet he couldn't stay here in camp. He knew that he needed a change. He thought momentarily of the woman who had befriended him in London. It seemed an age away and there was a measure of guilt in his mind over that brief episode anyway.

He was surprised by the longing that he felt for his wife. It wasn't particularly sex that he needed, he argued with himself.

He wanted to see Pamela, to see the new roundness of her now that she was expecting his child, and he felt a certain pride in the fact of his coming fatherhood. Perhaps Mary Turner would allow him to use Pamela's room for the two nights of his leave? The idea was attractive. He hadn't spent much time in Devon since he had joined up and he wanted to see what was going on. Perhaps he could get a look into the restricted area? he thought hopefully. And Mrs Turner would be able to tell him all the news that was never in the newspapers, secrets known only to those closely involved with the evacuation.

Feeling a little nervous about his reception, he parked his motor-cycle at the edge of road outside her house a few days later and knocked on the door. A cacophony of barking greeted the sound and he felt a moment's irritation. The dog! Binks would be here, of course, as well as Mrs Turner's two. Why did people want to keep dogs for pets? In wartime it seemed almost immoral. He tried to stifle his annoyance.

When Mary Turner opened the door to him he could see that at first she didn't recognise him for it was almost dark. 'Alan Saunders,' he said quickly. 'Forty-eight-hour leave. Just thought I'd call and see how things are going here.'

Her first hesitation disappeared. 'How nice to see you,' she said quickly. 'Come in, Mr Saunders, or is Sergeant now?'

'Not yet. My training isn't quite finished,' he replied. 'But please call me Alan.'

She led him through to the sitting room. 'I'll make a cup of tea.' She smiled at him and her voice was welcoming. 'Make yourself at home.'

Alone in the room he looked around and remembered the previous time he was here. He and Pamela had been ill at ease at first, but later they had made love together and it had been good, better than at any time before in their marriage, and she had conceived their child – their son, he hoped – that night. He felt a measure of pride and a surge of self-confidence, and when Mary returned with a tray set with teapot and cups he smiled at her. Even the three dogs sniffing round his feet didn't disturb him too much. 'Thank you for looking after Pamela for me,' he

175

said. 'And Binks,' he added with a grim little laugh at the idea that he had any interest in the creature. Hearing his name the dog looked up expectantly and Alan forced himself to pat the shaggy head. The big round eyes looking so soulfully into his distracted him and he tried to turn his thoughts and the conversation to other things.

'I hope to get up to Scotland on my next leave,' he said. 'It'll be a longer one, I think.' To his annoyance he realized that his words were slightly defensive, almost as if he felt some lack in himself, and that his hostess might think he ought to be there now. Foolish, of course. You couldn't get right up to Craemore and back in forty-eight hours!

'You'll need a special pass,' Mary told him unnecessarily. 'It's a restricted area, like this.'

'That shouldn't be too difficult.' He took the delicate china cup from her and stirred two spoonfuls of sugar into the tea, and then realized that he shouldn't have been so extravagant with her meagre ration. Still unsure of himself, still slightly defensive, he blushed. 'Sorry,' he muttered, 'shouldn't have taken two.'

She laughed at him. 'Don't worry. I don't have any in mine so that evens it up.' She offered him cake and he took it awkwardly, wondering again if he should.

'Have you anywhere to stay?' Mary asked suddenly. 'Pamela's room is still empty if you would like it?'

He accepted gratefully, wondering at her easy assurance and wishing that he possessed it too, but such self-confidence had never been his. He was always ill at ease with strangers, always lonely. He felt lonely now.

Mary showed him up to the big front bedroom with the lovely view over the bay. 'The bathroom is next door,' she said. 'I'm afraid that I can't provide a meal tonight as I'm going out, but please accept the freedom of my kitchen and make yourself something if you wish. My few hens are still laying regularly so there are some fresh eggs.'

'Thank you very much but you've been too kind already,' Alan murmured. 'I'll try to get something to eat somewhere. I'm not very good at cooking.'

Mary laughed again. 'Pamela spoils you, I expect,' she said. 'All men should be able to cook.'

The words were meant to be lighthearted and kind but they increased Alan's feelings of inadequacy.

It was not until Mary left him to unpack his few things he began to feel slightly more relaxed. This was the room his wife had used, the room in which his child had been conceived. He reminded himself of the fact again and immediately felt better for the remembering.

He opened the wardrobe door and looked at Pamela's clothes, the few things she had left behind, and pushed them aside to make room for the spare shirt he had brought. Then he looked at her books that were still on the bedside table. There was a volume of poetry and a couple of novels, not the kind of stuff he would ever wish to read. He'd had no idea that she read poetry. He leafed through the pages a trifle condescendingly and realized that he knew little about his wife. There was a sheet of writing paper folded up inside the cover. He took it out, saw that it was in Pamela's writing and read the verses through. What on earth did they mean? And why should she choose those particular lines? He read them again, and then shook his head. Women were strange creatures. He'd never understand them. But he'd have to make more effort after the war, he told himself, try to get to know her properly. He put the paper in his pocket. He would ask her about it when he saw her again.

It was a lonely evening. He sat in the local pub, talked to a couple of people, played darts, and eventually managed to get a meagre and unappetizing meal. Mary's eggs would have been a much better bet! Much later, when he lay in the big double bed, he discovered for the first time since he had joined up he longed for the war to end, longed to hold his wife in his arms, and most of all longed for Morelake and the security of his own house and his land around him. It was a long time before he fell asleep.

The following day he remembered the ration card that he had been given for his leave and handed it to Mary as he sat down to breakfast in her little kitchen. At least he wouldn't feel so bad

177

about eating her food now, he thought. 'They issue them to us when we leave camp,' he told her. 'I don't know what you'll be able to get with it, but it might help a bit.'

She took it gratefully. 'Thank you, Alan,' she said. 'What are you going to do today?'

'I shall go around the edge of the whole evacuation area,' he replied. 'I want to get as close to Morelake as I can. It's over the other side.'

'Yes, of course. I'm sure your house, all the houses, will be all right, though. They were sealed up, remember.' Mary handed him a plate with two eggs and a slice of crisply fried bread. 'Don't attempt to get through the fences, will you?' she said. 'One or two foolhardy souls tried it at the beginning but it's not safe, all mined and so on, I believe, and you'd be arrested if you were found.'

Alan laughed bleakly. 'Don't worry. There are enough people getting blown up in this war without inviting it to happen.'

'Be careful then,' Mary said half an hour later as she stood at the door and watched him kick the motor-cycle into life. 'The road surfaces are pretty awful now.'

He smiled at her and roared away, longing to go down towards the sea and along the familiar road that ran close the beach. Instead, and unwillingly, he turned inland. Then suddenly he thought of Ben Yates. Pamela had mentioned that he was in his brother's place over at Shercombe. Alan made up his mind that when he'd had a good look at as much as he could, gone as close to the forbidden area as was possible, he'd call on Ben. He'd always been known to have a good nose for the latest events, the newest bits of gossip. Alan reckoned that if there was any way of finding out just what the Yanks were really doing, Ben would know about it.

# FOURTEEN

*Olivia's Journal – 27th April 1923*
*Yesterday the family came back to Ash Manor again. I think they have taken it for the summer. I saw the boy swimming in the afternoon. His sister sat on the beach and watched him. At least, I suppose she is his sister. They look about my age. There was a woman too, very elegantly dressed in the latest style. I wish Maud would let me make friends.*

*There was a royal wedding yesterday too. Maud showed me the photographs in the newspaper. Lady Elizabeth Bowes-Lyon looked so beautiful. I wonder what it is like to get married? Will it ever happen to me?*

Alan drove more slowly than usual. He wanted to savour the familiar Devon air, the sounds of spring and the sight here and there of life returning after this most dismal of winters. It was April and he thought of all the work he would usually be doing on his land now that there was a promise of warmer weather. The cows would be restless. He looked at the sky. Today was right for letting them out.

He swerved to avoid a large pothole in the road, heard the report of an explosion over the lovely fresh greening of the fields, and gripped the handlebars of his machine more tightly in sudden rage at events which kept him separated from all that he knew best, all that he loved.

To the right of him were more favoured farms, untouched by

179

the war, and he could see lambs frisking beside their mothers. He stopped in a field gateway and watched two sturdy horses pulling the harrow which would prepare the land for the spring sowing. He frowned, wondering how long it would take to get his own acres back into cultivation again after a year or perhaps more of neglect. He shuddered and refused to think about it. There were more important matters even than that. Hitler had to be finished off, he reminded himself sternly. The newspapers were full of stories lately of the heavy bombing of Germany. He was longing to get his training over and to be part of it. He was sure now that he was to be a gunner, a rear gunner in a Lancaster most likely. Up there in the blue of the spring sky, or more likely at night with only stars for company, he would be able to forget all about the cattle, the corn, the barley, the ruining of his land.

The journey was a long one for he frequently took lanes that he knew well but which now led only to barbed-wire fences and large 'Keep Out' notices. Then he had to turn round and go back again, find another way. At last he was on the main road that led through Frogmore and looked around him, bemused, at the signs of the American invasion which were everywhere. Shercombe was a couple more miles in the direction of the sea and eventually he reached his destination. He drove carefully down the narrow lane and saw at the end of it the small thatched cottage that had belonged to the hero brother of Ben Yates.

There was a girl standing at the open doorway, obviously drawn there by the unaccustomed noise of the motor-cycle. She shielded her eyes against the sun and peered at him. He could see her untidy hair and grubby apron, but she was pretty. Of course, Molly Yates, the wayward daughter!

'Well now,' he heard her say when he turned off his engine, 'if it ain't Mr Saunders an' all!'

He didn't know how to reply. He was nonplussed to be greeted by the girl and hoped she wasn't alone. 'You're Molly, of course,' he said eventually. He removed his goggles and hung them carefully on the handlebars. 'I've come to see your father.'

'He'll be back for his dinner. He goes down to Kernwell to help out. They got extra animals, you see, double what they usually got, all crammed in from the evacuated farms. 'Tis a lot of work.'

Alan looked at his watch. There was an hour at least to go before dinnertime. He hesitated. 'I'll come back,' he said at last.

'No need for that. You'm welcome to come in and sit down. I'll make a cup of tea. Weak, mind. We got to make the ration last, but there always be plenty of milk.' She laughed. 'Nice rich creamy milk like you'm used to. I bet you get that white chalky stuff in camp.'

'Yes, we do,' Alan said. 'All right then, I'll have a cup of tea.' He hoped that he didn't sound too unwilling, but there was nothing else he could reasonably do, he thought. He made his motor-cycle secure, walked up the path and followed her into the house. He watched while she took the kettle from the hob where it was simmering gently. The little cottage was clean and homely and the girl, in spite of her apron, was wholesome and friendly. 'You were lucky to get this place,' he commented. 'Better than living in someone else's house.'

'Yes, you'm right. 'Tis nice. Sit down.' She indicated a large ancient armchair. 'That's me dad's. We had to bring en. He said he don't feel right without en. Men! All they thinks about be their comforts! I should be away enjoying meself in the forces or something if it weren't for they Yanks and theirs!'

Her meaning at first escaped him and he was sure that she was too young for the forces anyway. She put two large cups and saucers on the table and then went out to get milk. When she returned, she grinned at him. 'In the family way I am, Mr Saunders, just like your Pamela.'

He felt the colour rising in his cheeks. You didn't talk to strange young women about such things. At least, if you were Alan Saunders you didn't! But he found himself staring at her stomach where he now saw a slight roundness that didn't fit with the slenderness of the rest of her. In spite of his embarrassment he was suddenly possessed with a rush of pride for his own coming child.

'She'm lucky,' Molly went on. 'Your wife, I mean. Her kid'll have a home and a name.' She poured the tea and handed him a cup. 'Don't know what I'd have done if it weren't for my mum. She says she'm going to adopt my little mistake and bring en up as hers. She and Dad always wanted more kids. Can't think why they didn't have any after me. I be sure it weren't for want of trying!'

Molly laughed brightly and sat herself down opposite Alan. She had taken off the offending apron now and he could see the shape of her figure more clearly. He looked away, stared into his cup and then into the fire. He was deeply embarrassed and wanted to escape from the animal earthiness of the girl.

'I reckon there'll be a whole load of little half-Yankees around in a year or so,' she continued. 'A pair of nylons and you've got more'n you bargained for!' She stretched out her legs to the fire and ran her hand along the thick and rather ugly brown lisle stockings she was wearing. 'Nylons what last a week, or p'raps two if you'm lucky, and a baby what you'm saddled with for ever!'

She appeared to be talking half to herself and Alan didn't know quite what to say. 'You've got a good home, Molly,' he managed at last. 'You'll be all right.'

She looked across at him. 'Yes, I'll be all right. I'm one of the lucky ones, but there are plenty that aren't. Chucked out by their parents and nowhere to go, that's the fate of a lot of 'em.' Her perkiness had disappeared. 'I sometimes thinks that 'tis rotten being a girl, Mr Saunders, and that's the truth.'

He gulped on his tea. He felt at a complete loss and couldn't understand why she was talking like this to him. They hardly knew each other, but she went on relentlessly, the words tumbling out one after the other without restraint.

'They was so 'andsome, all they Yanks, and some of the officers fair took your breath away, like that Lieutenant Lawson that was sweet on your Pamela.'

It was a few moments before the import of her words dawned on Alan. When he realized what she had said his whole world seemed to collapse around him like a shattered building, only a pile of bricks and rubble remaining. 'What did you say?' His voice was at first deathly quiet and then it rose in pitch and volume. 'What did you mean by that, Molly Yates? Sweet on Pamela? What did you say? What are you suggesting?'

The girl looked terrified now and he felt suddenly quite merciless. He put the cup down on the floor with a crash and stood up, towering over her. 'Say it again, Molly. Let me hear you say it again – if you dare.' He wanted to shake her, shake the life out of her for the terrible thoughts that she had put into his mind.

Frightened by what she had said and by the fury on the face of the man standing so menacingly in front of her, Molly wished that she could unsay the damaging words. Whatever had made her tell? She had promised her mother faithfully that she would never breathe a word about Pamela's friendship with the American officer. ''Twas nothing, Mr Saunders, honestly,' she gabbled. 'He was lonely like all of them. He taught her to drive, that was all. They was just friendly. Nothing else. He was a poet or something. I remember she told me about him writing poetry. He wasn't like the rest of them, all out for a bit of . . .' She broke off, alarmed at the look on Alan's face.

'Shut up, you little bitch!' he shouted at her. 'Shut up, do you hear me?'

Molly jumped hastily to her feet. It looked as if he was about to strike her. She stumbled to the door. 'You got no right to call me that,' she shouted, tears springing to her eyes. 'I bet you'm no better than you ought to be. You men be all the same, just like I said.' Anger and a sense of injustice surged through her now, overcoming her fear. Rage at this man, her anger with all of them, suddenly prevailed. 'And what if she did have a bit of fun with her nice officer?' she shrieked. 'What if she did, Mr Oh-so-pure-Saunders? 'Tis all right for you men, but not for us women – and we got to bear the consequences an' all. You just uses us, don't you? Well, it be time we stood up for ourselves like all they suffragettes years ago what I heard tell about when I was at school.'

She paused for breath and looked at him. He was still standing there immobile, his huge fists clenched, looking as if he wanted to kill someone. 'Get out,' she said. 'If you'm going to behave like a great bully, just get out of here.' She flung open the front door and waited until he had passed through it. Then she turned and ran upstairs to her room and threw herself, sobbing, on to her bed.

Even when she heard the motor-cycle spring into life in the lane outside, even after the sound of its engine had long disappeared, she still lay there, angry and frightened, wondering what awful string of events she had set in motion. She liked Pamela Saunders and now she had wounded her terribly. Women ought to stick together, she thought woefully. She had let the side down! But there was nothing she could do about it. It was too late. She had to get on with life for the sake of her baby. She thumped the pillow angrily.

'I hope 'tis a girl,' she said aloud. 'A girl what I can bring up to know the truth about men. She'll never be stupid and soft like me if I can help it!'

Alan rode furiously along the narrow lanes, caring nothing now for the potholes in the road, the sound of explosions, the pillaged land. All he could think of was Pamela in another man's arms, her child the son of some unknown Yank – an officer too and a poet. Now he knew the meaning of those words she had scribbled out. His sense of outrage increased with each mile. He drove not towards Mary's home, where everything would remind him of his wife, but further away until the road took him towards the sea again. He could smell it, even hear it, and he pulled his machine on to the verge and was still for a moment trying to calm himself. The sun was shining and there were primroses in the hedge. It seemed that nature was mocking him, looking beautiful when he would prefer everything to be grey and bleak.

Molly Yates had accused him of having double standards. He thought of the woman in the pub, Brenda Barker. She had been generous with him and he had felt warm and fulfilled that night. He tried to condone his own behaviour. He was in the forces, wasn't he? It was natural. And as for Brenda, well, she was a widow. She wasn't betraying a husband. He left his motor-cycle and strode down the path towards the headland. He longed to go to Scotland and confront Pamela with her monstrous deception. He began to feel almost murderous. How could he ever make love to her again, how even look at the child she was to bear? All his triumph over her pregnancy had collapsed, leaving him with nothing but the vision of a faithless wife and a bastard offspring.

He had been brought up not to cry. It was a weakness his mother would not allow in any circumstances. But now, for perhaps the first time in his adult life, he felt tears in his eyes. He threw himself on to the damp earth and gave way to his grief.

In Craemore, as March passed into April, spring appeared to be coming at last to the little Scottish town. The air lost its bitterness and a few hardy flowers could be seen here and there. But it was still not as warm as Devon would be at this time of year. Pamela sometimes felt homesick, but then she would remind herself that she had no home but this at the moment. She tried not to think of Burlcombe as it used to be, for that way lay a sense of loss. One day she would go back and start a new life, but for now this was where she must be. She must find contentment here.

There were only two rooms downstairs in the little house so once Aunt Maud and Jane were in bed, she and Uncle Richard and Mrs Baines would sit round the kitchen fire, often in companionable silence. Sometimes Richard went out for a drink and for some male company as he had done at home. Usually he went to The Craemore Arms just five minutes' walk away, and when he returned Pamela and Mrs Baines were always waiting for him with the kettle on the boil, and both of them hoping for a bit of gossip, for whatever was happening both here and further afield would be discussed in detail at the bar.

'A couple of lieutenants were in,' he said one night, and Pamela felt her pulse quicken at the words. 'Naval ones,' he went on. 'Them what runs the Patrol Service. Said something about a contingent of RAF coming shortly for training. Now if your Alan were up here for a while, that would be nice wouldn't it, maid?'

185

'Yes, it would, Uncle,' she replied quickly, but when she thought about it she wasn't sure if her answer was strictly truthful. Life was easy and uncomplicated now. Alan didn't fit very well into the picture somehow.

She had been writing longer, fuller letters to him than she had thought possible, though, and in his replies he seemed to respond. The letters she received from him were a constant surprise. He commented on the things she told him as well as telling her about himself. He even remarked on Jane, expressing in one letter his pleasure over Pamela's obvious happiness in Scotland. Gradually a future with Alan was appearing more hopeful to her, but in spite of this she didn't feel ready yet to face him again, to resume her marriage as if nothing had happened.

She could feel Mrs Baines looking at her and she knew that the stolid countrywoman understood more than she gave away, and certainly more than Uncle Richard did.

'Not very likely that he'll come all this way,' she commented. 'Now if he'd gone in the Navy, he might have got hisself up here, what with all them flying boats out there on the sea. Can't think what they be here for meself, what with the Jerries being so far away.'

'Alan hopes to be flying soon,' Pamela said. 'He's nearly finished his training. I can't imagine him being a gunner, but he seems to be happy about it. It sounds awful to me. He went in too late to be a pilot. That's what he'd have liked, I think.'

'They all wants the glamour of that, though what glamour there is in getting yourself shot down, I don't know.' Mrs Baines sniffed derisively and glared at her knitting as if the thick khaki-coloured sock she was making was responsible for the foolishness of mankind. 'I wish this old war would hurry up and get itself over,' she said, 'before your man and my Jim got to do anything dangerous. Jim be still training as well but that won't last much longer.'

'I reckon it'll be over soon,' Richard said. 'Then us'll be able to go home and see what they Yanks have done to all our houses. I be dreading that day in some ways as well as looking forward to it.' He laughed. 'If I stays here much longer I reckon I'll be wearing the kilt. I wonder what they'd say at the Red Swallow if I went there with a skirt on!'

'You'd cut quite a dash, Uncle,' Pamela said. 'By the way, I had a letter from Mary this morning. Apparently Alan called on her and stayed a night. But she didn't say anything else of importance, nothing about what the Americans are doing or about what's going on beyond the barriers.'

Pamela felt a little uneasy about this visit of Alan's, but kept her thoughts to herself.

'Well, her mustn't gossip,' Mrs Baines said reprovingly. ''Tis forbidden. 'Tis all secret.'

'I know,' Pamela replied, and then was silent, thinking of her husband, wondering what he had done on that leave and where he had slept. She was glad that she had brought Lawrence's book of poetry with her. She must see that it was always locked safely away in her box.

There had been no letter from Alan for two weeks now and she had to admit that she longed for the next one, if only for reassurance that all was well. Nothing could have happened, she told herself firmly. I'm being silly. Mary wouldn't have said anything about Lawrence, and no one else knows. Then, like a shaft of foreboding, she remembered Molly Yates. Surely he hadn't gone there? And even if he had . . . Pamela refused to allow herself to think of the possibilities, but she was suddenly aware of the fragility of her happiness.

During the next few days she tried to forget the uneasiness that Mary's letter had brought. No news was good news, she told herself. Alan was becoming operational. He'd write soon, and meanwhile there was plenty to do to keep her occupied.

She had soon begun to feel at home in Craemore. There was a friendly bustle about it and a sort of excitement. The almost complete absence of barbed wire was wonderful. Pamela remembered the vicious barriers that had been part of life on the South Coast for a long time, but here she and Jane frequently went as close to the waves as they dared and one day when the sun was shining they even took off their socks and shoes and paddled.

'It's nice here,' Jane remarked as they sat together on the beach and wiped their feet dry afterwards. 'I wish we could stay for ever and ever.'

'Don't you want to go home?'

'No,' Jane said with determination. She jumped up and ran down towards the water again, dancing along at the sea's edge avoiding the small lapping waves.

'Except to see Sheppey,' she called back. 'Uncle Richard wants to see Sheppey too.'

Pamela laughed and packed the towel quickly into her bag. She joined the child and took her hand. 'Don't get yourself wet again,' she said. 'We must go back now.'

Jane was suddenly thoughtful. 'I wonder how the angel is with no pretty flowers?' she said.

'Angel? What angel? What are you talking about?'

The little girl stopped and looked at Pamela with a strange expression on her face. 'You know,' she said. 'Olivia's angel in the church garden. We give her flowers.'

'Who gives her flowers?'

'Me and Aunt Maud.'

Pamela had not known about this particular little ritual. So Aunt Maud had taken Jane to the churchyard regularly before they came here, to put flowers on Olivia's grave? There was nothing wrong in that, of course. She had often seen some blooms there when she took her own small offering.

The past returned suddenly to hurt and to haunt, the past that she had thought safely buried since she came to Scotland. Once more she felt the old burden of reproach, the blame for being born, for causing her mother's death.

Then she remembered the last time she had seen the graceful marble statue. She had been there with Lawrence and he had run his fingers over the cold stone. 'You are beautiful,' he had said. 'Beautiful like your mother.'

They walked along the beach to the spot where the harbour wall jutted out into the cold grey sea and Jane gripped Pamela's hand more tightly. 'If I hold on to you, can we walk right out there?'

'Yes, but only if you promise not to pull away.'

'I won't.'

Pamela always thrilled at the feel of her little daughter's hand so trustfully in her own. She looked down at her and smiled. It was another moment of special closeness, replacing some of the bitterness of the past.

They walked slowly out along the stone jetty. There was no wind today and no threatening waves. At the end they stopped and stood together looking at the array of shipping on the Firth and across at Invergarth on the other side. 'It's a nice place,' Pamela said aloud, but more to herself than to the child. 'Yes, I could be happy here.'

Jane glanced up at her and then pointed out to sea with her free hand. 'Look at all those funny wee aeroplanes on the water with boats on their feet.'

Pamela laughed at the remark and tried to put more serious thoughts out of her mind. 'They're flying boats,' she said. 'And I suppose by "wee" you mean small? They're not small. It's only because they're away over the other side of the Firth. Sunderlands and Catalinas, I think they're called.'

'Aunty Baines said they was, but her wasn't sure.'

'She wasn't sure,' Pamela corrected. She realized with some amusement that by the time they got back to Devon Jane's speech would probably be a mixture of Scots and Mrs Baines! Her uncle too had allowed his broad Devon vowels to come to the fore again now that Aunt Maud seemed not to know what he said.

They retraced their steps, and once back on the safety of the broad road beside the sea, Jane loosed her hold on Pamela's hand and skipped ahead again. Then she stopped and stared with solemn blue eyes. 'Pammy,' she said, 'why can't you be my mummy? I want a mummy like the other children at Sunday School. They've all got mummies except me.'

Pamela took a deep breath and stopped too. She held out her arms to the little girl, and then with sudden inspiration she whispered, 'I know. I'll be your secret mummy. You can call me Mummy all the time we're out of the house. How about that?'

'Ooh, lovely,' Jane said as she ran into Pamela's arms. 'I love secrets. Just me and you'll know. Mummy, Mummy, Mummy. I've got a mummy!'

Pamela lifted her off her feet and twirled her round, and then they ran together up the cobbled street and back to Lighthouse Lane, mother and daughter at last.

Only an hour later she opened the front door in answer to impatient knocking and in an instant all her precious happiness was destroyed. Alan stood there unsmiling, his lips set in a determined line and a frown on his face that chilled her to the depths. 'Alan,' she stuttered 'Alan! How . . . ?'

'Nice to see me? You won't think so after I've had my say. Get your coat.' He offered no explanations, merely looked at her with eyes fierce with anger. There was anger too in every line of him so that she flinched, gripping the door for support. 'What do you mean? I can't . . . I'm just . . .'

'Don't argue. Fetch your coat or I'll drag you out as you are.'

He turned away from her and strode the few steps to the gate. Pamela was filled with terror. She knew that she dared not disobey. Her fears had been realized. Someone must have told him about Lawrence. The thought turned her whole body to ice and her feet refused to move. She hoped desperately that Mrs Baines had not recognized his voice or heard the bitter words. She probably had not for there was another door to the kitchen which Pamela had closed carefully before opening the outer one. This was habit and must always be done, for the wind blew straight in from the Firth. Even today when there was only a breeze it was still cold and Pamela shivered. She could see Alan standing at the gate. He had not opened it but had turned and was looking at her, daring her to disobey. Although every inch of her wanted to rebel, she knew that she could not. 'I'll just have to make an excuse to Mrs Baines,' she said. 'She'll wonder where I've gone.'

'Then be quick!'

Pamela willed herself to move, to think logically. She tried to summon every vestige of strength that she could muster, and then walked back into the kitchen. It was no use telling lies to Mrs Baines, she decided, but she needn't know everything. 'It's Alan,' she announced. 'He's arrived unexpectedly. No time to let me know. He just wants to walk out on to the jetty. We won't be long.'

'Well now, that's a nice surprise. I'll have a cup of tea ready.' If she was bewildered by Pamela's words her voice betrayed nothing. 'Me and Jane are going to make some little cakes, and I've got a nice bit of fish for our supper. Don't be long. Now the sun's gone, it's getting chill.'

Pamela forced a smile and thankfully escaped before she needed to say any more. She was trembling violently as she threw on her thick tweed coat and her efforts to fasten the buttons were clumsy and awkward. She pulled the belt as tightly as she could around her thickening waist, tied a woollen scarf on her head and went out to face her husband.

# FIFTEEN

*Olivia's Journal – 2nd May 1923*
*Maud says that I may not speak to the new people in Ash*
*Manor. She says that they are unsuitable. I have no idea why.*
*I saw the brother and sister on the beach again this morning.*
*I watched them from a distance and I had to be very strict*
*with Mallory. The boy was throwing stones into the sea and*
*he wanted to run after them.*

Alan waited impatiently. He drummed his fingers on the gate,
trying in vain to contain his anger, trying to find some way of
coming to terms with the impossible. When Pamela at last
appeared he turned and strode along the way he had come, down
the cobbled street towards the sea. The sound of waves on sand
and shingle comforted him a little, reminded him of home.

'Wait for me, Alan,' she called desperately. 'Wait, will you?'

He paused for a moment and looked at her disdainfully. 'And
why should I wait? You didn't wait for me, did you? As soon as
I was away you were off with your fancy Yank!' He spat out the
words and Pamela gasped in dismay at the hatred and disgust in
them.

'It wasn't like that,' she whispered. 'It wasn't like that at all.'
Yet she knew of course that it was. It was just as he stated, no
more a magical fairy tale but rather a sordid reality, at least in
his eyes. She ran to keep up with him and wondered just what
he had heard.

They reached the sea wall, a low stone structure which ran along the whole length of the beach. 'Then what was it like?' he said. 'Something poetical and lovely you're going to tell me, are you? Is that why you've started reading poetry, and writing it too?' He pulled out the now crumpled piece of blue paper and thrust it at her. 'Is this what your fancy man means to you then?'

She looked at it in dismay. It would be no use denying anything now. 'What have you heard?' she whispered.

'That you're no better than that little slut Molly Yates! That the bastard you carry isn't mine at all. That he'll be some half-caste Yank – black, I shouldn't wonder. There are plenty of them around all over the place.' He threw the paper from him on to the beach where the wind took it, swirling it along the tide-line and into the piles of oily sea-weed. Then a wave caught it and Pamela could see it flattened out in the water, washing to and fro like some dead thing.

She sat on the wall and covered her face with her hands. So it was Molly who had told. She might have known. 'Don't say such terrible things to me, Alan,' she implored. 'Please don't say such terrible things.'

'Then what am I supposed to say, for God's sake? That I'll take you back and care for you and another man's child? Never!' He felt cruel. He wanted to bruise and hurt her just as he himself had been hurt. The triumph which he had thought was his, the triumph of Pamela's pregnancy, was now shattered and in ruins. He was sure that he would never again want to hold her in his arms, never again make love to her. Thoughts of a son of his own, flesh of his flesh, a child to inherit his beloved Morelake, would have to be abandoned now, perhaps for ever. Even if he could one day bring himself to overcome his revulsion, he might not be given the chance. He knew that his hopes of surviving the war were not very great. He expected to be posted soon, and air gunners were pretty vulnerable.

He slumped on to the wall and looked at the flying boats out on the Firth. They were big lumbering things and seemed out of place amongst the slim and elegant destroyers. There was a flotilla of small boats too fussing around between the more impressive craft. They looked for all the world like a swarm of fussy ants. And there was the ferry boat on which he had come to Craemore from Invergarth after a long and tortuous train journey. He bunched his hands into angry fists. What in the world was he doing in this faraway place? So long to get here, and for what? Of one thing he was completely sure – he'd be on that ferry at the next sailing.

Pamela was still sitting on the wall beside him and he glanced at her and saw the tears wet on her face. She wasn't bothering to wipe them away. She was just sitting there on the wall, looking out now at the expanse of choppy water with its white-frothed waves that chased each other on to the beach. He had no idea what she was thinking about: whether she was truly sorry, whether she loved this Yank, or whether it had just been a quick and thoughtless fling like his with Brenda Barker. But that was totally different, he told himself angrily for the hundredth time. He was a fool even to compare the two things. A woman's body was her husband's. A man might do as he pleased, but Pamela was his and no other's. He sat there with at least three feet of cold wall between himself and his wife and tried to believe in the double standards that would make her guilty and himself innocent. Everything that he had been conditioned to believe all his life reinforced his silent arguments. There was no doubt about it. Pamela had betrayed him, and with an American too! It was the final and most terrible disloyalty. In his tortured mind he lumped the Yanks together with the enemy for they had put him out of his land, taken his farm.

Suddenly she turned a tear-stained face towards him, but there was fierce determination in it. 'The child is yours,' she said. 'Don't you remember that night – Christmas Eve? We made love and it was good, Alan. Better than ever before. And it wasn't just once either. Your child was conceived that night. Believe it! You must believe it!'

Pamela wanted to believe it now herself. She had no idea how her body worked, but Alan had made love to her many times on that leave so perhaps that made the baby mostly his?

She held our her hands to him, pleading. 'It's your child I carry.'

He looked at her in suddenly renewed hope, desperately wanting to accept what she was saying. Yet he couldn't rid himself of the nightmare picture of some Yank holding her in his arms, making love to her, despoiling what was his. He looked away again and stared at the little town of Invergarth across the water, saw the gently rising hills beyond, and longed for Devon, longed for the comforts and security of his own home. But he was thinking of Morelake as it had been long before the evacuation. Before Pamela.

'But you slept with him, didn't you?' He wanted to grip her shoulders, shake her violently, but he sat on the wall, grim-faced, completely still and controlled.

She was silent for a long time, then she too stared out to sea. 'Once, Alan. Just once. And I shall never see him again. Can you believe me? Can you forgive me?'

'I shall stay at The Craemore Arms,' he said, ignoring her questions. 'I left my things there. I'll be getting the early ferry back to Invergarth tomorrow. I'm to be posted to an operational squadron soon, somewhere on the East Coast probably.'

She stood up and moved towards him, forcing him to notice her. He saw for the first time the slightly thickening figure and was filled with further suspicion and distrust – and then revulsion. He couldn't believe what she said about the child. For the first time he was glad that his chances of surviving the war were not very great. All he wanted to do was have a go at the enemy, shoot down a few Jerry fighters, take out all his anger on them. And if he failed to return, as the war office euphemistically put it, well then, his problems would end and Morelake would go to . . . to an American bastard! He clenched his fists even tighter. Never! He would never allow that.

He searched his mind for an answer to this further problem and realized with a stab of anger that there was only one solution. He could not be sure about this unborn child until he saw it. There was a chance then that he might know if it was his. But until that time? If he was killed before the child was born then Jane should have Morelake. Pamela could make of that whatever she liked! He determined to find a solicitor in some place where he wasn't known and get it seen to.

He looked at his wife coldly, staring at the belt around her waist, let out now two notches or more. 'I might write,' he said, and then turned swiftly and marched back along the way they had come. He went in at the door of the pub which stood, a secure and comforting refuge, on the corner facing the sea.

Pamela watched him go and felt fear rise in her like a swelling tide. She wanted to run after him, to clutch at him, even perhaps to plead for forgiveness, for although she knew that she would never forget Lawrence and that her love for him would always be like a bulwark underlying her life, Alan was her husband. He was the man with whom she would have to live after the war, the man who must give her coming child a name and on whom she depended utterly for sustenance and a home. And if he refused to accept this child, then its future as well as that of Jane and herself lay in tatters. Adultery was what everyone would call it, just like the Bible. To bear an illegitimate child was bad enough but to cuckold a husband who was away in the forces was the ultimate sin. She would be an outcast in her own village.

She stood quite still for a long time and then, shivering, started to walk along the sea-road in the opposite direction. She hoped that no one had overheard any part of the conversation between herself and Alan. Craemore was small and she and her family were well known now. But there were plenty of men in uniform about. It was a bustling little place with a naval camp on the top of the hill, an army camp just below it and numerous RAF personnel frequently in from the flying boats. One of their noisy little motor launches had come in earlier so she was fairly sure that Alan's uniform would not have attracted too much attention.

As she walked, the cold bracing air began to work its usual magic. It was not like the sultry and often humid atmosphere of Devon. Since the afternoon a wind had sprung up and the waves were larger, the weather altogether more wild. It challenged her and she responded to it, gradually beginning to feel a trace more hopeful in spite of the shock of Alan's accusations. She wasn't sure for how long she walked and then she turned back, wondering what she would say to Mrs Baines, and to Uncle Richard too if he were home.

The kitchen was warm and welcoming, Mrs Baines was smiling and cheerful and Jane was mixing something in a bowl when Pamela walked through the door. She didn't wait for the difficult questions that she knew Alan's absence would bring forth. 'He's not coming,' she blurted out. 'He's going back.'

'What now, straight away?' At first Mrs Baines obviously failed to understand. 'You mean he've come all this way just to see you for an hour or so. That shows love then.'

Pamela stood before the fire and warmed her hands. 'No. Well, yes, he did come to see me, but not like you think. He's staying at The Craemore Arms and going back on the early ferry tomorrow.'

Jane had never had any sort of relationship with Alan and her small intent face registered no emotion. She was still concentrating on the sticky mess in the bowl on the table in front of her. She licked her fingers and then offered a spoonful of the mixture to Pamela. 'Have some, Pammy,' she said. 'It's going to be wee round sweeties when I've done them.'

Pamela smiled automatically but with no happiness in her heart. 'Not now, darling,' she said. 'Later, when you've finished.' Suddenly she longed for Mary Turner. She would know what to do and wouldn't be too shocked. Pamela was fairly sure of that. But Mrs Baines? She was a countrywoman with strict views about life and morality. Yet more than anything in the world Pamela wanted to feel comforting and motherly arms round her, wanted to confess all her feelings about Lawrence, her doubts about her marriage, about the coming baby, everything. She felt that she had lived a pretence for long enough. She wanted to face the truth of what she had done, to talk it out and come to terms with it. But she could say nothing in front of Jane. She pulled herself tall and straight. She would not break down now. She looked at Mrs Baines, willing her to understand and to co-operate. 'It's all right,' she said. 'We'll talk later when Uncle Richard has gone out and after Jane's in bed. I'd like to tell you about things, if you'll listen.

'I'm good at that, deary,' the older woman said. 'Listening, I mean. I did a lot back at home, what with neighbours and their troubles. Nothing's ever as black as folks make out, you mark my words.'

Pamela blinked, forcing herself not to cry. 'Not as black as folks make out,' she repeated. 'That's good. Thank you.' Then Mrs Baines smiled at her, an understanding sort of smile.

I shall manage, she thought. I shall bring up my two children myself if I have to and we shall survive! She turned to Jane. 'Can I have a stir?' she said. 'It looks scrumptious!'

It was not until the late evening that Mrs Baines and Pamela were alone. It had been difficult explaining Alan's brief visit to Uncle Richard, but at supper it was not discussed. Pamela knew that he would be worrying and that he was deliberately keeping his own counsel. She wondered how much he knew about her marriage and whether he had any idea of her feelings for Lawrence. Although he was a quiet man, never gossiping or listening to gossip, yet she had often wondered if beneath that serene exterior there was a more complicated person, someone who was very much aware of what went on around him even if he gave no sign. She intended telling him the truth later, but it was to a woman that she wanted to talk first.

Apart from the clacking of knitting needles there was no sound in the quiet room. Aunt Maud and Jane were both asleep and Richard had gone for his nightly pint. 'Think I'll go up The Royal tonight,' he had said. 'I'd like a change!' He had smiled at Pamela and she knew his reason and was grateful. She had mentioned that Alan was staying in The Craemore Arms.

Mrs Baines, her eyes fastened on the pullover she was knitting for her son, spoke levelly and without emotion. 'You don't need to tell me about that nice lieutenant,' she said. 'I've knowed all along that you was in love, that 'twas him you wanted, and I can understand it too. Don't forget that I used to work for Mrs

199

Saunders now and then before she died, so I know about Mr
Alan and how he was brought up. Not easy. Not easy at all.'

Pamela wondered whether she meant it had not been easy
for Alan living with his possessive and domineering mother, or
whether the comments were for her own marriage? 'How much
do you know?' she asked quietly.

'I've guessed a bit, and I'm on your side, deary. You can count
on that. I don't hold with men, and I should think you'd had
enough of them after what happened to you all them years ago
when you was still a little thing.'

'You know about that too?' Pamela was horrified.

'Course I knows. You was still at school and he was a monster
whoever done it to you. I love little Janey, of course, but that
don't make it any better. So I reckons if you got a bit of pleasure
with your nice officer, well then, you was welcome to it!'

Pamela blushed, suddenly embarrassed. Although she had
intended to tell Mrs Baines about her present problems, ask her
advice perhaps and hopefully find some comfort, she had not
thought to go back into the past. The rape . . . She shivered. It
still haunted her even now but she believed it to be a carefully
hidden secret. If it was known to Mrs Baines then who else had
discovered the secret of Jane's birth?

Reading her thoughts, Mrs Baines looked up from her knitting.
'Don't worry, deary,' she said. ''Tis only me what knows and
I'm close, never gossip. Your aunt told me about little Jane
before she had that wicked ole stroke. I was that shocked I can
tell you but it'll never get past my lips, you can be sure. For the
sake of the little maid I'll never tell. 'T'wouldn't be right, so you
can count on me. I reckon that they ought to have found out
who done it, though. He should be locked up for ever.'

'It was a long time ago,' Pamela said, trying to put the unwel-
come memories behind her as she always did. 'I want to forget
now.'

'Of course you do, deary, and you got no need to worry about
anything. You'm the wronged one.'

'You don't understand.' Pamela shook her head. 'I do have
cause to worry.' She paused for a moment and stared into the

fire. 'My baby . . . I don't know who the father is.' She blurted out the words, shocking even herself with their awfulness. Although she had lived with this nightmare thought for weeks, it seemed worse now that she had actually spoken it aloud. She had tried to make endless excuses for herself, tried to cover her betrayal of Alan with thoughts of the beauty of her love for Lawrence. But suddenly there were no excuses left. She knew that she had stooped to common unadorned infidelity.

But Mrs Baines' knitting needles didn't stop and she appeared not at all shocked. 'This is how I see it,' she said. 'You been wronged all through. What with your aunt bringing you up too strict and with no love, and then the . . . rape . . . well, what could anyone expect of you after all that? Things was too much against you. You needed a mother, deary, to tell you what was what, to love you. Then you wouldn't have been forced to marry that Alan Saunders, a man you didn't love.'

Pamela gasped. She'd had no idea that she had such an ally, such a champion, in Mrs Baines. 'So you don't think that I've done such a terrible thing after all?' she demanded.

'Course not, deary. If I'd been in your shoes, well, I 'spect I should have done the same. Especially with a lovely lieutenant like yours coming courting me.'

Pamela felt that the older woman's logic must be faulty somehow but the words were just what she needed to hear. 'Thank you, Mrs Baines,' she said. 'You've cheered me no end. I know I've done wrong, but I've got to keep up my self-confidence and my courage, haven't I?'

The knitting needles stopped for a moment. 'That's right. You got to believe in yourself. For the sake of your babe, and for Jane too, you got to do that.'

'And I will,' Pamela said. She reached for her own knitting, a tiny blue matinee coat that was half finished.

"Believe in yourself." She was silent for a few minutes thinking about the words. If only she knew more about her own father, Olivia's lover, it might help her to do just that. Perhaps Mrs Baines knew his identity. The thought struck her suddenly and she felt a little shiver of excitement. 'My father,' she said quietly.

'I've never been able to find out anything about him. I don't suppose you . . . ?'

'No deary, I don't. It was a well-kept secret and if your aunt knows she never confided in me. We wasn't close in them days. I remember your sweet mother though, a lovely bright girl. We was all heartbroken when she died.'

The sudden flicker of hope disappeared as quickly as it had come, and was replaced by a little of the old sense of blame, as though she herself was personally responsible for Olivia's death. Pamela tried to shake it off. She glared down at her knitting and at the end of the row she counted the stitches anxiously in case she had made a mistake in the complicated pattern. Then she deliberately switched her mind to the coming baby and to more positive thoughts. 'What shall I call him?' she said. 'I thought about Mallory but that isn't a proper given name, is it?'

'Mallory!' Mrs Baines repeated the word. 'I like it though. An explorer, wasn't he?'

'Yes, died on Everest, and my mother called her wolf-hound after him too. The dog's grave is at Burlcombe. There's a headstone.'

'Well now, fancy that. I think I'd have something a bit more ordinary for a name if I was you, though. I've a feeling your hubby isn't going to like Mallory!'

At last Pamela laughed. 'No, Alan certainly wouldn't like Mallory, and if he's ever going to accept this child the name will have to be very sensible and down-to-earth. Perhaps it should be Alan?' The laughter died on her lips as she spoke. She could never have a son called Alan.

But of course the baby might be a girl. For the first time she began to think of her child as female and belonging neither to Lawrence nor to Alan, only to her. It was a far more acceptable idea. A look of determination crossed her face. She would not be intimidated by anyone. The wrong she had done suddenly became a little less terrible. It was the future and how she dealt with it that mattered. She looked at the little blue coat she was knitting and smiled to herself. The next one would definitely be pink!

In Devon Molly Yates too was knitting baby clothes in her spare time. Her father meanwhile was busy trying to discover just what was happening on the beaches and out at sea. He came home one day in late April with a glum expression on his face. 'Something big's going on,' he muttered as he pulled off his muddy boots just inside the door. 'Hundreds of boats be gathered together in the bay and the place be running over with men everywhere. I never seen so much toing and froing. I reckon that the whole of Devon be just one great army camp.'

Molly thought of her baby's father, the handsome Delmer whom she would probably never see again. 'When's it going to be then, d'you think?'

'When's what going to be?' Ben pulled an old towel from the hook just inside the front door and carefully wiped Sheppey's feet before he looked up.

'The invasion, of course. I ain't completely stupid.' Molly put her knitting down and got to her feet.

'They'm still busy with their practices and exercises by the looks of things,' her father replied, 'and if I knowed the answer to your question, my girl, I'd be as good as Mr Churchill, wouldn't I? It's top secret, and a good thing if you ask me. We don't want they Jerries coming over bombing us just to get at the Yanks.'

Wendy Yates appeared from the scullery. 'I don't reckon they got much of an air force left,' she said. 'Not as good as ours now anyway. I wonder when that nice Alan Saunders'll be flying. I hope he don't get shot down, what with Pamela expecting.'

Molly's heart beat a little faster. The visit that Mr Saunders had made to their home a short time ago had not been noted by anyone apparently, and she had kept quiet about it. She frequently wondered if he had written to Pamela or confronted her with the awful things that she herself had revealed. She thought of it mostly at night when she lay listening to the steady drone of bombers, wave after wave of them heading out over the Channel to France or Germany. She frequently shivered, clutching the bedclothes to herself in fear. It was not fear for herself but for the men up there in the darkness, many of them destined never to come back. The unknown crews of those aeroplanes all seemed to look like Alan Saunders in her imagination.

When she slept she also dreamed of him, and in her dreams his plane was spiralling to the ground in flames and the look he turned on her was one of disgust. She would toss restlessly in her sleep. Because of her foolish and thoughtless words, he was probably going to his death an angry and miserable man. ''Twas only a dream,' she always told herself with relief when she awoke the next morning. 'For all I know he hasn't even finished his training yet. 'Tis my Delmer I got to worry about!'

She tried hard and often unsuccessfully to banish the gloomy thoughts that persisted. All day she worked. An extra pair of hands was welcome in the overcrowded cottages and farms all around for every household was brimming over with people and animals. Most of the evicted families had tried to cram themselves and their stock into accommodation and land that was as near as possible to their abandoned homes. Molly frequently looked after the noisy children of the two families living in the small cottage down the lane. She did most of the work at home while her mother was charring elsewhere, and she cooked meals that were as nourishing as she could make them, both for her own family and for the two old people who lived in squalor in a tiny two-roomed shack nearby.

But after supper, just before the sun went down, she usually allowed herself a little time alone. She liked the dimpsey when it was still light enough to see but not quite dark. She always called to Sheppey and they would walk out on the path above the sea. It led to one of her favourite places, a small scrubby wood as close as she could get to the evacuated area. From there she could look down on part of the stretch of forbidden coastline unobserved, and would stand and look at all the activity below and think about her life, and about Delmer. Sometimes she allowed herself to dream that he would come back after the war and claim her, take her away to the magic land called America where she would be rich and learn to drive a motor-car. She would have a big house, perhaps a ranch, and a horse to ride . . . She knew that it couldn't happen, but it was nice to dream. He became in those magical moments more a prince on a white charger than the laughing, smoking, drinking GI she had known and to whom she had given herself for those few fleeting minutes behind the hedge at the village hall.

Occasionally everything was quiet, the men elsewhere, only the ugly artefacts of war marring the beauty. Molly liked it on those evenings. She loved to hear the seagulls instead of the gunfire, the sound of waves on shingle instead of men's voices.

On one such evening, as the night clouds gathered over the strangely quiet sea, her attention was suddenly caught by something odd on the beach below, something floating down there at the sea's edge. Backwards and forwards it flopped, at the mercy of the waves. She shielded her eyes and tried to see more clearly in the fading light. She realized that there were two of the dark inanimate shapes in the water, sometimes together, sometimes thrown apart. Then she screamed and turned and ran stumbling back to the cottage.

'Mum, Dad,' she called as she pushed open the door. 'There's bodies down there on the beach. Bodies, I tell you, in the sea!'

# SIXTEEN

*Olivia's Journal – 1st August 1923*
*The family are back again in Ash Manor. They have been away for some weeks, the school term I suppose. Maud seemed quite put out when she heard of their return.*
*There was a beautiful rainbow this morning. I feel that it is a good omen. Its colours bring the promise of something special. Perhaps, in spite of my sister's strange displeasure, I shall become friends with the brother and sister? That would be so wonderful.*

Lawrence Lawson lay in a hospital bed and could remember nothing. Gingerly he put up a hand to his head and groaned. He appeared to be swathed in bandages and couldn't move at all. The past days were a horrifying blank. He had no idea where he was, what day it was, or even what month. He could see a figure in a white apron across the other side of the room. He must be in some sort of hospital. 'Nurse,' he called weakly. 'Nurse.'

'You mustn't talk. The words came to him from a great distance and the face bending over him swam alarmingly.

'Where am I? What's happened?'

'An accident.'

He closed his one good eye, the one that was not bandaged, and tried to remember, but there was a total blank where knowledge and recall should be. It was strange, almost terrifying, to be lying there, to be helpless and to know nothing. 'What kind

207

of accident?' he managed, forcing himself to look at her again.

'You mustn't talk,' she repeated.

'But I'm going crazy. My head's all confused.'

'I can't tell you anything. I'm as ignorant as you are.' She whispered the words, bending low over the bed. 'Something happened during your practices. You'll be all right, though.'

'What happened, for God's sake? Don't leave me in this nightmare, honey.' He felt that he was rapidly losing consciousness. The girl, the light from the window, the ceiling above him were all receding, and the blackness in his mind was enveloping everything.

The young nurse looked at him closely and placed his arm, which was the only limb unbandaged, carefully beneath the blankets. She sighed. A stream of ambulances filled with wet and shivering men had been pouring through the hospital gates for much of the day. Many of them were badly wounded like this one, but others were merely cold and shocked, having been in the water for hours. She had no idea what had been going on. They were only supposed to be practising but a lot had died, drowned mostly. She hoped this one would survive. From the little she could see of him he looked nice. She had shaved some of his dark wavy hair before the doctor had stitched up the horrifying wounds on his head. He was asleep now anyway. She moved on to the next bed.

Molly Yates had been told not to be so fanciful when she rushed into the cottage with her tale of bodies on the beach. Her father had been adamant that she was mistaken. 'Plenty of logs and bits of wreckage gets washed up,' he had said firmly. 'And when they be all tangled up with sea-weed and rope and the like 'twould be easy to think they were something nasty. You forget about it, girl. And not a word, mind.'

Hearing the tone of his voice Molly had her doubts, but she tried to believe him. She decided that she wouldn't go back to her little wood above the sea for a bit. The beach held a more ominous threat now than the war-games that had been going on for so long.

But two days later her father returned home with a grim look on his face. 'A mishap,' he stated. 'Something terrible have happened out at sea, so they say.'

'What d'you mean?' Both Molly and her mother spoke together. They stared at him for he seldom looked so shaken.

'I don't know much. 'Tis all hushed up. I heard something. That latest big training operation have gone wrong by all accounts, and a lot of men been killed. But it won't be in the papers. No one got to know.'

At once Molly thought of Delmer. 'Who's been killed?' she said. 'What are you talking about? If it's not the invasion, how can they be killed?'

Ben looked at her a trifle scathingly. 'Well, they be training with live ammunition. You know that, girl. The past couple of days they been sending in assault craft on to Slapton, pretending it's France. But there's whispers of something worse than the odd few injured. 'Twas all a mix up – some landing craft went down. Some say the Germans got wind of what's going on and some E-boats come in when the practice was in full swing. The Yanks was sitting ducks if you ask me. Others say 'twas just an accident, and that the poor buggers died in friendly fire.' He laughed grimly. 'Friendly fire! That's a funny thing to call something what kills you.'

'How do you know all this?' Wendy stared at her husband critically. She was used to his fanciful tales, but was also aware that he had a nose for news and if there was anything important or secret to be discovered, her man would be sure to sniff it out. He frequently sneaked into the forbidden area to snare rabbits and often came home with frightening bits of information. But this was different, and by the look of him he was quite shaken. 'Where did you hear about it?' she persisted.

'Never you mind, woman,' he said. 'And not a word outside the four walls of this cottage. It happened quite a ways from here, along the coast. Well past Sidmouth, I think 'twas. No one knows for sure. But 'tis rumoured there are bodies.'

'Bodies?' Molly thought of what she had seen and of her father's disbelief the other evening.

'Only rumours, I expect, so let's have something to eat and forget all about what don't rightly concern us.' Ben went to wash his hands, and his wife and daughter knew by the expression on his face that the subject was closed. Molly wished that he had said nothing. It was better not to know than to hear fearful bits of information that would set your mind imagining all sorts of horrors. She had tried so hard to believe that what she had seen was merely flotsam, just bits of wood and seaweed. Even if Delmer was not for her she still wanted to imagine him alive and well. She didn't want to think of his rotting body washed up on the beach. And there was Pamela's handsome lieutenant too. She shivered and reluctantly went to help her mother dish up the meal, the stew that she usually enjoyed but that now made her stomach heave. Bodies on the beach . . . The words went round and round in her head as she ladled out the food.

'I feel ill,' she gasped suddenly. She plonked the large spoon she was holding back into the pan, wrenched open the back door and rushed out into the yard to vomit on to the potato patch.

'Sorry,' she whispered to her worried mother when she returned white-faced to the cottage a few minutes later. ''Tis Delmer, I'm sure of that. He's dead. I just knows it.'

Pamela often wondered how much Aunt Maud understood of what was happening around her. Had she heard Alan's angry words spoken on the doorstep, and if so did they mean anything to her? The room in which she spent all her time was at the front and from there his voice would surely have been audible. There was indeed a strange look in the faded eyes. Once they had been shrewd and cold, but now they had lost their power to hurt. Maud seemed to have mellowed, and Pamela sometimes caught her smiling to herself, an odd enigmatic smile that could have meant anything or nothing. Sometimes Pamela had the definite idea that her aunt wished to talk to her, but no words came. There must be so many secrets locked away in her mind.

Pamela still wondered if she knew the identity of Olivia's lover. Surely she must? To have kept quiet about it seemed unpardonable for, Pamela told herself, the man was my father, my real flesh and blood father.

Daniel. She often said the name aloud when she was alone and tried to picture him in her mind. But he was also the one who had caused her mother's downfall, her death, and he had gone away and left her to her fate. No wonder that to Maud, who loved Olivia so much, he would be beyond redemption, someone never to be thought of or named. But of course there must be more to it than that, Pamela decided. There was surely some further reason for Maud's silence through the years?

And there was the other great mystery in Pamela's life. She frequently thought it strange that neither she nor Jane had named fathers. Sometimes she felt that she was a person without a past, without an identity.

Pamela usually carried in the evening drink to her aunt. It was a sweet milky concoction which Maud had always liked. Then she would sit beside the old woman, sometimes holding her hand, sometimes reading aloud, even though there was seldom a glimmer of response. She longed to communicate, to seek answers to the questions which plagued her, but it was too late now. The stroke had sealed everything away for good. Pamela had to be content to sit there reading quietly with all the problems, the mysteries unsolved.

Aunt Maud not even capable of indicating what book she wished to hear read, but it was not difficult to choose something suitable. There were usually one or two novels around borrowed by Mrs Baines from the library, always romantic idylls from which Pamela omitted any bits that she felt were rather too slushy. Then there was the *Daily Telegraph* which Uncle Richard still bought every day, more from habit than choice, and occasionally the Bible would seem the best choice and Pamela would read a psalm or two or something from the New Testament. She tried to choose comforting, gentle passages that she thought would please her aunt.

On the evening following Alan's angry visit, however, the old leather-covered book fell open at the story of Noah and his ark

211

of gopher wood. Pamela glanced at it and remembered Jane's colourful picture of the day before. She had been given a colouring book by Uncle Richard. In it a picture of the ark tossing on a lurid blue sea was topped by a giant rainbow which Jane, with the help of Mrs Baines, had crayoned over with every colour that her small pencil box afforded. Pamela smiled to herself as she thought of the picture. She turned to the beginning of the story and read it through slowly until she came to the bit about the rainbow.

'I do set my bow in the cloud, and it shall be for a token of a covenant between me and the earth. And it shall come to pass, when I bring a cloud over the earth, that the bow shall be seen in the cloud: And I will remember my covenant, which is between me and you . . . and the waters shall no more become a flood to destroy all flesh. And the bow shall be in the cloud . . .'

Pamela stopped at those words and a sudden rush of hope surged through her. Instead of the small room and the pathetic invalid beside her she saw Burlcombe, saw the wide sweep of Start Bay and the rainbow resplendent over the sea.

'The rainbow shall be seen in the cloud,' she whispered. It seemed to be a message sent just for her, and she remembered how often the rainbow featured in her mother's diary. For Olivia Belmont too the glowing colours seen through cloud and rain had been a token of cheer and hope.

Suddenly there was movement from her aunt's chair. Her one good hand shot out and grasped Pamela's dress. The cup, empty now, which had been placed on the table at her side fell to the floor with a crash, but Maud seemed not to care. The shattered china which once would have caused her great annoyance went unnoticed. Pamela jumped to her feet and stared at her aunt. There was an odd expression on her face and she obviously wanted desperately to communicate something of importance at last. It was as if the simple Bible story, so often related as a children's tale, held a message for her too. Pamela bent close to her, wiped the saliva from her mouth, held the clutching hand gently in her own, and kissed her aunt on the forehead.

'Forgive me,' Maud whispered. 'Burlcombe. It will be yours. Look after Jane and Richard. Forgive Alan.' Then she closed her eyes and appeared to sleep, but it was only for a moment. 'And Olivia,' she said. 'Look after Olivia.' Then her head sank forward and she slumped in her chair.

Pamela stared at her in fascinated horror. She had spoken . . . and what strange words. And now her eyes were still wide open, but vacant and coldly empty.

'Quick! Uncle Richard, Mrs Baines, come quickly,' Pamela called. She had never seen death before. But she didn't run from the room. She just stood and stared down at the shell of the woman who had moulded her life. She felt strangely detached. Then Richard rushed in, took one look at his wife, lifted her hand and cradled it in his large ones while he wept.

They all pondered those strange last words as well as her ability to form them. Pamela repeated everything she had said except the bit about Alan. That she kept to herself. What could Maud have meant? What was there about Alan that she didn't know and which needed forgiveness? However much she turned the words over in her mind, she could come to no sensible conclusion.

As for Olivia . . . how was she to look after Olivia? Was it just an old woman's ramblings. Olivia Belmont had been dead nearly nineteen years now, the whole span of Pamela's life.

Eventually she told Mrs Baines about the mysterious words. As she expected, the older woman thought little of it.

'Don't you worry about it, deary,' she said when they were sitting in the little front room the day after the funeral.

The room was cleared now of the bed, the wheel chair, and the other necessities of her aunt's latter days and had a bare un-lived-in look about it.

'She was just wandering in her mind. I'm surprised that she

spoke so clear to you like that. She hadn't said nothing for weeks. A miracle I call it. I 'spect it was just something in her mind from the past.'

Pamela hoped that this was so. Perhaps her aunt had been thinking about Alan as a boy or a young man? Maybe he had done something to displease her? Yet these explanations didn't satisfy her. Surely it had to be something of importance to bring out that forthright demand just before her aunt died? It was a troublesome thought, another mystery. She had hoped that the mysteries of her life might one day be unlocked by her aunt, not increased.

'Her talking about Olivia,' Mrs Baines went on, 'well, she always loved that sister of hers more'n I thought was healthy. When Olivia died, it really took her hard.'

And she never forgave me for it, Pamela thought.

Jane was playing with her doll. She looked up at them both. 'Aunty Maud meant we have to look after Olivia's angel, I expect,' she said. 'You know, Pammy. The one by the church. I want to go home and see her.'

Pamela looked at the child in surprise. She had no idea that she was listening or that she understood what they were talking about. But she remembered that Jane had mentioned this before. 'Perhaps you're right. That's what she meant,' she said. 'When we go back to Devon, we'll go straight away and visit the angel. But I thought you liked it here? You said you wanted to stay for ever.'

'I do. It's only the wee angel I want to see.' The words were decisive, and with the subject closed, Jane returned to the difficult process of putting the long elaborate nightdress that Mrs Baines had made on to her doll's unyielding body. Pamela found herself thinking yet again, and unwillingly this time, of the magical day with Lawrence when they had walked round the churchyard: when, beside her mother's grave, he had told her she was beautiful. It was the day she first realised what other people meant by falling in love.

Mrs Baines soon brought her back to the present. 'Now that your poor aunt have died,' she said, 'well, there's no need for both you and me to be up here looking after Mr Lindhurst and Jane, is there? You'll be giving me the sack, I'm thinking.'

Pamela stared at her in pained surprise. 'You're not serious? We couldn't do without you, Mrs Baines. You're like part of the family. And where would you go, for goodness' sake?'

'I'd like to stay, I just thought I might be in the way.'

'Never never think that. Perhaps it's me that ought to go.'

Jane stopped in her efforts to put the doll to bed once again,. 'No, Pammy! You mustn't go and leave me. You promised. We played mummies. You're my secret mummy and mummies don't leave their little girls.'

Pamela scooped her up in her arms, doll and all. 'Of course I won't leave you, my precious,' she said. 'How about calling me Mummy all the time now?'

'Not just for secret any more?'

'No. Not for secret any more!'

Thoughts of the future now occupied much of Pamela's mind. Her aunt was dead, and to her annoyance Pamela felt strangely rudderless. Being up here in Scotland felt wrong now. It had been Aunt Maud's choice. Pamela felt uneasily that the direction of all their lives was still being dictated by her aunt. This was a state of affairs that mustn't be allowed to continue, but they couldn't go home yet for there was no home to go to. She wondered how much her uncle thought about it, and whether or not he felt slightly superfluous now, just like Mrs Baines. She broached the subject at supper a few days later. 'How long do you suppose we'll have to stay in Scotland?' she asked. 'There's not much point in being here, is there, now that . . .'

'Now that your aunt's gone to be with the Lord,' Richard piously finished for her. 'Well, I've been thinking about it. It shouldn't be too long before they give us back our land. Until then us be pretty comfortable here. It might be better to make the best of it. They'm overcrowded down there by all accounts.'

Pamela nodded. 'I suppose you're right,' she admitted. It was strange to find that she now owned Burlcombe and yet it was completely closed to her. 'I can't wait to get back to Burlcombe

215

though,' she said sadly. 'Olivia said in her journal that she loved it and wanted it and it was never hers.'

Suddenly she thought or Richard's feelings and could have cursed herself for her insensitivity. It had been his home too for all the long years of his marriage to Maud. 'You won't leave me, Uncle Richard, will you?' she said quickly. 'You'll stay and get it back into shape, won't you, and manage it like you used to? I never, never want you to go anywhere else to live.'

Richard smiled at her and she saw the happiness in his eyes. 'I had thought to buy myself a nice little cottage with a few acres of land,' he said. 'But if you really want me to stay on for a bit, love, then I'll do it. But what will I do, rattling about in that great house all on my own?'

Jane looked up at him. Her spoon was poised halfway to her mouth and she dripped gravy all over the white cloth. 'Me and Pammy will be there, Uncle Richard,' she said. 'You won't be on your own.'

Pamela said nothing for a moment. In her dreams she saw herself as mistress of Burlcombe, but she was Alan's wife. More-lake, the gloomy dreaded Morelake, was the place where her destiny lay. The thought of settling down there again was suddenly too horrible to be borne. All she wanted to do now was to go to Burlcombe, to her very own Burlcombe, and to live a free and independent life for the very first time.

'Maybe Morelake and Burlcombe won't be in a fit state to go back to,' Mrs Baines said gloomily, 'or my cottage for that matter. You know, I had a letter from Wendy Yates this morning. She says there been lots of firing, more than usual lately, and they been storming up the beach just for all the world as if 'twas Jerries there waiting for them. It makes no sense to me, killing each other just for practice!'

'Whatever are you talking about?' Pamela was immediately worried. 'She shouldn't have put such things in a letter anyway.'

'She was careful not to put any address on it.' Mrs Baines was defensive. 'Nor no names of places. She didn't say nothing what's secret. There were bodies though.'

'Bodies?' Pamela's voice sounded incredulous.

216

'Yes. Just that they seen bodies. Might have been anywhere. Just bodies on the beach.'

'From a torpedoed ship, I expect,' Richard said. 'The tide brings them in now and then.'

Pamela shivered. She hoped that this conversation would be lost on Jane.

'I'm not so sure about them being from boats.' Mrs Baines' voice was sinister. 'Ben Yates told his wife and that silly little Molly of his that 'twas only lumps of sea-weed what they saw. He said they wasn't to mention it to a soul.'

'So Wendy Yates immediately puts it all in a letter to you!' Pamela laughed grimly. 'Oh, well, it probably was just sea-weed. That's what I'm going to believe anyway, or I shall dream about it tonight.'

'Please yourself, deary. Maybe you'm right. 'Twas only sea-weed!' Mrs Baines finished her stew and got up from the table to clear away the dishes. 'I hope we can get back soon,' she said. 'Then we'll know for sure what them Yanks have been doing down there.'

'I'm sure it'll be all right,' Pamela said cheerfully, but although her words were confident, in her heart she was fearful. Later that night she lay sleepless in bed and the lumps of sea-weed took on other forms in her mind just as they had done for Molly Yates. When eventually she slept they became, in her dreams, bodies just as Molly's mother had said in her foolish letter. Bodies that were American, young American faces with Lawrence's features, Lawrence's smile. But this time the faces she saw were dead ones, the expressions blank and the eyes empty sockets that looked up at her mockingly from the surf at the sea's edge.

In spite of the hens clucking around the cottages, and the kitchen gardens carefully cultivated, food was none too plentiful during that spring of 1944 and Ben Yates was determined that his family should not go hungry. His secret escapades into the forbidden area brought forth many treasures. He knew of places where the barbed wire had been cut so that it could be removed then put back and no one would know. He wasn't afraid of mines or unexploded shells. 'If my name's on one, then that's it,' he cheerfully confided to one of his mates, the only man who knew about his adventures. They went in together sometimes and returned with carrots and potatoes from overgrown and deserted gardens, and always with rabbits which they snared with great skill. One night they ventured further than usual, spurred on by Jack Partridge's desire to get a look at his own cottage and small-holding. They went by back lanes that they knew well and which weren't likely to have been in the thick of the mock-battles. But the devastation shocked them. They had chosen a bright moonlit night and the ghostly scene of shattered trees and shell-pocked buildings seemed unreal in the shadowy silver light.

'If they goes on like this much longer, it'll get to look like the Somme,' Jack said. 'I was there in the last lot. I never reckoned to see it happening here.'

Suddenly Ben stopped. 'Listen,' he said. 'There's someat going on.'

The two men stood quite still. The recent big practice was over and the night had been fairly quiet, but there were distinct noises now of trucks in the distance. There was machinery too.

'I reckon that's bulldozers,' Jack said. 'In the field over there.'

'Rotten buggers,' Ben said. 'What do 'em think they'm doing with our land? 'Tis going to take us months to get it back to growing things again.'

'I'm going up closer. 'Tis near my cottage.'

'Praps we shouldn't. We've come a fair old way tonight.' Ben was beginning to regret that he'd agreed to this crazy scheme to get to his friend's home.

'Now we've come this far, I'm not turning back.'

The men stooped and made their way quietly in the shadow of the high hedge. They crept for another mile or so, going always in the direction of the noises that they could hear just over the hill. They came eventually to a field gate and a gap in the hedge and both stopped and peered down at the small pin-points of light from the vehicles below. They stood in silence for a long time and then Ben grabbed his hat from his head. 'It be bodies they'm burying down there,' he said. 'That's what I reckon they'm doing.'

Jack Partridge felt prickles of horror all over. Then he tried to grab hold of some shreds of common sense. 'Could be anything,' he whispered. 'Yanks don't do things like that. They give their lads the best of everything. If there've been a big accident like some say, then they'd bury 'em proper in marked graves. You'm being fanciful, Ben Yates.'

Ben put his hat on again and picked up the brace of dead rabbits that he'd been holding. 'Praps you'm right,' he said. 'What with my Molly rushing home and talking rubbish about bodies on the beach, and the fighting all round, I began to think I was in the trenches again too.' He turned and started back the way they had come. 'Reckon we'll not go down to your place tonight after all.'

Jack took one last look at the scene below him, and at the wood which hid his little cottage from sight. 'Reckon you'm right,' he said. 'Another time, praps.'

At last Alan was flying, really flying. He had been over Germany five times and returned safely. His squadron was using Wellingtons and he had great admiration for the large ungainly machines, and for his pilot too. For the first time in his life he felt fulfilled. Farming had brought him a certain pleasure, but the exhilaration of flying couldn't be compared with day-to-day drudgery on the land. He sometimes thought about Pamela and wondered if he would ever see her again. For the moment it hardly mattered to him. He had managed to get his affairs sorted out to his satisfaction during a short leave which he had taken in Bristol. There, in the anonymity of the big city, he had found a solicitor, made his will, reluctantly named Jane his heir, and settled a small amount of money on Pamela and a fraction more on her unborn child, just in case. He felt that he had done all that was required in the circumstances. He knew that his wife was to be the future owner of Burlcombe so she wouldn't want for anything. He was totally carefree at last and this was the best way to be when you had to go up there in the darkness almost every night and face enemy fire and the possibility of sudden death.

Eventually the enemy targets were changed to military installations and supply lines in France. 'It must be to soften up the second front,' the Squadron Leader said. 'Tactical bombing to knock out Jerry coastal defences and cut off their supplies.'

Alan listened in silence and said nothing about the practices that went on most of the time over his precious bit of Devon in preparation for this feared but longed-for assault. The evacuation was still hardly known about, still a secret carefully kept by all those involved.

A few American fliers, as well as other nationalities, appeared here and there, and Alan regarded the Yanks with dislike for they disturbed his inner peace, the careful sense of satisfaction with things that he had built around himself just lately.

'Hi there,' one of them called to him one day. He held out his hand. 'Joe Hoffner – Flying Officer. I've been assigned to your squadron.

Alan looked at the proffered hand and forced himself to take it. 'Alan Saunders,' he said stiffly. 'Rear gunner.'

'Swell,' the American replied. 'You'll be the guy we rely on when we meet up with enemy fighters. Any good combats lately?' He laughed, a great annoying guffaw.

'A few,' Alan said. 'I've downed a couple of theirs. They've got good cannon though.' He determined that his prejudices shouldn't show. 'It out-ranges our Brownings.'

'I know. It's real bad. I bet the back-room guys'll come up with something just as lethal pretty soon, though.'

'Shouldn't be surprised.' The conversation stopped there and Alan was grateful that the handsome Joseph Hoffner wasn't assigned to the same plane, but the American's presence on the station irritated him, made him think of Pamela and her Yank when he wanted to forget her.

The power of the Luftwaffe night fighter defence system was brought home to Alan forcefully on a moonlit night at the beginning of May over northern France. His plane had just turned after releasing its cargo of bombs when a burst of cannon fire caught them underneath the body and flames started to flare up all around him.

He was surprised by his reaction. A great surge of adrenalin flowed through him and he felt exultant. This was it! This was the end – and before he went he'd show them a thing or two! Ignoring the terrible heat and smoke he gave burst after burst of fire at the fighters swarming around and had the satisfaction of seeing two of them spiralling to the ground in flames. He had never been so happy and so triumphant in his entire life. The crew of his plane were struggling to control their own fire and when his guns refused to perform any longer, he turned to help.

'Get ready to bale out.' He couldn't hear the words but he knew what the thumbs down signal from the pilot meant. He saw a large hole in the floor of the plane where shells had been pumped upwards by the enemy. It was a new tactic of the Luftwaffe that he had heard about but never experienced until this minute. He stared at it in disbelief, and then before he had time to think he was through and falling downwards into the black hell below.

His training took over where his brain refused to function and he pulled the ripcord of his parachute and eventually found his headlong flight checked and controlled. He tried to remember all the drill he had received to prepare him for this moment . . . and in spite of his earlier thoughts about death being a welcome release, now he wanted to survive. Dear God, how he wanted to survive!

For the second time Pamela was standing in stunned silence staring at a telegram. She had rushed to answer the doorbell thinking that it was the groceries being delivered or perhaps the three sacks of coal that she had ordered. But it was no such comfortable, ordinary thing.

She tore it open and read the brief message inside. Alan's plane had failed to return. He was missing, believed killed.

The freedom she had longed for now seemed an empty and desolate thing. If it was achieved through Alan's death then she wanted none of it. And she would never know what she had to forgive him for. Her aunt's words still haunted her.

She had not thought that she would cry for Alan, but now the tears flowed and would not be stopped. She rushed to her room and threw herself on to her bed. She buried her head in the pillow and sobbed for a long time until she realized that she was crying not only for her husband but for all those others – the bodies on the beach, the thousands preparing for the invasion of Europe . . . for Lawrence. Already in her mind he was dead too. Killed like millions more in this crazy, senseless war.

# SEVENTEEN

*Olivia's Journal – 5th August 1923*
*The Ash Manor family were not in church this morning. I*
*had hoped that they would be there and that Maud would*
*acknowledge them. They seem very respectable and very rich.*
*I still cannot understand why we are not allowed to call on*
*them officially. It's a complete mystery to me.*

Alan struggled in the blackness to free himself from his parachute. His training had been thorough and he should know just
what to do, but this bore little resemblance to the practice drops
that he had actually enjoyed over the friendly English countryside. He wasn't sure where he had landed, and was ashamed of
his fear and the shivering that was making every action difficult.
He could hear the sound of guns and the screech of bombs
but in between every ear-shattering burst there was an uncanny
silence. It was more profound than the quietness of the soft
Devon nights at home. No small creatures appeared to be stirring, no owl's eerie cry pierced the stillness. Every living thing
was holding its breath for the next explosion, the next outrage.

He struggled to his feet and made an effort to gather his
parachute together. It was a big unwieldy thing, graceful and
purpose-built for the skies but unimaginably difficult on the
ground. Eventually he had it in an acceptable bundle and groped
for a bush or a hedgerow in which to hide it. He pulled off his
leather gloves, and with his bare hands fumbled with the briars

223

and debris of what he thought was a ditch. Eventually he had the thing concealed to the best of his ability. He hoped that in daylight not a sign of it would be visible. It was supposed to be buried but how he could accomplish that with the shaking of his hands and the pain that shot through his body he couldn't imagine.

He started to limp away in the darkness, not knowing where he was going but hoping that he would find shelter from the steadily falling rain. His hands were scratched and torn and then he felt the slow trickle of blood on his face. As his fingers tried to trace the source of the wound he realized that he had left his gloves behind and, cursing his foolishness, retraced his steps. Nothing must be found that would betray his presence. For a long time he circled the place where he thought he had landed and then, as if in slow motion, swayed on his feet and sank to the ground. He lay for a moment on the wet grass staring at the searchlights sweeping in great arcs across the sky above him, and then there was a blessed feeling of release, a total blackness, and peace at last.

The peace ended. Alan awoke to find two faces looking down into his. They were a blur in the early morning light and he closed his eyes, wanting to blot out the sight of them. Memory returned and with it all the fears of the night. But the language he heard was French. His fuddled mind grasped that fact with relief. At least they weren't Germans. He tried to make sense of the words.

'Can you walk?' He realized with a shock that the voice was female and the question was in English.

'I . . . I think so.' He tried to struggle to his feet and failed, falling back heavily on to the wet earth. A stream of rapid French followed this display of weakness. The other voice was male. He struggled again and then, holding on to the hand that was stretched out towards him, he forced himself to stand. He was icy cold and very wet.

'These are yours.' The girl held out the lost gloves, sodden now and useless. 'It was a good thing we found them before the Boche.' There was slight condemnation in her voice. 'But if we

224

had not then we probably shouldn't have found you either.'

She smiled at him and relief surged through Alan's body. It was going to be all right. He would live. He would see Pamela again and the child. His mind was fuddled with shock and pain. The thought of the son that she carried gave him sudden courage. It was only much later that he remembered . . .

June arrived with unusual gales and rain, and when it was not raining it was murky and chill. The atmosphere along the Devon coast was heavy with apprehension, a strange disquiet that affected everyone. The waiting troops, more than a hundred thousand or so it was guessed, were mostly kept cramped in various embarkation areas and airfields for the sake of security. The careless laughing GIs were not seen around the towns and villages any more.

Mary Turner, walking her dogs on the cliff top from where she could see for some distance inland as well as the whole vast sweep of the bay, was aware of a brooding intensity like the lull before a great storm. She was impressed and yet uneasy too as she saw the vast armada of men and machinery that filled every vacant space. It was not only the evacuated area now that was commandeered. Wherever there were discreet fields that could be used as parking places equipment was stored, and every small bay and river was crowded with ships and strange-looking craft of every conceivable size and shape. The whole area seemed to be waiting breathlessly for something immense that was about to happen, the great battle that was to break shortly and would change the course of the war. Though all was secret, though nothing definite was known, and even the newspapers retained a fairly discreet silence, yet everyone who lived within a few miles of the sea knew that the assault on the Germans over the Channel must take place soon. Only the weather failed to co-operate.

Each day Mary walked and looked and said nothing. She thought of the men she had come to know, the Americans who had helped with the evacuation, Lawrence Lawson in particular. Pamela had not mentioned him in any of her letters, but Mary

225

knew that they had been in love. Yet she hoped the silence meant that the affair was over for good. The war would probably sort everything out anyway, she thought grimly.

Ben Yates, much to his delight, had managed to get the job of official Coast Watcher for his bit of cliff-top, and was thus more knowledgeable than most. Sometimes he did night duty, and in the early morning of June 6th he stood in the rain and the wind and pulled off his hat as a symbol of respect and awe. Wave after wave of bombers passed overhead towards France and as he watched he saw the dark Normandy sky lit vividly by flares and searchlights and then by the fires started by the British bombs. He could feel the vibrations of explosions. Even here, more than ninety miles away, the very cliff top seemed to throb in sympathy. He knew that the stormy sea below him was full of ships and longed for daylight yet feared it too.

''Tis a sight worth seeing,' he reported to his wife when he arrived home later for a quick breakfast. 'The sea be jam-packed with the poor devils going over there to their deaths.'

'That don't sound very patriotic,' Wendy Yates told him as she handed him a plate of fried eggs and bread. 'And don't say nothing like that in front of her.' She nodded up towards the ceiling. 'Molly's feeling a bit poorly and she'm having a lie in. She still can't forget them bodies on the beach even though 'twas a few weeks ago now. Keeps thinking 'twas that Delmer of hers.'

'Don't be sentimental, woman,' Ben said, his mouth full of egg. 'He weren't never hers anyway, and the sooner she forgets all about him the better. She'm still a pretty girl and when her've dropped that baby and we've adopted en, then she'll be better. You mark my words.'

Wendy sat down opposite him and pushed her egg around her plate. 'That's as maybe,' she said. 'But she'm pining if you ask me.'

'Women!' Ben shrugged his shoulders dismissively. 'All they wants is a fellow, and when they gets their comeuppance they complain.'

'And every reason to,' Wendy retorted. 'There'll be plenty of 'em left alone and complaining after this day's out. Them Yanks was determined to leave their mark behind. There'll be a load of little uns for us to remember them by.'

'That be a bit heartless,' Ben said. He looked at his wife in surprise. 'What with the poor buggers out there getting sea-sick I shouldn't wonder, and then being shot to bits as a reward, well, I think they was entitled to some fun before they went.'

'That's as maybe, and just the sort of thing I'd expect from a man. And don't swear, Ben Yates. Not in this house anyway. I keep telling you!' Wendy sniffed and got up from the table. ''Tis time you was gone,' she said. 'And mind not to say nothing over at Kernwell about what you saw.'

'No need to keep quiet now,' Ben commented. 'It's started, woman. We're going to give those Jerries the surprise of their lives!'

'I hope you're right,' Wendy said as she cleared the breakfast dishes. 'I just hope you're right or there'll be no future for any of us.' Then she went out into the wind and the rain to feed the clucking hens which ran to her at the sound of the opening door.

Alan had been in the loft above a small barn for three weeks. He had been very frightened at first. All his clothes had been taken from him when he was brought in cold, wet, and half dead. He had been given some thick unwholesome garments to wear and knew that if he was discovered dressed in the rough clothes of a French peasant, the Germans would probably shoot him as a spy. Without his uniform he'd have no protection. But after two days the girl carried his clothes back to him. She smiled and put them carefully on the box under the window.

'They are dry now, Monsieur,' she told him. 'I have washed some of them. You had mud and blood everywhere and they were very wet. I am sorry that it took so long.'

Since then he had been incarcerated in this place, never speaking to anyone but the girl, never able to breathe a whiff of fresh air, and nothing to do but read the books she brought to him. They were all French. 'I'm sorry about that, Monsieur,' she said. 'We daren't risk having English books here. The Germans come

227

occasionally and twice they have searched the farmhouse.'

'You speak good English. Where did you learn?' He had not been able to keep the surprise from his voice and she'd laughed at him.

'You call us peasants, but we go to school, you know!'

He flushed in shame. 'I'm a farmer,' he told her. 'And I went to school, too, but my French is very bad.'

'Then you will make it better.' She pointed to one of the books. 'See, there is a dictionary. If you spend all your time here reading French books you will be fluent, and I will speak to you in French too. You may as well make good use of your time.'

She brought him food regularly, washed his clothes and emptied his slops, a chore that gave him considerable embarrassment but which she had shrugged off. 'I do many unpleasant things,' she said briefly.

He didn't even know her name. 'It is better that you know nothing about us,' she said, and night by night he lay under an old blanket thinking about her words, shivering at their sinister implication and cursing his own vulnerability and helplessness. Most of all he feared the danger that his presence might bring to these simple good people who were sheltering him. For hours he would listen to the incessant bombardment, recognizing the sound of British bombers above him, longing to be up there in the freedom of the night sky. He was better now, his wound almost mended and the fever that had racked him for that first awful week gone completely. When he thought of Pamela it was with indifference. If he thought of the future at all it was in a detached and dispassionate way. The only thing that mattered was getting back into the air, back to his guns, back to smashing the Jerries. All his fury was directed at them.

He longed to talk more to the girl who looked after him but her visits to the stable were short and she seldom said more than was necessary. She was small and dark and had a sort of quiet efficiency that irked him somewhat. He realized that he was totally dependent on her, dependent on a woman once more as he had once been dependent on his mother long ago. At least it seemed long ago, another life altogether.

228

One day there was a difference in the girl. The headscarf that she normally wore was missing and her hair flowed about her shoulders. She came to him with excitement shining in her eyes and a buoyancy in her step that he had never seen before. 'They have landed,' she told him. 'The allies. They have landed and everything is going well for them. Soon perhaps they will be here and you will be free.' She set down the bread and cheese she carried and came over to him. Then she continued in French – rapid excited French that he would have found impossible to follow before he came here, but now he understood her almost without effort. Suddenly and unexpectedly she took both his hands in hers and planted a kiss on his cheek, two kisses in fact, one on either side of his face in the French way.

As she spoke he saw clearly in his mind the long stretch of curving beach near Morelake, the Yanks, the guns and the tanks. He took her in his arms and crushed her small body to his, kissing her firmly on the lips. 'Thank God,' he said as he released her. 'Thank God they've come at last.'

She stood back from him and stared into his eyes. 'You will be able to get back to your Pamela,' she whispered.

'Pamela? How did you know?' He was instantly on the defensive.

'You talked a lot when you had the fever,' she said. 'A baby too, and a little girl called Jane.'

He felt a tremor of unease wondering what he had given away. There must have been something for she moved over to the tiny cobwebby window and stared out at the yard below, not waiting for an answer.

'What is past is past,' she said, 'and a baby is precious.'

He could hardly hear the words for her mood had changed and there was sadness suddenly in every line of her. She reverted to English, speaking slowly and thoughtfully.

'You have . . . ?' He didn't know what to say.

She turned to face him and he saw a haunted look in her eyes. 'Not me,' she said. 'My mother. She went with the Boche. I am so ashamed. That's why we have no friends. We're hated by everyone who knows. She was very pretty then in the early days

229

of the war. My father was so angry that he nearly killed her. But she died anyway when the child was born and I'm bringing him up. My father wouldn't look at him for a long time, called him a German bastard. But . . . but I love him, Alan. He can't help his beginnings. I love him, and I think that my father one day will accept him.'

Pamela switched on the wireless set for the news. Then, as she heard the clipped and perfect voice of the announcer telling her that the momentous day had arrived at last, she put her hands to her mouth and closed her eyes, her whole body filled at once with a mixture of emotions. The allies had landed on the beaches of Normandy. She could hear Lawrence's voice, see his face in her mind, and she was sure that he was dead, killed on those French beaches that were supposed to be just like the ones around her home. And Alan too, both of them gone from her life for ever. She sat down and tried to calm herself. It might not be so. She could be sure of nothing except the things the news reader was saying. She tried to concentrate. It had been at first light and so far things had gone well in spite of the appalling weather. The beaches were taken and the allies were forging inland.

She and Jane were alone in the house and Richard was the first to return after his daily walk. As soon as she heard the click of the front door she ran to him and threw her arms around him. 'Uncle Richard,' she gasped. 'Have you heard? They've landed. It's happened at last.'

'Careful, lass,' he said. 'You mustn't get so excited, not in your state.'

Excited? Hardly excited, she thought, but emotional, yes. She felt highly emotional. She led the way back into the kitchen and sat down. 'It was on the news,' she said quietly. 'The allies landed in France this morning.'

'God bless them,' Richard said. 'Those poor lads need our prayers.' He pulled out his handkerchief and blew his nose in embarrassment.

Mrs Baines, coming in soon after, was equally taken with the need for supplication to the Almighty. 'Us'll have to pray for them,' she commented. Then her thought turned to more selfish matters. 'And now that the Yanks have gone, perhaps us'll be able to go home. Scotland be all right if you're born to it, but give me Devon any day.'

The comment made Pamela laugh and lightened the atmosphere a little. 'Yes, Mrs Baines,' she said. 'I'm longing to see Burlcombe again.' She paused and added guiltily, 'And Morelake too, of course.'

'We want that babe of yours born at home, don't we, not up here or he'll be wearing a kilt and that'll look pretty funny down home.' Richard too had caught the sudden mood of optimism.

The mention of her baby however brought Pamela back to reality. Where would he be born? Morelake or Burlcombe? Would he be fair or dark, fathered by Alan or . . . she clasped her hands over her stomach and tried to think about holding him in her arms, a child of her very own, hers and no one else's. 'He's not due until September,' she said. 'We'll be home by then.'

'Aye, lass, you're probably right,' Richard said, using some of the Scots words that especially appealed to him and which he had adopted with amused gusto. 'The wee laddie'll be born in his own native land, I hope. And by September us'll have chickens round the door and some cows and sheep in the fields.' He became thoughtful. 'I doubt there'll be much to harvest, but by this time next year . . . well, us'll see!'

Pamela was suddenly weary. There was so much to do and she guessed that Uncle Richard was being more than optimistic. From the few bits of information she had gleaned from Mary's letters the land was in a terrible state. But he was so cheerful and confident that she didn't want to destroy his day dreaming.

'Us should write to the authorities and find out about going back,' he went on. 'You do it, Pamela. You're good with letters.'

'All right, Uncle Richard,' she said. 'I'll do it now.' But as she went to fetch her writing case she could only think of Lawrence. Going back to Devon would bring the memories flooding back and for a few moments she thought that she would prefer to stay here for ever, surrounded by strangers and with an identity that she could forge for herself, an existence that she could invent and which would be just as she wished it to be. I wouldn't have a past to come to terms with, she said to herself as she looked out of her window over the cold waters of the Firth. But she knew that it could never happen. Running away from your problems was no good at all. You had to stand up and face them. She knew that she would be strong and resolute, and anyway Burlcombe was waiting for her, beautiful Burlcombe, her inheritance.

'Aunty Baines says we're going back to see Olivia's angel,' Jane said when Pamela returned to the warmth of the small kitchen. 'Then we can give her some flowers, can't we, Pammy? I mean, Mummy,' she added. 'Will you still be my mummy when we go back home?'

'Yes, darling,' Pamela said with a glow of happiness. 'I shall always be your mummy now.'

Olivia's angel! She thought of her own mother. She still read the old journal from time to time. Burlcombe would have been Olivia's now had she lived. For a moment Pamela wondered yet again about her unknown father. There were so few details in the journal on which she could base any true picture and she wondered if she would ever know more than it revealed. Aunt Maud had consistently refused to acknowledge the fact of fatherhood, both Pamela's and, later, Jane's. Pamela's thoughts veered, as they often did when she began questioning and remembering, to the awfulness of Jane's conception. She had thought those memories were fading at last, but here they were, suddenly back, trying to terrorize her again.

Then she saw in her imagination the graceful marble statue, Olivia's angel, as Jane always called it, and remembered Lawrence looking at it with her in the quiet graveyard. In imagination she felt his kiss and blushed for the memory, but she had to admit that if she thought about that long enough it helped a little to erase the other. And with her child's eyes upon her and the word 'Mummy' on her lips, the memory of the rape hadn't the same power to hurt as it once had.

232

But would she ever be able to forget Lawrence? No, she never would, she decided. But whether he remained in her mind as just a wonderful dream of the past or a very real concern of her future years depended on the coming baby. She thought of the little one growing so strongly inside her. She could feel him kicking now and her heart was filled both with love and with disquiet. Well, she would know in September. Would the first glimpse of his downy hair tell her for sure? Would he look at her with a baby version of Lawrence's eyes or with the appraising stare of Alan?

Molly Yates was also thinking about her coming baby and for her there was no doubt about the identity of its father. The only worries she had were for Delmer's fate. She wandered disconsolately on the cliff top near Shercombe and as near as she could get to the beach. She often took longer walks too up to the barriers of the evacuated areas. One day her mother walked with her.

'I could do with a bit of sunshine,' Wendy Yates commented. 'Now the invasion be started the weather seems to have come to its senses.'

At last the skies looked more as they should in mid-summer but Molly fretted as she puffed up the slope trying to keep up with her mother. Her cotton frock was tight and uncomfortable, adding to her discomfort.

'And it'll get tighter,' her mother said without sympathy in answer to her moans. 'I'll see if I can let it out for you.'

'Thanks.' Molly stared out at the sea which was blue now and calm and for a moment she could see Delmer's careless laughing face in the white puffy clouds. 'It looks lovely, don't it? But thinking about all them men what got drowned even before they had a chance to fight the Jerries, well, it makes me think I'll never enjoy the beach and the sea again.'

'Oh yes you will, especially when that baby of yours wants to go and build sand castles.'

Molly shivered. 'That's as maybe,' she said. 'We'll see. I wish September was here. I just wants to get rid of the kid and give

233

'im over to you, Mum. Then I wants to forget all about Delmer and the Yanks and the war. I just want to go off somewhere and start living all over again.'

They had reached part of the barbed-wire barrier that stretched across the road and both women stopped and stared over into the now desolate and empty landscape. The hills rose all around them and everything was silent and forlorn, a landscape of ghosts. ''Tis all empty,' Molly said at last. 'I never seen it like this. I can't even hear no birds.'

They both stood, subdued and almost frightened by the brooding stillness. They could see trees below with ugly leafless branches ripped and torn, and hedgerows and fields with huge brown gaps where shells had exploded.

'I wonder what the houses be like,' Wendy whispered. 'And the churches. Surely they haven't practised round them?'

'I dread going home,' Molly said. 'When'll we have to go, do you think?'

'The sooner the better.' Wendy's voice sounded ominous. 'I wants to see what the damage is.'

Suddenly a pigeon flew from the wood nearby and Molly stared at it. 'Look, Mum,' she said. 'That's the first bird I seen. All the little ones have taken fright. Perhaps the others'll come back now?'

'Praps,' Wendy replied. 'Let's get back anyway. It makes me shiver looking over there. It's sort of threatening somehow, all empty and strange as though it been cursed.'

Molly looked at her mother with surprise for she wasn't usually given to such fanciful thoughts. 'Only cursed by people,' she remarked. 'It be full of unexploded shells and things, I heard tell. And worse things,' she added darkly.

'What worse things?'

'Bodies,' Molly said. 'I keeps thinking about it. Bodies in the fields. I hope 'tisn't true or I'll never go walking on my own again.'

'That was only rumours,' Wendy declared. 'The bodies, I mean. And as for the shells . . . well, the authorities'll have to clear them all up, won't they, before we can go back. And that'll take a long time.'

'I reckon my baby'll be born afore we'm back,' said Molly with a sniff. 'And a good thing too if you ask me. I don't feel like facing all that work in this state.' She looked down with distaste at her swollen figure and was reminded of Pamela. 'And Pamela Saunders'll be coming home soon, I suppose,' she added.

'And her poor dear hubby missing, believed killed,' Wendy said.

Molly glanced at her mother and saw no glimmer of anything in her face other than slight sadness. If Alan did indeed fail to come home though, she thought, well then, a lot of problems would be solved. She immediately felt guilty for her wicked thoughts. 'Perhaps he've landed in France and he'm just hiding somewhere?' she murmured, trying to make her voice sound hopeful.

'Praps,' Wendy replied. 'We'll know soon anyway. France'll be free before long if things go right. I reckon that ole Hitler must be shivering in his shoes at the thought of all they Yanks out to get him.'

Molly laughed and together the two of them retraced their steps to their cottage. She wasn't going to worry about anything, Molly decided firmly. If this old war was going to be over soon then that was the only thing that really mattered.

# EIGHTEEN

*Olivia's Journal – 12th August 1923*
*I have spoken to the brother and sister from Ash Manor!*
*After lunch I was allowed to go for a walk on my own as*
*Maud had a headache. It was Mallory who made my wishes*
*come true. He ran down to the beach and almost knocked*
*the boy over in his excitement. He went into the water, then*
*came out and shook himself all over them and ran back to*
*me. Of course I had to reveal myself and the boy was*
*entranced with Mallory. He said that he had never seen such*
*a huge dog. We talked for quite ten minutes. They are twins*
*and both so nice. Their names are Daniel and Sarah, names*
*from the Bible. I wonder why they don't attend church and*
*why Maud forbids me to mix with them?*

Alan wondered about his precise whereabouts. The girl who
looked after him had said that she couldn't risk giving him a map
just yet. She wouldn't tell him where he was either. 'The less
you know the better, for the time being,' she had said. 'When
the allies arrive, then you'll be able to have all the information
you want.'

He knew that when he baled out his plane had been some
considerable way inland and that the allies were advancing
slowly, but he had no idea how long they would take to get here.
Sometimes, when there was something definite to report, the girl
was excited, and especially so if the latest village to be freed was

237

one she knew. But in the midst of her happiness Alan was aware that there was fear too for the small half-brother whom she said she loved.

'Do you think they will turn on him when the Allies come?' she asked one day in July when the news was good, when the sounds of gunfire could be heard faintly in the distance, and the air was heavy with the heat of midsummer carrying the scent of honeysuckle which had pushed its way through the broken window-pane. 'He's such a little boy. Surely they couldn't . . .'

'Of course not.' Alan tried to sound confident. 'And your mother is dead. They will say it was the will of God.' He spoke slowly so that she could follow his words, just as she did when she replied to him in French.

'Yes. They have always said that she was punished for what she did. but the baby is here, isn't he? We've kept him.'

Alan was filled with a sudden wild rage, almost despair. He was angry not with her but with the war, with people's unreasoning prejudice, with himself, with everything. 'What the hell does it matter who his father is? He's just a kid, isn't he? They can't take it out on a kid!'

She looked at him sadly, obviously not understanding all that he said. 'While the Boche are here the villagers will do nothing,' she whispered. 'But after the Germans have gone, who knows?' She shrugged her shoulders.

She suddenly appeared very vulnerable, very young. Alan wished that he knew her name and was filled with a desire to protect her and the unknown German bastard whom she said she loved. He surprised himself with his feelings.

'Do you know that five of our men were lined up and shot in revenge for a German officer killed?' She continued in French and he had to strain to hear her. His understanding of the language had improved but her words were scarcely audible. 'They were the sons and husbands, Alan, of the people here, our neighbours. They will never forget.'

There was silence between them then, broken only by the sound of clucking hens in the farmyard below. At last she spoke again. 'After things like that, revenge will be sweet.'

The silence descended again. Alan felt that there was nothing he could do, no comment he could make that would help. He could find no way of coming to terms with all the miseries of the world, his own included. The girl was standing at the window and he looked at her back, at her hair which today was tied in two thick plaits which hung down either side of her head. She looked so young – young enough to be at school, playing games, enjoying life.

She said without turning round, 'They shave the heads of collaborators, you know.'

'They won't do that to you!' Alan's words were fierce and he realized that his voice was raised dangerously. He paused and speedily collected his wits. He must be quiet, almost silent at all times. 'It was your mother who collaborated,' he whispered angrily. 'Not you. What could you do with the child, for God's sake? Throw him in the ditch?'

She turned and looked at him. 'Will you hurry with your soup, please?'

'God, how can you think about food?' He suddenly wanted to fold her in his arms, keep her safe for ever.

'Because there is not very much of it. Because I have to scrape and save every little bit to make enough for all of us.'

He was ashamed. He turned to the enamel bowl and started to eat quickly. It was delicious and he was aware of her eyes watching him as he ate. 'I'm sorry,' he said.

'It's nothing. I can understand your anger.'

A sudden thought struck him. 'I shall be here when this village is liberated,' he said. 'I shall tell them of all that you have done for me. I owe my very life to you and to your father. That must count for something.'

She laughed bleakly. 'Perhaps.'

'You are risking your lives to keep me here. They'll know that.'

'It's nothing,' she said as she gathered up the now empty dish and the tin mug. 'We have to do it.'

Alan laughed a little bitterly. It was the biggest understatement he had ever heard. If he was found by the Germans the whole family would be shot, one by one.

'When we're liberated by the Yanks or whoever arrives here first, then I shall talk to your villagers,' he said. 'I shall make sure that they know. I shall make them promise to accept your . . .'

'Our German bastard! Yes, Alan. Thank you. It might work.' She smiled at him as she lifted the trap door. It was a grim little smile. She had placed the cup and dish on the floor. 'Just hand those to me,' she said, 'when I'm on the ladder.' Her voice was matter-of-fact now. 'Keep hidden and quiet. Soon you will be back with your Pamela and you will forget all about us.'

When she was gone and the trap door closed again on his solitude he felt ashamed. He had been handing out advice to the girl, telling her that the fact of a child's parentage shouldn't matter. Well, of course it mattered. Why had he sounded so impossibly priggish? He could sometimes hear the German baby crying. He could hear it now and was consumed suddenly with longing for a son of his own, a boy who was flesh of his flesh and not some Yank's bastard. He clenched his fists hard and thumped the mattress violently until dust flew out and enveloped him in its stale and foetid odour.

In spite of the affection he felt for the French girl he was desperate to be away from the need to stay cooped up in this hot dusty place. He longed for his fields and the open skies, and even, in a perverse way, for Pamela.

He had frequently suggested to the girl that he should leave, try to make his way back to the coast. But although the wound on his head had healed, his leg was painful and he knew he was still weak. But he hated being the cause of danger to her. Whenever he mentioned this the girl would smile at him, and the last time she had put her fingers firmly onto his lips. 'It's a risk we've taken all through the war,' she said. 'There have been others like you, and the resistance used to have an escape route. But now it is not possible, and it won't be for much longer. We shall be liberated soon.'

Occasionally he had considered leaving without her knowledge, but she had always guessed at the reason for his restlessness and on the days when his impatience had been almost too much to bear she had usually come with some special morsel of food, sometimes a little wine, and with a certain grim determination in her voice. 'If you want to survive, and if you want us to live too, then for just a little longer you must be patient. Please, Alan, obey orders. Just for a little while more.'

Obey orders! He had laughed bitterly at the words. How he hated taking orders from a woman, even this special woman who had saved his life! But there was no choice. He must stay until the village was liberated, and then he would plead for the German baby. It would repay her a little for all she had done for him.

Frequent nightmares didn't make his life easier. On the ancient horse-hair mattress that served for a bed he would often fall into a troubled sleep, and during the worst nights, his dreams took him far back into the past . . . He shouted in his sleep and thumped the mattress so that dust filled his nostrils and he awoke coughing in the stifling heat, and terrified in case his English voice should have been heard by some German or collaborator on the road that ran alongside the yard.

As July gave way to August Pamela was less and less inclined to walk far and had to be persuaded by an anxious Mrs Baines to go outside at all. 'You'm pining for that man of yours in spite of all you do say about the other one!' she stated frankly. ''Tisn't no good for baby if you'm just sitting around here all miserable, and 'tisn't no good for Janey either.'

'A lot of our airmen are being found,' Pamela said as she heaved herself from the chair. She indicated something she had just read in the newspaper. 'They've been hiding until the allies get to them. Do you think . . . ?'

'I don't think nothing,' Mrs Baines said. 'If Mr Saunders be alive then you'll be hearing soon, but they got to go slowly, them poor lads, what with all the mines and bombing and things.'

Pamela wasn't immediately sure who had to go slowly. She presumed that Mrs Baines meant the allied forces. Her thoughts turned to Lawrence. He had said nothing about what part he expected to play in the invasion. Sometimes she had asked him, but he had always replied with a laugh and often with the irritating words she had become so used to: 'Careless talks costs lives!' She could remember him now so clearly enunciating the words from the posters that were displayed all over the place. He had tried to imitate an English upper-class accent and they had laughed together at his efforts.

She thought of him on the beaches of Normandy, or further inland perhaps by now if he had survived the April mishap. She often felt that both of them, he and Alan, must be dead. But perhaps they were not? Perhaps Alan was hiding somewhere? Perhaps Lawrence would enter some French village victorious and find Alan, liberate him!

She tried to shake the silly ideas out of her head. She was getting fanciful. It must be the baby kicking and thrusting about inside her, the child of one of them. 'I'll walk along to the point,' she said quickly. 'Coming, Jane?'

Together they walked at the sea's edge and she considered the future once more. She could see the long curving beach at home in her imagination and it was without its barbed wire, clear and golden and waiting for them. 'We'll go back to Devon soon,' she said to Jane. 'And we can go on our beach and swim. It'll be warm.'

'And we'll have the baby, won't we?'

'Yes, darling. You'll have a little brother.'

'Will he be my real brother?'

Pamela paused and her heart raced a little.

'Of course. What else could he be?'

'He might be my sister,' Jane said seriously.

Then they looked at each other and laughed and the world was right again.

'Can we race, Mummy?' Jane said, tugging at her hand.

'I'm too fat to race,' Pamela protested. 'In a few weeks' time. Then I'll race you, I promise!'

* * *

The news came towards the end of August. Alan was safe, liberated, in hospital. He would be home soon.

'Hospital? What's wrong with him then?' Pamela held the telegram and had visions of horrific burns, totally disabling injuries.

'Don't be so mazed, girl,' Richard said. 'They wouldn't say he'd be home soon, would they, if he was seriously ill?'

Mrs Baines added her assurances. 'Course not, deary. Just a check up, I should think.

The realization that he was alive dawned on her slowly at first. Then gradually the fact of his imminent reappearance began to take hold of her. He would be here soon. He was her husband. He would expect things. He would look at her baby with . . . with hatred perhaps? She shivered and put her hands protectively over her stomach.

The letter arrived a few days later, a long letter from Alan himself posted from some hospital in the South of England. It was merely his leg that was the problem. It had been injured in the drop and they were keeping him in for a couple of weeks. Then followed three closely written pages. She read them over many times with increasing amazement. He talked of a girl who had saved his life, of a German baby whom he had tried to protect when the local people were bent on revenge. It wasn't that the child would have been physically hurt, he wrote, but he had been able to stay with the girl and the child, refusing to go until he had the villagers' promise that there would be no reprisals of any sort. He would return, he had told them. He wanted to see the child after the war.

Pamela held the letter in her hand and was almost convinced at first that it must have been written by someone else. Not one sentence of it sounded like her husband. Yet it was definitely Alan's handwriting and he had signed his name clearly at the end. There was no mention of herself or of her coming child. He just went on and on about this girl and the German baby. Perhaps he was injured more than she knew? Maybe he was slightly mad? Or could he have fallen in love with this French girl? Something had certainly changed him. She anticipated his arrival with more anxiety than ever, but also with a glimmer of hope.

By the end of August Paris was free, Alan had still not come to Scotland and there was no word yet from Devon to say that Burlcombe or Morelake could be reoccupied.

'Some folks be going back,' Mrs Baines remarked. 'But it do look like your baby'll be born here in Scotland after all. Well, who'd ever have thought it? Them Yanks left Devon back in June and here we are, still with no place to go to!'

''Tisn't as bad as all that,' Richard commented. He was sitting in the old companionable armchair by the fire and Pamela, looking at him, guessed that he had almost come to like Craemore.

'There'll be a lot of work to do when we go back,' she said. 'Perhaps a few more weeks here will be best all round.' Privately she felt that she couldn't face the trauma of going home and all that it would mean just yet. When her child was born she might feel more enthusiastic.

On September 1st 1944 Pamela looked down at her new baby daughter and revelled in the knowledge that no one would take this child away from her. She remembered Jane's birth, and the love she felt then for the little blonde scrap in her arms, and finally the tearing grief when Aunt Maud had claimed her and decreed firmly that love must be completely denied.

Pamela smiled to herself. She was more confident now. She knew that the difficult years since Jane's birth had changed her considerably, and now she was rich, the owner of Burlcombe. Even if Maud had been strict and unloving in life, in her death she had been generous.

'Baby must go back to the nursery now.' The nurse bore down upon her and prepared to take the little warm bundle out of her arms. 'Mother must get some sleep after all that hard work.'

'Please can I keep her a little longer?' Fear rose in Pamela's heart and this woman assumed the proportions of a tyrant, became for an instant another Aunt Maud.

'Just while I get the others then,' she said grudgingly. 'They all have to be changed before I go off duty.'

Pamela shifted herself painfully in bed and cradled her baby in her arms. She looked down at the blue eyes that seemed to be staring into hers and brushed the cloud of dark hair from the little round head. Were they Alan's eyes or her own perhaps? But the hair was Lawrence's. A sudden chill encompassed her body, replacing the previous euphoria. Secretly she had wanted Lawrence's child, Lawrence's son in fact, and now there was this little girl lying placidly in her arms and she could belong to either one of them. Alan would look at her and see only the hair, the dark hair that was nothing like his own short fair crop or hers. This was another child that he would not want. She shivered slightly and wondered how long it would be until he came here to Scotland.

The nurse broke into her thoughts again. 'I must take baby now,' she said. 'You'll have her back in the morning. You need a good night's sleep. Make the most of it.'

Pamela relinquished her hold on the precious little bundle and managed a smile. 'I shall call her Rachel,' she said. She had read again part of Olivia's journal just before she was rushed into the hospital. It was the bit where her mother had written that the two young people from Ash Manor had Bible names. Daniel – Olivia's eventual lover – her own father? – and Sarah. Well, her child too would have a Biblical name.

The nurse looked down at the baby. 'Yes,' she said. 'That suits her very well. She's really bonny, like Rachel in the Bible. I expect your hubby's dark, is he?'

'She has blue eyes,' Pamela said defensively, unable to say that Alan's hair was as fair as the summer corn.

'Most babies have blue eyes, deary,' the woman replied. 'They're sure to darken down later on!'

Alan came at last. One golden day towards the end of September he arrived on the ferry from Invergarth, feeling a strange mixture of emotions. Sometimes there was the twisting agony of betrayal, but there was apprehension too. He feared to look at the new baby, the child who might be his daughter. He had heard of her

245

birth with a strange emptiness, a lack of feeling. But the knowledge that she was female lessened the torment in his mind. He could hardly have borne to accept a male child who was not his . . . probably not his. He would have been a rival, a threat for the future, a Yankee bastard who would be there every day of his life to remind him, to challenge all his assumptions about himself. A girl would be less provocation. He could forget a girl. And there would be other children. He was determined about that now. As soon as Pamela was recovered from the birth, he would waste no time.

He had not told them the precise hour that he would arrive. As he strode purposefully up the cobbled street to the little house, he remembered the last time he had visited it. He had been so angry. How long ago it seemed. The weeks in France had changed him, he knew that. He considered himself to be quite a different person now. He thought of the days he had stayed in the French farmhouse after the allies had arrived, not as a prisoner any more but as a welcome guest.

There had been jubilation when the Yanks had triumphantly entered the village, cheering such as he had never heard before. He had looked at the peasants crowding round the armoured cars and tanks, and for the first time in his life had shed tears of joy, sharing their happiness. But the girl was not there. He knew her name now. There was no more need for secrets.

'Nicole Verlain,' she had told him. 'You may call me Nicole.'

She had stayed behind in the farmhouse when she heard the cheers and the shouting, and he had known that she was frightened for her little half-brother because of her mother's betrayal, the tainted German blood. He had been disinclined to believe her fears until he saw, to his horror, two other village women hounded out of their homes and hustled into the square.

There they were subjected to a ramshackle trial. A trestle table had been quickly set up on the cobbles and behind it sat a group of angry, grim-faced men. The women were held roughly, and after sentence was passed upon them their hair was savagely shaved from their heads. Then they were sent away, one of them with a baby in her arms. 'Collaborators! German whores! We spit upon them.' The words echoed round the square and Alan had shivered for Nicole.

He had gone quickly back to the farmhouse and had stayed with her until they came. Then he stood in front of her, thankful for his RAF uniform which she had sponged and pressed for him when she knew the allies were close. She had said she wanted him to look good for this special day.

He would never forget how they had poured through the unlatched door and then stopped suddenly at the sight of him. He had forced himself to speak calmly, in the best French he could muster. It was her mother and not she who had collaborated, he said, telling them what they already knew. The child was innocent, and if they harmed one hair of his head or of Nicole's then he would bring all the might of the combined allied forces down upon them in retribution. At that moment he almost believed his ability to do so. Were they going to stoop to the depths of degradation of Nazi thugs? he had asked. He had pulled himself to his full height and all the command and authority of his public school upbringing had suddenly come into its own. His voice held barely concealed scorn and rage and he had glared at them all, daring them to say a word or lift a finger against the woman and child cowering behind him.

Alan was proud of what he had done that day. As he walked up the little Scottish street and heard the gulls calling in the afternoon sky, he remembered again the heat of the French noon and the way the men had backed away from him. He had not let them go easily. He had forced a promise from them that they would not take out their anger with the Boche on the child or his family after he had gone, and he had told them that he would return when the war was finally over to see that they had kept their promise. He would bring his wife and children, he said, in a sudden inspired effort to bring back a sense of normality. They had finally shaken hands with him and returned later with some of the best wine that had been carefully hidden away for four years. The day that had begun with fear had ended with festivity, good nature restored and friendship promised. It was a day he would never forget, a day that had changed him, set all his values on end.

He stood now at the door behind which he would find his wife and the new baby, and Jane of course. He closed his eyes for a moment in a quick prayer for help. He had achieved a kind of faith during those weeks in France in addition to the other changes in his attitude to many things. Yet he was still apprehensive. He had thought about this moment so much, wondering if he was being given a second chance to mend his marriage.

He raised his hand to knock and then lowered it again, standing irresolute. He stood for a long time before he could bring himself to lift the brass knocker. Then he banged it purposefully three times and stood back and waited.

# NINETEEN

*Olivia's Journal – 30th August 1923*
*Daniel and Sarah are such fun. I meet them secretly when-*
*ever I can. Today Sarah had to stay indoors because of a bad*
*cold and I spent the time with Daniel. I have never been able*
*to talk to a boy alone before. I was quite scared at first, but*
*he is a perfect gentleman, as my sister would say. We went to*
*Fairy Bridge on the old packhorse route through the woods. I*
*told Daniel about the stories I used to make up of the fairies*
*who live in the boulders in the stream beneath. He didn't*
*laugh at me. He just looked at me with those strange blue*
*eyes of his and said that it was a magical place.*

It was Mrs Baines who opened the door. She took one look at
Alan and her homely country faced flushed with pleasure. 'Mr
Saunders,' she gasped. 'We been just longing for this day. Come
in, come in.'

He followed her through the outer porch and past the lobby
door which now stood open instead of being fastened securely
as it had been when he was last here. He remembered staring at
the stained glass set unsuitably in it and recalled with a pang of
remorse Pamela's white face etched against the ornate pattern
as she stood listening to his angry words. Judging by Mrs Baines'
welcome, Pamela had said nothing of what had passed between
them on that awful day back in the winter.

She was sitting on a low chair nursing her baby. As he entered, she looked up at him and pulled the child's shawl protectively over her breast. He took in every gesture, every line of her, and longed to stride over, to push the shawl aside, to gaze at mother and child, and to know, at last to know! Instead he smiled, a forced wooden smile. 'Hello, Pamela,' he said. It was all he could manage.

Mrs Baines had walked past him out to the small kitchen and had pulled the door shut behind her. Jane was nowhere to be seen.

In spite of her determination to remain calm and face him with confidence, when the moment actually arrived Pamela was terrified. She groped for something to say. She wanted to shout at him to come and take the child, acknowledge her, love her. She wanted to thrust the baby into his arms and so end all the months of doubting.

But instead she murmured, 'You're well again then?' The words sounded hollow, cold. 'Your injuries have mended properly now?'

'Yes. Nicole did her best, but she couldn't get a doctor. There were problems. I'm fine now, though. And you?' He was still standing across the room from her, his feet apparently rooted to the spot.

'I'm well too.'

The conversation was almost laughable, Alan thought grimly. Was this how two people who had suffered such traumas should behave to each other? He recalled the easy friendship with Nicole, the quickly flowing and spontaneous conversations they had enjoyed in the stuffy little barn during the last two or three weeks of his incarceration there. In spite of the barrier of their backgrounds, their differing language, they had never lacked for things to say.

He watched as Pamela rearranged her clothes, stood up, leaned the baby over her shoulder and gently patted its back. Then she wrapped the shawl more closely around the child and looked at Alan. Challenging him perhaps? There was a staircase leading from the room and she walked over to it. 'I'll just put her in her cot and we'll have a cup of tea.'

His heart sank. He was painfully aware of the terrible pallor of her face, the fear in her eyes. So the child wasn't his?

'I've called her Rachel,' Pamela said suddenly. 'I'm sorry you weren't here to help me choose.' She paused at the bottom of the stairs. 'Do you want to look at her, Alan?'

She held the little bundle out towards him and at last he felt the power of movement return to his leaden feet. He took the necessary few steps towards the two of them and looked down into a tiny screwed-up face, saw the dark fuzz of hair, and his heart sank. Then the eyes opened and seemed to be looking directly at him. He peered down, actually touched the shawl so that he could see more clearly. The eyes were blue, wide blue eyes staring into his. He looked at the little hand waving about so close to his and put his finger into the tiny fist and felt the baby softness of it. Delicate fingers closed around his large one. He had never seen anything so small, so perfect.

Feeling himself overcome with an emotion that only a few weeks ago would have been totally foreign and unknown, he pulled his hand away and took a step back. Angrily he blinked the threatening, shaming tears from his eyes and turned from her to sit down heavily on an old sagging armchair.

With Mrs Baines now bustling about there was no more time for emotion, for heartsearching or difficult conversation. She pulled out one half of the drop-leaf table and threw an elaborately embroidered cloth upon it. 'Afternoon tea! That's what we'll have today,' she announced. 'I made a cake for your homecoming, Mr Saunders. 'Tis still difficult what with all the rations and things, but we got three hens out in the back yard and they been especially obliging this week!'

'That's very kind of you, Mrs Baines,' he said automatically. He glanced at the best china she was setting out on the table and thought of his mother and the afternoon ritual of long ago. The last thing he wanted was cake!

Upstairs Pamela put the baby into the wooden cradle that had been borrowed from a neighbour. She tucked the shawl in carefully and looked at the tiny dark head. She was amazed at the change in Alan and for a second wished that she could go down to him and tell him that Rachel was certainly his. But would she ever know? Those blue eyes were her daughter's only hope of acceptance. She had seen the surprise in Alan's face as he saw them, the sudden tenderness. 'Please, God,' she whispered, 'don't let her eyes turn brown like the nurse said they would. Please, please, let her keep her blue eyes.'

In Devon, Molly Yates, standing in the garden of her old home, looked around at the desolation and listened to the uncanny silence. ''Tis bewitched,' she whispered.

'Don't be so daft, maid,' her father said. ''Tis just a mess, and we got to get it right again.'

Ben Yates, along with a few other farmers, had been given permission to return to his land and on one golden day in autumn he and his daughter had trudged over from Shercombe to see what had to be done before they could move back in. His wife had been left behind with Molly's baby. Wendy Yates had taken one look at her tiny grandson in the hospital a few weeks before, and had vowed that whatever the Yanks had done to the land, this precious little scrap of humanity made it all right. She could forgive them anything. She had the son she had always longed for. Molly had merely laughed. 'Then he's yours, Mum,' she had said. 'He can grow up thinking he'm my little brother!' The arrangement suited them all very well.

Ben Yates pushed open the front door. It swung drunkenly on one hinge. He went inside, followed closely by Molly. They stared in dismay at the leaves and other debris blown into heaps in every corner by the wind. Windows were smashed, hardly any panes remaining intact, and the rain had found its way inside. Wallpaper was peeling from the walls and the ceilings were stained and mildewed.

'You locked it up, Dad. I remember you handing the keys over to the information officer. How did it get in this state?' Molly was horrified by what she saw.

''Twas all the shelling, I suppose,' Ben replied. 'Blew doors off and windows in. I seen lots of other places in the same mess.

We get compensation, though. It'll all be put right.'

'I should hope so.' Molly went up the dirty stairs to her little room, the little sanctuary where she had sobbed out her grief over Delmer. That had been just before they moved out. She traced her finger along the dusty windowsill and then peered through the small cracked pane of glass. She could just see to the edge of her father's fields. One seemed to have been ploughed or dug. She called to Ben.

'Come and look, Dad. What have they done to the end field, do you think?'

She moved away for him to see and he rubbed the glass clean with his sleeve and then stared through it for a long time. 'Well,' he said at last, ''tis probably just shells that been and disturbed it.'

For some strange reason Molly shivered and then she ran down the stairs again, not wanting to stay up there. 'I don't know that I want to come back,' she said. ''Tis nice where we are.' She went out into the overgrown garden. There was no sound of bird or beast, just an eerie silence. She looked at the honeysuckle and brambles growing together in unbridled abandon where this time last year her mother had been picking the remaining few kidney beans. 'Mum's not going to like it,' she whispered as her father joined her. 'What with the baby an' all, she'm going to have a lot to do.'

Ben closed the door behind them but the lock was broken. He put a large stone at its base and then turned to her. 'Us'll go and report all this and then forget about it for a bit, maid. No good thinking about coming back till the road be repaired. Couldn't even get the cows here, let alone all our other clobber.'

They retraced their steps, avoiding the field with the strange uneven ground. 'Might be unexploded shells there,' Ben declared. 'They'm still clearing up. Us got to keep to the proper paths for now.'

'Could us go a bit further round by Morelake?' Molly said. She still thought frequently of Pamela. The news of Rachel's birth had reached her a week ago via Mary Turner. Mrs Turner had also said that Alan was safe and had gone to Scotland. Molly tried to imagine what had happened between him and Pamela. Was the baby fair like Mr Saunders or . . . She remembered the American lieutenant with his good looks and dark intelligent eyes. She wondered what had happened to him. Had he died on those awful Normandy beaches, or was he drowned like so many others on that April exercise, as her Delmer might have been? The thought always made her sad. Such a waste to be killed like that for no purpose.

It had all been kept secret and even now only a few local people knew about the hundreds who had been drowned weeks before D-Day. She remembered what she had seen on the beach and a few tears slid from her eyes.

Morelake stood desolate and silent, its ugly pebble-dash exterior made more unprepossessing by the shell marks that now covered the front. There was no glass at all in the windows. ''Tis even worse than our place,' Molly said. 'Mr Saunders won't be very pleased.'

'He'm in the same boat as all of us,' her father commented dryly.

'But him being a flier, it makes it worse somehow.'

'The authorities'll get it put to rights before he comes home for good.'

Molly sniffed. 'They better had too! What about Pamela's other place?'

'Burlcombe? I think from what I hears that 'tisn't as bad as some, though that's not saying much. That fussy old Maud Lindhurst won't be coming back, any road.'

'Dad!' Molly was shocked. 'You shouldn't speak bad of the dead!'

'Well, 'tis the truth. Her was always a thorn in the flesh. I couldn't never understand why Richard married her.'

'I expect he had his reasons,' Molly commented darkly. 'It ain't done him much good though. She didn't leave the place to him, did she?' Molly had heard about Pamela's legacy, that the house had been made over to her on Maud Lindhurst's death, and had been consumed with jealousy.

'He never expected to get it. Richard Lindhurst be a good

254

chap, and there's one thing I be sure about – whatever it was he married Maud for, it wasn't money!'

'Could we go over there now? I'd like to get a look at it.'

'I'm not walking no further on these roads,' Ben said firmly. 'When the authorities have made 'em right again, then praps we'll go.'

With that Molly had to be content and they retraced their steps in near silence back to Shercombe. On the way, as they passed close to the field that had been dug up so strangely, she suddenly shivered. 'What did they do with all them bodies, Dad?' she said. 'You know, all them what was drowned back last April. Hundreds of 'em, so they say.'

Ben looked at her. 'Buried somewhere hereabouts, I heard. But 'tis only rumours. And if they did, then they'd have taken 'em back to America by now.' His eyes followed hers as she stared at the uneven surface of the field. 'Don't get no fancy ideas, maid,' he said. ''Twasn't in this part anyway. 'Twas over t'other side near Strete if there's any truth in it.'

Molly looked doubtful but tried to believe him. She didn't want Delmer's ghost haunting her for the rest of her life.

Burlcombe stood proud and defiant against its backdrop of trees and shrubs which were mostly red-gold in their autumn glory. Richard stood and stared at it and was almost glad that Maud was not here to see the desolation. There was not one window left intact and the beautiful rowan tree that grew beside the path had several branches ripped from its trunk. There was a general air of desolation, and yet the house was still beautiful. It brought a lump to Richard's throat. He had always known that it was not to be left to him, that it was Pamela's inheritance. He didn't mind. That was only right and proper for she was a Belmont. Maud had left him enough to buy a small cottage and that was all he wanted. But first he must see to the restoration of this beautiful house and get it ready for Pamela and the two children. He had decided to come back alone. He would write and tell them when it was habitable again, he had stated firmly.

Mary Turner had insisted on meeting him at Newton Abbot

and driving him all the way here. She stood beside him, staring at the house. 'Well, I've seen worse,' she said. 'Come on, Mr Lindhurst. We'll go inside. I expect the door is unlocked.'

''Twas a bit stupid, all that locking of doors and handing the keys over before we had to leave,' Richard commented. 'From what I hear, nearly all the houses were broken into or the doors ripped off.'

'And it wasn't the soldiers who did all the damage either,' Mary said. 'A lot of it has been done since they left, since June. We don't know who the culprits are but the authorities think that gangs of louts came to steal whatever they could when they heard the houses were empty.'

'I'd like to strangle the lot of them,' Richard said. He walked towards the house, touching the rowan tree as he had often watched Pamela do.

Mary saw him and laughed. 'I didn't think you'd be super-stitious,' she remarked. 'But I must admit that whenever I see a rowan, I try to touch it if I can. It's supposed to ward off evil.'

'Do you believe that?'

'Not really. Just habit.'

Once inside the house they looked around in increasing amaze-ment. Door handles were missing, wires hung everywhere, there was no electricity and no light bulbs, and wallpaper hung from the walls in dismal trails.

'Have you been to Morelake?' Richard asked. 'Is that as bad?'

'Worse,' Mary said. 'But the authorities are going to pay full compensation and put everything right.'

'I don't know what to do first.' Richard sighed. 'We ought to get the land to rights and some stock back in the fields, but I need a place for Pamela and the kiddies.'

'They can come to me.' Mary's voice brooked no argument. 'I should love to have them. Is Pamela going back to Morelake or does she plan to live here?'

Richard shrugged his shoulders. 'I don't rightly know. I should think she'd come here until Alan gets demobbed, and that won't

be until after the end of the war.' Privately he doubted that he
would survive that long with so many aeroplanes being lost, and
then he felt immediately guilty as if thinking such a thing might
make it happen. They were standing in the sitting room and he
thought of the long brocade curtains that Maud had been so
proud of. Surprisingly the curtain rod was still in place. 'Good
thing we packed everything up,' he said. 'I suppose all our furniture and stuff is safe.'

'I'm sure it is,' Mary said hopefully. 'I'm working in the information centre again so I'll be able to trace it all for you now that
you're back.'

Pamela felt that a new era in her life was beginning. Scotland
was in the past now, Craemore a place she would always remember with affection, but this was home. They had managed the
long journey back without too much trouble. Jane had been
excited and Mrs Baines had taken almost complete charge of
Rachel. Then there had been a week spent with Mary, and now
they were on their way to Burlcombe at last.

'Do you think Rachel will like Burlcombe?' Jane wanted to
know.

Pamela laughed. 'I don't think she'll mind where we are as
long as she's warm and fed.'

'Was I like that, Mummy? Did I just want to be warm and
fed?'

'Just like that.' Pamela didn't add that it was Aunt Maud who
had given the regular four-hourly feeds and supplied all the
love and care. Bitterness towards her aunt was swiftly fading,
especially now that Jane had slipped easily into the habit of
calling her Mummy.

They were sitting in the back of Mary's van, the three of them
– or four if you counted Binks. Pamela's reunion with her little
dog the previous week had been boisterous and noisy but he was
now sitting quietly on the seat beside her, sniffing occasionally
at the strange bundle on her lap but otherwise content. Jane was
restlessly peering out of the windows, first one side and then the
other.

257

'Look, Mummy, the sea. There's the sea. Can I go and make castles?'

'I shouldn't think so. Not yet. When you're bigger and the war's over perhaps.' Pamela thought with a pang of fear of the mines that she believed had been buried in the innocent-looking sand at Goldpool beach.

'They cleared the mines,' Mary interrupted, guessing her thoughts. 'But there may be unexploded shells. It's still fenced off. In fact, there's a danger of shells everywhere, they say.'

'Then I wish we'd stayed at Craemore,' Jane pouted. 'It was lovely there. There was a long beach you could walk on, and pretty pebbles to find, and Uncle Richard helped me make castles.'

'Us'll make castles before long, lovey,' Mrs Baines said from the front seat. 'Goldpool's great for making castles.'

Pamela, with her new spirit of optimism and cheerfulness, was tempted to sing something about building castles in the air, or was it blowing bubbles? She resisted the desire, but ever since Rachel's birth she had experienced this wish to be irresponsible and carefree.

''Tis all them lost years of your childhood,' Mrs Baines had commented darkly. 'They got to come out somehow!'

Pamela had laughed but she guessed that there was a grain of truth in the words. It wasn't her childhood that she regretted so much as the years since the rape, since Jane's birth. Those years had been full of stress, repressed anger and frustration. Her marriage to Alan had made things no better, perhaps worse at first. But gradually she had felt that she had grown up, had learned to cope with life. She knew what love was really like now, and even though she was convinced that she would never see Lawrence again he had helped in the maturing process. And because of him, and because of her two lovely daughters, she was beginning to find happiness.

'My love for Lawrence was like a fairy tale,' she once confided to Mrs Baines. She wanted to add that it was a sort of magic that she could hug to herself for ever although nothing real would ever come of it, but Mrs Baines had no time for magic. The thought had made Pamela laugh. Alan had no time for magic either! Yet he too was changed. The war had done something to him, mellowed him. This thought added considerably to her optimism. Perhaps life was going to be good at last?

'We'll go to Fairy Bridge,' she said to Jane. 'It was one of my favourite places. Olivia liked it too. She wrote about it.'

'Are there really fairies there?'

'If you want them to be.'

Jane turned from the van window and stared at her. 'Olivia has an angel,' she said. 'You remember, Mummy, in the church-yard. Is an angel the same as a fairy?'

'A little bit the same. They're both special. We'll go and see the angel too,' Pamela said.

Richard was at the door to greet them. He strode over to the little van as Mary pulled it to a halt in front of the house. 'There's a fire in the sitting room, food in the cupboard and the kettle on the boil,' he said proudly. 'Welcome back to Burlcombe.'

Binks was the first one out. He bounded on to the drive and rushed round and round the garden in a frenzy of joy. Rachel, wakened suddenly by all the noise, started to wail, and then Sheppey rushed from the house and joined in the excitement, barking loudly. When they had all clambered out of the small van it was only Jane who was suddenly quite still. 'Aunty Maud would have liked to come back home, wouldn't she?'

For a second Pamela was shocked by the feelings of relief she felt that Maud was not in fact here! Was it a very sinful thing, she wondered, to be glad that someone was dead? Would she be punished for her wicked thoughts? She quickly passed Rachel to Mrs Baines and then scooped Jane up in her arms.

'Yes. Aunty Maud would have liked it. But even though she can't be with us, she'd want us to come back, . . . wouldn't she? We'll have to make Burlcombe nice again, just like it was when she was here.' She planted a kiss firmly on Jane's fair curls and set her down again. 'Now let's go in and see what Uncle Richard has already done,' she said. 'And I'm dying for a nice cup of tea.'

She was determined that her newfound happiness would not be spoilt by any ghosts. Only Lawrence's spirit would remain to haunt her, she hoped, and haunt was the wrong word anyway for such a desirable presence.

Mrs Baines' cottage, lying a few miles further inland, had not been so badly damaged as some. 'I'll stay as long as you want me,' she told Pamela. 'Then when you think you can manage, I'll go and put my own place to rights.'

Pamela wondered if she would ever be able to manage. The big house was a constant challenge. Now that winter had arrived again there were fires to be made every day as well as all the other myriad demands on her time and energy.

Then one day Richard dropped his bombshell. 'What would you think to me and Mrs Baines getting wed?' he said calmly, in a voice as impassive as he would use if he were asking for another piece of cake. He had just come in from his afternoon's work in the fields and was standing at the kitchen door in his socks. He padded over to the chair by the Aga and groped beneath it for his slippers. 'I don't mean right away,' he continued. 'Us wouldn't go and leave you in the lurch, but that cottage of hers'll be pretty lonely, and it needs a lot doing to it.'

Pamela was sitting in the other comfortable chair darning a pair of his socks. She looked up at him and was filled with dismay. Whatever would she do without the pair of them? She quickly strove to be less selfish. 'Well,' she said, 'that's grand news, Uncle. I had no idea . . .'

'We been talking things over, me and Mrs Baines,' he went on. 'And I been talking to Ben Yates too. His Molly needs a place and we thought this might be right for her.'

Pamela's spirits sank right into her shoes. Molly Yates here every day! Molly with her sluttish ways and knowing winks. 'Oh, no,' she said. 'I couldn't face Molly Yates every morning of my life!'

Richard laughed. 'Well then,' he said, 'think no more about it for the time being. We're in no hurry.'

In the days that followed, however, Pamela did think about

it. She felt differently about the two of them now. When they were all together at meal times, and in the evenings when Richard was reading his newspaper and she and Mrs Baines were sewing or knitting, there was a difference. The two of them were a couple and Pamela was the odd one out. It wasn't a comfortable feeling.

At last, just before Christmas, she made up her mind. 'You two had better get wed in the new year,' she announced. 'Jane's just dying to be a bridesmaid!'

# TWENTY

*Olivia's Journal – 12th August 1924*
*How can I write about the wonderful thing that has hap-*
*pened to me? I am in love! I am in love with the beautiful*
*Daniel. He is tall and strong and dark. Dark hair and blue*
*eyes – such striking eyes. He kissed me today. We walked*
*again to Fairy Bridge as we have done many times. There is*
*magic there.*
*I wish I could take him to Burlcombe. I wish Maud would*
*accept him and Sarah. Why will she not?*

Pamela thought she would never forget those first months of
1945. Each week brought something important to be commented
upon, rejoiced over or criticized.

At the beginning of February she discovered that she was
pregnant again and the knowledge brought mixed feelings. Mrs
Baines was considerably put out by the news. 'Too soon,' she
said. 'I don't know what he was thinking about. A pity he ever
got that last leave, if you ask me.'

But no one was asking her. Alan at least was delighted when
he heard. A child of his very own! One that he was quite sure
was really his. He had a new and jaunty look about him that one
or two of his fellow airmen crudely commented upon. And for
once he didn't mind, just laughed with them and shared his
triumph. And when he flew over Dresden and watched the city
below him burning, a vast fireball, he had no qualms. His sense

of fulfilment in his personal life overflowed into everything else.

Mary Turner was not so happy about either event. 'You haven't got your strength back yet from having Rachel,' she said to Pamela. 'You'll have to look after yourself.' Although she had quite liked Alan Saunders, the thought of him now was slightly distasteful. She could picture him in one of those great Lancasters as well as in Pamela's bed. She'd just been reading about the latest raids over Germany. 'I really didn't think we'd feel that it was necessary to bomb Dresden,' she said bitterly one bright February day, almost implying that it was Alan's fault. She had come over to Burlcombe for one of her frequent but hasty visits. 'James and I were there before the war, a beautiful city full of priceless paintings and wonderful old buildings. It always reminded me of Florence.' Her voice was full of regret. 'It's a smoking ruin now from what I hear.'

Molly Yates, knowing nothing of Florence or Dresden or anything more stimulating than Kingsbridge, breezed into the room with Rachel on her hip and a feeding bottle in her hand. 'Here you are,' she said to Pamela. 'She wants her feed. You just got time to do it before you fetch Jane from school.'

In spite of her earlier misgivings about Molly, Pamela was finding that the girl was of great use around the house and an acceptable companion too, always willing to tackle the worst jobs, and usually cheerful. She lived in, and in spite of all the differences between them, the two girls had achieved a certain careful kind of friendship.

Molly handed the baby to Pamela and prepared to take herself off again to the kitchen. She preferred the room with its two comfortable old armchairs and constantly warm Aga to the large drawing room that was only used now and then. She had lit a fire today in honour of Mary's visit. 'And to keep it aired,' Pamela had said. 'We must have it warm once a week at least.'

But Molly resolutely refused to sit there herself. In fact, she was not quite sure of her position in this house. Was she a maid or a companion or a sort of paid friend? 'A mixture of all three,' she had confided to her mother on her first weekend off.

'I bain't used to drawing rooms,' she had remarked to Pamela when she first saw its splendid proportions. The beautiful family portraits set once again on the refurbished walls had further disconcerted her. 'I couldn't sit there with all them ancients staring down at me,' she had said. 'Miss Olivia now, she's different. Her picture's all right.'

The painting of Olivia had been rehung in its place of honour in the hall. Molly had stared at it for a long time. 'I reckon that she's beautiful. Nice and friendly too.' Then she had frowned. 'And her cold and dead in the churchyard.' She had shaken her head and uttered only one word: 'Men!' before turning and marching back to the kitchen, just as she was preparing to do now.

Mary Turner glanced at the girl's bright country face and was glad that Pamela had someone to help her. She got up and smiled at Molly. 'I must go,' she said. 'Look after Pamela, won't you?' She stooped to kiss the baby's dark head, and gathered up her things. 'I'll be over next week to see what you want me to do for the wedding.' Then she looked at Pamela who was contentedly cradling Rachel close while the baby sucked at the boat-shaped bottle with enthusiasm. 'She seems to be quite happy with her new regime,' she said. 'Is everything going well?'

'Fine,' Pamela replied. 'I should have liked to go on feeding her myself, but everyone insisted that it wasn't a good idea now that there's another on the way, so I've given in. I won't let anyone else give her the bottle though. Molly keeps trying to persuade me, but it's a pleasure I'm determined to be selfish about.' She smiled up at Mary, but didn't add that the early forcible weaning of Jane had been so traumatic that she was quite resolved to form a close bond with this new small daughter. 'I shall be glad of all the help I can get with the wedding though,' she added. 'I've a long list of things to be done.'

After Mary had chugged away in her little van and Rachel had finished her feed Pamela carried the baby into the kitchen. Her mind was full of this coming wedding between Richard and Mrs Baines. It was the next event of note and would need a lot of careful planning.

Molly too was thinking about it as she peeled potatoes.

'I can't get over Mrs Baines being the new Mrs Lindhurst,' she said. 'Though I reckon that your uncle'll be happier with her than with that sour-faced old Maud.'

Pamela, who frequently had identical thoughts, nevertheless flinched hearing them from someone else. 'You shouldn't speak like that of the dead,' she said. 'And I think he was happy with Aunt Maud, in spite of everything.'

Molly laughed. 'I told my dad off in them same words when he said something about your aunt. But you got to be honest, there's no accounting for tastes. Some of the oddest couples seem to get hitched and live happily ever after.' She sighed. 'Can't think who I'm going to find. What with so many blokes getting theirselves killed, there bain't many left around. Don't know that I even want one. He got to be rich anyway. I made up my mind about that.'

'The right one'll come along one day,' Pamela said. 'He'll probably drive up in a great big car and sweep you off your feet.'

'Some hopes,' Molly said. 'Pigs might fly. I'll make another cup of tea anyway. You just got time to have one if you drink it quick.'

Pamela put the sleepy baby against her shoulder and patted her back gently. The conversation had made her think about her own marriage. Alan was hoping to get another short leave for the wedding. Perhaps this time she might persuade him to hold Rachel? With the promise of another child, he might be more at ease. She thought of his last visit. They had gone to church together and outwardly he had appeared to accept the baby. Pamela was deeply grateful for this for it had quietened many gossiping tongues. Yet she wasn't sure what he really felt. He had been pleasant on the whole, and had made love to her with care and gentleness, resulting in this new pregnancy. But he had looked hard and long at Rachel and wouldn't take her in his arms yet.

The thing that had most displeased him was that Pamela continued to live at Burlcombe. 'Morelake is your home. When are you going to move back there and see to things?' he asked impatiently.

'Burlcombe is mine too,' she had said, and thought she would never forget the closed look that swept over his face.

'I've a rich wife, of course,' he said. 'I hadn't thought you would inherit so soon.'

'Be glad for me, Alan. You could come and live here.' The words were out before she had considered them.

'I'll never live here.' His eyes had swept the beautiful room. He had stared at the portraits, the ones which had so badly disconcerted Molly and sometimes bothered Pamela too. 'Morelake is mine and that's where I intend to live. A wife's place is in her husband's home.'

'Yes, Alan.' Pamela had sighed and wondered how they would work things out. What would become of Burlcombe? She was determined that she would never sell it. One day it would belong to her daughters. She must keep it for them. She knew that if her next child was a son Alan would insist that he inherited Morelake. He would never consider the girls worthy of his precious house and land.

Every afternoon Pamela stood with several other mothers at the school gate in the village and waited for Jane. She usually left Rachel at home with Molly so that she and Jane could have a short time on their own together. Today the sun was shining, the ground frozen hard and the air crisp. 'Shall we go home by the old road?' she said when Jane had whirled out of school, fair plaits coming undone, hat askew, and coat unbuttoned.

'Ooh, yes please. Then we can look for fairies beneath the bridge.' Jane thrust a crayoned drawing into Pamela's hand. 'Look, I did Burlcombe. I put all its front windows in, seven of them. I can count past seven now. Up to twenty actually.'

Pamela looked at the picture, folded it, and put it carefully into her shoulder bag. 'I shouldn't like a house with twenty windows, would you?' she said, laughing. 'Too much glass to clean.'

Jane wasn't interested in cleaning windows. 'Come on,' she said impatiently. 'Let's go and find the fairies. Perhaps we'll really see them today and then I can count them.'

267

'They'll be too quick to count.' Pamela allowed herself to be pulled along the road past the school and down the street. 'Olivia couldn't count them.'

'Did she see them?'

'Well, she didn't say so in her journal. She just said there was magic there.'

'What kind of magic?'

Pamela wondered how to reply. She couldn't say to a child 'the magic of a first kiss', the magic of being with your first love, Daniel of the dark hair and the blue eyes. She had read that bit again only last night. There was nothing in the journal of his other name. Olivia had kept that a secret. He just remained Daniel, the young man to whom she had eventually given herself. Suddenly Pamela was jolted out of her reverie. Dark hair and blue eyes! Rachel's colouring exactly. Was her baby taking after her grandfather and not after Alan or Lawrence? Were the eyes and the cloud of glossy dark hair, so much hair for so young a child, an inheritance from this unknown young man, this Daniel, the man who was her own father? Would the mystery never be solved?

'Mummy, mummy, what's the matter?' Jane looked up at her and tugged her on. 'You're laughing.'

In March Richard and Mrs Baines were married. The sun shone for them, and all the guests had turned out long-forgotten finery for this special day. It promised to be one of the happiest events the area had known for a long time.

Pamela was glad that she was only three months' pregnant and still able to wear her one pretty frock. She intended to make a special effort to look her very best for the occasion, and to her delight had found a frothy little hat in one of the trunks that had been away in store. She had no idea who had worn such a thing before – certainly not Aunt Maud. It would be just right to jazz up her old blue coat. She stitched its veiling into becoming swirls on the crown – for there was no brim – and then perched it on her head, fastening it with long hat pins. She pinned her hair up into large firm rolls on each side of the hat, and the back, just shoulder length now, she allowed to flow loose so that it curled softly on the collar of her coat.

'I look quite refurbished, like the vicar said about the church,' she had remarked to Molly with a laugh when she tried on her outfit. 'I've even found gloves to match the hat. They cover my rough hands.'

'You looks really nice,' Molly said. 'But I don't know about refurbished. I don't rightly know what that means.'

'Made like new,' Pamela told her. 'That's how I feel too. A wedding must be a good tonic for us all.'

The church had definitely been refurbished, brought back almost to its pre-evacuation state. The treasures had been unpacked and everything lovingly cleaned and replaced. There were even daffodils for the wedding, their bright golden heads bringing promise of summer to come.

'How did you get them to open so soon?' Pamela had enquired of Molly when she saw them before the great day.

'Us picked 'em last week,' Molly told her. 'Me and Mum. Then we put 'em in buckets and kept 'em in the warm room so they opened up. You couldn't move at home for the things.'

Looking at them now, on the wedding morning, looking at her uncle and his bride at the altar, looking at the lovely old church, Pamela felt a sudden stab of joy which was followed quickly by a traitorous thought that she wished she could banish.

She thought of another day, a grim and dismal November day when she had stood in this same church with Lawrence. There was nothing beautiful to be seen then. Everything had been packed away, the rain had fallen relentlessly and the sky had been dark with clouds. Yet it had been a golden day.

She held her hymn book firmly in her hand and looked around at the ancient walls and at the tomb of the knight and his lady. They had survived the onslaught of guns and bombardment undamaged. Pamela remembered Lawrence touching the cold stone, marvelling at the years that had passed since they had

269

been interred here, promising to come back to see it all one day in the future. She shivered and for one moment felt that his ghost stood at her side.

Then she was filled with guilt at the direction of her thoughts and jerked herself back to the present. It was not a ghost who stood beside her but Alan, handsome in his RAF uniform. He had managed to get the leave he had asked for. She listened to his pleasant baritone. He was singing the rather poignant hymn with enthusiasm. ' "That theirs may be the love which knows no ending . . ." ' he sang. She wondered if he was thinking about the words . . . ' "Whom thou for evermore dost join in one." ' She had been surprised that he liked to sing, that he had a good voice. She had discovered this soon after their marriage. It didn't fit the image she had of him. In fact there were a lot of things lately that didn't fit that first image. She glanced up and for a moment their eyes met, but she couldn't decipher what he was thinking. Then she stared at her hymn book again. ' " . . . peace which calms all earthly strife . . ." ' She joined in as the hymn came to a close. ' "And to life's day the glorious unknown morrow, that dawns . . ." ' She felt tears spring to her eyes and groped for her handkerchief. In front of her Richard was looking at the ample figure of his new bride. She knew there would be tenderness and love in their home.

As March and April gave way to May the ugly signs of war began to fade from the fields and woods around Burlcombe. 'There's some birds nesting in the spinney,' Molly announced one morning. 'And if that bain't a good omen then I don't know what is!'

'Robins,' Pamela told her. 'I saw them flying around yesterday. Well, the war's nearly over. Perhaps we'll hear something definite on the wireless soon.'

'When that old Hitler be dead, everything'll be all right.' Molly was folding breeze-fresh nappies that she had just collected from the clothes line. She sniffed them appreciatively. 'A good blow do get them nice and fresh, that's for sure,' she said, her mind happily making the jump from the fate of Hitler to the well-being of Rachel's bottom, and then back again. 'What about all them poor prisoners that I been reading about? Them Jews. Hitler wants boiling in oil, I reckon, not just dying in his bed.'

'I don't suppose he's very comfortable, not with Berlin falling in ruins all round him and the Russians marching through the streets,' Pamela said. 'And I shouldn't think he's very likely to die in his bed either.'

For a second Molly allowed a dreamy expression to cross her face. 'I think the Yanks be there too. Wouldn't it be wonderful if my Delmer was in Berlin, all victorious and handsome, instead of lying cold and rotting in that field over yonder?'

'Stop it,' Pamela commanded. 'You've got to stop talking like that, Molly. You mustn't go on believing the tale of a field with Americans buried there or it'll become a great big rumour and other people will listen to you and before we know where we are everyone will be saying it's true, and then where shall we be?'

Molly looked taken aback. 'I thought you believed in the field story too?'

'Well, I don't. It's a rumour that's got to stop. And Delmer isn't there anyway. He might be in Germany, he might be in Berlin, he might be in a military hospital back in America being looked after, or he might . . . well, he might be dead. But you must try to forget him, at least until you know something definite.' Pamela was surprised at herself, at the strong emotions the girl's remarks had evoked. She could only suppose that it was because of Lawrence. Since coming back to Devon, her new pregnancy, and those wayward thoughts during the wedding service, she had tried to put him out of her mind. She wanted to forget Lawrence now, or if not to forget, then to place him in a separate compartment of her life, a compartment that was of the past, precious but finished. But each time Molly mentioned Delmer the memories came flooding back to disturb and haunt.

Pamela could see that Molly was looking at her now with a measure of understanding.

'Sorry,' she murmured. 'Thoughtless of me, but we both got memories and I don't suppose they'll ever go away, will they, not with the kids to remind us of them?'

'Do you think about your baby often then?' Pamela asked. Molly's infant son was growing up fat and jolly, the delight of Ben and Wendy Yates, but like her own Jane long ago, it had been decreed that he would not be told who his real mother was.

Molly laughed and shrugged her shoulders. 'Me? No, not much. He's happy as a sand-boy, and so are Mum and Dad, so why should I worry? I been able to give them what they've always wanted, and I've got my freedom. There'll be time enough for babies if ever I get properly wed. They'll come too fast then probably.'

Suddenly Pamela realized the other thing that Molly had said. She had implied again that Rachel was Lawrence's child. She must get this idea out of the girl's head before Alan came home for good, and completely out of her own head too for that matter. At all costs she must maintain her conviction that Alan was Rachel's father.

'Molly,' she said, and her companion stopped the folding and looked up, arrested by something in Pamela's voice, some earnestness that had not been there before.

'Molly, please, please, will you understand that Rachel is Alan's daughter? She is Alan's daughter, I tell you!' Pamela almost shouted the words. 'I believe it and so must you.'

'Righto, if you say so, if that's what you want. I think I believe it anyway, what with those great big blue eyes of hers.' Molly laughed again and went back to her folding until the pile of fragrant snowy nappies was complete.

Then suddenly Richard burst through the door. 'Heard the news?' he asked. 'Berlin has fallen, Hitler's dead, and I've just heard the announcer's voice on the wireless telling us that it's Victory in Europe and we're all to have a holiday.'

Molly let all the nappies, which she had taken into her arms to put away, fall to the floor in a great disorganised heap. She grabbed Pamela and pulled her to her feet and they pranced all round the room, kicking nappies everywhere in their excitement. Binks joined in the fun.

'Hey, you'll have to wash them all over again,' Richard said, laughing and trying to scoop some of them up.

'Who cares? The war's over, the war's over! It's OVER!' Pamela shouted. 'It's all finished.'

They all eventually collapsed on to the chairs and sat for a moment looking at each other.

Richard was the first to speak. 'Thank God,' he said. 'Now the men can come home.'

Pamela felt her heart beat a little faster. The men could come home. Alan would be coming home for good. Morelake was waiting for her, Morelake and Alan.

Suddenly Richard had a chilling thought but didn't voice it aloud. He couldn't say anything just now to spoil the excitement. But there's Japan left, he thought to himself. It's not quite over. We've won the war in Europe, but there's still Japan.

There was a Victory tea in the village hall for the children, a Victory dance for the adults in the evening, and celebrations everywhere. 'Except for them what's lost folks,' Molly said, voicing the thoughts of quite a few and probably thinking of herself too, Pamela thought. Although Delmer's fate was unknown, he was just as lost to Molly as if he did indeed lie beneath the soft Devon earth. And Lawrence? Lost too, with only his slim little book of poems and the small photograph to prove that he wasn't just a dream, a figment of the imagination. He had disappeared from Pamela's life as surely as all the other GIs who had filled the countryside with their noisy laughter. They were just ghosts now, remembered in many hearts and homes, but ghosts nevertheless.

'I wonder if any of them'll ever come back?' Molly remarked a week later. She was doing the ironing, a job she liked. There was an excuse to stop in between, while the iron re-heated itself on the Aga. She liked being close to the warmth too. She always placed the ironing board as near to the source of heat as she could. Even now in May there was sometimes a chilly breeze that found its way beneath the kitchen door.

'Some might,' Pamela replied. 'They'll come in a few years time probably, for holidays. And they'll bring fat, contented wives and strings of children. And they'll look at us as though we are curiosities, leftovers from the past.'

'You'm cheerful, I must say.' Molly held the iron close to her face to judge its heat. 'Perhaps we'll be rich by then and we'll be able to go to America and see just what they was talking about?' She grinned merrily. 'That'd be good. Can you just imagine it? Going on the *Queen Mary*, all posh and pampered. I'd like that.'

Pamela laughed and then dismissed the idea. She had more pressing things to think about. She was standing at the sink preparing vegetables for their evening meal. Uncle Richard was to share it with them tonight for he intended working late, making use of the lighter evenings. But while her hands worked automatically, scrubbing and peeling, she was thinking about the changes that would soon have to come about in her life. She had decisions to make. She decided to talk to Richard about it at dinner.

She waited until the first course was finished. Then she carried the steamed jam pudding from the cooker and placed it on the table. She stared at it absently.

'I'll have to make some plans, Uncle Richard,' she said. 'More-lake is getting more and more derelict. The longer I stay here, the more difficult it's going to be to move. And with the baby coming, I ought to get the worst of the work done soon. What do you think I should do? I hate the thought of leaving Burlcombe. It's like some kind of nightmare.'

'What's a nightmare?' Jane wanted to know.

'A nasty dream,' Pamela said as she served the pudding.

'Morelake's nasty,' Jane agreed. 'All dark and witchy.'

'Not really, darling,' Pamela said quickly. 'It won't be when we've painted it.'

'It'll always be witchy.' Jane was quite determined not to like Morelake. But now she was more interested in the gooey jam that was running down the sides of the pudding on to her plate. 'Yummy, yummy,' she said, and started demolishing it, Morelake and its witchyness set aside for the moment.

Richard looked at Pamela and felt sorry for her. She'd been

pushed into marriage with Alan Saunders, but what was done was done and there was no going back. She'd have to go and live in the gloomy place. 'If you'd like me and the wife to live here part of the time as caretakers, that's what we'll do,' he said to her.

Pamela was filled with relief. 'Would you really, Uncle Richard? Would you really come back here, and wouldn't Mrs Baines mind?'

Richard grinned at her. 'She's agreeable. She've worked here most of her life after all.'

'You and me'll stay too, Mummy. If Aunty Baines is here I really truly want to stay.' Jane had finished her pudding and was looking from one adult to the other. 'We can, can't we, Uncle Richard?'

'No, we can't.' For once there was an edge of annoyance to Pamela's voice. 'We have to live where Daddy wants us.'

'Then I wish he wouldn't come home. Can I get down now?'

'Yes. You can go and play, but be quiet. Don't wake Rachel.'

Jane looked from one to the other and then jumped down from her chair and ran out of the room without saying anything more.

'I'll go and see to her,' Molly said. 'She don't mean it.'

'I'm afraid she does. I must be more careful what I say in front of her in future.'

'You can't watch every word,' Richard said as Molly left the room. 'Children have to fit in.'

As we all do, Pamela said silently to herself, women anyway. Then she looked at Richard and smiled. 'If you're really sure about coming back here to live when we go to Morelake, I'll be so grateful,' she said.

It was the almost perfect solution. The house would always be a sort of refuge, a place of her own, a bolt-hole if she should ever need one. With Richard and Mrs Baines looking after it, she could come any time. 'I couldn't wish for any better tenants,' she added. Then she blushed at her last unfortunate word. 'I'm sorry,' she said. 'I didn't mean . . .'

'Never mind, maid,' he said. 'That's what we'd be. I never felt it was mine even when I was wed to your aunt. It was always her home and I knew that 'twas being kept ready for her descendants.'

For me, thought Pamela, and for Jane and Rachel. Our home. Not Alan's, mine.

'It might be a long time before Alan is demobbed though,' Richard added, thinking of Japan. 'No rush. You don't want to move there until you have to.' He finished his pudding and placed his spoon and fork neatly side by side on the plate as Maud had always insisted he should. Then he padded across the room in his socks and pulled on his wellingtons which stood on the mat just inside the door. 'No need for you to do any of the work on Morelake yourself anyway,' he said. 'You just choose what you want done, colours and things, and I'll see to it. The land is being put to rights. I've arranged all that.'

Pamela got up from the table and went over to him. She kissed him gently on the cheek. 'What would I do without you?' she said. 'Thanks, Uncle Richard.'

'By the way,' she added, 'we seem to be saying "Mrs Baines" still.'

Richard grinned at her. 'She likes it that way in spite of her marriage lines. That's what she's been for a long time and she can't get used to no other name.'

'It doesn't seem quite right though,' Pamela persisted.

'She don't want to be the same as your aunt,' Richard explained. 'She knows that's what she is officially, of course, but she says that Mrs Lindhurst don't sound right. Just go on calling her Mrs Baines, I don't mind.'

'That's good of you,' Pamela commented. She wondered what Alan would say if she refused to call herself by his name.

Richard laughed. 'Do you know what her first name is?' he said. ''Tis Pansy, and as she says, could you possibly think of anyone less like a pansy?'

Pamela hadn't known and she too was amused. 'Right then,' she said. 'If everyone is happy with Mrs Baines, that's what it'll be. After all, she couldn't be less like Aunt Maud, could she, so perhaps Mrs Lindhurst wouldn't fit her either?' Although she didn't say so, Pamela considered that this last remark was definitely a compliment.

'I call her Pansy,' Richard admitted as he let himself out. 'But only when us be alone. She likes it then.'

With her thoughts cheered by the picture this revelation conjured up, Pamela cleared away the dishes, and when Jane came back into the room she kissed her and then fetched the box of sweets that were kept for special occasions. 'Let's have two each,' she said.

'Four each,' said Jane.

A letter arrived from Alan a few days later. Pamela read the opening sentence twice over. 'Burma,' she said to Molly. 'It sounds so far away.'

'He'll be bombing the Japs. Aren't you worried?'

'Of course I am. I'm going to start on Morelake. It'll take my mind off things,' she said.

Morelake was nearly derelict but this gave Pamela the opportunity to refurbish it just as she wanted. With Alan absent she could do as she liked and when scarlet poppies cheered the corn fields and the hedges were bright with foxgloves, the once gloomy old farmhouse stood resplendent too. Some of the older inhabitants of the village considered that it looked brighter and more habitable than it had done for twenty years or more.

There was even a garden with flowers. Pamela had employed an old man to dig and plant. There were bright curtains at the windows, carpets instead of the old brown linoleum on the floor, and only the best of the furniture was reinstated. Richard had marshalled several willing helpers to do most of the work and in spite of all the shortages had contrived to find all things that Pamela set her heart upon. It was almost ready to move into and even Jane was impressed.

'I think the witches have gone,' she said one hot August morning when they came over to make some last arrangements.

'Quite gone, my pet,' Pamela said happily, thinking with relish

277

of Alan's mother. 'Do you think Daddy will approve?'

'He might,' Jane said wisely. 'If he doesn't I shall tell him he's silly.'

'You mustn't do that,' Pamela told her, immediately alarmed. 'Little girls don't tell their daddies that they're silly. That would be naughty and rude.'

'But he's not my real daddy, is he, so I can say it?'

'You most certainly cannot! And whether he is or is not your real daddy makes not one bit of difference. Is that clear?'

'Yes, Mummy.' Jane at five and a half years old was becoming more and more sure of herself. Sometimes, Pamela had to admit, even a little cheeky.

'She needs a father,' she confided to Molly later that day.

Mrs Baines had just come into the kitchen and overheard the last sentence. 'Then I reckon she'm going to get one soon,' she said, excitement spreading all over her face. 'Heard the news, have you?'

'No, what?'

'On the wireless,' she said. 'Two great bombs have been dropped on them Japs and they've surrendered. The war's going to be over proper.'

Pamela and Molly stared at her as if she had announced the end of the world. At first they both failed to take in her momentous news. The war had been going on for so long, and they'd expected it to be much longer. The Japs were fierce fighters and not likely to give in very quickly.

'Tomic bombs,' Mrs Baines explained, sounding as if she knew everything there was to know about such things. 'Some place called Hiroshima and 'tis all flattened, all of it. No survivors. Serves them right, I say, for all they done to our boys.'

'So they'll all be coming home?' Molly said. 'No more fighting. 'Tis been war almost all my growing up. Are you sure 'tis true, Mrs Baines?'

'True as I'm standing here, love. Yes, 'tis all over at last. 'Tis peace.'

Pamela looked round at the Burlcombe kitchen, at the Aga comforting even now in August, at the shelves with their gleaming pans, at Binks sleeping happily in his basket in the corner, and at Rachel. Through the window she could just see the baby asleep too in the big family pram which had been placed outside in the fresh air.

Everything was about to change. Peace! The word had a curious sound. Mrs Baines had stressed it, relishing it. What would peace be like? Alan would be coming home for good.

'I reckon we should celebrate.' Molly stood up, undecided what to celebrate with.

'A nice cup of tea,' Mrs Baines said.

'Wine,' Pamela said. 'Some of Aunt Maud's home-made.' She disappeared and returned a few minutes later bearing two bottles of deep red liquid. 'Blackberry. Find the best glasses, Molly.'

They stood, the three of them, in the kitchen, each holding one of the delicate glasses, each wondering what peace meant, what it would bring.

'Here's to peace then,' Pamela declared.

'And no more wars,' Mrs Baines added.

Jane ran in at that moment. She looked from one to the other. 'What's peace?' she asked.

Pamela smiled at her. 'The most wonderful thing in the world.'

# TWENTY-ONE

*Olivia's Journal – 20th August 1924*
*I have been meeting Daniel secretly all this year. He comes*
*without his sister now. Maud would say that I am being very*
*wicked, yet is it wicked to love someone so much?*
*Mallory is always with me when I go to meet Daniel. And*
*of course if it had not been for Mallory I might never have*
*plucked up courage to speak to him at all.*

Jonathon Alan arrived easily towards the end of October. He
was a big happy baby with his father's features stamped clearly
on his fair round face.

Alan, back now from Burma, was granted special leave. He
rode through the winter drizzle and mist on his motor-cycle and
everything that had troubled him about his marriage seemed to
fade into insignificance now that he had a son.

He left the motor-cycle on the forecourt of the hospital and
suddenly was nervous. And he realized that he had brought
nothing. No flowers, no chocolates. There hadn't been time. He
stood for a few moments trying to summon the courage to go in,
and then resolutely pushed open the swing doors, asked a
starched little nurse where his wife was, and followed her into
the ward and the uncomfortable smell of disinfectant. He had
planned his arrival for visiting time and had managed to get it
just right. Pamela was waiting for him.

She was sitting up in bed, her face a little paler than he

281

remembered it, her hair was loose about her shoulders, a golden halo. She saw him and smiled. He strode past all the other beds. He looked very handsome in his uniform but was unaware of the sensation he caused, the admiring glances that followed him through the ward. He appeared to have eyes for no one but his wife, yet Pamela, watching him, knew that it was his baby he was looking for.

'Is he all right?' he said, confirming her thoughts.

'Yes, he's fine. The babies aren't allowed in the wards at visiting times in case of germs,' she explained. If she felt slightly hurt at his first words she didn't show it. 'You'll be able to look at him through a special glass window in a minute.'

Relief flooded through Alan. Of course he should have known that he wouldn't be able to hold his baby yet. Fathers were considered very undesirable carriers of all sorts of ills. But his child was all right apparently. 'And you?' he asked belatedly. 'How was it? Are you OK now?'

'A piece of cake,' Pamela said. 'Yes, compared with the other times it was a piece of cake.'

Alan was amused at her use of the familiar RAF slang but it put him at ease, lessened the awkwardness between them.

'I came as soon as I could,' he said. 'I haven't bought you anything, but I will. I promise I will.' He put his hand over hers. 'Thank you,' he murmured, then kissed her gently.

Before he left the hospital he was allowed to peer through the glass window to see his son. A nurse held the baby up and Alan looked at the small red face with its shock of blond hair. 'Can't I hold him?' he pleaded.

'Sorry. Not allowed. You'll have to wait until he leaves hospital.'

Two weeks later the longed-for day arrived. Alan was stationed not too far away and was able to get another forty-eight hour leave. This time he managed to borrow a friend's motor car and as he bowled along the road that led to Devon was suddenly happier than he'd been for a long time. He was soon to be free of the RAF, free to cultivate his land again and watch his son grow up in his own house, surrounded by his own fields.

He had a present for Pamela this time too. It was a slender gold chain with a little cross hanging from it. He had chosen it with care and was sure that it would meet with her approval. It had been wrapped by the jeweller and now lay safely in his inner pocket.

They reached Burlcombe towards the end of the afternoon. 'In the dimpsey,' Pamela said. 'My favourite time.'

Molly had been watching for them and flung open the front door. 'Come in out of the cold,' she ordered. 'Quick. We'm all longing to see the little lord and master.'

Pamela laughed. She was not quite sure whether she liked her son's new title. But she held him out for inspection, and wondered for a moment if Molly thought of her own little boy. There was no sign of anything other than excitement and pleasure on the girl's rosy face.

'There was a rainbow in the sky this morning,' she said as she peered into the folds of the shawl. ''Tis gone now, but I know you set some store on rainbows so I thought I'd tell you in case you couldn't see it from that hospital.'

Pamela nodded. 'Thank you, Molly. I did see it actually, and yes, it did seem like a good omen.'

'Well, I hope he don't cry in the night.' Molly's pleasure diminished slightly at the thought of endless broken nights. 'Rachel didn't much, and still don't. He'd better take after his sister.'

Later, in the drawing room, Alan had eyes only for the new baby. 'He won't cry,' he said, thinking of Molly's earlier remark. 'He's perfect.'

Pamela smiled at him. She was happy. She had given him what he most desired and now perhaps it was the beginning of better things for the whole family. She was sitting on the settee with the baby on her lap. She held out her other hand to Jane who was standing beside Mrs Baines. 'Come and look at your brother,' she said. 'He'll be glad of a big sister to help look after him.'

'I wanted another sister,' Jane said. She pouted and refused to look. 'I don't like boys. They're rough.'

283

Rachel sat on the floor and waved her rattle at everybody. Then she stood up unsteadily and toddled over to her mother. At fourteen months she was still not too sure of the ability of her legs to support her. 'Be-be,' she said, thrusting the rattle towards her brother.

Pamela intercepted the toy and glanced up at Alan. She saw the sudden look of alarm on his face.

'Don't worry,' she said. 'Babies are pretty tough. He'll survive.'

'Keep that child away from him,' Alan said. 'She might do him some harm.'

Pamela said nothing, but her happiness suddenly had a great dent in it. She scooped Rachel up with her free hand, for Jane had run off to play with Binks, and she cuddled this middle child into her side. 'We must be gentle with Jonathon,' she whispered. 'He's very little.' Rachel too was little, an elfin fairy child, and Pamela guessed that in a few years' time Jonathon would quite outstrip her.

The move to Morelake was scheduled for the end of November. 'Just two years almost to the day from when we all had to move out,' Pamela said, remembering. Alan was to be demobbed in time for Christmas, their first Christmas at his old home. 'I shall try to make it really nice. We'll have a tree and candles, and I shall make puddings.'

'No, you won't. You'm still not strong enough.' Mrs Baines was adamant. 'I shall make the puddings, and I shall put them in the old wash boiler to cook. Don't you worry about nothing.'

'I feel fine,' Pamela objected. She had recovered quickly from Jonathan's birth, and he was, as Alan had predicted, almost a perfect baby. He slept long and soundly, grew steadily, and caused not a minute's concern. The rainbow seemed to be living up to its promise!

They accomplished the move without too much heartache in spite of Pamela's foreboding. Only Jane refused to be comforted. Her delight in the small room set aside for her was short-lived when she discovered that Binks was not allowed to come upstairs.

'But I'm lonely,' she objected. 'Why can't I have Binks in with me, like at Burlcombe?'

'Because Daddy doesn't really like dogs, and we must start as we intend to go on,' Pamela said. 'He'll be home for good soon and we don't want him to be cross, do we?'

'If it was Jonathon wanted a dog, he'd be allowed to have it,' Jane said wisely. She had already summed up the situation, and knew that, as far as Alan was concerned, she and Rachel counted for very little.

Pamela looked at her three-week-old son and was saddened by Jane's remark. 'He's too little for a dog,' she said. 'I'll buy you a big furry dog for Christmas, a toy one. You can have that right in your bed. And it'll be better than a real one. It won't snuffle and bark and wake you up, or go out and roll in nasty things and smell.'

'I don't want a toy dog.' Jane was adamant. 'I want a real dog. Rachel can have a toy one. I'm too big for that. I'd like one of my very own really. Binks is yours. He likes you better than me. I want a friend. And if he smells, you can help me to bath him with carbolic like you do to Binks sometimes.'

Suddenly Pamela remembered reading something very similar to her daughter's statement in Olivia's journal. Not about the carbolic soap, she somehow couldn't imagine her beautiful mother sloshing about with that, but she had been a lonely child too and had recorded how much she needed a friend. Richard had given Mallory to her, the wolf-hound who was buried at Burlcombe with his very own headstone in a peaceful corner of the garden. It was Mallory who had caused her to speak with the family at Ash Manor. Perhaps without Mallory . . . well, who knew what might or might not have happened?

And suddenly Pamela made up her mind. Why shouldn't Jane have a dog of her own? Why should Alan lay down the law so? In fact, he hadn't actually said anything about not having another dog, she reminded herself. Perhaps she was being unfair to him? She had just assumed that he would refuse. As soon as the idea formed in her head she became determined that she would do something about it. She had almost three weeks before he came home for good. Perhaps Richard knew of a puppy? It would be just the thing to cheer Jane up, help her to come to terms with living at Morelake. It might even enable her to suffer her small brother with a little more grace, get over her jealousy in time. Alan had his son now. He would surely agree to a special present for Jane? A little dog, Pamela thought. Something small. A terrier maybe.

It was all quickly arranged, but it was not a small dog that arrived a few days later. Richard appeared with the biggest puppy Pamela had ever seen. 'Mallory's great-grand-daughter,' he said. 'You don't want a yappy terrier. These are wonderful with children. I'll help train her.'

In spite of Pamela's misgivings, Jane was delighted and christened her dog Belle straight away. And the two were friends immediately. Whatever Alan said when he came home, the deed was done. After that first introduction there was no going back.

'Why Belle?' Molly wanted to know. 'Not a very doggy name, is it? And it starts with a "B", like Binks. They might get their names muddled up.'

'No, they won't. They're not stupid,' Jane said, almost implying that it was Molly who lacked intelligence. 'And Belle is Belle because it's a princess's name, and she's beautiful, and she's my best friend.'

The first battle of wills occurred at bedtime on the first evening of the puppy's arrival.

'I want Belle in my bedroom all night,' Jane said. 'I told you, she's a princess and she's my friend, and you can't put friends in the barn.'

'I'm sorry.' Pamela's voice was as firm as she could make it. 'You know that I've put a lovely warm box there right beside Binks . And Belle isn't completely house-trained yet. She'll probably make a puddle. We couldn't have that on your nice carpet, could we?'

'I can clear up puddles.'

Pamela sighed. This child was sometimes as determined as Alan. She could foresee battles ahead when he came home for good. But she too could be firm. 'Do you want to take Belle out and settle her before you go to bed, or shall I do it later?'

Jane was cradling the puppy in her arms. 'If you're really certain sure that I can't take her up with me, I suppose you'd better do it. Then she'll have longer in the kitchen. You take her out, Mummy, when you take Binks, last thing.'

'That's my sensible girl,' Pamela said, relieved at her fairly easy compliance. She had expected more resistance. 'Daddy won't mind us having another dog as long as it's outside at night.'

'How do you know he won't mind?'

'I've got a feeling in my bones,' Pamela said, hoping that she was right. 'He'll be in a good mood because he'll be home for good and it's going to be Christmas. And if you're especially nice to him, then he'll be happy about it.'

'He won't know if I'm being nice or not,' Jane said. 'He'll only notice Jonathon.'

'He loves Jonathon because he always wanted a little boy to help on the farm. But he . . .' Pamela paused, wondering how she could further help Jane come to terms with her resentment. 'He loves us all too,' she added, hoping that the small lie would be forgiven, and might in fact come to be no lie at all eventually.

'Jonathon can't help on the farm,' Jane said. 'That's silly. He's too little.'

'He'll grow. Now, come on. Bed. Put Belle in her box. She's fast asleep like Rachel, and like you should be too.'

Reluctantly Jane carried the puppy over to the cardboard box beside the stove. 'You'll see she's warm over there in the barn, won't you, Mummy? Tuck a blanket all round her like you do for Rachel and me.'

'Yes, darling, and there's lots of hay in the bottom of her box. Hay keeps you warmer than blankets.'

Suddenly Jane brightened. 'I suppose she's lucky really. She's got two beds, a daytime one and a night-time one.' She stood looking down at the puppy, and for a second Pamela saw on her face the same look of wonder and adoration that had been so obvious in Alan's eyes when he first looked down at Jonathon. The similarity in their features took her by surprise.

'I'm so glad you've got Belle,' she said quickly. 'I can see that you're going to love her more than anyone.'

'Not more than you, Mummy,' Jane said. 'I love you more'n anything.' She turned and threw her arms round Pamela, and they hugged each other.

'Now, bed,' Pamela said again.

'And I want the story of the princess and the frog.'

'I want doesn't get.'

'Please can I?' said Jane.

By the time Alan came home just two days before Christmas, wearing his ill-fitting demob suit, Belle was fully established, part of the family.

He arrived in a taxi, and to Pamela's surprise carried a small bunch of flowers.

'I should have given you these in the hospital,' he said, and held them out to her. Chrysanthemums. She took them and looked at their golden beauty, remembering that he had now given her two gifts. Her free hand went instinctively to the cross on the chain that hung around her neck, the present that he had given her in gratitude for Jonathon. She wished that he had chosen anything other than a cross. Every time she felt it she remembered Olivia's cross, the precious piece of jewellery that she had given to Lawrence. Alan had had the name 'Pamela' engraved on the back of this new one, and the date of their son's birth. On her mother's there was the one word 'Olivia', and a date too.

Pamela sometimes regretted that she had given this precious possession to Lawrence, and wondered where it was lying now. Far beneath the sea perhaps, or in some grave, or even in the fertile Devon soil, the field which Molly persistently believed held the bodies of the many GIs drowned in that fatal April exercise. Or was the little cross put away in a box or drawer somewhere in that unknown place called America, an embarrassment now possibly? Yet maybe he was wearing it still? When her thoughts ran in this direction she would resolutely turn away from them, for that way lay discontent.

288

She watched Alan pay the driver and then gather up his luggage. He put it all down again in the hall and kissed her briefly. His next words were entirely predictable.

'Where's Jonathon?' he said, and then Pamela realized, with a stab of mixed emotions, that no one really existed for him at that moment except his baby son.

'In his pram outside.' She wondered if this would meet with his approval. She always put the baby out to have some fresh air, whatever the weather. Now she glanced at the puppy snug in its box and grinned to herself at the incongruity of it.

Alan had not even noticed the dog or remarked on the absence of Rachel and Jane. Within seconds he was outside looking down at his sleeping son. She watched him through the window. He stood for a long time in the fading afternoon light. She could just make out his face, see the tenderness there. She saw him take out a handkerchief and wipe his eyes. Quickly she turned away from the window. She was deeply moved, yet saddened too.

Why can't we be a proper family? she thought. If only he could love Jane and Rachel as he loves Jonathon. I suppose it's my fault. Then she pulled on her apron and started preparing vegetables.

Molly had gone to fetch Jane from her friend's house today, taking Rachel in the pushchair. Pamela longed for her eldest child to rush through the door, longed to scoop her up in her arms and hug her. It would be a kind of compensation. Seeing Alan's love for his son she found herself wondering again who Jane's father was. Poor Jane. The puppy awoke at that moment and Pamela quickly dried her hands and scooped up the dog and took her outside. It was the waking-up ritual, the training to be clean.

She had to pass Alan to get to the patch of grass just outside the gate where the puppy was supposed to relieve herself. He looked up, surprised.

'What's that?' His voice was not angry, more curious.

Pamela shut the gate behind her and deposited the dog on the grass. 'Busy,' she said to it. 'Busy. Be busy.' She looked at

289

Alan and her heart thumped uncomfortably. 'Jane's Christmas present,' she said. 'She's had it early. I hope you don't mind too much. She was sad and rather lonely when we first moved here. Two moves, of course. She missed Scotland a lot at first, had friends there. She set her heart on a dog. Richard got this one for her, the same breed as Olivia's Mallory, very big but gentle, he says.' She was aware that her words were spilling out nervously.

The puppy was obediently being busy. She squatted on the grass and did as she had been trained to do when given this strange command. Then she got up and started to sniff around and run on unsteady though huge baby paws. She was very appealing in spite of her size.

Pamela opened the wooden gate again and the puppy gambolled through it and up to Alan. She tried to eat his trouser legs and Pamela waited for the impatient movement that she was sure would come, the angry pushing away, perhaps even a small kick, the storm of reproach.

Instead he stood quite still, suffering the animal's playfulness. 'Couldn't Jane have done with the dog we already have?' he enquired. 'You know I don't like them.'

'Binks is my dog,' Pamela said. 'Jane needed one of her own. She needed a friend.'

Still feeling the joy of coming home, the thrill of seeing his son, Alan felt benevolent. And he wanted to do something for Jane, especially now that he would have to change his will again and leave Morelake to his son. Perhaps if he managed to put up with this huge animal, it would help to make up for the past? (But no . . . nothing could ever make up for that. Nevertheless this was something he could do, and he wanted to make Jane happy.) 'Then I suppose she'll have to have the dog,' he said. 'But both of them go out at night. I don't want them in the house after supper.'

'I know.' Pamela's voice was deliberately meek. 'They have warm boxes in the barn. They're used to it. I knew you'd want that. Thank you, Alan, for not being cross about Belle. Jane will be so pleased when she knows you don't mind. she's been worried.'

'I've brought her a present,' he said. 'A doll I got overseas. I hope she'll like it. I don't want her to think that I'm . . .' He didn't finish his sentence and Pamela had no more time to realize how amazed she was.

She heard Molly coming down the lane with Jane and Rachel. Jane bounced through the gate, roses in her cheeks and a smile on her face, but saw Alan and stopped. She looked at Pamela and the smile was replaced by apprehension. 'Is it all right?' she said. 'Can I keep Belle?'

It was Alan who replied. 'Yes. You can keep her.'

But there was no answering warmth or gratitude in Jane's voice. 'I was going to run away to Aunty Baines if you said I couldn't,' she said. 'Me and Belle was going to Burlcombe for ever and ever.'

'Bow-wow, bow-wow-wow,' yelled Rachel, struggling to get out of the push-chair into which she was firmly strapped. The puppy ran up to her and licked her face.

'Come on, Belle,' Jane called immediately, jealous even of her sister. She turned and ran out of the garden gate and into the field beyond, followed by the dog. There she threw her arms around the puppy and Pamela heard her words shouted into the dank afternoon air.

'I love you, Belle. I love you better'n anybody.' Then there was a pause. 'Better'n anybody except Mummy, I mean.'

# TWENTY-TWO

*Olivia's Journal – 20th December 1924*
*Christmas will soon be here, yet I am more miserable and*
*frightened than I have ever been in my life. I am going to*
*have a child! What am I to do? Maud is bound to know soon.*
*I long for Daniel with all my heart yet I have made up my*
*mind that he must not know. Is the terror and grief that I feel*
*the result of loving someone? Yes, it is. How stupid I have*
*been. I shall never tell anyone about Daniel.*

Every time Pamela read the last entry in her mother's journal
she felt great sadness that her own begetting should have been
Olivia's downfall. And now with the war over at last and Alan
home for good, she determined that she would put the little book
away. It would be a symbolic act.

The present and the future are what matters, she told herself.
I will make a success of my life from now on. I owe it to Olivia.
She died giving life to me and I know that she would want me
to be happy. I mustn't waste what she gave me. I'm lucky in all
the ways that she was not.

With three children to bring up and a farmhouse to run she
wanted to banish all the ghosts and dreams of the past and to
concentrate now on Alan's future and hers, the two of them
together. She put Lawrence's book of poems and his photograph
away too. She sealed them in an envelope and placed it at the
bottom of the small inlaid box that stood on the lower shelf of

a table in her bedroom. On top of the envelope she put a few mementoes of her childhood, two of Jane's early drawings, a lock of Rachel's dark curly hair, and a fair curl of Jonathon's. Then, finally, the journal. The box possessed an insubstantial lock with a tiny brass key, but it was enough to form a barrier with her past.

That part of my life is finished, she told herself firmly whenever she felt the urge to remember and to dream: whenever she wanted to take out the envelope at the bottom and to hold in her hands again Lawrence's little book that she knew could set her heart racing and bring a flush of colour to her cheeks even now.

Yet there were other things that brought back memories, things she could not lock away or escape from. Jane still insisted on taking flowers to the graveyard. For Olivia's angel, she said. The ritual started long ago by Aunt Maud had somehow caught Jane's imagination. Pamela guessed that the marble angel must be mixed up in her mind with Olivia herself for Jane had always been fascinated by the great painting in the hall at Burlcombe.

'Has Aunt Maud got an angel?' Jane asked one wild but sunny March day. 'I suppose hers is an old angel.'

Pamela laughed, and the remark confirmed her thoughts. 'I don't think angels ever get old,' she said. She was secretly glad that Maud had been buried in Scotland and that there was nothing here to accuse silently, no grave to visit. 'But no, she hasn't got an angel,' she replied. 'Just a headstone. I don't think Aunt Maud would have wanted an angel.'

'I want an angel on my grave,' Jane said. 'You'll buy me one, won't you, Mummy?'

'You're not going to die,' Pamela replied. 'Not for ages and ages. Come on, put your flowers down and let's go. The dogs will hate being tied up at the gate in this cold wind.'

Mention of Belle made Jane hurry to do as she was told. 'Aunt Maud has got a headstone like Mallory then,' she said as she skipped down the gravelled path between the graves. 'Belle must have an angel though when she dies, because she's special.'

'Stop being so morbid,' said Pamela, hurrying after her.

'What's morbid?'

'Headstones.'

'Alan wouldn't want an angel, would he?'

'No, I suppose not, and I've told you enough times not to call him Alan.'

'Uncle Alan,' Jane amended.

'Why not Daddy?'

'Because he isn't. But I do say Daddy sometimes, don't I? When I forget.'

'I wish you would say it always.'

'I might one day, when I can pretend enough.'

Jane reached the gate first and started to unfasten the dogs, but their leads were tangled and they were too excited at the prospect of imminent freedom to stand still. They pranced about almost strangling each other. Belle, now five months old, was getting enormous.

'Stupid animals! Be still,' Pamela said as she struggled to separate them. Then suddenly Binks started to growl and his hair stood up in a line down his back. Pamela looked up and saw a stranger hurrying towards the churchyard. He was smartly dressed, certainly no local. His overcoat was immaculate, and he was holding his trilby firmly on his head against the wind. Pamela noticed that a camera was slung around his neck. She held both dogs firmly and stood aside to let the man pass.

He nodded to her briefly. 'Good afternoon,' he said. 'I don't seem to have chosen a very good day.'

'Not too bad for March,' she said. She glanced up at the sky. 'At least it's sunny.'

'Of course. I spend most of my time in London. I had forgotten how fierce the wind can be down here.'

His voice was very English, very cultured, and Pamela wondered what he could be doing in Devon out of season like this.

He must have sensed her curiosity. 'I'm in the South-West on business,' he said. 'And I want some photographs, so perhaps the day isn't too bad after all.'

He smiled and half bowed to her, indicating that the

conversation was at an end, and then went through the gate into the churchyard.

Jane had skipped ahead and the dogs were straining at their leads to catch up with her, but Pamela stood as still as she could in spite of their tugging. She watched the man. He appeared to be looking for something. He went from grave to grave carefully reading the headstones. Finally he reached Olivia's grave. He traced his hand over the words and took photographs of the marble angel from several angles.

Pamela was not surprised by his interest. The statue was considered to be the finest in the whole churchyard and strangers were frequently entranced by its beauty. It was a favourite subject for visitors' holiday snaps and featured on some of the post cards in the village shop.

Suddenly Belle, unable to contain herself any longer, broke away and bounded after Jane, almost pulling Pamela over into the mud. But she quickly regained her footing and bent to unfasten the lead from Binks' collar too. Then, embarrassed lest the stranger should turn and realize that she had been watching him, she hurried away after Jane and the dogs.

Whenever Pamela and Jane made their pilgrimage to the churchyard they came alone. It was a special time that Pamela liked to share with no one but her eldest child. The other two usually stayed at home with Molly. Rachel at eighteen months was too active and impatient to remain for long in the pushchair and yet too small to walk very far, and Jonathon had formed such an attachment to Molly that it seemed natural to leave him with her whenever possible. He was an easy uncomplicated child and their natures seemed to fit each other perfectly. Rachel was different, a child of quicksilver, bright and sensitive. Molly frequently complained that she found it difficult to cope with this middle child. She would sometimes give Pamela a knowing look. 'She do get them heady ways from somewhere, I'll be bound,' she would say enigmatically. And Pamela knew just what she meant.

On this wild windy day Pamela was looking forward to getting home to the cup of tea and the delicious scones that Molly usually managed to contrive in spite of the shortages and continued rationing.

But to her surprise there was no kettle singing on the hob in the kitchen, no comforting smell of baking, no sign of Rachel running to the door to greet her. Instead Molly was sitting in the rocking chair, Jonathon held tightly on her lap.

She glanced up as Pamela pushed open the door and there was a terrified look on her face. 'Thank goodness you've come,' she said. 'It's Rachel. She . . .'

Pamela had seldom seen Molly cry but now the tears streamed down her face. She had struggled to her feet and with Jonathon in her arms couldn't wipe her eyes or her nose. She just stood there alternately sniffing and sobbing as though her heart would break.

Pamela felt herself go quite cold with foreboding. 'What's happened?' she said. 'Where is she?'

'Mr Alan have taken her to the hospital,' Molly gasped. 'She . . . been an . . .' She appeared to sway as though she was about to faint and Pamela crossed the room in two or three rapid strides and snatched Jonathon from her, depositing him in the pram which stood just inside the door.

'Now tell me, for goodness' sake!'

'She toddled outside.' Molly, her hands free now, groped in her apron pocket for the piece of white rag that, to Pamela's constant annoyance, she always used instead of a proper handkerchief. 'Jonathon was dirty. He got the runs, see, and I had to change him. I had to take him to his bedroom and get fresh clothes. He was in a proper mess.'

'Yes, all right. What's happened to Rachel?' Pamela was beside herself with terror. What was the matter with the girl? What was she hiding? 'Molly, what's happened?' Pamela's voice was no longer quiet and controlled but came out in a shriek.

'Well, there was this awful noise, a bang, and then screams . . . Mr Alan was nearby. He came running and carried her in. I held her while he tied her arm, tore up the table cloth, then got the car. Your Uncle Richard was here helping out with the lambing and he came. He held her in the back seat while Mr Alan drove ever so fast out of the yard. That's all I know. Said they were going to the hospital.'

'Which one? How can I get there?'

'You can't. 'Tis too far for the bike. He said to stay here and he'd come and fetch you.'

Pamela started automatically to rock the pram to stop Jonathon's screams which were cutting right through her head. Molly's words terrified her. 'What was the bang?' she demanded. 'Tell me, Molly. You still haven't told me what really happened.'

'I think it must have been one of them devilish shells that my dad says are still around the place. She might 'ave found one and picked it up. But 'twas only her hand, honest, Pamela. Her face was all right. I looked for that special.'

'My God!' Pamela left her son to his own devices and sank down on the rocking chair. She started to rock herself backwards and forwards instead. Only her hand, only her hand! Then Jane, whom she had quite forgotten, came over and put her small arms around her.

'Will she be all right, Mummy?' she whispered.

'Just pray that she will,' Pamela murmured. 'Pray very hard, there's a good girl.'

'I'll ask Olivia's angel,' she said with doubtful theology. 'Olivia's angel loves us all. She'll make Rachel better.'

It was two agonizing hours before Pamela heard the car engine in the lane. She had done nothing, eaten nothing, prepared nothing. Molly had fed Jane, seen to Jonathon, and even put some pasties in the oven in case anyone should want to eat.

As the car came to a halt Pamela was out of the house and rushing madly into the yard in seconds. She threw herself into Alan's arms, gripped him, stared at him, demented. 'Tell me! Alan, please tell me!'

He held her tightly. 'She'll be all right.'

The words reached her tormented brain and she relaxed a little. 'Just tell me how she is, what happened to her.'

'We think she picked up a shell, but she must have thrown it away from her before it exploded. So it's not too bad.' His voice was gentle, reassuring. 'The doctors say it's a miracle that she's no worse.'

'How bad is she?'

Pamela noticed Uncle Richard standing just behind Alan. 'Tell me the truth,' she pleaded. 'Please, just tell me the truth.'

It was Alan who replied. 'It's her hand,' he said. 'Her right hand. She lost a lot of blood. She's had a blood transfusion, but she's all right. She will be all right.' He emphasized the last words. 'Believe me, Pamela. We can go back to see her tonight.'

She pulled away from him. It sounded even worse than she had imagined. 'I must go to her straight away,' she said. 'I can drive myself if you can't come.'

A spasm of pain crossed Alan's face. 'Of course I shall come. I want to come. You mustn't go on your own. They told me to come back at eight, not before. Come inside, Pamela. You're shaking like a leaf.'

She allowed herself to be led back into the kitchen where Molly, also pale and trembling, thrust a cup of tea into her hands.

'It's all my fault,' she said. 'I could kill myself. If I hadn't been so fussy about Jonathon, I'd have noticed her wandering off. If I had a gun I'd shoot meself!'

'A lot of good that would do,' Alan said. 'Be a good girl and look after everything while we go back to the hospital.' In spite of his anguish he smiled at her. 'Rachel will be all right, you'll see.'

Jane, playing with Belle in a corner of the kitchen, looked up at them all. 'I know she'll be all right,' she said solemnly. 'Olivia's angel told me that she'll look after her. She's our guardian angel. We did about guardian angels in Sunday School.'

It was dark when they set out for the hospital. Alan was very quiet and after the first mile Pamela's imagination began once more to conjure up all sorts of frightening possibilities. 'It's worse than you said, isn't it?' she queried.

Instead of replying he surprised her by suddenly pulling the car into a field gateway. He switched off the engine and turned to her in the darkness. She felt that her heart was taking a nosedive right down to her feet.

'No, no worse,' he said. 'But there's something I haven't told you. Something that to me is quite wonderful.'

'Wonderful?' What was he talking about? How could anything be wonderful with her child lying in hospital badly hurt? 'Have you gone quite mad?' she said brutally. 'How can . . . ?'

'Rachel has a very rare blood group. There was a problem about getting blood. They asked me if mine was the same, and it is. I gave blood for her. AB Rhesus negative. We have the same blood group, a very rare one. You know what this means, Pamela?'

She closed her eyes and tried to make sense of what he was saying. 'She's your child,' she whispered at last. Relief flooded through her. No more guilt, no more doubts. Rachel was Alan's child.

He pulled her into his arms and kissed her, and then she was vaguely aware of the engine springing into life again and the headlights making a path of light that pierced the blackness of the empty road.

They drove in silence for the next few miles as if the news, coming now at this time, was too dramatic for further comment. Pamela held the shopping bag into which she had crammed some of Rachel's things tightly to her breast, her arms around it as though it had life, as though it was Rachel she was holding and cherishing. The terrible disaster had revealed the truth that she had longed to know. Now, at this awful moment when she had no idea how badly Rachel was hurt, even if she would live, now Alan had pronounced the words that should make for happiness. 'She's my child.'

Two weeks later Rachel was well enough to come home. They fetched her at the beginning of April when the hedgebanks were bright with daffodils and wild campion, and the cherry tree that Pamela had planted in the garden was proudly showing its first blossom. There were lambs calling from the field near the house too. 'A happy time of year,' Pamela said. She was sitting in the little car beside Alan holding a silent and frail Rachel in her arms.

'She'll like the lambs,' he replied. 'The tame one especially.'

'Yes, she will.'

They turned into the yard and he parked the car and came round to help her out. He was very protective, very concerned. 'We'll have to take great care of her,' he said. 'Build her up. Lots of creamy milk, that's what she needs.'

They hadn't talked much about the momentous news of Rachel's blood group. Both were hesitant of stirring up old memories. For Alan the discovery that Rachel was really his daughter had been both wonderful and challenging. He had disregarded this child, somehow transferred the shame and disgust of Pamela's betrayal on to her. Now he had to reverse all that. And there was his will. He had visited the Bristol solicitor again to ensure that his son would inherit Morelake, and had left some money to Jane and a letter for Pamela, a letter that had taken a vast amount of courage to write. But at that time he still hadn't been able to accept Rachel as his. She would have hardly anything if he died. He decided that he would have to go to Bristol for a third time to put this right, but there was no hurry. He had no intention of dying for many a long year yet.

Pamela was glad about Alan's happiness and the new concern he showed for Rachel. She hoped that he would come to love the child as he loved Jonathon.

'Course he will,' said Molly. 'He just got to come to terms with it, that's all, like all of us.' She was sitting in the kitchen with Jonathon on her lap and a bottle plugged into his mouth. 'Whoever would have guessed that you could tell things with blood? 'Tis a real bit of luck finding out like that.'

'Well, if you can call having your finger blown off a bit of luck, I suppose it is!'

'You know what I mean. Pity it couldn't 'ave been without the accident though.' She pulled the teat of the bottle out of

Jonathon's mouth and held it up for inspection. 'Greedy little beggar this one. Nearly finished all this lot.'

Jonathon's fat baby hands groped anxiously for the bottle and Molly thrust it back. 'I been reading about blood in my last library book,' she said darkly. 'Like you say, we all got different kinds. The only thing I knows about mine is that 'tis red. 'Tisn't blue like royalty's for sure! Do you really think Princess Elizabeth and Princess Margaret Rose got blue blood?'

Pamela laughed. 'No. That's just a fairy tale. Their blood is red, just like ours.'

'That's a relief then. Fancy bleeding blue blood!'

'You shouldn't read such silly books.'

'I like romances. I don't think I shall need to read them no more though. I'm going to have me own romance.'

'What d'you mean?' Pamela glanced at her suspiciously.

'Met a Yank down by the field where the bodies are.' There was a hint of triumph in Molly's voice. 'He come back to have another look at the place. We talked. He asked me out.'

Pamela was immediately alarmed. 'I told you not to go on about bodies,' she said. 'You know it's only a rumour. No truth in it. And who is he anyway?'

'Sam, he said his name was. He's nice. He was in that Operation Tiger that they keep all hushed up. Nearly got hisself drowned like hundreds more, he says, but he was rescued.'

'You're not going to see him again, are you?'

'You bet I am! Nothing else doing round here, is there? And he weren't no ghost neither. He's got a motor car too – borrowed it from a garage. I reckon he'm rich.' She laughed and took the now empty bottle firmly from Jonathon's protesting mouth. 'That's all for you, young man,' she said. 'You'm going in your cot for a bit and you better be quiet. You got a rival now for your dad's attention. No more spoiling.'

'No 'poiling,' said Rachel, pulling herself up. 'Kiss Jon-jon.'

She put her thin little arms round her brother's fat body and planted a kiss on his sticky face.

Although Pamela was concerned over Molly's bombshell she told herself firmly that it was none of her business. After Delmer the girl was surely old and experienced enough to look after herself. She tried to put these unnecessary worries out her mind and to think of her children instead. As she looked at her two youngest she was filled with a sudden glow of happiness. There was only Jane now to pull into the close security and love of her family circle.

'Time to fetch Jane,' she said. 'Will you finish this ironing, Molly, while I take these two to meet her from school? They can both go in the pram. Rachel can sit on the front.'

'Kool,' said Rachel. 'Go kool.'

'Yes, my darling,' Pamela said to her and she scooped her up into her arms. 'We'll go to see the lambs first, shall we?'

'Daddy,' Rachel said. 'Daddy lambs.'

Pamela closed her eyes and buried her face for a moment in the child's fragrant dark curls. 'Daddy's lambs,' she whispered.

Molly looked at them both and at the baby on her lap and grinned a trifle wickedly. 'Out of the mouth of babes,' she quoted. 'Daddy's lambs! No more doubts.'

Then Pamela laughed too. 'You were the doubter,' she said.

'Glad I was wrong. Truly.'

'Come on,' Pamela said to Rachel. 'We'll find your coat while Molly gets Jon-jon ready.'

Rachel, set down on her feet again, now clung firmly to Pamela's hand. Since her stay in hospital she had become timid. Together they went into the hall and then up the stairs to the little room that was Rachel's own. It overlooked the farmyard and through the open window came the sound of Alan clattering about below. Rachel broke away from Pamela and ran to the window and looked down at him. 'Daddy,' she said.

He glanced up and waved, and Pamela marvelled again at the way Alan had changed. Yet as she looked at her daughter and then down at her husband she felt a sense of bewilderment too. Rachel was so unlike Alan. Surely there was something in this beautiful dark fairy-like child that came from some other source? What in her begetting gave her that magical quality?

Then Pamela laughed at herself. She was getting as fanciful as Molly. Molly! The new American . . . She would try to find out

303

a bit about him. Perhaps Molly was her concern after all. Wendy and Ben Yates wouldn't thank anyone for a second little Delmer to bring up!

# TWENTY-THREE

Molly was very taken with the American. 'He'm a real gentle-man,' she confided to Pamela a few days later. 'Not one to sweep a girl off her feet like Delmer, but none the worse for that. He'm the marrying kind.'

He certainly seemed reluctant to go home. To Pamela's con-sternation he found lodgings in the village and eventually started to court Molly with determination. He became a frequent visitor to Morelake. By the autumn they were engaged and he had produced enough dollars to buy the small tumbledown cottage that lay at the end of the Morelake lane, and the few fields that went with it.

'I always liked them Yanks,' said Molly in triumph on the eve of her wedding day. 'I told you he weren't just a good-timer.'

'You're lucky,' Pamela said. She had overcome her earlier fears for Molly. Sam Welton, for that was the American's name, seemed a good catch, a nice enough lad with no plans to go back to the States. The only problem for Pamela was his voice. Every time he spoke she heard Lawrence's accent, and when he called Molly 'honey', her heart thumped a little with remembering.

Alan knew nothing of this. 'I've asked Sam Welton to work for us,' he told her after the wedding. 'And he agreed. He's glad of the job. He farmed in the States apparently. I think he'll be a good worker.'

And so he proved to be. The year passed easily and

uneventfully and the year after that in the same way. Molly produced a son, still worked at Morelake and helped with Jonathon, and only the sound of Sam's voice continued to disturb Pamela's peace of mind from time to time. But gradually she became used to it. He was Sam, she reminded herself, Molly's good and worthy husband, not the ghost of Lawrence. He must certainly have been killed. Or if he had not, then he obviously wanted to forget her. He was nothing to do with her life any more, had no part in it nor ever would have.

And Alan had mellowed, become a family man. He was concerned with his farm, his children and his wife, in that order. Little else bothered him. And if life at Morelake was a trifle dull, Pamela had many small pleasures which compensated. Alan had finally given reluctant permission for her to drive the car and this brought many pleasant changes in her routine. Because of it she had been able to renew her friendship with Mary Turner, go more frequently to Burlcombe with all three children, and sometimes venture further afield for picnics or shopping.

Burlcombe stood for most of the time beautiful and eerily silent. It seemed to be waiting for her, but by the summer of 1948 Pamela was beginning to wonder if it was such a good idea to keep it after all. She invited Mary over one day in August when she had a few precious hours to herself. She liked company when she visited the house, for its emptiness was doubly poignant when she was alone.

They wandered through the lovely rooms looking sadly at the dust sheets which covered much of the furniture. There was a slightly musty smell mixed here and there with the more pungent aroma of home-made furniture polish.

'Uncle Richard and Mrs Baines look after it and live here for a week or more every month,' Pamela said. 'The farm just about pays for its upkeep, but I know I should sell it really.'

'It's beautiful,' Mary said. 'Couldn't you persuade Alan to sell Morelake instead?'

Pamela laughed bleakly. 'Never in a thousand years,' she replied. 'He won't hear of it. Morelake is his home, always has been, and that's where we have to live.'

Suddenly Mary turned to her and looked her full in the face. 'Are you happy, Pamela?' she asked. 'Really happy, I mean?'

She was momentarily startled by the question. It was one she pushed away from her, tried not to think about. 'What does anyone mean by happy?' she said at last. 'I have the children. Alan is good to me, and we've enough money. Yes, I suppose I'm happy.'

The door to the garden stood open and Binks ran through, closely followed by Belle and by Mary's dogs. Pamela patted them enthusiastically, glad of the diversion they made.

'Alan has never become used to the dogs,' she said. 'I don't think he ever will.'

'How did he come to let you have Belle?'

Hearing her name, the huge dog wagged her great tail slowly from side to side and licked Mary's hand.

'I've often wondered about that,' Pamela replied. 'It was soon after he was demobbed and he probably felt that he couldn't start his new life with an argument. Belle is Jane's dog. I know Alan finds Jane difficult. I used to think that he resented her being with us, yet he often does things to please her.'

'He may feel sorry for her,' Mary said. 'Or guilty.'

'Why guilty?'

She shrugged her shoulders. 'Because Jane is the odd one out, I suppose, and because he can't feel the same about her.'

'That's why I'm so glad she's got the dog,' Pamela said. 'Belle worships her. They worship each other. They're almost inseparable. Jane even asked if she could take her to school.'

Mary laughed. 'Not on, I suppose.'

'No. I usually take her to meet Jane though, and she always gets a kiss before I do.'

'Quite natural,' Mary said.

'Alan won't let the dogs stay in the house at night,' Pamela continued. 'Jane keeps on about it and it's a constant source of strife but he's quite adamant, won't budge an inch.'

'But you can't really grumble, can you? You can't expect him to give way on everything.'

307

It's I who do most of the giving way, Pamela thought. Aloud she said, 'No. You're right, I suppose.'

Belle, getting bored, brought a rubber ball and laid it at Mary's feet and they all went outside, where the sun was shining on the summer lawn and the berries were just beginning to show red on the rowan tree.

'It's so beautiful here,' Mary said as she threw the ball towards the gate. All five dogs bounded towards it and Pamela laughed at the confusion that followed.

'No one can have everything,' Mary said thoughtfully as she watched them.

Pamela broke a small piece of branch from the rowan tree and held it in both hands. 'No,' she said. 'Not everything. But I think I'm happy, Mary. On the whole, I think I'm quite happy.'

Sometimes Pamela thought that she would like to stop the weekly pilgrimage to take flowers to Olivia's grave, but a sense of obligation as well as Jane's insistence that the angel must not be neglected forced her to continue.

One Saturday in September she set out with all three children, as well as Binks on a lead, to walk the whole distance. 'Daddy is busy ploughing the stubble, the sun is shining, and the walk will do us good,' Pamela had announced. 'Belle must stay. She's too boisterous.'

Jane accepted this ruling with a certain amount of petulance, but had picked a large bunch of chrysanthemums from the garden, and come to terms with her pet's temporary banishment. Her mind was now on her mission.

'Do you think Olivia's angel likes chrysanthemums?' she said, looking at them critically.

'I'm sure she does.'

'Are angels always girls?'

Gulls were crying and wheeling in the sky overhead as they walked along the path at the edge of the beach, and the wind was gently swaying the rushes of the Ley as Pamela answered. 'No, I don't think so,' she said. 'I don't think they're boys or girls, really.'

Jane was skipping ahead. She stopped and turned round. 'That's silly,' she said. 'They must be one or the other.'

Pamela laughed at her. 'Not necessarily.'

'Well, I think they're girls. They're too nice for boys.'

Rachel, oblivious of this theological discussion, was busy trying to restrain Binks. At four years old she could only be persuaded to walk this distance if she was allowed to hold the end of his lead. Jonathon, as always when he was in the pushchair, was fast asleep.

They saw the car before they went into the churchyard. It stood on the road outside looking opulent and out of place.

'He's here again,' Jane whispered. 'You know, him with the camera.'

Pamela's heart gave a lurch. Ever since that first meeting she had wondered who he was. When she had met him a second time she had allowed herself to speculate a little more, and now he was here yet again. As on the other two occasions he was standing near Olivia's grave.

He looked up as they approached. 'Good afternoon,' he said, and raised his hat. 'So we meet again, and in the same place.'

'Yes.' Pamela was suddenly filled with excitement. Dare she hope? Words deserted her. Could all her dreams be coming true at last? Was her mother's journal about to come to life before her eyes? Or was it just coincidence? Perhaps he was a historian or a writer, someone with a quite ordinary and legitimate reason for being here?

She had allowed herself, now and again over the past months, to think that the tall stranger might possibly be Olivia's lover . . . and therefore her own father. She had told no one of her very secret hope and had tried to banish the thought when it came, fearing disappointment.

But now perhaps was the time for her to solve the mystery and find out why he was so fascinated with this place. His presence here seemed to indicate more than just natural curiosity.

She straightened her shoulders and told herself to be calm, to say the right things. At this most important moment she must be in full control. She looked at Jonathon and was glad to see that

309

he was still sleeping soundly. She parked the pushchair and put its brake on.

Jane must be given something to do. There must be no distractions. 'Take the dead flowers and put them in the bin,' she told her unnecessarily.

Then Pamela took a deep breath and addressed the man directly. 'This is my mother's grave,' she said without preamble. 'She died when I was born.' She threw the words at him, and they were not at all what she had secretly rehearsed whenever she'd thought about this moment.

He paled visibly. He took a step backwards and seemed suddenly to lose his confidence and air of self-possession. He looked at Pamela closely. 'Your mother, you say?' There was a long pause. He closed his eyes for a moment then looked again at the date on the plaque beneath the feet of the angel. 'Died May 1st 1925.' He read the words quietly to himself. 'So it was as I feared.'

'Feared?' She hadn't expected that reaction.

They stood quite still and stared at each other. Then he lowered his eyes and traced the word 'Olivia' with long artistic fingers. 'She died nine months after we parted, and I didn't know until I came here nearly twenty years later.'

Pamela noticed with some satisfaction that there were tears in his eyes. So he really had loved her. But why then had he . . .?

'My family never came back to Devon.' He spoke slowly and shook his head. 'If only she'd told me. I thought it was for the best that we shouldn't meet again. I wanted her to forget me completely, although I knew that I would never forget her.'

He seemed to be lost in a world of his own, a long-ago world in which Pamela and her children had no part, but suddenly he looked up and there was a ravaged expression on his handsome face. 'How can I ever expect you to understand? My desertion of your mother must seem the most callous, the most heartless thing you have ever met.'

'I've never understood.'

'You didn't know that I'm Jewish?'

Then suddenly she did understand. The mystery of Aunt

Maud's refusal so long ago to accept the family who were on holiday at Ash Manor was quite clear now. She had heard her aunt hold forth on the subject of race many times. It had shocked her, but there was always something else to think of that was more immediately important. And she herself knew no Jews, no black people. After the war there had been news of Hitler's atrocities in the newspapers and like everyone else she had been deeply shocked. But there had been no personal feelings in her reactions, for she had had no notion that her mother's lover was Jewish. The names in the journal, Daniel and Sarah, had intrigued her, but they were Bible names. Pamela had thought that the family must be religious. And she had liked the names, used a simliar one for Rachel.

'No, I had no idea,' she replied. 'No idea at all, but it explains things. My mother wrote about you, but said nothing of that.'

Pamela could see her mother's graceful writing and the name 'Daniel', written over and over again. And now he was here in front of her, the word made flesh.

'Wrote?'

'Yes. A journal. I have it locked away at home.'

'Will you . . . could you show it to me?'

Olivia seemed to be standing there in the quiet churchyard, standing between them, arms around both of them, drawing them together.

But Pamela shook her head uncertainly. 'Perhaps. Perhaps not,' she whispered. 'She loved you very much, though.'

'And I her.'

Another awkward silence, with both wondering how to span the years of unknowing.

'Does it make any difference to you?'

She looked at him, surprised. 'Difference?'

'My being Jewish?'

She hesitated. 'No, I don't think it does. In fact . . . in fact it makes me Jewish too, doesn't it?'

'Not strictly,' he replied. 'Jewishness is only recognised through the mother.'

Pamela did some quick thinking. 'So if you and my mother

had married, none of your children would have been Jewish.'

'Correct.'

'And that would matter to you of course.'

'It's why we try to persuade our children not to marry out.'

'Was that why you left her then?'

He shook his head. 'I realize that to you it must seem like that. But no. I would have married Olivia had it been possible and the right thing for her. But her sister would never have allowed it. Olivia would have been cast out completely from her home, as I would have been from mine. We were very young and neither of us had any resources. Had I known about her pregnancy . . .' he hesitated. 'About you . . . things would have been very different. As I said, I didn't know. I was sure she would forget me much sooner than I would forget her. In fact I knew that I would never forget.'

There was silence between them as each tried to absorb the momentous thing that had happened. Pamela was vaguely aware of gulls wheeling and crying in the sky above and of Jane returning from her job with the flowers, but neither of those things had any reality.

She was the first to speak and her words came out hesitantly, wonderingly as if from someone else. 'I always wanted a father.'

'And I a daughter.'

She was jolted out of her reverie. 'Have I any brothers and . . .?'

'None. My wife was unable to have children. You are my only child.'

The barriers of embarrassment came tumbling down, the inhibitions disappeared. He held out his arms to her and Pamela went to him, hesitantly at first. He embraced her gently and after a fleeting second they stood back and stared at each other again.

Then she was suddenly aware of Jane standing at a distance, looking a little lost and slightly defensive. 'This is Jane,' she said quickly. 'My eldest child. You've met her before.'

He held out his hand to her as though she were grown up. 'You should have been called Olivia,' he said to her. 'You're just like your grandmother.'

Jane didn't return his smile. Her big blue eyes were filled with distrust. 'She's not my grandmother,' she said. 'She's Olivia.'

'We call her Olivia,' Pamela said, trying to account for her child's brusqueness. 'She seems permanently young, never a grandmother.'

Further explanations were ruled out when Rachel, who had remained at the gate where Binks was tied, suddenly became bored. She ran towards them and then stopped suddenly, staring at the stranger.

'This is my other little girl,' Pamela said. 'Rachel, come and say hello.'

She had no inhibitions. She looked up at him and grinned. 'Hello, photo-man,' she said.

If any tension remained, it was broken by the remark.

'Photo-man? he qeried.

Rachel pointed to the camera. 'Yes. You take photos of Olivia's angel.'

He laughed. 'Yes I did last time I was here but I'd rather have a real little girl today. I knew another Rachel once and she looked very much like you.'

A lot of posing followed. He wanted all of them. Jonathon had awakened and was grizzling to be let out of his pushchair. As Pamela bent to deal with him she felt that this was all some bizarre dream. She had found her father at last! After years of wondering who she was, who he was, she had found him, and now he was taking photographs just like any . . . any grandfather. There ought to be something dramatic happening, she thought. It was one of the most emotional moments of her life and yet it seemed suddenly quite ordinary. He was her father. Her father! She looked at him and saw the dark hair, greying now, the blue eyes of Olivia's journal.

Then when the photographs were taken he stared at Rachel again. 'Why did you give her a Jewish name?'

'It's a Bible name,' she replied. 'Like yours. Daniel in the lion's den and all that. I suppose my mother's journal gave me the idea.'

'My niece was called Rachel,' he said. He paused and looked

313

away across the churchyard and the peaceful Devon fields. 'Your Rachel is so like her.' Then, quietly, 'She and her mother, my twin sister, were in Auschwitz.'

Pamela gasped. The horrors of the concentration camps suddenly became real, events that had happened to identifiable people, a child called Rachel and a girl called Sarah. The Sarah of the journal.

'That's awful.' The two words sounded hollow and completely inadequate but she could think of nothing else to say.

'My sister married a young Jewish scientist from Germany in 1928,' he explained. 'Jews have always been persecuted. That was why I wanted to end my friendship with your mother. I knew that it could only bring her trouble.'

'As it did!'

He bowed his head. 'If only she had told me.'

'She was determined that you shouldn't know. Of course, she didn't expect to die.'

'No.' Another long pause. 'And you were brought up by her sister?' he continued at last.

'By Aunt Maud, yes.'

'And your name? It seems so foolish but I don't know what my own daughter is called.'

'Pamela,' she said, confused for a moment.

'Pamela Belmont?'

'Saunders now. Belmont is the family name.'

'Mine is Rosenbaum. Daniel Rosenbaum,' he supplied.

And mine too, Pamela thought. So I am a Rosenbaum. Aloud she said, 'If Olivia had written that, then I should have known the reason for everything.'

'Yes, you would have known.'

How was this interview, this extraordinary afternoon, going to end? Pamela wondered. She couldn't leave him like this. What should they do? How did you cope with a new father? What did you do with him?

She realized that it was beginning to get cold, and all three children were restless. Rachel tugged at her coat. 'My hands are shivering,' she said. 'Can we go, Mummy?'

As usual Rachel had supplied an amusing remark just at the right time. Then Pamela had an inspiration. 'There's a beautiful painting of my mother in the hall at Burlcombe,' she said. 'Would you like to see it?'

They all packed into his splendid car. He folded the pushchair and put it into the boot as though he had been used to doing such things all his life. Even Binks was allowed to go on the back seat.

A short time later they stood together in the old house and stared at the painting. Daniel was quite still, devouring it with his eyes. Pamela tiptoed out of the hall, taking the children with her into the garden. He needed to be alone for a while, alone with his memories and his guilt, for she was sure that he felt guilt. Undeserved perhaps, but there nevertheless.

She refused his offer of a lift back to Morelake. 'We shall walk,' she said. 'It's not far and we need the exercise.' But the reason went deeper than that. She too wanted time to think, time to sort all her jumbled and jangled emotions before she encountered Alan. And she wasn't sure yet that she wanted to share her news. There would be a right moment.

She stood with the three children at the gate of Burlcombe and watched Daniel drive away, after promising to keep in touch, and then she turned and walked up to the rowan tree, Olivia's rowan tree, and realized that she should have told him about it, told him that her mother liked to touch it when she went in and out. Superstitiously she put both hands on its small but sturdy trunk. It was a link with her mother. 'Thank you,' she whispered.

'Why are you talking to the tree?' Jane immediately wanted to know.

She laughed. 'I'm not. I'm talking to Olivia.'

'You ought to say it to the angel then.'

'No. Olivia loved this tree.'

'She loved that man. You can't love trees.'

Surprised, Pamela looked at Jane. 'How do you know about . . . about Daniel?'

'I heard you say that she did. And you said he was your father.'

'Yes, he is.'

315

'If you were my real mummy, he'd be my grandfather. I've always wanted a grandfather.'

Pamela took a deep breath and cursed Aunt Maud for the continuing problems she had created. Perhaps now was the time to get things straight? She could explain everything later when Jane was older and could fully understand. 'I am, darling,' she said. 'I really am your mummy, and Daniel is your real grandfather.'

'Hooray!' Jane grabbed Rachel's hands and glared at her. 'She's my real mummy,' she said. 'Not just yours.' Then she looked up at Pamela and said casually, 'I always thought you were. I just wanted to know for sure. What's a Jew?'

Pamela was nonplussed for a second. Then inspiration came. 'Jesus was a Jew,' she replied. 'It means you're special.'

'That's all right then,' Jane said. 'If Jesus was one, it'll be good. Are we Jews?'

'You have to have a Jewish mummy to be one,' Pamela replied.

'Oh well, we're a little bit Jews if that man is my grandfather.'

'Yes, I suppose we are.'

It was, of course, Jane who broke their momentous news to Alan. 'I've got a Grandfather,' she shouted exuberantly as soon as he opened the back door. 'And he's like Jesus.'

Alan stood poised with his hand on the latch and he stared at her with total incomprehension. 'What on earth are you talking about?' His voice held a trace of irritation. It had been a long hard day on the farm. He wanted his tea and some peace and quiet.

'Like Jesus.' It was Rachel now who continued the story. 'That's what Mummy said, so he's special.'

Pamela looked up a trifle apprehensively. She was laying the table, setting out egg-cups and plates ready for the meal that they all shared regularly at half past five each evening. She had guessed that Jane would blurt out the news, but she had not wished to spoil the child's excitement. She'd been bubbling over ever since they returned from Burlcombe. It was as if a grandfather made up in some way for the lack of a father. 'Are you ready for a shock, Alan,' Pamela said. 'A pleasant one I think, though.'

He removed his boots, walked over to her and kissed her briefly, then slumped on the settle. 'What now?' he said. 'Another of Jane's fantasies?' He picked up his son who had been playing with a toy lorry on the rug at his feet.

'It's real. He's truly real,' Jane continued. 'He's called Daniel and he was Olivia's lover.'

Pamela blushed at her child's use of the last word. 'Go and wash your hands at once,' she directed. 'Take Rachel and Jonathon and leave me to tell Daddy all about it.' Jonathon scrambled from his father's arms and ran to join his sisters as Pamela shooed them all out of the room, closed the door behind them and then sat down opposite Alan. 'We told you about the man in the cemetery,' she began. 'Well, I've wondered about him from time to time and now . . . it's quite amazing.' She was suddenly lost for words.

'You mean that he's your . . . your father? Are you quite sure?'

Pamela nodded. 'Yes. I'm quite sure.' Then she couldn't speak for the tears that filled her eyes and the lump that seemed to control her throat.

For some minutes they sat there, Alan staring at her as though she had taken leave of her senses and Pamela trying to regain control.

'And what's this about being like Jesus?' Alan had conjured up visions of the bearded and white-robed figure in the painting in church.

'He's Jewish. That explains almost everything,' Pamela managed after she had wiped her eyes and blown her nose.

It wasn't until the children were in bed and fast asleep that they really talked. Pamela fetched Olivia's journal and read to Alan many of the references to Daniel. It was a time of closeness that they had seldom experienced.

'Are you going to keep in touch?' Alan wanted to know. 'Will it make much difference to you?'

Pamela thought about her answer carefully. 'Yes, we shall keep in touch of course. I promised to write regularly. But, no, it won't make any difference to our ordinary everyday lives, I shouldn't think. I might tell the children something about the Jewish faith, but I don't know much myself, and apparently we aren't true Jews. You have to have a Jewish mother to be one.'

'Well that's a relief,' Alan remarked.

'Why do you say that?'

He shrugged his shoulders. 'No reason I suppose, other than that it's a strange idea. Will I ever meet him?'

'Perhaps he'll come to stay very occasionally, if you don't mind.'

'As often as you like,' said Alan, hoping fervently that it would be very very seldom. 'He's your father after all.'

'My lost father,' Pamela mused. 'It'll make a great difference to how I feel about things though.'

Alan looked at her quizzically. 'What do you mean?'

'He gives me a sense of identity. And I've never liked mysteries. It's another one solved. There's just . . .' She didn't finish her sentence. She had wanted to add, 'Jane's birth . . . Jane needs a father too,' but she forebore. There was no point in reminding herself of what had happened to her long ago. She tried never to think of it now and certainly never to mention it aloud.

Alan appeared not to have heard those last words. 'I'm pleased for you,' he said. 'Very pleased.'

There were presents for all of them in December. Not at Christmas but at Hannukah. Handsome presents sent from London. 'Your father is rich,' Alan said at breakfast after they had opened the parcels. 'I've been finding out. He owns a lot of companies. You're probably an heiress.'

'What's an heiress?' asked Rachel as she dripped some of her cornflakes on to her new doll's splendid dress.

'A princess in a tower,' said Jane. 'I've been reading about one in my book at school. She has to be rescued by a prince.'

'What's a prince?' said Rachel.

'A man who loves a princess, silly,' Jane told her. 'Then they live happily ever after.'

# TWENTY-FOUR

Pamela hated winter at Morelake. Burlcombe had a huge fire-place with ample supplies of logs, and the kitchen with its Aga was always warm, but the Morelake fireplace was small. 'Mother had the old one bricked up to save fuel,' Alan had told her when she first saw the ugly little grate. 'She just put extra clothes on when it was cold.'

Now in a particularly bitter week Pamela remembered his words and shivered as she made bed-time drinks. The kitchen fire was no better than the one in the parlour. She was determined to replace it with an Aga as soon as she could, but there was no spare money for luxuries like that yet. The old black monstrosity with its oven and hot plate had to do. Alan was sitting beside it smoking his pipe. He had taken to a pipe recently. The pungent smell filled the room.

Pamela stirred sugar into mugs of warm milk and placed them on the scrubbed table in front of each child. 'Drink up and you'll feel warmer,' she said. Then she refilled the black iron kettle and put it on the fire. 'Hot water bottles tonight,' she told them.

'Goodee!' Rachel grasped her mug and sipped with apprecia-tion. 'I like having a hotty for my toes.'

'Belle and Binks haven't got hot water bottles,' said Jane. There was an aggrieved frown on her face. 'They'll be so cold out there in that horrid old barn. They should be in by the fire.'

Pamela sighed. Here we go again, she thought. More

321

arguments about the same thing. Over and over again it went, and still Alan was adamant. It had become a point of honour not to give in.

Jane looked at the milk in front of her and gave it an angry stir. 'I've just looked out and there's more snow,' she complained. 'And there's wind and draughts. I want Belle in with me, and Binks too. He's old.'

Pamela thought she saw a glimmer of tears in her child's eyes.

Then Jane's grumpy voice changed to one of wheedling femininity. 'Please, Uncle Alan,' she said. 'Please let them come in tonight.'

Alan knocked out his pipe and for a moment Pamela thought he was going to relent at last. He took out his tin of tobacco and began slowly to stuff more of it into the bowl of the pipe before replying. She held her breath.

'No,' he said. 'I've told you that you only have dogs on one condition – that they go outside at night. There's hay in the barn. They'll be warm and dry.'

Jane clenched her fists and glared at him. 'I hate you, I hate you!' she screamed. 'I shall go to Burlcombe and live. I hate you!'

Pamela was horrified by this outburst. It was worse than usual, and Jonathon, looking from Jane to his father, began to cry while Rachel's mouth drooped as though she too was about to let out a monstrous wail. Pamela wanted to run outside and fling open the barn door and call to both dogs to come and share the warmth of the house as they did all day. But she had long ago made a pact with herself. On this thing she would never give way to Jane. Alan had accepted the dogs against his will and she was determined to do her part.

She glared at Jane although it broke her heart to do so. 'Go to bed this minute,' she said. 'You're a naughty rude child to speak to your father like that.'

'I hate you too,' Jane flung at her. 'I shall go and live with Aunty Baines – me and Belle will go tomorrow. And he's not my father!' She jumped down from the table, leaving her mug of milk almost untouched.

'Aunty Baines wouldn't want such a bad girl,' Pamela said. 'Now off with you to your room. And you will tell daddy that you're sorry for being so rude and saying such wicked things.'

'They aren't wicked because they're true,' Jane said with her usual logic. Then she stamped out of the room and Pamela heard her going upstairs, thumping on each stair, and finally slamming her bedroom door. She sighed audibly but said nothing.

Alan took his pipe from his mouth and stared into the fire. He had not joined in the argument, he never did. 'That child gets worse,' he said at last. 'I wish to heaven I'd never made the rule about the dogs. I can't give way now, though.'

Pamela looked at him in surprise. 'No, I suppose you can't,' she admitted reluctantly.

When she went into Jane's bedroom half an hour later there was just a silent mound beneath the bedclothes. Whether Jane was asleep or merely pretending she couldn't tell. She touched the quilt gently. She had wanted so much to have a good relationship with this child. She often thought about the months in Scotland when everything had seemed to be going so well. And at Burlcombe too Jane had been happy. But since coming to Morelake the problems had begun to pile up. 'Good night, my darling,' she whispered, and there was an answering sniff from the bedclothes, followed by silence. 'I'll put the oil-heater in the barn,' she added. 'That'll keep the dogs warm.'

Pamela awoke suddenly some time later to the smell of smoke. At first she thought it was Alan's pipe, but he never smoked in the bedroom. She sat up and rubbed her eyes. They were smarting. Then she leapt from the bed and stared in horror at the scene outside. A bright glow filled the night sky and the snow shone red as it fell thickly, its beauty illuminated like some magical firework display. Then she saw a small figure outside in the yard and was filled with terror as in one blinding flash she realized the whole frightening scenario that was taking place below. She threw herself at Alan who was still sleeping soundly. 'Quick!' she shrieked. 'The barn! The barn's on fire.'

She remembered the oil heater.

Alan had never moved so rapidly in his life. He careered down the stairs wearing only his pyjamas and in seconds was outside, his bare feet crunching on the snow. Suddenly he saw Jane and realized, as Pamela had done, what she was doing. The dogs were in there, in that inferno. And in that moment he was seized with a fierce love for the little girl who was struggling desperately with the bolt that held the door so firmly closed. He tore across the yard and pulled her away but she fought him fiercely.

'Daddy, Daddy!' she shrieked. 'Daddy, get them! Get them out.' Even in the trauma of the moment he realized that she was calling him Daddy at last. At this terrible time he was hearing the words he had lately longed to hear. 'Go back,' he said to her. 'Go back. I'll get them.'

Pamela was close behind him and he thrust Jane into her arms. 'Take her back, for heaven's sake, and call the Fire Brigade.' He struggled with the bolt, cursing himself for not having oiled it, using every ounce of strength. Gradually, bit by bit, it slid back and the door burst open. Binks was the first out, wild with fear but unhurt. The dog dashed past almost knocking him to the ground. Then Alan heard the terrified howls of the larger dog. Belle was inside still, trapped somehow. Jane's dog. He had to get Jane's dog out.

He put his hand over his mouth and plunged into the smoke-darkened hell beyond. He had to fight the dog to get her collar off for it had caught, and she was making frantic efforts to free herself. Usually gentle in spite of her size, she was now formidable, crazed by the flames. Alan felt that he was about to lose consciousness. 'Jane's dog,' he gasped. 'Jane's dog.' It was all that mattered. He must rescue Jane's dog, whatever happened.

His fingers were clumsy and the dog twisted and turned in terror, making the job almost impossible. But at last he managed to get the collar undone and with one bound Belle was away from him and out of the door. He felt unable to move, unable to force his legs to follow. He had won. Jane would have her dog. He had made recompense.

Pamela stood at the kitchen door, transfixed with fear. 'Alan,

Alan!' she shrieked. 'For God's sake, come out.' Binks and then
Belle had streaked past her into the comparative safety of the
house and Jane had followed them, so that Pamela was alone
now with the blazing terror in front of her.

Then, galvanized into action, she grabbed the hen-food bucket
that stood just outside and thrust it into the sink, turning the tap
on hard so that she could feel the splash of water through her
nightdress. 'Dear God, help me,' she said. Water! The Fire
Brigade! She rushed into the hall to the new telephone, the pride
of Alan's life, installed a few weeks ago. She dialled nine-nine-
nine and gave the details in a strangled, terrified voice then
slammed the receiver down and staggered to the door with the
bucket. She crossed the yard, slipping on the snow, and hurled
water into the flames. The bucket dropped at her feet and she
wanted to run into the heart of the fire and find Alan, was about
to do when an American voice yelled at her: 'Hey, Ma'am, get
back from there, will you? The roof's going.'

She turned and saw Sam Welton's large sturdy frame running
towards her. He grabbed her and hustled her, slipping and sliding
on the rapidly thawing ice and snow, unwillingly back into the
house. He thrust her into a chair but she sprang up again, protesting. This time it was Molly who held her back.

'Tidden no good,' she said.

Then, confirming her words, there was a great thunderous
crash as the roof of the barn gave way. Acrid smoke, a terrible
searing smell that Pamela knew she would never forgot in a
thousand years, filled the room, her lungs and her eyes.

'Alan!' she screamed again. 'Alan!'

After that she was aware only of the sound of buckets in the
sink, water gushing, and eventually the raucous and welcome
sound of the fire engine.

She sat for a long time the next morning saying nothing, drinking
the tea that was thrust into her hands again and again, listening
to the voices around her. One after another they told her how
brave he had been, what a good thing it was that there was no
wind to fan the flames, to burn Morelake too, how sad to give

325

your life for a couple of dogs. How quickly the fire brigade had got here. They went on and on, Molly, Sam, Mrs Baines, Uncle Richard, all trying to console and help.

Then Jane crept up to her and stood white-faced beside her chair. 'My daddy died to save Binks and Belle,' she said. 'He was brave and good, wasn't he, Mummy?'

Pamela smiled at last. 'Yes, darling. He was both brave and good.' She said nothing then about the oil heater, but she knew there would be a well of remorse in her heart for ever.

Alan's will was a shock for Pamela. She learnt that he had gone to Bristol to make it. There had been two in fact, one made on his way back from Scotland, and the later valid one after Jonathon's birth. The farm was left to his son. There was a small bequest for herself, a larger one surprisingly for Jane, and almost nothing for Rachel, just a small token, a few pounds.

She stared at the solicitor, trying to take everything in and wishing that the day was over. The funeral had been a big one. Alan was a local hero now. The fact that he had died rescuing his daughter's dog had captured the imagination of the press as well as neighbours and friends from all over the area.

When most of the invited guests had eventually left and all three children were in bed, Pamela sat, still numb with shock, beside the small parlour fire that Molly had lit and kept fed with logs. She remembered suddenly the letter that the solicitor had handed to her after the official reading of the will. 'Your husband gave this to me on his second visit,' he had said. 'He instructed me that you were only to have it if he should die.'

She had glanced at the typewritten envelope and thought it probably contained some documents, perhaps something relating to the farm. It looked too official to be interesting and she had placed it in her bureau to be dealt with later.

Uncle Richard was sitting at the other side of the fire. He and Mrs Baines were staying the night. 'Can't leave you all alone,' he had said earlier, and she was grateful for the company. Mrs Baines was in the kitchen making a nightcap for them all.

'There's a letter that I haven't read yet,' Pamela said. 'The solicitor gave it to me this afternoon.' She got up and fetched it and slit open the thick brown envelope with some difficulty. Inside she found not the official document she expected but another envelope, and in that a letter written in Alan's own handwriting. She glanced at it and felt the colour drain from her face. It was like receiving a message from the grave. The words blurred before her eyes, but then she gathered herself together and started to read.

Dear Pamela,

I don't know how to start this letter or how to tell you the thing I have to tell. The facts that you are going to hear now have come between us ever since we were married although you weren't aware of them.

That night when you were raped, I was the man. I can't tell you how ashamed and full of remorse I've been during these past years. You will never know how ashamed. All I can do is ask for your forgiveness. I can't expect your understanding, but please try one day, for Jane's sake, to forgive me, Pamela, for Jane is my true child as much as Jonathon. I've never found it easy to love Jane for she was always a reproach to me. Make it up to her if you can.

To try and excuse my behaviour in any way is both abhorrent and distasteful, yet I've spent a lot of time trying secretly to do just that. Remorse is a very terrible thing and every day I was confronted with the result of my crime. Although Jane is sweet and beautiful, she was still a constant reminder. I always kept my emotions hidden though and hoped that you would never know how I really felt.

Why did I do such a shocking thing? I've tried to tell myself that my mother was to blame, that the near-bondage in which she kept me triggered this terrible response. She made me both fear and hate women. You won't believe this because I hid my fears beneath my bullying behaviour and my anger. I've tried to improve a little on that score lately. But the more I think about what I did to you all those years ago, how I ruined your life, the more I've come to see that

327

there's no possible excuse. I was guilty of the worst crime that any man can commit.

I must leave to you the decision about what to tell our children. Perhaps you won't find it necessary to tell them. If you can bring yourself to destroy this letter and keep the matter a secret between you and me then, from the grave, I shall be grateful. Only your aunt knew, no one else. You will wonder, of course, why Maud chose not to expose my guilt. She had her own secret reasons and never enlightened me about them. She was always determined to have power over other people, and of course this knowledge gave her control over both our lives.

You won't receive this unless I die before you. If that happens I hope that this terrible truth won't hurt you too much. I could have kept it a secret for ever, but I know that would have been wrong. Maybe I have been a coward not to tell you face to face. Please forgive me for that too. And please try to remember the happy times.

With my love, Alan

She sat very still for a long time. Richard, puffing on his pipe, wisely said nothing but merely stared into the comforting little fire. The smell of tobacco reminded her poignantly of Alan. It was as though the man who had penned these pages had suddenly come back to life.

She felt totally numb, unable to take in all that had happened in so short a space of time and especially this last paralyzing blow. But she was sure that she must keep Alan's secret. No one, not even dear Uncle Richard, must know or guess the truth. But how was she to live with this knowledge and tell no one? Could she ever do it?

She glared down at the page and her hands were shaking so much that the words were blurred now, dancing before her eyes and making no sense. But here at last was the final clue to the puzzle of her life. Of course she should have guessed long ago. Her distress turned to rage, and she clenched her fists so that the paper became crumpled in her hand.

Eventually she forced herself to speak. 'A last letter,' she said slowly. Then she carefully screwed it into a little ball and threw it onto the glowing logs. 'Better burnt,' she added. She watched the paper curl and then flatten as the flames took it and she shuddered thinking of the fire, the flames, and Alan dying so horribly, just as his words were dying now in front of her eyes. He had talked of remorse, but she was suffering from remorse too and probably always would. One of the dogs must have knocked over the oil heater on that fateful night. How stupid she had been to leave it. Her thoughts blurred again and she closed her eyes, wondering if she would ever be able to come to terms with the events of the past few days.

But later that night, alone in the large double bed, she thought, not about her own shortcomings, but about her marriage and the lie Alan had lived for all the years of it. It was the most staggering piece of news she had ever been given. Alan was the man who had caused that moment of supreme terror so long ago, and the terrible months that followed. She thought of the horror, the pain, the wrecking of her teenage years, the destruction of her youth. Could the fire possibly have been a just retribution? Surely not! She tried to banish the uncomfortable thought. She couldn't believe in a God or a fate which ordained such awful things.

And Aunt Maud had known too! She was suddenly aware that she had been doubly deceived. She cast her mind back and remembered many things that had not made sense and now did. She tossed and turned and remembered Alan's lovemaking and she shuddered at the thought of it. And he wanted her forgiveness? Would that ever be possible? Would it make any difference to him if she forgave him now? Could people have any knowledge about the living when they were dead? And did she too need forgiveness from him? She shivered but her anger dissipated a little and was replaced by pity. Alan and her aunt were indeed both dead while she was alive and free and even rich! She must certainly find it in her heart to forgive them both. She could see now that they had both, in many ways, been unhappy. Alan had achieved a kind of contentment since the war though, she thought, and there had been some happy times. And of course he was Jane's father! Another difficult thing to accept. So all her three children were Alan's. She wondered if Jane should ever be told. Perhaps when she was a woman, when she could take the truth, or maybe not. No decisions need be taken about that now. At least Jane was not the child of a tinker. There was a relief in that, she thought wryly!

Eventually, when it was almost morning, she fell asleep but not before she recalled that in Jane's eyes Alan had totally redeemed himself, for he had died saving a dog. It was incongruous, but in that one act, that had partly been Pamela's fault, he had at last found favour with Jane. To his daughter now he would always be a hero. Nothing could take that away from his memory whatever else might one day be revealed.

# TWENTY-FIVE

## 1954

Pamela stood on the beach in the drizzle and looked around at the assembled company. 'Not many here,' she said to Molly, 'considering it's to mark the tenth anniversary of D-Day.'

'What d'you expect with this weather? Lots of handsome sailors over there though.' Molly indicated a detachment of seamen from the Royal Navy. 'I don't suppose many of them were in it – the invasion, I mean. Too young probably.' She sighed. 'Ten years ago. Don't time fly? Makes me feel old.'

Pamela laughed. 'You shouldn't be looking at them. You're a respectable married woman with four children.'

'So I am.' Molly was contrite.

'I shall be thirty next birthday,' Pamela added.

'And umpteen years without a man,' Molly chided her. 'There be plenty looks at you with you-know-what. 'Tis time you was wed.'

'Shh,' Pamela whispered. 'Here they come.'

The Guard of Honour gave their salute and a short but impressive-looking man dressed in the uniform of a general of the United States Army strode towards the improvised platform.

'It's General Gruenther,' Pamela said. 'He's going to make a speech.'

The crowd listened in polite silence to his thanks for their sacrifice of ten years ago, his remarks about Devon and the part it had played in the preparations for the assault upon Hitler.

331

And then the atmosphere was suddenly electric as he started to talk about the seven hundred American soldiers killed in the April before the invasion.

'Told you,' Molly said in an undertone. 'The bodies what I saw on the beach. I thought no one knew about it.'

'Not many did, till now,' Pamela replied. Then: Lawrence, she thought. I heard nothing from him after that April. What a useless wasted sacrifice. Seven hundred men killed for nothing, a tragic mistake.

She heard no more of the General's speech but was lost in a sea of memories until the playing of the Star Spangled Banner and God save the Queen brought her rudely back to the present. She looked up at the Union Jack and the Stars and Stripes flying now from flag-poles on either side of the memorial obelisk and quickly brushed a few tears from her eyes.

'I'm soaked through with this drizzle,' Molly said when it was all over. 'Come on, let's get back. I could do with a nice cup of tea.'

He was standing in the churchyard with his back to her, staring at the marble angel, his hand tracing the word 'Olivia'.

Pamela had walked over to the church later that same day. The rain had eased off a little. Jane, now fourteen, was old enough to be left in charge of the other two children and Pamela frequently made this journey alone. Even the dogs had stayed at home today. Binks was far too old to go further than the garden gate and Jane wouldn't part with Belle. The old days of Jane's fascination with Olivia's angel had gone.

'It's just a marble statue,' she had said to Pamela a couple of years before. 'I used to think she was magic. Silly, wasn't it?'

Pamela had smiled, but sadly. 'Maybe there's still some magic left if you look for it.'

Jane had stared at her mother with a superior knowing look but now, suddenly, the magic was back. Or was she dreaming? Pamela looked at the man beside the marble angel and her whole world turned upside-down.

He turned, stared, came towards her with outstretched hands. 'Pamela?' he said.

She ran to him, dropped her flowers and was in his arms before she knew what was really happening. Then he held her away from him to look closely at her, devouring her with his eyes.

She shook herself away from him, stepped backwards. 'Is it really you, Lawrence, come back from the dead?'

'You could say that, almost,' he smiled.

'What happened?'

'I was in that exercise that went wrong. I nearly drowned, and lost my memory. I didn't even know who I was.'

Pamela, needing to do something, stooped and picked up the flowers she had dropped. 'When did you know?'

'It took about a year.' He opened his jacket and pulled out a small gold cross on a chain – a thick sturdy chain now, not the thin delicate one she had given him. 'It was partly this,' he said. 'I kept wondering who Olivia was, and the date intrigued me. I knew that I couldn't have been in love with a girl who had been around in 1907.'

Pamela took the vase from the grave. She wished her hands would stop trembling. She poured out the rain water that had accumulated in it and absently started to arrange the fresh flowers. 'So when did you remember . . . remember me?'

'It was the painting that I recalled first, the one of your mother at Burlcombe. Then I began to see this church, and gradually I saw you too, and your name came to me through a mist. But then I tried to make enquiries. I was not very successful at first but as my mind became clearer I managed to contact some guys who had been here in forty-four. We had a reunion each year and eventually I heard about a guy who was returning to England, wanted to stay and farm apparently. He'd been left a bit of money and had taken a fancy to the place.'

'Not Sam Welton?' Pamela interrupted.

'The very one. I wrote to him and gave another name, just pretended to be vaguely interested. I was determined not to make any move if you were happily married still.'

333

Pamela pushed the last flower stem carelessly into the vase and looked up. So she had given him the impression that she was happily married back in 1944, she noted. She felt a small measure of satisfaction that even if she had betrayed Alan, she had not given away her deepest feelings about her marriage. But several things still puzzled her. 'Why did Sam tell you about me, and why didn't he tell Molly?'

'It was of no interest, I suppose. I had a brief note from him saying that he was getting married and settling down and was helping at a farm called Morelake. He mentioned that the owner had been in the RAF and was a decent sort. That was all he said but it was enough for me. I knew that your husband was back, and so I tried to put you right out of my mind. Unsuccessfully!'

'So when did you hear about the fire?'

'Only recently. At our last get-together some of the guys were talking about coming to the tenth anniversary celebrations. One of them wrote to the same Sam Welton about arranging digs. When he wrote back he gave us this new address, said he'd moved into Morelake. That sent alarm bells ringing for me. So I enquired some more.'

'And found out that I was at Burlcombe and Alan had been killed.'

'Right.'

'And Sam had no idea that you knew me?'

'None at all I guess, honey. I didn't want him spilling the beans until I came here myself.'

'Oh, Lawrence.' She couldn't say any more for a moment or two and he took her in his arms and kissed her again right there in the quiet churchyard with no one to hear or see except the sea gulls calling eerily in the sky above. Then, as if by mutual consent, they walked together along the gravelled path and entered the church at the main north door.

'I came here last night,' Lawrence said. 'It's so beautiful now, just as you said it would be.'

'You promised to come back, didn't you?'

He nodded. 'And I kept my promise. The knight and his lady survived too.' He nodded in the direction of the large tomb, and when they reached it he put his hand upon it, stroked the cold stone. 'I remember the sand-bags.'

'A wet day in November,' Pamela said. 'Everything packed up in big wooden crates and the gloom outside matching how we felt.' She shivered. 'It's always cold in here though. Let's go, Lawrence.'

Suddenly she realized how little they knew of each other. She had no idea where he was staying or for how long. She began to feel slightly embarrassed. Had she taken too much for granted when she first saw him just now? Was the person she had secretly dreamed about for so long really the same as this flesh and blood man at her side? 'You must come home,' she said. 'Meet my children.'

At Burlcombe they were greeted by Molly who still came in to help even though she had plenty to do in her own home now that she and Sam had taken over the complete running of More-lake. She eyed the visitor up and down and then winked at Pamela behind his back. 'Well now,' she said when they were both in the kitchen hurriedly preparing a meal. 'There's a turn up for the books then. Come right back from the dead he have! I just hope Delmer don't do the same. Sam wouldn't think kindly on that!'

'Are you sure that you had no idea,' Pamela questioned, 'that Lawrence had written to Sam?'

'Course not. D'you think I could 'ave kept me mouth shut about something like that if I'd a knowed?'

'He said that he wouldn't ever have come if Alan had been alive.'

'I always said that he were a nice chap,' Molly said. 'You could do much worse than marry him. You been lonely these past years.'

Pamela stiffened. 'No one said anything about marrying, and how could I leave Burlcombe?'

'No one said nothing about leaving Burlcombe, neither,' Molly replied. 'Them Yanks seems to like settling here. Look at my Sam, happy as Larry. Larry, there's a joke!'

335

Pamela remembered that this play on words had once dis-comfited her. Now it made her laugh. 'Well, we shall see,' she said. 'Now let's find out how he's getting on with the children. I didn't like leaving him to Jane's tender mercies.'

In the sitting room Lawrence was surrounded by dogs and children. Pamela opened the door to hear Jane's clear voice proclaiming, 'Yes. She really is my mummy. She told me. I don't know much about it yet, and I don't have a father, but when I'm twenty-one she promised to tell me everything.'

Pamela blushed with annoyance. She wondered what could have brought forth that confession from her elder daughter. But then she remembered that Lawrence knew nothing of her relationship with Jane. 'I see that you've been learning all our secrets,' she said quickly to cover her mortification at the words.

'And I told him about the blood,' Rachel said, not to be outdone. 'How Daddy had to give blood to make me better, and how he loved me a lot more after that, almost as much as he loved Jonathon.'

'Where did you get that idea? About the blood, I mean?' Pamela was horrified by this further revelation. She had no idea that Rachel remembered anything about that distressing incident. She was minus one finger it was true, but she seldom remarked upon the fact, managing quite well with the remaining ones.

'Molly told me. I asked her one day about my finger what's not there. She tells us lots of things.'

Pamela sank weakly onto the settee. 'I'll bet she does,' she said with horror. 'But now you can all go and wash your hands, brush your hair, and make yourselves look nice for supper. Uncle Lawrence is having it with us and he doesn't want a load of dirty little monkeys sitting down at table.'

'Goodee,' eight-year-old Jonathon said as he made a rush for the door. 'I'm fed up with women. Hope you'll stay a long time, Uncle Lawrence. I'll show you the body field. There are lots of soldiers buried and sometimes you can see ghosts.'

Jane was the last one to go. 'He's talking rubbish,' she said just before she closed the door. 'Absolute rubbish, but then boys nearly always do, don't they!'

Pamela closed her eyes and put her hands over her face after they had gone. The room seemed strangely quiet. She could feel her heart pounding in her chest. 'I shan't blame you if you take the earliest opportunity of escaping back to America,' she said as soon as she felt able to speak.

He came over to her and knelt on the carpet. Gently he pulled her hands from her face. 'There's so much I don't know,' he said, 'but if you'll let me stay there'll be plenty of time to find out.'

Suddenly Pamela knew that she had to tell him the worst, had to get it out before she could sit politely and hand him roast chicken and vegetables, plum pie and cream. 'Jane,' she began. 'I was raped, Lawrence, when I was fifteen. Jane is the child of that rape. You didn't know before, no one did except Maud and Richard.' She nearly said 'Alan' but stopped herself in time. She would never tell that secret, never betray him a second time.

'Raped.' Lawrence almost spat out the word. 'Gee, honey. That's frightful and you only a kid yourself. And Jane is . . .'

'Don't blame her will you?'

He looked at her, deeply shocked. 'Blame her? What kind of monster would that make me? You still don't know me very well, Pamela honey.'

'No, I don't, and you know so little of me.'

'Then I'm going to stay right here in your little old Red Swallow until that's all put right.' He was silent for a moment and then Pamela felt his body grow tense. He clenched his fists. 'Who was the guy who did this to you, raped you. My God, just tell me who it is and he'll feel the . . .'

She laid her fingers quickly and gently on his lips. 'I can never tell you who it was, my dear, but he's dead and I've forgiven everything now. Without forgiving there's no future.' She took his fists in her hands and tried to straighten out the long artistic fingers.

'By God, you're an angel,' he said, relaxing a little.

'Not quite,' she replied. 'Not as good or as beautiful. And now I must go and carry the dishes. Molly helps out, but she has to go and see to her own family now.'

He jumped up. 'Can I do something?'

'No. Just amuse the children when they come back. That's the hardest job of all.'

None of the children wanted to go to bed that night. Lawrence proved to be a popular and entertaining guest. But eventually Pamela was confident that the two youngest ones were asleep and Jane, curled up in bed, was deep into her latest book.

'They're great,' Lawrence said. 'Your children.'

Pamela smiled at him. 'Thank you. It hasn't been easy, bringing them up. They all have a trace of Alan's stubborn will.'

'Caught rather than inborn in Jane's case,' he said casually, and Pamela flinched, realizing how easy it would be to tell the truth by mistake. One day she knew that she would tell, but not yet. Jane couldn't cope with that knowledge for a few more years. And the identity of the rapist was of no concern to anyone but Jane. But she would tell Lawrence everything else. 'Rachel,' she began. 'I suppose you want to know what she was talking about, the blood I mean?'

'Not unless you want to tell me.'

'I do.'

She told him of her pregnancy, of her longing that the child should be his, of Alan's anger. Then the accident, the rare blood group, and Alan's happiness when he knew that Rachel was his child after all.

Lawrence sat beside her on the settee, not touching her. He was quite still and silent. She continued with the story of the dogs, of the rule about them staying out at night, and then her own folly in lighting the oil heater, forgetting to turn it off before they went to bed. She finished with Alan's spectacular bravery.

He said nothing for a while. Then surprisingly, 'Scotland?' It was a question. Just the one word.

'Scotland?' she echoed not understanding. 'What do you mean, Scotland?'

'You went away. That was why I was unable to see you again. I thought that you went to avoid seeing me. I wondered about our night together. I didn't want you to have any trouble because

338

of me. I would have supported you somehow.'

'But we had agreed not to meet any more.'

'Yes, but I couldn't have left you in the lurch, Pamela. Surely you knew that?'

It was her turn to be quiet, not to answer. They sat for a long time staring at the large arrangement of flowers that filled the fireplace. Then she put her hand out across the gap in the middle of the settee that separated them. 'It's all a long time ago,' she whispered. 'Does any of it matter now?'

'Did you go to get away from me?' he persisted.

'Oh, Lawrence! No, I didn't. Of all the mysteries we have to unravel for each other that one is the simplest. My aunt had a stroke. I went to help. Rachel was born in Craemore. We must go there some day. It's a wonderful little place and gave me a lot of happy times.'

He pulled her into his arms then and for a long time they did no more talking.

'Will you marry me,' he whispered at last, just as the old grandfather clock was gathering its strength to strike midnight. But before she could reply the door opened a crack and Jonathon peered around it.

'I just wanted a drink . . .' he began, and then he sighed. 'Oh, gosh, they're being sloppy,' he said loudly.

Lawrence disentangled himself, sat up and grinned at the boy over the back of the settee.

'Say, a drink's a good idea,' he said. 'How about us all having one. Got any coke around? I believe your Mom and I have some good news to celebrate right now.'

'You're going to marry her then.' Jonathon's words were matter-of-fact. 'Jane said you probably would. Well, at least it means I shan't be the only man around. It gets a bit tiresome with so many women.' He gripped the door knob. 'No, we haven't got coke. Just homemade blackberry wine that I'm not allowed to drink.'

'Blackberry wine sounds perfect, and I'll persuade your Mom to let you have a few sips, shall I?'

'Sure thing,' said Jonathon. He abandoned his place of safety near the door and, crossing the room to the sideboard, opened the cupboard and removed a bottle. Then he stood and cradled it in his arms and, looking searchingly at Lawrence and his mother, he nodded his head wisely. 'Yes,' he said. 'As long as you don't go around being sloppy it'll be nice if you marry each other.'

'I think it will be nice too,' Pamela whispered to Lawrence. Then she jumped up and smiled at her son, including him in her happiness. 'I'll fetch three glasses.'